SORROW AND JOY

SORROW AND JOY

GALLOWS HILL ACADEMY™ YEAR ONE

D.R. PERRY

LMBPN Publishing
PMB 196, 2540 South Maryland Pkwy
Las Vegas, NV 89109

Version 1.01, June 2021
ebook ISBN: 978-1-64971-843-3
Print ISBN: 978-1-64971-844-0

NIGHT OF SORROW

PART ONE

CHAPTER ONE

The bus to Danvers stank intolerably. I wasn't on it. I'm a raven shifter, so I never set foot or feather on public transportation. But sometimes I take it, in a manner of speaking.

Since I could fly, you might be wondering, why not use the shortest route instead? I like my privacy. My family was murder. Literally and in more ways than one. So, I rode the bus's fragrant wake. When I shifted behind the low stone wall separating the brick building from the street, I didn't have to worry about my clothes. The shell locket I'd had for as long as I could remember meant I didn't have to lose them when changing from one form to the other.

I'm getting ahead of myself. Story of my life.

The entire reason for following the bus in the first place was visiting my asshole brother, who was lucky to be in Danvers Sanitarium instead of max security for trying to kill his girlfriend and a boatload of her friends and classmates.

Our mother forbade the rest of us from visiting him. There I was, doing it anyway.

Or trying. The automatic glass doors opened to a lobby, mostly empty on Sunday at the dinner hour. Chairs and tables sat on the other side of a low wall painted to look like fieldstone. One pink-cheeked young woman in a pale blue dressing gown hummed as she snapped pieces into a jigsaw puzzle. I knew she couldn't see or hear me, so I walked on.

Danvers Sanitarium was a psychiatric hospital, but absolutely not one that belonged in a horror show. Faeries ran it, treating the residents with surprising humanity and kindness. Rumor had it, the doctors appointed by the state of Massachusetts held ducal ranks in the Fae courts. But they didn't do direct patient care.

That duty fell to the pure fae, which I still had three years to learn about at Gallows Hill Academy, the local charter school for shifters and changelings. The pure weren't human, though some supposedly came close. I'd only seen them from a distance before that night.

One of the walls and the entire floor was wood. Murals covered the rest, most of magical creatures in an Impressionist style. Soothing was a decent word for it, but I liked bucolic better.

The fact that I'd never been in here before didn't matter. I knew the drill. Before he'd left for college, my brother's ex-best friend Bartholomew told me how things worked here. So I faced that wooden wall and announced myself instead of fumbling around like an ignoramus. Always a good thing not to be.

"Mavis Merlini, here to see her brother Crow, same last name."

"We have no records of a Samelastname."

"Crow Merlini. Uh, Cornelius. Sorry."

"Apology unneeded. Proof of blood requested."

"Okay."

I went to the wall, which upon closer inspection, did have some actual rock incorporated into it.

"Ow." I winced. Something sharper than any of those rocks stabbed me.

"Blood relation confirmed. Prepare for vanishment to Aggression Wing, room 111."

"Oh no, not vanishm—"

I blinked and found myself in a much smaller and more rustic space. Like the inside of a cabin in the woods. Not the creepy kind you see in horror movies. This place was a secure and tidy domicile but the sort that took hard work to live there.

Of course, they'd glamoured it. Pure were far better at that sort of thing than the teenage changelings I knew, or even the tithed faeries they'd eventually become.

Even with illusions likely, the brick building didn't have room for all of this. So the ward Crow was on might be situated in the space between the mundane world and the fae Under. One glance at the nonexistent bars on my phone confirmed that theory.

The cabin had a fireplace, banked and smoldering, with a hook and pot hanging over the flames on a hinged arm. The aroma of a fish-based stew wafted from it. An unfinished table, chair, and bed frame were the only furniture. Hides on the bed partially covered a rough straw mattress. I saw a locket hanging from a nail over the bed, the same as mine but more battered. One thing was missing, the most important.

"Um, I came to see my brother, and he's not here."

The voice didn't answer. Instead, I heard a *creak* then felt a gust of unseasonably nippy air behind me.

"Of course he is. Look again."

I turned and walked out the door into a small, brush-ringed yard. The babbling sound of a stream or creek sounded from somewhere out of sight but nearby.

A lanky fellow stood across the yard from the door, splitting firewood. He wore a red and white flannel shirt and blue jeans. His hair was short, uneven stubble as if he'd shaved it all off maybe a month ago. My brother wouldn't be caught dead looking like that on the streets of Salem. Still, I'd have recognized him even if he'd been wearing a ballgown and painted orange.

I stepped carefully over a bundle of green branches.

"Hello, Crow."

"What are you doing here, Mavis?" He stopped in mid-swing, back still turned toward me. "Snitches get stitches. So do the sad sacks who associate with us. You don't want that kind of trouble from the Boss."

I grimaced. His life took a turn for the worse once he started calling our mother that, which was one reason I never would.

"No one followed me. In case you were, uh, worried about that."

"Thank the gods." He raised the ax again, chopped through the log on the stump, and paused. "It's harder work than you're cut out for, being in here. Doesn't suck as much as expected. You'll be in a world of hurt if she finds out you came here, though." He set the ax down and turned.

"I know."

"After what I did, I'm not worth this kind of trouble. So, why?"

"I'm starting school tomorrow."

"You never make sense. You know that?"

"I make sense to myself. I know you don't always get me. Why else would you say stuff like this all the time?"

"To get you out of my face." One corner of his mouth tilted up. "Seriously, what's the deal? You can't be here just to annoy your littlest big brother. Third time I'm asking, and this is a faerie-run facility. They like their tidy threes. So spill it."

"I'm keeping our promise, Crow."

"What?" He blinked. "That's old news. Zombie horse. Water under the bridge. Wearing cement overshoes. A doornail. I failed."

"It's not over. Because I'm still here. I refuse to fail." I crossed my arms over my chest. "Or give up on you."

"You should. Could have refused that last order the Boss made, let her kick me to the curb." He hung his head. "Couldn't leave you behind. If only I knew it was no-win."

"It's not." I cleared my throat. "We promised each other, and I quote. '*We're* getting out of here. That house. This town. No matter what.'"

"In case you haven't noticed." He waved a hand at the cabin, the ax, the sky. "Kinda stuck. With good reason."

"So consider this a warning. You've got three years to do the work in this place."

"Work?" He snorted. "Chopping wood is redemption?"

"Rehabilitation, duh." I rolled my eyes. "It's why Uncle Paolo got you in here, remember?"

"He's not our real uncle. But whatever." He shrugged, turned his back on me, and hefted his ax again.

My eyes narrowed, jaw set, nostrils flared. Out of all seven Merlini siblings, Crow and I were the only ones who hadn't let the competition built into our upbringing break the bond between us.

"No whatevers. I'm graduating."

Three years ago, the night before he'd started at Gallows Hill, we'd made a vow. One he thought he'd failed at, irrevocably. He'd forgotten it had two sides.

"Good for you. That taskmaster principal is no joke. So make like a tree and get out of here."

"No. Not until you understand this. Do the work, and I'll take you with me."

"You think that's still happening?" He put a hand over his middle, laughing. With the other, he wiped his eyes. "I was supposed to be the one getting you out."

"That's on Mom."

"Don't call her that." He pressed his lips together. "It's a mistake. You know what she really is. And what she's capable of if you let your guard down. How will you keep her out of your hair?" He bent and collected an armload of firewood.

"I haven't figured that out yet."

"You suck at planning. Get better." He walked toward the tiny cabin. "I'll give their boring-ass therapy sessions another shot. For now, I've got to chop enough wood, or it'll be a cold night. That's how this aggression program works. Burn the rage out with survival. Don't come back, Mavis. It's too dangerous."

"Thanks, Crow. For caring even a little." I nodded, then stared up at the high ceiling that looked exactly like an overcast sky at sunset. "I'm done with my visit now."

A moment later, I was back in that calming lobby. I stepped outside and made the short walk to the bus stop, then hid behind a shrub to shift into raven form. Following the bus back to Salem was easy, though still unpleasantly fragrant.

If my parental unit or any of my uncaged siblings saw me on the way to or from Danvers, this stop was a futile exercise. Hopefully, I was wrong.

I landed in Irzyk Park, lingering before remembering Crow's old buddy Bar was in Rhode Island at college. I stuck around anyway. If I stayed long enough, saying I'd been there wasn't technically a lie. Taking some time to think about keeping four hostile family members at talon's length couldn't hurt, even without anyone to run my thoughts by.

Crow was the most recent in a long line of siblings and even a few cousins to try breaking free before being broken. I was the youngest. Also the last.

If I'd been a magus at Hawthorn Academy, I would have lived in the dorms like everyone else. But my school wasn't private and privileged. Gallows Hill was a charter school with living quarters only available to out-of-state students, starting this year.

The one upside was, nobody at home could prevent my attendance by holding tuition over my head. Something like that had happened to a guy at Hawthorn a couple of years ago.

I took off, winging from my perch on top of the decommissioned tank and away from the unfortunately empty park. My student handbook was at home, and I wanted to read it. Maybe I'd missed something. Special cases might be flexible, like a weak spot in a wall separating me from the future I wanted.

Maybe there was another way to ask. Or a string to pull, as Paolo Micello had done for Crow with the sanitarium. An unwritten rule, a loophole, or a convoluted connection perhaps. Rules aren't breakable, but bent is an entirely different story.

I shifted into arms and legs on the back porch. As easy as it might have been to do it on the fire escape outside the window of my attic room, I didn't want anyone to accuse me of sneaking. Instead, I pushed the door open and stepped into the cavernous kitchen that took up half the first floor in the triple-decker building I only ironically called home.

I walked into a murder. Of crow shifters, not a crime scene. As the only raven in the family, I didn't add to it. The long, scarred pine table had seven place settings, though only three of my siblings occupied theirs.

The head seat was only temporarily vacant, like mine. The spare two belonged to Babs and Marge, my sisters both doing time for separate crimes. They remained in the family's good graces because neither had squealed.

Crow had ratted them out, part of his plea deal. That's why the span of wood in front of his chair was barren, without the honor conferred by an empty set of dishes and silverware.

The twins bickered over the biggest pork chop. Hugh lost his bid for that prize, glaring as Manny slapped it on his earthenware plate. They were twice my age and acted half of it instead. For all their uncouth posturing, they didn't dare start eating. Not until our mother arrived.

Branwen heaped beans, rice, and cornbread on her plate, ignoring the latest episode of our brothers' nightly battle. Her one act of defiance in this family had been declaring herself vegetarian. In all other ways, she followed our mother's orders to the letter. I grabbed a plate from the counter and sat across from her.

"Hey, Bran." I reached for the rice. "How's tricks?"

She'd made her bones for the family by running an escort service in the noughts when Backpage was still a thing.

"Don't give me any of that horse shit, Mav." She slapped my hand away. "Where you been?"

"The park, duh."

"Good answer." She mimicked the sound of a game show buzzer. "Wrong. Try again."

I decided to lie along the lines of our mother's preferred reality, in which each sibling fit a set of traits she based on bones thrown on our birthdays. My role was a trickster. I gave an entirely false but more in-character response.

"Fine. Dodge Street Café." I rolled my eyes, the only genuine part of that false confession. "Trying to pass myself off as old enough to drink."

"That I believe." She chuckled. "Go on, kid."

I portioned out small helpings of each item on the table, contemplating the nest I came from but never quite fit into.

Bran was the oldest and canniest of my siblings, heir apparent to the family business, which wasn't actually a courier service. She hadn't married or had kids, which also made her the most trustworthy of the bunch as far as our mother was concerned.

The twins, Hugh and Manny, were all brawn no brains, previously directed first by Marge and then Babs. My middle sisters were both in the state pen but had managed apartment buildings Mom owned before that. The twins had that job now.

Everybody who wasn't in lockup or dead came to the nest for dinner each night. Even if they'd had a meal.

It wasn't about the food. It was about proving loyalty. Everything was supposed to be in my family. I didn't even dare glance at Crow's empty seat for fear Mom would walk in and see me looking.

But she didn't walk in at all. Of course not.

Finally, I realized what I should have suspected all along.

My mother was there the whole time, leaning in a sliver of shadow in the corner to my left. Watching. Listening. And judging, of course.

There's an old saying about two wolves that live in each of us. The one you feed wins. Morgan Merlini's judgment was more like a shark, constantly moving because stopping meant starvation. If there'd ever been a kinder predator inside her, it hadn't survived long enough for me to meet it.

My mother was a diminutive woman. Tiny, the one word we never spoke aloud in her house, and with good reason. Her capacity for rage was as limitless as the vast emptiness of outer space. Size didn't matter. She terrified us all.

When she paced toward the chair at the head of the table, the twins fell silent. Bran's facsimile of a smile didn't reach her eyes. I meant to set the spoon back in the bowl gently. Big mistake. It clattered, tipping out along with a small hill of beans.

"Mavis, honestly." She put her chin and both hands on the high back of her chair, eyes twinkling like graphite from beneath the dusky fringe of her bangs. She reminded me of a penanggal, one of those nearly-headless Malaysian vampires. "You're sixteen, not six."

"Sorry, Mom." I pulled my napkin off my lap and reached out to sweep away the offending legumes.

"You're almost too old to call me that, too."

I only nodded, containing my food mess in the cloth as I rose from my seat and walked toward the garbage can at the end of the kitchen counter. Her next words hit me like a knife in the back.

"I smell fae." The sound of earthenware grating against wood turned the pit of my stomach to ice. "Why is that, I wonder."

Mom could move silently when she wanted to. I heard each footstep clearly. This was a psych-out. My brain knew this fact, sure as water is wet. My body reacted as if she'd read every transgression in the history of my life out of my brain.

I dropped the beans into the trash, hands shaking. The napkin followed like Vlad the Impaler's wife diving out of her tower. Mom stepped to my left, peering into my eyes like she'd pluck one of them out and make a trinket from of it.

"Nervous?"

"Uh, yeah." I swallowed, then forced the corners of my mouth up. "First day of school tomorrow."

"That's right." She nodded, expression flatter than roadkill. "I have an idea about that."

"Oh?" I tried to freeze my features, maintain that smiley veneer of benign ignorance.

My eyebrow betrayed me, hoisting itself like a mainsail.

"Let's see how you do over at Gallows Hill after a night sleeping on the streets."

"Mom, no." I blinked.

"Mavis, yes." She snapped her fingers.

I don't know who caught me under the shoulders and dragged me out the door. I didn't fight them because I'd seen this happen before. One of my earliest memories was watching Babs do it to Hugh. One sibling or another getting tossed out for a night was a regular occurrence here.

This was my first time, though.

It's possible to learn from someone else's mistakes. Probable, maybe not. Still, I'd had six examples. That's why I walked away without looking back. No amount of knocking or even crying at the door would get me back inside. If I tried shifting and flying to my room's window upstairs, I'd find it locked.

Salem's a small town, but the streets were never empty at night from Labor Day until November first. Sure, I was stuck with the clothes I stood in, but I wasn't entirely without means. Emergency bus fare sat folded in my back pocket.

I headed to the local pizza place, Engine House. The two slices I got were cheap, hot, and filling but needed a ton of crushed red pepper to taste halfway decent. If I wanted breakfast in the morning, I couldn't afford a beverage. The water fountain between the bathrooms was good enough to wash my meal down.

Out on the street, I flitted from one group to another, pretending to belong at their fringes while thinking. It wasn't easy, considering where to sleep in town. Any of Crow's old haunts had too many memories attached, things that might break the autopilot triaging all my decisions.

I had no friends. That's only partly true, but the two I still had weren't in town. Bar was in Providence at college orientation. Cadence was on Cape Cod with her roommates playing a Piercing Whispers gig. Kids from middle school only knew me as an odd duck. The ones who hadn't crossed the street when they saw me in town over the summer weren't people I knew much about, let alone where they lived and whether they had a couch I could crash on.

Salem had four influential families. Ours was one and Mom considered the other three enemies. She'd slowly been eroding the Ambersmith's grip on local businesses, with funds she'd acquired mysteriously the year before. The Micellos got pushed across the bridge to Beverly back before I was born.

That left the Morgensterns, who were practically untouchable. Also unapproachable now that the younger two were grown and off being their best selves. Still, their entire house including the yard was a no-go zone according to Mom. Maybe I'd pass the night safely in their mulberry tree. Shifted into my bird form, of course.

I paused on Hawthorne Street, out in front of the psychic parlor and Diego's house. Which he'd banned me from visiting during our breakup. Even if I'd had the money, I couldn't have asked for a tarot reading to guide me because of that.

Hanging my head, I stepped around the corner—and got knocked out of the driveway, back to the sidewalk, and directly on my backside. Luckily, it turned out.

A car had hit me. A van, to be exact.

CHAPTER TWO

The *click* of gears shifting and an insistent series of *bings* preceded heavy footsteps crunching on gravel. I peered up into a broad, familiar face, framed by exactly no hair.

"Mavis?" When he recognized me, his glamour dropped long enough to reveal ruddier skin and a set of coffee-yellowed tusks.

He was a faerie of the troll variety, fully tithed. Which meant I'd better not ask him any questions. Three of those in one day to a faerie meant you owed them a favor. Too many favors meant owing your life.

"Sorry, Mr. Micello." He didn't like being called by his courtly rank, which despite his fifty years was only baron but at least better than a mere lord.

"Don't apologize." He helped me up. Stiffly. Rumor had it his knees had no more cartilage after a recent injury in service to the Faerie monarchs. "What are you doing out the night before school starts?"

"Um, nothing much." I chuckled, crossing my arms and staring off at the tippy-top of the Morgenstern's mulberry tree, which I could faintly see over the eaves of their house.

"Can I drive you home?"

"Um, no." I sniffled.

"Anywhere else, then?"

I shook my head, knowing full well that if I spoke another word, I'd end up ugly crying right there in the street. Merlinis weren't supposed to weep in public, let alone in front of the head of a rival family. I was already in heaps of trouble.

"How about a frosty beverage, then?" He shuffled toward the van's passenger side, momentarily blocking the bubble-lettered airbrushed words Moonstruck Music on the side. "Least I can do after knocking you over."

I was thirsty so I nodded and got in when he opened the door. I'd been in Paolo's van before, with his nephew Bar driving. The odor of old coffee highlighted by a hint of ozone from the audio equipment in back brought hopeful memories back.

Ones from last year, when we thought Crow would pull off graduation and getting out. Before the entire weight of escape from Salem rested solely on my shoulders.

Tears rolled down my face.

Long years in the nest had given me plenty of time to rehearse a silent weeping routine. Paolo didn't say a word about my pathetic sniveling. I'd managed to hide it.

When he pulled up in front of Tropica Mart and handed me a tissue, my delusions fell like a picture window struck by a fastball.

"I don't expect you to talk about whatever it is to me, but I hope you find somebody to trust with it soon."

"Thanks, Mr. Micello."

"Paolo."

"Um, Paolo." The name felt odd, like biting a red gumdrop expecting cherry and getting cinnamon. Not quite right, but still true. I wrinkled my nose. "Yeah, Paolo works for now."

"Do you want me to bring you something?"

"Nah. The Mart calms me down. Just let me blow my nose." I did, then held the damp tissue gingerly as I exited the vehicle. Fortunately, I could deposit it in a wastebasket beside the door before going into the *bodega*.

I'd been there before, over the summer while hiding from Piercing

Whispers. They practiced in the basement apartment across the street, where most of them lived, including one of those two aforementioned older-than-me friends. I spied on them more often than I liked to admit.

Speaking to Cadence was forbidden for several reasons. The closest I could get to my old friend was haunting Palmer Street over the summer. So I'd seen the inside of Tropica Mart a time or ten. Thousand. The man behind the counter tolerated me because I helped his dhampyr son stock the shelves without asking for pay. It'd be rude not to greet him.

"Hi, Mr. DelSangre." I grinned, hoping he wouldn't say anything about my puffy eyes, which he'd noticed because he was a vampire.

"Hello, *avita*." He grinned. "Excited for school tomorrow?"

"Uh, yeah." I nodded. "I'm just gonna, uh."

I jerked a thumb at the row of refrigerated cabinets at the back of the store. He nodded.

I paced along, gazing almost past the rows of drinks in the coolers, unsure what I wanted. Or even how I'd gotten kicked out of the house in the first place. It didn't make sense. How did she know where I'd been?

Shifters had enhanced senses of smell, but I'd stayed in the park long enough for the faerie scents from the sanitarium to wear off. I stood in front of a random glass-fronted case, tugging the locket on its chain around my neck. Still, I couldn't figure it out. I sighed and shook my head.

"Try the Snapple. Peach tea. It's my favorite. Maybe you'll like it too."

I didn't jump at the unexpected voice despite its newness, mostly out of habit. Acting startled at the nest had consequences and habits carried over like remainders in long division. The speaker took it in stride by tugging on the chrome handle, releasing a cold front over my still tear-sticky face.

"Here." A pallid hand pulled a glass bottle off the shelf and held it out to me.

"Uh, thanks?" I reached for the beverage and looked up at the same time. I got an eyeful of chestnut brown hair in need of a trim and corrected my gaze's angle downward a little. "Oh, hi."

The guy standing in front of me was short, fine-boned too. Definitely not a shifter either because he smelled almost mundane. His eyes smiled. A glance down told me his mouth wasn't on board. I'd barely ever seen that, a mismatched expression that meant the opposite of trouble.

He wore all black, which might've made him look smaller than he was. I would have guessed his age younger than mine, but those smiling eyes had depth to them. Maybe he'd seen a thing or three. I got the impression he was older than he looked. Was he a vampire, like Mr. DelSangre?

My fingertips brushed his and destroyed that idea. His hands were warm, like mine.

"Sorry," he said.

"I'm not. I mean, don't be." I didn't bother pasting a smile on my lips as I had in the nest earlier. Faking it for someone who seemed this genuine felt wrong. "I'm Mavis."

"Ed." He cocked his head to his left as though listening. "Uh, Redford. From Providence." He did the listening thing again. "I'm here for school."

"Gallows Hill?" I asked, hopeful. Folks from in town knew my infamous last name. Here was someone from away who'd make up their mind based on me, not the Merlinis in general.

"Messing Academy." He sighed.

"Oh." I sighed too. "Figures."

"What?"

"I'm at Gallows Hill. Sort of hoped I'd met a classmate."

"Same." He grinned, then swept his too-long bangs away from his face. "They don't have dorms, so I'm staying with the Gallows Hill folk at their new boarding house. My roommate's one of your classmates."

"Really?"

"Yeah, Cosmo's a shifter. We grew up together."

"And you?"

"Not a shifter."

"No, I know Messing's for psychics. What's your talent?"

"Oh." He swallowed, then dropped the word like it weighed a metric ton. "Medium."

"That's so cool." This time, I grinned for real.

"Really?" He raised an eyebrow.

"It's only the best psychic talent." My grin turned into a smile before I could stop it.

"Most people would argue that point." He shot a dirty look off to his left, which finally made sense. He'd been interacting with a ghost this whole time. "Are you a changeling?"

"No, just an odd duck." I chuckled. "Figuratively. I'm a raven stuck in a nest of crows. Anyway, thanks for recommending this." I jiggled the bottle of tea. "Tell your ghost friend hi for me."

"Rob can hear you. He says greetings and salutations back." Ed smirked, then put on what I could only describe as a hoity-toity accent. "He's colonial."

"Wow." My face made a genuine smile that time. I swallowed and took a step back, shocked by my expression like a total weirdo.

"Thanks." Ed grabbed his bottle of tea like it was no big deal. He'd seen a thing or few, then. "Anyway, I have to get back, so—"

"You gotta go." I nodded. "Thanks, Ed."

"See you again sometime." He turned and headed back toward the front of the store.

"Bye."

I took my time making my way through Tropica Mart. I had nowhere to be, for one thing. Also, I didn't want Ed aware of my entire plight. Weakness happened. I wasn't supposed to show any. After perusing chicharrones and cans of Café Bustelo, I finally went to the register after he'd left.

"Is that all?" Paolo asked. "Are you sure?"

"Yeah." I passed the bottle to Mr. DelSangre at the register. Paolo paid a dollar, and we stepped out on the sidewalk.

"What are you doing after you drink that?" His eyebrows lifted, wrinkling his brow.

"Uh." I swigged tea to avoid answering.

He said nothing, just walked toward the van, a cane I hadn't noticed him leaning on before tapping the pavement at his side. I went along, drinking more peach tea. Ed was right. It was good. I'd try the other three flavors before deciding whether it was my favorite or not, though.

"So, you got kicked out."

"I never said that."

"You didn't have to." He sighed. "You're Morgan Merlini's daughter."

"Fair point."

"Listen, I have an idea—"

"No." I stopped walking. He stopped with his back to me, head tilted. "It's my fault I'm in trouble. You shouldn't clean up the mess I made."

Paolo surprised me by throwing his head back and laughing, full from the gut, rich as ninety-two percent chocolate. He leaned on the van with one hand, made a shuffling turn, and faced me, grinning.

"It's not funny."

"Sorry." He reached up with one substantial hand and wiped his eye. "Seems like yesterday I heard the same thing from another bird shifter down on her luck. Anyway, you can spend the night in a tree or avoid this situation altogether in the future."

"That's impossible."

"Not with my connections." He shook his head. "Would a shared roof and three squares four blocks from campus make a difference?"

"If you burn a connection, I'm in debt, questions or no." I put my hands on my hips, sloshing a drop of tea on my shoe. "And in even more trouble. Merlinis and Micellos might as well be Capulets and Montagues."

"Helping you means losing a favor, yes. It also lets me pay somebody else back. It's a wash."

"You'll have to promise I won't owe."

"I swear by the Goblin King, my help with your living arrangements won't put you in my debt, extrahuman or otherwise. I swear it twice. And thrice."

I swallowed. That promise was serious business. The monarchs were the be-all-end-all for Fae.

"Lead on, Paolo."

We got back in the van to save his knees, he said. A few minutes later, he stopped it in front of an old brick building. It had four steps in front and a red door framed by Doric columns. In the orange glow of the street light and the shadow of the van, one looked crimson and the other indigo. Upon closer inspection, I discovered both coated with a thick layer of white paint.

The door opened before we could knock on it. The light inside made the person holding it seem like a cardboard cut-out. I let Paolo go ahead, glancing to my right at our greeter as I walked by.

I knew her. Not personally, but I'd seen her at Crow's ball games, and her face was all over the brochures for Gallows Hill School. The name that went with the pictures the year Crow started there tumbled from my mouth.

"Principal Hawkins?"

"Formerly." She tilted her head, appraising me as she shut the door behind me. "It's Klein now. You're Mavis Merlini. Apologies in advance for the coming outburst."

CHAPTER THREE

She turned, pursing crimson lips and narrowing amber eyes at Paolo. Then, she planted her feet and put her hands on her hips, nostrils flaring. Flour streaked the blue apron she wore over her knee-length floral dress.

"This had better be good, Uncle P." The tip of one brown patent Mary Jane shoe tapped the foyer's marble floor. "You've got a lot of nerve, coming here while I'm trying to get the boarders settled in."

"I've got one more."

"Please. I wasn't born yesterday." She rolled her eyes. "Mavis lives in town."

"All the same, she needs a place to stay. By my last count, there's room for one more freshman. With a full house, you can petition the Harcourts for another grant."

"True." The principal nodded. "I'll need a reason I can put on paper."

"I found your locally registered student here on the street. Unstable living situation, family history of same."

He seemed to be trying awfully hard to convince her to take me in. If she was the person he owed, I'd kiss a gnome.

She turned that gaze on me, raising an eyebrow. It softened unexpectedly. Her eyes wandered over my wardrobe of threadbare unisex hand-me-downs, streaked with dirt where I'd fallen. And my lack of luggage. By the time her eyes met mine again, her foot had stopped tapping.

"Is this true?"

Principal Klein was a dhampyr. Which meant her powers included an air of goodwill and trustworthiness. After the night I had and the chance she offered, those made little difference.

"Yes, ma'am."

She opened the door, letting us into a small foyer with benched coat trees on either side. The double doors into the gleaming hallway beyond stood propped open with rubber wedges.

"It's Matron in this building." Her hands fell from her hips like leaves in October. "Principal on campus. You'll need bed linens. And something to wear while I have Sid launder your clothes. I hope spare gym uniforms will do. Size small?"

"Medium, actually." I let out a too high-pitched chuckle. "Uh, I'm not really—"

"The athletic type. I've heard." One corner of her mouth turned up. "Everyone at Gallows Hill starts the day with a PE session. They're sweats, comfy enough for pajamas."

"Since you put it that way." I shrugged.

Matron Klein held the watch on her wrist against her temple. At first, I thought of an actress in a melodrama. As she moved it away, I heard footsteps on the stairs inside the hall to my right. A guy who looked like he might be a senior ran down them two at a time.

He was on the burly side, with a round freckled face and reddish hair that clashed with the red slouchy beanie on his head.

"Matron Klein tells me you're Mavis Merlini."

"Uh, what?" I blinked because she'd said no such thing.

"I'm John, RA for the freshmen." He held out his hand, but I didn't shake it. He shrugged and lowered it, slowly enough that I noticed he wore the same kind of watch as the matron. So, our principal and chaperones communicated with magipsychic devices. Good to know. "Wanna see your room?"

"Sure."

He led me up the stairs. As I followed, I heard Paolo and Matron Klein talking in hushed voices behind me.

"—got a hard road ahead of her."

"If only we had this house last—"

Their words faded as we rounded the corner at the landing. John stopped and turned.

"Hey, I wanted to say I played Bishop's Row last year with your brother." John's nose wrinkled. "But Bar kept saying you're—"

"That's an uncomfortable subject, John."

I tilted my head and neutralized my expression the way Mom did when she wanted to be intimidating. Despite the fact that this guy had almost a foot of height on me and was probably a redcap changeling to boot, it worked.

"Sorry."

"I didn't catch your last name."

"Uh, Clayton."

"Lay off the topic of my family from now on, Clayton."

"I can respect that." He winced.

"Thanks." I'd played the scary death omen bird card and discovered I hadn't liked it. "Sorry."

"It's all good." We climbed the rest of the steps to the second floor in silence.

"Whoa." I stopped at the top, blinking. "Does she have a time machine or something?"

The second-floor hallway was paneled in deep amber marble, striated with waves of gold and silver. The floor was a lighter color. Though it was all stone, the effect was inviting and warm. Doors segmented the walls at even intervals, their wood stained to match with doorknobs. The hinges and doorknobs were crystal instead of metal.

"This is next door to impossible."

"Huh?" John looked over his shoulder at me.

I flapped my hands at the décor. "I just walked into *The Great Gatsby*."

"Movie buff?"

"No, read it." I ran my hand down a marble column. "I can't believe all this. It's got to be glamour."

"It's real." He pointed at his hat and his eyes. "Come on."

He kept walking as if he was in a hurry. Sensible of John after I'd turned the intimidation up to eleven. Unfortunate for me because I could have used the ten-cent tour and this wasn't even a penny.

Mom's tactics hadn't worked for Crow here at Gallows Hill. No wonder they had me batting zero. This guy was the RA, too. The person I'd need to ask for help in emergencies. I should have apologized.

Before I could, he knocked on a door at the far end of the hall on the right, 204. It opened almost immediately, framing a girl my age and height but pretty much my exact opposite in every other physical way.

My skin was pale and dull, like scuffed ivory. Hers was dewy and golden. My black hair hung in lank tangles over my shoulders. Rich brown coils framed her face like a corona. She bounced on her toes. I wanted to sink into the floor.

"I'm Kiara." She smiled, showing off a charming set of dimples. "Are we roommates?"

"Yeah, Mavis here is rooming with you." John nodded. "I've got to go help Matron Klein finish baking. See you."

"This is so awesome!" Kiara clapped her hands, then stepped aside and waved at the room. "They said I'd be alone in here, rattling around like the last bean in the bowl. Come on in. Is your luggage downstairs? I can get one of the boys in 203 to drag it up. I'm from Amherst, sort of. How about you?"

"Uh, other side of town." I walked in past her. "What do you mean, Amherst sort of?"

"People assume it's Georgia when I say Lenox." She grinned. "Are you a changeling or a shifter?"

"Shifter." I headed toward the large window, which was right in the middle of the exterior wall. It opened enough for me to fly out of in bird form, thank goodness. "Raven."

"Oh, so the window's got to be important for you. I'm a Sidhe changeling, but my family's all lion shifters. Dad has a mane and everything." She giggled. "Did you know the matron's serving cupcakes downstairs? Now that you're here, it'll be almost like a party."

"Party." I snorted. "Fun."

"Hey, are you okay?" She leaned on the wall beside the window, which I still stood looking out of. "You don't seem happy. Are you homesick?"

Our differences weren't entirely physical. Kiara put the extra in extrovert, and I liked keeping my head down. She didn't know that. Or anything about me. The Merlinis in general, either.

Also, she was kind in the way that makes walls fall and guts spill. I refused to drop mine. It wouldn't be fair, dumping all my drama on Kiara. She was here for school, to learn and make friends. Not be my counselor.

"It's been a rough day."

"Hmm." She held her hand out, palm toward me, gazing at the back of it. "Everyone else got here on Friday, unpacked, had orientation. Here you are, the night before class. Do you want a tour or something?"

I closed my eyes. "I kind of need a few minutes to myself, if you don't mind."

"I grok that."

"Grok?" I opened my eyes and tilted my head to one side.

"Yeah, from this." She reached for a book on the shelf by her bed, then handed it to me.

"*Stranger in a Strange Land*?"

"You can borrow it. It's sci-fi though because I'm an enormous nerd. Anyway, I'm out of your hair and off to visit the ladies in 202. I'll be back at eight with those cupcakes, though."

The door closed behind her. I turned the book over in my hands. The back didn't have an actual description, only a collection of flattering quotes from critics. I had no idea what it was about.

Reading was my favorite escape, so I wasn't picky. I kicked my shoes off, sat on the stripped bed, started reading, and promptly lost track of everything until a knock on the door startled me.

I sprang up, determined to hide the pulpy paperback somewhere as usual. Then remembered I wasn't at the nest and didn't have to. Nobody here would care that I'd been reading, and fiction no less. I shook my head and tucked the book in the crook of my arm.

"Um, come in."

The door opened, and there was my older new friend, Ed Redford from Providence. He tugged a white canvas sack across the threshold, panting slightly. After hauling it to the foot of my bed, he leaned against my desk, pulled a gray inhaler from his hoodie pocket, and took two puffs.

"Sorry." I lifted the bag easily and set it at the foot of my bed. "And thanks."

"Huh?" Ed lowered the inhaler. I noticed he'd painted his nails black sometime in the last hour. "I mean, you're welcome. But I don't get the sorry part."

"Well, you know." I put one hand on the back of my head.

"Because I use my inhaler, you have to apologize? No." He shook his head.

"It's more like, if I hadn't been a twit to John, he would have—"

"A-s-s-u-m-e." He grinned. "Ass. You. Me."

"Assume?"

"I volunteered for linen hauling duty."

"Why?"

"I know what it's like, ending up someplace unexpected with just the shirt on your back."

"Oh." I opened the bag and peered inside because I didn't know how else to react to someone my age sounding wise.

The bag contained everything Matron Klein had asked for and then some. In addition to five sets of Gallows Hill sweats, sheets, pillows, and a thick wool blanket, it had an unopened pack of Hanes women's briefs, some sports bras, and socks. One thing was missing. "Dang it."

"Dang what now?"

"No toothbrush." I sighed. "Or soap."

"That kind of stuff shows up in the bathroom cupboard when you need it."

"How?"

"Faerie architecture." He waved a hand at all the glorious craftsmanship.

"Looks mundane to me."

"Untrained eye. But it is. I know it well."

"You're no ordinary medium, Ed."

"Bet you say that to all the psychics."

He sounded like me. Evading. Deflecting. Pretending around what he couldn't or wouldn't say. If the Merlinis were good at one thing, it was faking it. Ed could have held his own at the nest.

"Nah. Just the ones risking severe respiratory distress on my behalf."

His snort was almost a chuckle. He opened his mouth to say something, but we both heard a voice shrieking his name from down the hall.

"Hope." He winced.

"What?" I swallowed past the inexplicable lump in my throat.

"My sister from another mister." He shrugged. "Gotta go."

"Yeah, I grok that." I nodded, unable to grin. "See you later."

"Later." He headed out.

I put *Stranger in a Strange Land* on the empty desk and made my bed. After that, I opened the Hanes packages, stowed their contents in the dresser's top drawer, took a pair of each along with a set of sweats, and headed into the hall to look for the bathroom.

It was easy to find, only one door with ebony inlay lettering that read "lavatory." The fixtures were chrome and porcelain white, and the floor was checkerboard tile. A row of sinks sat along the wall on the hall side, with mirrors above them and tables in between.

I turned to find four more doors. Like the main one, ebony inlay marked them. Ladies, gentlemen, gentlepersons. The fourth, I read aloud.

"Supplies." I turned the knob on that one and pulled, unsure what to expect.

Every personal care item I could imagine was inside, neatly arranged on shelves. I grabbed an assortment of toiletries, including a hairbrush and toothbrush, then headed through the door marked ladies, which opened on a tiled wall. That bewildered me until I noticed I had to turn right into the room.

Three-quarters of the space was devoted to toilets and shower stalls. A large clawfoot tub sat in one corner with a screen leaning on the wall nearby, a luxury I'd use some other time. My stomach rumbled when I remembered the cupcakes.

The shower stalls had full-length doors, with a bench and hooks inside and a waterproof curtain between that and the part with all the water. I hung my clean clothes on the hooks, then leaned my forehead against the cool tile and closed my eyes because there wasn't a towel.

Right as I decided to shower anyway and dry myself with the cleanest part of my t-shirt, I noticed a basket under the bench. With a pile of fluffy towels inside, of course.

"I grok nothing about this place," I said to nobody in particular. Which, of course, was one excellent reason to get educated formally. The school of hard knocks taught me that what you don't know will hurt you. As I showered, I tried making sense of the strange facilities.

Ed had mentioned faerie architecture. There were all kinds of water-affiliated faeries and pure. Gallows Hill educated and employed plenty of them. The school hadn't used this building before, though.

One of Crow's teammates had to live with a cousin in an apartment for almost three years. The bits of conversation I'd overheard between Paolo and the matron supported that.

Could Paolo owe whoever remodeled the boarding house? If so, they were no small fry, what with all the fancy décor and magic supply closets.

What if they were new in town or a powerful infrequent visitor allied with the Micellos? Could that explain Mom's shortened fuse? She'd recently backed the wrong magus during her failed power grab.

I shut off the water, wishing I could abandon the gyre of unprovable hypotheticals as easily. Once dry and dressed, I noticed a second empty basket under the bench labeled toiletries. The soap, shampoo, conditioner, and lotion went in there. My dirty clothes went into a laundry hamper I hadn't noticed before by the bathtub. I brought the brushes and toothpaste out to the sinks, where I put them to good use.

Once done, I noticed my name on the back of the brushes. So I took them back to my room, where Kiara had arrived with two cupcakes and a small carton of milk for each of us.

Her chatter about the admittedly delicious desserts distracted me from my troubles, and she seemed content with my cake-muffled monosyllabic responses. Somehow, despite my worst intentions, I felt better. More normal, maybe. Because I still wasn't sure exactly what that meant for most people.

"Hey, Kiara?"

"Hmm?"

"I just wanted to say thanks." I nodded at *Stranger in a Strange Land*, which still sat on my desk. "For the book. It's good so far."

"So far?" She stared at the book then glanced at me. "Damn, girl. Looks like you read almost half already."

"I read a lot." My face felt warm.

"Yeah, me too." She grinned.

We sat talking about books until we both yawned. After brushing my teeth a second time but in good company, I went to bed. I was asleep before my head hit the pillow.

CHAPTER FOUR

The giant bee from my dream faded until only its insistent buzz remained. Threatening, too. Because every sense except sight told me someone else was in the room. Also, my alarm didn't sound like that.

The Dremel Mom used in her pewter-smithing hobby did. She'd threatened me with it before. Put a couple of holes in books she didn't want me reading, too.

I leaped from the bed in the slate-colored morning light, shifting into my bird form automatically and streaking toward the nest's bare gable-peaked rafters.

Then ended up clonking my noggin on a plaster ceiling instead.

"Mavis?"

Looping in a circle didn't help the dizziness but gave me a view of the unfamiliar room. The pretty deep-brown face peering up at me from the other bed brought the entirety of last night back. The brocade fabric covering my headboard made an excellent perch.

Being in bird form saved me tons of embarrassment. Nobody can see you blush through feathers. Plus, preening after landing looked better than hand-wringing or fist-clenching.

I hopped down among the tossed bedclothes and shifted back.

Kiara averted her eyes, then glanced back at me. Her mouth dropped open.

"How'd you do that?"

"Huh?" I blinked. I'd told her I was a shifter the night before.

"Keep your clothes?"

"Oh." I pulled my shell locket out from the collar of my sweatshirt. "It's this."

The clock at her bedside buzzed, which explained everything. I'd panicked over an alarm like a birdbrain.

"Cool." She grinned, pressed a button on the clock, then got out of bed. "Time to get ready or we'll be late."

I got up and made my bed, noticing in the process that my laundered clothes from yesterday were at the foot of it, along with a battered brown satchel and a schedule.

"Gym? First thing? Really?" I rolled my eyes.

"Yup, recreation twice a day." She collected a toiletry case and a set of sweats.

"Bummer." I pointed at my attire. "At least I'm dressed for that already."

"Bring your regular stuff in the bag." Kiara stepped into a pair of cozy-looking slippers and headed toward the door. "I'm not. So, see you downstairs in a few."

"Yeah." I gave her a moment, then grabbed my hair and tooth brushes from the night before and used them at the sinks in the bathroom. Afterward, I took Kiara's advice and packed my regular clothes in the bag, which already had a spiral notebook and a pack of pencils inside. It had the letters HL stamped on the front flap.

"Wonder who you belonged to." My stomach rumbled. "Food first."

Out in the hall, my high top sneakers squeaked on the marble floor. I stared down at them, startled, but forgot to stop walking. Which is why I ran into another girl, tripped over her foot, and hurtled headfirst toward bare stone.

"Whoa!" an airy voice said.

Unexpectedly strong arms darted out, faster than mundane speed, and caught me a centimeter before my nose made contact with the floor. Then, they set me on my feet.

"Uh, thanks." I took a look at my rescuer, whose voice didn't match her build at all.

Her hair was red and styled in a bouncy bob with bangs, and she had the height and build of a professional basketball player. Her face was more handsome than pretty, and she didn't wear jewelry.

"No biggie." She shrugged. "Hi, I'm Hope Dunstable, from 202. You must be Kiara's new roommate."

"Yeah, Mavis."

"Are you okay?"

"Yeah, thank you." I shook my head. "The last thing I need on top of everything else is a broken nose."

"Wouldn't that heal, though?"

"Hmm."

"You're a shifter, right?"

"Uh, yes. But we haven't met, so—"

"It's Ed. He tells me practically everything."

"Oh. Okay."

"Djeet?"

"Gesundheit." I wondered whether she had allergies.

"Sorry, I forget not everyone speaks Rhode Island. Did you eat?"

"No, I was on my way to do that, actually."

"Well, come on then. Before our upstairs neighbors eat all the bacon and eggs, and we get stuck with oatmeal. Or worse, cold cereal."

I followed Hope down the stairs, bemused that her idea of a harsh fate was cold cereal for breakfast. Though clearly, she was as athletic as I wasn't, so not enough protein might be a problem for her.

The aromas wafting down the hall had me drooling like a dog shifter. Or how I imagined they might, I'd never met one.

Hope needn't have worried. The room we walked into showed no signs of a food shortage. A series of round tables filled it, each set up family-style with serving dishes of breakfast fare. However, something was missing.

"Do we eat right off the table?"

"Nah." Hope chuckled. "Watch."

When she sat, a place setting appeared magically. Nothing fancy, the proper usage of dessert forks and appetizer spoons wasn't part of our education. Instead, it felt homey.

Except I had less idea what that was actually like than the dog shifter drooling matter.

"Life is a battlefield," I mumbled before sitting.

"Huh?"

"Life is breakfast," I enunciated. Then, I poured grapefruit juice.

"Damn skippy." She raised her glass of soymilk. "Salut!"

"Cheers." I clinked glasses with her.

"Hey." The resonant baritone came from my left. I turned.

This fellow reminded me of a bulldog, broad and powerful but compact. A red ball cap perched haphazardly on his head, backward over buzz-cut hair. He would have looked right at home in Irzyk Park.

"Hi," I said.

"You're Kiara's roommate, right?"

"Yeah." I shrugged. "And you are?"

"Wyatt. What's your name?"

"Nunya."

"Huh?"

"Nunya Business."

"Ha. Where's Kiara now?" His toothy smile reminded me of a shark. "In the shower?"

I'd never had anyone talk to me that way, though I'd heard it happen to others. Having six scary older siblings had given me some level of immunity to creeps in general. Refusing to give my name might have been a bad idea.

"Ask her yourself." The voice behind me was cold as ice, despite the New England old-money accent. "And leave our table at once. You uncouth little toe-rag."

"Uh." Wyatt stared past me and stepped backward, swallowing. "Yeah, okay."

He turned and beat a hasty retreat toward a table full of upperclassmen, which included the RA. Surely, my reputation would precede me the next time I tangled with Wyatt.

I turned to find a reptile behind me. Or more accurately, a dragon shifter who'd begun transforming her partially shifted jet talons, sea-green scales, and silver eyes back toward human. No wonder Wyatt left.

"I would've chased him off eventually, Say."

"You wouldn't." The girl tossed glossy waves of black hair with green highlights over her shoulder. "You're way too nice, Hope. And stop calling me Say."

"What do you want?" Hope said around a mouthful of bacon. "You know what I am."

"Hush about that." Saya looked down her nose at me. "Who are you?"

"I'm Mavis."

"Yes, yes. I know your name and other details." She sniffed. "I'm talking about *who* you are. What sort of people you come from."

"I don't know what you mean." I did. I also didn't want to answer a question like that. Right as I thought silence equated a free pass out of admitting to my infamous family, someone else sauntered over.

I froze. At first, I thought the newcomer was my brother, escaped from Danvers Sanitarium. He had the same kind of well-worn trench coat, gangly height, and wavy black hair. His olive complexion and the big goofy grin he wore shattered the illusion.

"Hey, Saya! It's breakfast, not a debutante ball."

"Wish it was." She rolled her eyes. "Leave me alone, Cosmo."

"Oh no, that won't do at all!" Cosmo mimicked her accent. "Your seat, Miss Harcourt."

He pulled the empty chair on the other side of Hope away from the table, bowed at the waist, and waved a hand at it.

"Can we stop ribbing the new kid and enjoy this fine dining now?"

Hope slapped a hand over her mouth, which was a good thing because otherwise, she would have sprayed soymilk and laughter everywhere. Saya sighed, placed her palm on her face briefly, and shook her head before sitting.

"Hey, Mavis." Cosmo took the seat beside me. "I know so much about you it feels like I already know you."

"I get that a lot." I jerked a thumb at the other girls. "You're Ed's roommate."

"Right." He reached out and heaped scrambled eggs on his dish, then scooped up some more and raised his eyebrows at my plate. "He said you're a bird shifter. So are you, I mean do you—"

"Consume the unborn, yes." I nodded gravely. "I'm an *evil* bird who defies and intimidates her enemies by eating eggs."

"And a comedian, apparently." Cosmo smiled and put the eggs on my plate, adding bacon a moment later. "Ed said you were cool. He didn't tell me you were so pretty, though."

Kiara waved at me from across the table before sitting on Saya's other side. The four of them could have been leads on a TV show, and there I was, getting complimented. I'd never seen a healthy way of responding to that in real life. When in the inspiration for a teen drama, do as the dramatists do.

"Hungry takes precedence." I turned back to my plate, unwilling to endure gym class on an empty stomach. Or threaten Cosmo for daring to drop a compliment, as my mother would have done.

He turned the conversation toward more comfortable topics, boasting about his friends. He and Hope wanted to try out for the Bishop's Row team. They kept trying to nudge Saya toward cheer squad. Apparently, she'd been into dance practically since hatching. She wasn't sure.

Wondering how the hour stood, I glanced up at the clock above the door. Ed stood under it, tugging the stiff collar on his uniform blazer, eyes wide as he looked at something or someone behind me.

I looked over my shoulder, but nobody was there. At least, not anyone I could see. Ed was a medium, and this was an old building. For all I knew, the room was full of ghosts obscuring his view. So I waved until he headed over. Slowly and with his mouth moving. Instead of taking a seat, he stopped between Cosmo and me.

"Hey, Mavis?"

"Yeah?"

"Did you do anything with the satchel before you used it?"

"No. Just put some clothes in it, like a regular person."

"Okay." He nodded at me, then looked past me and nodded again.

"It comes with a ghost, huh?"

"Yeah, old friend." He sat on the other side of Cosmo and let his eyes wander over the food on the table. "Didn't expect him to show, though."

"Cool." I grinned. "So far, I like your other friends. So what's his—"

A bell rang. Not the buzzing claxons you expect in schools, either. A handbell, courtesy of Matron Klein, who tapped her watch and spoke with an amplified voice.

"Five minutes."

"Fewmets." Ed winced. "I'm late."

"Eat a sandwich," Cosmo said. "Sorry if I sound parental, but no skipping meals on my watch."

"Yeah, on it." He grabbed two pieces of toast from a basket in front of him.

The scrambled egg spoon lifted out of its bowl and dropped its contents on one piece of toast. Seemingly on its own but probably a ghost. Maybe the partner Ed mentioned the night before or his old friend from my borrowed satchel. He added cheese, closed the sandwich, and took an enormous bite.

Already done with my breakfast, I decided to be helpful on my way out and poured him a glass of orange juice. When I set it down in front of him, he looked up and smiled.

"Thanks."

"There goes my good deed for the day."

"My brother would say kindness matters so do more than one."

"I'll keep that in mind." I nodded. "See you later."

On my way to the hall, I realized I should have replied by asking what Ed himself would say. Everyone I'd met so far except for Wyatt seemed to know how to act around people. Friendly, too. I felt like I'd grown up on another planet.

Also, I hadn't gotten the memo about how to get to class. Nobody was at the door to the street, which was closed unlike the night before.

Was I too early? So what if I was? There was a saying about early birds for a reason. Maybe leaving before everybody else would work to my advantage.

Someone tugged my sleeve.

"Um, Mavis?"

"Yes?"

I turned to find Kiara grinning while pointing over her shoulder with her thumb.

"We're taking the shortcut."

"The what now?"

"Come on, or you'll end up getting there after the rest of us."

I followed her to the other end of the hall, where a line of mostly upperclassmen stood. A door opened, bright lights and a scent of citrus wood soap invading the hall like heralds of future migraines.

"Ow."

"Sorry, dude."

I turned to find a tan guy with sun-bleached hair in board shorts and a Billabong t-shirt in line behind me.

"Dudette."

"Sorry. Again." He flashed white teeth but in a wince, not a smile. His tan reddened. "Because I just misgendered you after stepping on your foot."

"It's okay. You didn't step on it. I was thinking how whatever's through that door is migraine fuel."

"So we're cool?"

"Sure."

"Thanks. Hey, are you—"

I turned away, not wanting to say my name. The last thing I wanted was to get branded Least Likely to Succeed before even setting foot on campus.

"Mavis." Kiara elbowed me, eyes wide. She cut her eyes toward the surfer then back to me, raising her eyebrows.

"What?" I shrugged.

"Sorry about my roommate." Kiara looked over her shoulder and introduced both of us.

"I'm Brandon Porter. Do either of you know if they have a pool at the gym? Doesn't smell like it, but I'm a selkie, not a wolf shifter so what do I know?"

"Not in the gym." I shook my head. "There's dock access, though. And a boathouse."

"Aces!"

"I don't know about Mavis, but I'm not." Kiara dropped him a wink. "Ace, that is. I'm into guys." He blushed again. The line started moving. "Nice meeting you, Brandon."

"Yeah." He grinned. "Totally stoked to meet you, too."

Kiara linked her arm through mine and paced forward. I preferred keeping up with her to tripping over my feet. She leaned closer and whispered, "He's cute!" She grinned but noticed when I didn't mirror it. "Something wrong?"

"Nervous." I swallowed the truth about why. "Worried about first day, uh, problems. School is—"

"Full of people. I grok it now. You're no social creature." She nodded. "You weren't at orientation, so I'll tell you what they said. Because we're at a school full of hormonal shifters and changelings, they have chill-out chambers. You'll see a blue door with a glass knob. If it gets really bad, like dropping glamour or fight or flight, find one and go in. Unless the knob's red. That means someone's already occupied it so just find the next one."

"Oh, thanks, Kiara."

"If I hadn't known, you would have told me, right?"

"Yeah." I wasn't sure whether I'd answered honestly. Being in a position to help someone just because was uncharted territory for me.

I hadn't noticed that we'd walked through the magic door and into the gym four blocks away. Or knew exactly when Kiara dropped my arm and headed off with Saya. That's how messed up I was.

A whistle shrilled three times on the other side of the gym. While heading toward the coach who'd used it, I glanced around. I already knew this place. Everything was wood, glass, or stone. The markings on the wood were enchanted on, movable to change the court for any sort of game or exercise.

It was a track, so I didn't have to listen to the burly young coach's instructions to know what came next—running and lots of it. I lagged, hanging back instead of starting with the rest of the crowd.

"Merlini, is it?" The coach nodded. "You got a doctor's note or something?"

"No." I shook my head. "It's just you weren't here when my brother played Bishop's Row," I blurted, face heating like the time I had pneumonia. "Didn't catch your name."

"Coach Bobby Tremain. I do morning gym for your section and also entertainment wrestling. Sorry about Crow. I heard he didn't graduate last year. Listen up. I'm a fair bear so I don't play favorites or single people out, either. But you've got to do the work just like everyone else."

I nodded. His eyes twinkled, making me think he did an impression of some other teacher. Maybe his coach talked like that, not long ago either. He barely looked old enough to be out of college.

"Now get ready, get it under control. And run!"

I did. Mostly because he'd reassured me. Exercise was for the birds as far as I was concerned. As in, something better done with wings in the air than legs on the ground.

He kept us on the track for three laps, which was three more than I would have liked. At least I wasn't completely winded. Coach Tremain blew the whistle in five short blasts, and a pile of yoga mats appeared.

Everybody took one. Saya unrolled hers nearby, which was comforting. Wyatt would avoid us, at least. But not Cosmo, who ended up to my other side.

I tried not to feel weird about that, which wasn't easy. Cosmo seemed like a joker, the class clown. So it was impossible to know whether his compliment at breakfast was serious. Probably not. None of my sisters were considered attractive. At least not in the conventional sense.

After Coach Tremain let us go, we washed up and changed uneventfully. At least until Saya met me by the door, eyebrows up and eyes wide.

"What?" I crossed my arms over my chest.

"I suppose we're technically *allowed* to wear what we want." She sniffed.

"Trust me. This wasn't my choice." I sighed, imagining the boots and leggings paired with my lucky red shirt and pleated black and white skirt. It probably still hung on my closet door where I'd left it the night before.

She rolled her eyes and pushed through the door, speeding up once I was through. As though she didn't want me walking near her. Considering her threads looked designer, was I surprised? No. Disappointed, yes. Someone tugged my sleeve. I kept walking.

Cosmo stepped in front of me, turned, and started walking backward.

"Don't fear the dragon lady." He waved his hand as though shooing a fly. "The family puts more on her shoulders than the rest of us."

"Are you her brother? A twin?" I blinked. "Ed called Hope his sister from another mister but looks nothing like her. You can't all be the same age. How many siblings do you have?"

"Just half a grown brother in the bio sense. But the Rhody crew all basically grew up together on Saya's compound. It's a long story, better for later. Do you mind?

"I mind more not knowing where class is." I glanced at the name on the schedule. "It says Mrs. Ambersmith, but no room number."

"Who knows the way and has two thumbs?" He chuckled and used them to point at himself. "This guy!"

I snorted and followed him through the crowded hallways. Most of the students here looked old enough for college, which I'd expected. Some of that went along with the sturdier shifter and changeling types.

Cosmo should have matched most of the ones inside the classroom because lions were part of that demographic. Though he certainly looked older than Ed, he wasn't on par with his peers. Maybe that long story had something to do with it.

The classroom had three tables with five chairs at each. Kiara, Brandon, Saya, Hope, and a plump girl I didn't know already occupied the one in front.

I would have grabbed a seat at the table in the back, but Wyatt was already there, yukking it up with the Thorne twins, wolf shifters I'd seen around town. They definitely knew all the dirt on my family.

The next best option, the middle, contained another familiar face. Ramon DelSangre wasn't an enemy. He knew who I was and didn't judge. He'd been something of a co-conspirator during my summer haunting Palmer Street through Tropica Mart's front window. I sat beside him.

"Hey, Ramon. Mind if we sit here?"

"Hey yourself." He glanced up. "No, I don't. You're in Dana Ambersmith's class too?"

"Um, did you say Dana?"

"Yeah, it's her first year teaching. She used to go here. I think the same year as—"

"My brothers. The twins." I put my hand over my mouth, suddenly queasy.

"Yeah, they make me sick, too." Ramon narrowed his eyes, studying my face. He had the wisdom to jerk his thumb at my escort and change the subject. "So, who's *el gato?*"

"*Tu parli?*" Cosmo blinked and sat next to my quasi friend.

"*Si, español. Comprendes, mis italiano?*"

They went on, sewing together something like a conversation from their cousin languages. That left me alone with the contents of my mind. One track, unfortunately.

Dana Ambersmith used to be Dana Clayton. She hated our family, with good reason. Hugh and Manny got kicked out of Gallows Hill in junior year when they put her in the hospital, but I wasn't sure why they'd fought in the first place. No wonder I'd scared John Clayton. They had to be related somehow.

I didn't want to be there, sitting in front of one of my family's victims. Before I could flee the classroom in search of the Registrar's office to transfer class sections, she walked into the room.

Her straight ice-blonde hair was caught up on the left in a bright red comb the length of my hand. The rest obscured the right side of her face, even one lens of her square-framed glasses, also red.

She dropped an enormous leather tote bag on her desk, emitting a *boom* that startled most of us. Anybody who hadn't noticed her entrance wouldn't make the mistake of overlooking her again.

"You will call me Mrs. Ambersmith. You will respond to attendance and only speak to answer questions instead of asking them. I'm tithed, so you must inquire on the subjects in Forum."

A fleshy, dimpled hand went up at the table in front.

"Excuse me—" The girl with nut-brown hair spoke.

"You must learn not to ask, Miss Connolly." Lady Ambersmith stared at me, not the girl trying to speak. "Learning the ways of faerie is part of your education. Consider it practical experience."

Saya stood.

"Some of us are aware of proper phrasing, Mrs. Ambersmith. She only wants to know, as I do, how to take notes."

"Attendance comes first. That's one strike against you, Miss."

"I'm Saya Harcourt, daughter and heir of the last dragon queen." She tossed her head. "You're a teacher, so teach us the rules."

"No questions is the rule in every first-year lecture, which tithed faeries like myself conduct. Lab covers the special phrasing practicum, where your instructor is a shifter, with good reason Miss Harcourt. I'm here to educate, not put my students in my debt."

"There must be more." Saya tilted her chin up but couldn't manage to out-snob our instructor.

Mrs. Ambersmith sneered with the left side of her mouth, revealing sharklike teeth. Saya was wrong. Our instructor wasn't only a teacher. She was also a powerfully intimidating redcap. Even a dragon couldn't deny her authority.

"Please be seated and let us continue."

Saya sat, but not before I saw her fists clench. The girl who'd initially raised her hand slouched in her seat as Hope patted Saya's shoulder. Kiara was the only one still sitting up, looking front and center.

Mrs. Ambersmith knocked thrice on the desk, though she didn't strike me as the superstitious type. The wood shimmered, revealing a tablet that appeared made of crystal. She pressed her palm on its surface, and it lit up. Magipsychic then, like the matron's watch.

"Clayton, Wyatt."

"Yes, Au—uh, Ma'am."

"Connolly, Fiona."

"Here." The name went with the slouching girl up front.

"DelSangre, Ramon."

"*Aqui.*"

"Dunstable, Hope."

"Aye."

"Gitano, Cosmo."

"Present."

She didn't call Saya, just tapped the tablet.

"Knight, Kiara."

"Here."

"Merlini."

I waited for her to say my whole name, but she didn't.

"Uh, Mavis? Here."

"Noted. Strike one, Merlini. Two more and you'll have detention to pay off your debt."

"But didn't you forget to—"

"Strike one, DelSangre. Any other objections? Remember, no questions."

Her lip curled, but only on the left. I wondered whether maybe the right side of her mouth didn't work for some reason. No. If it didn't, I knew why. My oldest brothers. The room remained silent.

"Porter, Brandon."

"Here."

"Thorne, Jaxon."

"Hey."

"Thorne, Jillian."

"Yeah."

"You may now access your tablets using the same method I did before taking attendance. If you weren't watching, imitate your more attentive peers. You won't get in trouble for copying anyone or anything here in this lecture. You must listen, watch and learn. The best way to do that is with attentiveness. Lecture is a one-way conveyance of information because learning to be cautious when speaking to the tithed is a survival skill and not optional. Are we clear?"

A jumble of affirmative responses filled the room. When they died down, she continued.

"Write your questions in your notes and ask them in Forum or Lab. Mr. Hickson has full knowledge of my entire curriculum, and we work together to write the exams he'll give. He's no easy grader. You'll get multiple chances to practice every practical skill in Lab with Doctor Aranha. Now, we begin."

Kiara helped Fiona get her tablet. Cosmo studied my hands intently and copied my movements. I couldn't see in back, but nobody else in the middle or front had any trouble.

That was a good thing. Mrs. Ambersmith's lecture was denser than last Christmas's fruitcake. The topic was basic types of extrahumans but more in-depth than what they taught in middle school.

I'd had no idea that some psychics went practically their whole lives without discovering their talent. Even after the Great Reveal, many life experiences that activated those remained rare. Especially mediumship and summoning.

She went on to discuss how extrahuman potential ran in families, along with a handful of maladies "ultimately incompatible with life," as she put it. She built on that by writing an outline of complementary, overlapping, and contradictory powers on her tablet. The words showed up on the board behind her.

I copied it all down, racing Ramon. I lost. Cosmo had simply given up writing on his tablet. Not on class, though.

He stared at the board, eyes wide and mouth slightly open, pinkies framing his face as the rest of his fingers lay in his sooty curls like snakes in midnight grass.

What had him transfixed? I opened my mouth, the question ready to spill out.

Ramon's elbow shook the impulse loose, and I continued recording everything. By the end of the two hours, my hand stung, and there was a stylus-shaped dent in my middle finger.

"Thank the gods we've got snack right now." Saya had turned to face my table, looking down at her nose at me.

"Um, yeah."

"Come along, featherbrain."

"What if she wants to go with me instead?" Ramon crossed his arms over his chest.

"I'm building an in-crowd here, DelSangre." She raised an eyebrow. "Are you suggesting everyone ought to fit in it?"

"Ramon's cool," Cosmo said.

Saya glanced toward the back of the room.

"I can't include everyone."

"Hey, I'm everyone." I stood. "So's she." I nodded at Fiona.

"But—" She blinked.

"I don't like crowds, in or otherwise. Too people-y." I slung the satchel over my shoulder and tucked my tablet inside it. "Also, the Merlinis are definitely the opposite of dragon high society. So, thanks but no thanks."

I turned my back on Saya, Cosmo, and the rest and stalked out the door. The Thorne twins stood in the back blinking, along with Brandon. Wyatt followed me into the hallway.

"Looks like the latest Merlini's antisocial. Gonna come to school packing cold iron, I bet."

"I'm harmless, just an introvert." I kept walking. Each step I took was a reminder of six siblings going down in a blaze of self-inflicted infamy, without graduating.

I spotted a blue door, the chill-out chamber. If his attack remained verbal, I might get there in time. But I couldn't let the redcap's threats break my stride.

"You need a lesson before you hurt someone. Like your brothers did."

I felt Wyatt's passage behind me, disturbing my senses. Heightened awareness of incoming blows was an indelible part of life in the nest. Universal, I thought back then. It seemed perfectly normal, imagining his hand outstretched and practically foreseeing an attack.

He'd get me by the hair, of course. Probably, he'd spit in my face and hope I threw the first punch. Plant my reputation as a bad seed. If it'd been one of the Thornes, I could have asserted dominance and gotten shifter cred. Birds are faster than wolves, and Crow taught me how to sweep a leg.

Redcaps are faeries but built like brick walls. No bird in her right mind deliberately collides with one. Winning was impossible and fighting back could put me in the infirmary. I couldn't afford to miss Forum, so I chose to suffer humiliation and stay out of trouble.

Popularity wasn't a graduation requirement.

I turned to face Wyatt Clayton, whose hand was where I'd predicted and dropped my hands to my sides.

"Fine. Do your worst."

"Stop."

The voice beside me resonated with commanding power, of a familiar sort. I stopped. Everything did.

"Cadence?" I breathed, glancing up.

It wasn't her.

Hope Dunstable stood with her hands out, strange magic shimmering between them.

"Thought you were from a faerie family, Dunstable." Wyatt snorted. "Way to sell one of your own out."

"Actually, they raised me to be fair." She tossed her head, shaking her hair off something slowly emerging behind her. "Unlike whatever you're doing here."

I tried lifting my foot, intending to move it and escape. It wouldn't budge. Wyatt's open hand trembled as though he wanted to raise his fist higher. Or lower it, maybe. Behind him, the Thorne twins whimpered. I kept my poker face on, but it wasn't easy.

For the briefest of moments, Hope Dunstable had wings. Enormous ones, with bright feathers in every color of the rainbow. They shimmered in the magical glow from her hands, which could only be glamour. She looked like an angel but wasn't. There was no such thing.

The wings shimmered out of existence, but not before a few more people noticed them.

"*Dios mio.*" Ramon put a hand over his heart and leaned against the wall.

Fiona nodded and stepped backward. I didn't blame them. If

Hope's magic hadn't kept me stuck in place, I might have done the same.

It made no sense. Changelings couldn't conjure and channel glamour like a magic element without special equipment for playing Bishop's Row. Even grade-schoolers knew winged faeries didn't have feathers. Maybe I'd imagined that part.

"What *are* you?" Wyatt paled. Okay, maybe I hadn't.

"A prodigy. Proven and tithed, which you felt after asking that." Hope's face held no whimsy, only authority. "On campus, this class section is now my crew. From now on if you want to fight, request a duel. Unless you want a turn in the ring with me. And nobody wants that."

"Guess that goes for Merlini, too." Wyatt raised an eyebrow.

"Every. One."

"Yes, ma'am." I nodded. Having someone besides the dreadful Lady Ambersmith claim authority here was a relief.

"That's captain from now on," Hope said.

"No way you got that rank." Wyatt blinked. "Or a ship."

"Sidhe Queen's Navy." Hope siphoned a stream of the glamour from her shoulder and revealed a hidden insignia. A set of embroidered amber bars appeared there, glowing with golden light. "Get your soggy bottoms to snack, already. I don't want any hangry swabbies in Forum."

"Aye, captain!" Cosmo gave her a snappy salute and marched toward the courtyard, whistling *Drunken Sailor*.

Kiara and Fiona followed, giggling with Brandon in tow. Jillian and Jaxon stalked in the same direction but on the other side of the hall, while Wyatt stomped into the bathroom alone.

"Thanks." I adjusted the satchel's strap. "Uh, captain."

"Thank Horace. I can't hear a word he says, but he's good at charades."

"I don't know a Horace."

"The ghost haunting your bag." Hope sighed. "Didn't Ed tell you about that?"

"He was running late."

"Talk to him after school. That's an order."

I nodded and went off to the courtyard. A glass ceiling covered it like an old-fashioned conservatory. All sorts of plants grew in cultivated beds, pots, and even on trellises against the glassed-in walls. I stood in line, where snacks appeared on a long marble counter, alone with my thoughts in a crowd of students from the other first-year sections.

It felt odd, calling the friendly girl who snarfed soymilk at breakfast captain. But Hope Dunstable was an actual tithed faerie, the youngest I'd ever met, even if I had no idea what type she was. Whatever she'd done to earn that must have been enormous. She probably deserved more respect than little old me could muster. And I'd thought for a minute that *I* belonged at Gallows Hill.

I took a Granny Smith apple off the snack tray and almost kept walking. But an unexplained breeze drew my attention to a cooler to the right full of bottled beverages.

"Peach Snapple." I glanced left then right before reaching out to grab one. "Thanks, Horace. If that was you and I'm not totally insane."

"Generally, questioning your sanity means you've still got at least some of it."

"Never thought of it that way," I murmured. Letting people hear me talking to myself was a bad idea, but it felt wrong somehow not to answer. Even if I wasn't supposed to hear ghosts as a garden-variety raven shifter.

"You don't have to whisper." The voice was louder this time and getting picked up by my ears.

I looked up to see a teacher gesturing at me with a bag of beef jerky in his hand. His hair was light brown but graying at the temples, held back in a long braid that lay over the shoulder of his green tweed vest.

"Thought I was hearing things."

"Rough first day for you too, then." He nodded. "Same thing, different year. They didn't have Snapple when I was a student here, though. I'm Mr. Hickson."

"You're my Forum teacher?"

"Guide. But yes. I've got First Year Forum, second section after this break. And you're Mavis Merlini."

"You knew one of my brothers. Or a sister."

"Had every one of your siblings in my classroom at one point or another." He shook his head. "I'm no stranger to your family."

"I'm sorry." I slapped my hand over my mouth.

"Me too."

"Oh no." The Snapple bottle shook in my hand. "What did they do to you?"

He popped a piece of jerky into his mouth and chewed, pondering that, and me. I settled my nerves as best I could, put the lid back on the bottle, and stowed it and the uneaten apple in my satchel. Hunger and thirst had flown the coop.

"It's more like what I didn't do." The left corner of his mouth tilted up. "I let all of them down."

"How?" I blinked.

"None graduated." He folded the top of the jerky bag over and put it in his pocket, where it crinkled.

"I'm going to."

"I don't doubt it." His grin was vaguely canine. "See you in five minutes. Second room on the right through there." He pointed over his shoulder at a doorway flanked by foxgloves.

I watched him go, then retrieved my Snapple and drank it.

Forum wasn't set up the same way as Lecture. The seating plan did away with the three long tables segmenting us into front, middle, and back. The fact they stood in a circle like a recovery meeting didn't bother me. Getting help when you needed it was important. If only the rest of my family felt the same way.

There didn't seem to be any particular chair designated for our instructor. Each seat was identical. I chose one facing the door, the better to see everybody else come in. Something felt wrong, but I couldn't put my finger on what. Until I remembered Mr. Hickson told me he'd be there and wasn't in the room.

He hadn't said what sort of extrahuman he was, though. He might be hiding with camouflage. Maybe he was a spider shifter, hanging in a web somewhere overhead. That wasn't a comforting thought, even if he acted nothing like Mrs. Ambersmith. Thank God. I wasn't sure I could go two more hours of school with another stern teacher.

My elementary classrooms were rowdily overcrowded. I'd kept my beak in a book the moment I learned to read, which made me an unremarkable but at least not annoying student for most of that time. In middle school, everything changed.

I finally activated myself. Not in the way anyone expected. I made the honor roll in seventh grade, was a peer tutor for English in eighth, and won the talent show for a scene from *As You Like It* in ninth. Mom hated all of it, especially the three months I spent dating Diego Mendez, my co-star in that scene.

Every time Mom yelled at me, Crow came around later and told me to keep going. If it hadn't been for him, I might've given up sitting in front, raising my hand, and speaking first in every class discussion.

Participating wasn't only for fun anymore. Education was the last lifeboat on the *Titanic*. I *needed* to learn.

Mrs. Ambersmith made that difficult. Even if she hadn't hated my family, interaction in there was all one way. Lecture was uncomfortably rigid, but as much as I wanted to blame the teacher, I had to admit it wasn't her fault.

"I'm being too kind. Again."

"Nothing wrong with that." Kiara took the seat next to me.

"You're not gonna tell me to stop talking to myself?"

"No, I've done that often enough as an only child." She shrugged. "I'm not judging."

"Thanks for that." I pulled my tablet out of my satchel and set it in my lap.

"Will it be like that lecture, you think?"

"Probably not. I met Mr. Hickson in the courtyard. He's kind of cool."

"You don't say." Kiara smiled, which lit her face up like the sun coming out over the ocean. I couldn't help but smile back.

I wasn't the only one struck by Kiara's expression. Wyatt Clayton stood in the door, eyes wide, staring directly at her. No surprise, with his inquiries at breakfast, before he knew who I was. Hopefully, it was only a crush because obsession was downright dangerous, another lesson learned secondhand from my brother.

"Get out of the way already." Jillian Thorne stuck one muscular arm between the door and Wyatt under his armpit, trying to get through somehow. It was no use.

Redcaps are the immovable objects of the faerie world. A teenage wolf shifter like Jillian Thorne wasn't an unstoppable force. I knew what I would've done but hesitated to offer a member of Wyatt's brute squad any advice.

"Are we the only ones who'll make it in, do you think?" Kiara asked.

"I don't know." I sighed, begrudgingly sharing my strategy for the common good. "Tickle him!"

"Oh. Right."

Jillian's fingertips dug into the jersey fabric covering Wyatt's armpit. He doubled over laughing, stumbled in through the doorway, then knocked a chair out of the circle. He sprang up a moment later, looking around to see who'd goosed him. Jillian was already gone, sitting in a chair halfway across the room. She winked at me, glanced at her brother who just walked through the door, then glared back at me again.

"That looks like a truce in the making," Kiara observed.

"If wishes were horses." I shrugged.

"You're smart. Maybe you're overthinking."

"Overthinking is the spice of life?" Cosmo took the seat on my other side. "That's what my brother says anyway."

"What is he a detective or something?" Kiara asked.

"PI. Before that, he was a diplomat with paranoia. Who turned out to be right. Literally, a tinfoil hat." Cosmo slapped his knee.

Kiara and I blinked in tandem.

"You've said enough." Saya grabbed Cosmo by the ear, yanking. He stood, shuffling away as she dragged him. I never thought I'd see the heir to all things dragon acting like a lion's grandma. But that's what happened.

"What's with them?" Ramon shook his head, then sat beside me. "The lion king and his sisters have a strange vibe."

"You mean Captain Dunstable's thing in the hall?" Kiara asked. "They're not siblings, by the way. Just grew up together."

"Saya did something like that before breakfast, Kiara." I shook my head. "Ramon's right. It was strange. I thought I saw wings."

"Wings aren't crazy in a place like this. Channeled glamour is." Ramon pointed at the corner of his eye. "During snack, I saw her do it again. She wasn't even wearing ballistae like they do for Bishop's Row."

"Dude, knock it off." Brandon sat next to Kiara, leaning forward to whisper at Ramon. "This isn't the time or place."

Kiara brightened up even more, which made sense. This morning she said Brandon was cute. He wasn't remotely my type, but I could see why she found the sunkissed surfer guy attractive.

The Thornes chuckled over their tablets while Wyatt rolled his eyes and kept stealing glances at Kiara. Brandon launched a description of his surfboard, which he couldn't wait to use this weekend. He kept asking how the local waves were, which I didn't have personal experience with. Growing up in a tourist town meant I always had stock replies to questions like that, so I gave them. Kiara listened, too.

Hope sauntered into the room, smiling and waving as if she hadn't commanded us into a copacetic state. Once she sat, Mr. Hickson faded into view at the center of the circle, shuffling his feet with one hand in his pocket.

I stood, knocking my chair backward. My face burned as I squatted to retrieve it. It felt like all my damage was on display again.

"Birdbrain." Wyatt snorted.

"Sorry," I mumbled.

"I'm Mr. Hickson, your Forum guide. Everything's valid in here."

Mr. Hickson jerked his chin at Wyatt. "Almost. I don't tolerate intolerance. But there's no such thing as a stupid or wrong question."

"What about stupid answers?" I asked.

"Those exist. If you put them on your tests, I will grade you accordingly. That's exactly why questions are so important in here. And why I let everybody ask what, why, how, and who on any topic covered in Lecture or Lab. The only true way to learn something, to comprehend and access knowledge without hesitation, is by questioning it." He stood, hands folded in front of him, waiting.

Saya raised her hand.

"Yes, Miss Harcourt?"

"Was Mrs. Ambersmith wrong? She gives us detention for asking questions in her class."

"She wasn't because the rule for faerie teachers here is that any debt a student gets into with them must be discharged the same day. Her job is to convey information and be sure you learn the gravity of questions in faerie society. In Forum, we analyze all those facts. Education is like making a mosaic out of what we already know. That way, when you find something new outside school, the skills you learn here will help you make your picture." He grinned. "So, Mrs. Ambersmith is correct regarding her classroom."

Cosmo raised his hand.

"Yes, Mr. Gitano?"

"Can't we have two Forum periods?" He cleared his throat. "Some of us already have too many facts. I'd rather ask questions all day than have to take notes for two hours every morning."

"Nope, sorry." He shook his head. "I teach three sections each day. You've got to share me and the space. The good news is, you get Forum every year. And Lab is all hands-on. You'll like it in there."

"Yeah, so, why you?" Jaxon Thorne asked.

"That's a good question, but you'd have to ask Principal Klein. She's the one who renewed my contract. I've got many years of experience as a guide here. So it's probably that."

"Or your fake nice guy act." Jillian tapped her nose. "I can tell you're a coyote, and they're always up to some shit."

"Language." Hope snapped her fingers. "Watch it."

"Fine, captain. Whatever." Jillian rolled her eyes. "Ambersmith said you're a hardass with the grades. Are you here to trick us into flunking?"

Instead of challenging Hope, taking offense at Jillian, or reacting like any normal teacher, Mr. Hickson threw his head back and laughed.

"Yes, I'm a coyote shifter, but not so great at the tricking people part." He nodded at Jillian. "Your question was valid. I'm not here to pull one over on my students. Is there more you'd like to know, Miss Thorne?"

"Not about you, no."

"What about magical shifters?" Brandon asked. "When do we talk about them? In Lecture this morning, Mrs. Ambersmith only covered nonmagical types. But not people like me."

"That's definitely coming up, don't worry. If you have information that differs from what Mrs. Ambersmith says in Lecture, absolutely share that here. Part of my job is to take notes on the experiences of students, especially rarer types, so our library is up-to-date, accurate, and equitable."

"When do we go to the library?" Saya wanted to know.

"During your R&R, which is the period after this. It includes lunch, research, and a recreational activity."

"Thank God." Fiona glanced at her tablet. "Mrs. Ambersmith said extrahumans are almost always only one type. How does that work?"

"Because most powers and talents are something you're born with," Mr. Hickson explained. "Magic elements, psychic talents, and standard shifter forms all run in families this way. You inherit genes from both sides, but only one set of extrahuman traits get expressed. Doctors are working on a blood test that shows it before powers manifest, but it's still in trials."

"There are exceptions, though," Brandon pointed out. "I was born an air magus, but then I inherited the magic pelt. So I can conjure and change forms. But I don't want to hog all the time."

"You can keep going." Mr. Hickson smiled. "If the rest of the class has questions."

"I do!" Kiara raised her hand. "Can you conjure while shifted, Brandon?"

We spent some fast-moving time learning about selkies specifically and conjuring in general. Brandon could breathe underwater by conjuring air but had to shift out of seal form briefly to make a bubble. Air magic didn't act like levitation. Because their pelt's magic came from the Sidhe queen, selkies could use glamour, which was much harder to channel and control than elemental magic. And no, Brandon didn't like raw fish in either of his forms, not even sushi.

"Any other questions?"

"Yeah okay, I've got one." Ramon raised his hand.

"Mr. DelSangre."

"Are we going to talk about what happened last year? To Cadence DelMar, and uh—" He glanced at me, wincing. "The seniors at the graduation cruise? The fallout's bad. I mean, there's been an awful lot of tension in our section already today. Do you plan to let us discuss that?"

"The easy answer is, this is Forum. We discuss whatever you ask. However, there's an exam at the end of each semester. So my answers will include related facts."

"Let's talk about it now, then." Wyatt leaned back in his seat and pointed at me. "Her brother went feral on his ex-girlfriend. Stabbed people with a null dagger, too. Then tossed her to a kraken and almost got the boat capsized. All after getting offered a free ride to play Bishop's Row at Oxford Occult. Why'd he do it, Merlini?"

"I'm not him." I ground my teeth together so hard they squeaked. "I can't answer that."

"I think you know more than you're letting on."

"She's his sister, you absolute toadstool." Saya snorted. "Not his shrink."

"Mr. Clayton, rephrase your question and ask it more generally so anyone with information can offer an answer."

"Fine." His nostrils flared. "Who here knows about New Order?"

"New Wave band from the 1980s," Cosmo offered. "*Blue Monday* was the first song my bro Ed learned to play on the keyboard." He shrugged with a grin. "A vampire taught him, what do you want?"

I blinked. Why were the kids from Providence so hell-bent on protecting me? Surely not because Ed met me for two minutes in Tropica Mart. It made no sense.

"Not the band New Order, the magisupremacy group." Wyatt bared his teeth. "They want to deport all us faeries and changelings to the Under."

"Yeah, and kill my parents." Ramon swallowed.

"Whoa." Brandon blinked. "You're a dhampyr?"

"So you know about the bigots too, Porter." Wyatt nodded. "Spill it."

"New Order's not really one organization. It's an alliance between Golden Dawn and The Magus Order." Brandon shook his head. "Those two are part of why you don't see many vampires from before the Reveal."

"The other piece was us." Jaxon's face reddened. "Our alphas, really. Too many wolf packs abandoned our old allies just because a few bad apples went on a turning spree."

"You paid attention in Reveal History last year, Jaxon. I'm impressed." Mr. Hickson's grin was gentler than a summer breeze. "Go on."

"The old version of the Magus Order murdered scores of my people." Saya sniffed. "They went by *Sancta Magica* back then, though."

"Slayers are also an offshoot of *Sancta Magica*," Ramon said. "Dad said they weren't a thing anymore. Then a few years ago, one showed up when Night Creatures played on the common."

"Right." Wyatt nodded. "They've been building a presence in this town ever since."

"So, let's bring this back to the cruise," Mr. Hickson said. "What's the connection to Crow Merlini specifically?"

"Null weapons," Wyatt said. "My brother said Merlini had one on the boat, and he got it from some New Order magi."

"Why would magi want null weapons around anyway?" Fiona asked. "Makes no sense to me."

"They block elemental conjures but are downright nasty for changelings and fae." Hope clicked her tongue. "Null magic can take the mantle right off a fully tithed faerie. Arming shifters with magical weapons is an ancient war tactic. Maybe even older than Bishop's Row."

"And why the magi don't use it themselves," Cosmo added. "I don't know much about these groups, which sound horrifying, but tactically it makes sense for magi to put shifters on the front lines against faeries. And give them null blades. Especially when the monarchs still arm magical shifters with their special weapons."

"Why not iron if they want to kill us, then?" Kiara asked. "Null magi are rare, and you need them to enchant the metal."

"Because they don't want all the faeries dead. Iron kills anyone who's got even an ounce of glamour," Saya replied. "Null leaves them all mortal. The ones with magic elements or psychic talents are left with those. Which means more citizens to rule over."

"Subjugate, you mean." Fiona's face reminded me of a sheet of paper.

"You're right." Saya nodded. "Genocidal fascists aren't concerned with good leadership."

"Good thing we're all set on that now." Hope smiled.

"We're not, though." Wyatt wrinkled his nose. "Captain. Merlini's not making a peep. Her whole family must be anti-fae. They've had beef with the Micellos and the Ambersmiths for a hundred years. Her brother had that dagger. He's on board with the magisupremacists."

"No." I shook my head. "Whatever else Crow is, that's not it. You don't understand."

"So explain it." He tapped his foot. "We're all waiting."

I opened my mouth, ready to tell him the only fact I knew. That the idea came from Mom and Crow said she'd forced him. I hesitated because I still didn't know why or how she coerced him. With that essential piece missing, would my classmates even believe me?

The bell rang.

I rose from my seat and hoisted my satchel, fleeing the fact of my family's crimes. In the hall, someone already occupied the only chill-out room in sight, the doorknob red. I needn't have worried.

Nobody stopped me that time.

CHAPTER SEVEN

I barely remember eating the ham and cheese sandwich. Probably because I ended up dumping more than half of it in the trash. The carrots and celery sticks on the side were crunchy but mostly flavorless. R&R sounded suspiciously like a second session at the gym, so I'd need some energy even if being singled out had turned my stomach.

Had Coach Tremain said he'd see us again? No. I checked my tablet, hoping to see it listed there, but the space beside the time slot only said Recreation. Mr. Hickson mentioned extracurriculars, which must include Bishop's Row. The last thing I wanted to do was play my brother's sport. It had helped make him infamous, apparently.

At least I knew where the gym was. I walked down the hall, relieved that Hope had made it impossible for anyone in section two to go after me. I kept my pace brisk, though. Gallows Hill had nearly three hundred students who weren't part of Captain Dunstable's crew.

Before I got to the gym, somebody tugged the strap of my satchel. I turned to find Cosmo Gitano standing with a sheepish grin on his face.

"Hey."

"Hey?"

"Uh, I noticed this morning you're not really the gym type. Maybe you shouldn't go in there. I mean you don't have to, but can if you want to." He gestured with his hands in the space between us. "I'm screwing all this up."

"That's me, Cosmo." I sighed. "I'm screwing up. I stuck up for my brother, even after everything they said. They weren't wrong about that knife or where it came from. They're right to think my apple's next to his under the tree."

"Okay, no accusations here, just a question." Cosmo shrugged. "Were you involved with what went down on that boat?"

"No." I shook my head. "I don't know Crow's whole story, but he got arrested. The judge sent him to Danvers Sanitarium instead of prison. I can't let go of the hope he'll get better someday. But I'm the only one who seems to believe that."

"Nobody believed my big brother, either. He said if I ever found someone in the same situation to give them a chance. So I'll take you at your word." He held out his hand.

"Thanks, Cosmo." I put mine in it, intending to shake on that. He clasped it instead, pulled up, then tilted his fingers toward me before letting go while waggling them.

"Secret handshake?" I blinked. I hadn't engaged in one of those since elementary school.

"Sorry, old habit." He shook his head. "Maybe it's instinct. You're a shifter too, you understand."

"Maybe. I don't grok all the PE here, though." I sighed. "They have cheer, Bishop's Row, and entertainment wrestling. I'm not cut out for any of them."

"It doesn't have to be like PE. It's supposed to be fun. I mean, they have a Drama Club too."

"Drama Club?" I blinked. "I had no idea. Nobody in my family talked about anything but sports."

"There's a music room and an art studio if that's more your style. Just saying."

"That's a relief. Can't sports, I have the klutz."

"Somehow I doubt that. Anyway, the auditorium's that way." He pointed around the corner from the doors to the gym. A much smaller door stood at the end of a short hallway.

I hesitated.

"Look, walk in there with that attitude from this morning, and you'll be fine."

"Huh?"

"Go to school, do the work, get the diploma, right?"

"How did you know?"

"Lion ears." He pointed at them. "I hear a lot of things, like how you're the seventh Merlini at this school and the others didn't graduate. Did you know my brother was the first Gitano to graduate high school, let alone college?"

"Really?"

"Our dad's a bad dude who got locked up before I met him. He raised Tony to be like him, but he did his own thing. If he made it, so can you."

"That means a lot, thanks." I blinked a few times rapidly like my eyelashes wanted to take off. "Are you coming with me?"

Cosmo shook his head.

"Bishop's Row is kind of my jam. Or least I want it to be, who knows if I'll make the team." He chuckled and pointed with his thumb over his shoulder at the gym doors. "See you later though, okay?"

"Okay." We turned and headed in opposite directions.

I didn't hear Cosmo open the door to the gym, only a wooden *thud* as it closed behind him. By contrast, the entrance to the auditorium squeaked like a family of rats trying to turn on a rusty garden faucet. I paid the noise no heed and walked on through.

Mr. Hickson sat on the edge of a scarred and scuffed stage. I had no idea he also ran Drama Club. Then again, it made sense. He was all about nonlinear learning. Creative art made sense. Maybe lousy tricksters made decent actors. I stayed wary, though. He hadn't done much to steer the discussion once it turned on me, despite his friendliness earlier.

I walked along the first row of seats, then grabbed the nearest aisle seat in the middle section. That talent show performance with Diego was my first. Along with several other things unrelated to theater. He'd auditioned at an integrated performance art magnet school but ended up at Messing anyway.

Kiara and Jaxon walked in, taking seats at the section by the door instead of joining me. I couldn't blame them after Forum. I'd speak with Kiara later if she were willing to listen.

A gaggle of upperclassman came in through the wings on stage. I tried to keep my head down, even though they'd noticed me. I didn't want to witness their knee-jerk reaction to seeing a Merlini in the auditorium.

I was right. They saw, knew, and judged. As it turned out, not in connection with my brother.

"Hey, aren't you Mavis?" A girl with wavy brown hair and a healthy beige complexion leaned over the chair to one side of me and smiled. "You're Cadence DelMar's friend, right?"

"I know Cadence."

"She talked about you all the time, called you her editor. You helped her find all the rhymes for her songs last year."

"Yeah, guess I'm kind of like a dictionary." I let out a nervous little giggle.

"I saw her at a gig on the Cape this past Sunday. She plays at the Dodge Street Café sometimes. I hang out there most nights because it's all ages. Drop by sometime and say hi."

"Maybe I will."

"Awesome." She held out her hand. "I'm Wanda."

"You were on cheer squad with Cadence."

"Yep. Bottom of the triangle. I'm a bear shifter."

"She said she couldn't have done half her formations without you." I grinned, putting a brave face on bittersweet nostalgia.

"Are you going out for squad? Plenty of folks do both."

"Not with my chicken legs and two left bird feet." I shrugged. "Cardio's not my jam."

"You'll have fun here in Drama Club, then."

Mr. Hickson called us up to the stage and gave a basic explanation of Drama Club activities. For the last few years, they'd done variety shows and one-acts, but we had space to do full-length plays or even smaller musicals. He said we'd do three productions each year.

"It's a small group, though." Jaxon had his hand up but spoke anyway. "They'll all have to be small shows, right?"

"Not necessarily." Mr. Hickson pointed at the door. "We'll see more over the next few days, after Bishop's Row, cheer squad, and wrestling post their rosters."

"Or people decide they can handle more than one." Wanda smiled. "I was on squad for two years and still made every rehearsal."

Mr. Hickson nodded. "Bartholomew Micello played Bishop's Row and blocked all our stage combat for The Fifteen Minute Hamlet last year."

I wished Bar wasn't off at Providence Paranormal College. Toward the end, when Crow pushed me away, Bar still let me tag along with him. If only somebody left at Gallows Hill had the same inclination.

A portly fellow with bushy salt and pepper hair and a matching goatee stepped out between the backdrop curtains. He had the male equivalent of resting bitch face, but Mr. Hickson smiled at him anyway. So did the upperclassmen.

"Sid's the school's jack of all trades. Also, he's in charge of tech and sets here. He'll give you a tour backstage. Since the upperclassmen already know their way around, I've got a list of potential productions for them to look over. When the first years finish exploring, you're free to hit the library or watch the end of the tryouts at the gym."

I lagged behind Kiara and Jaxon on the way to the wings, where black curtains hung to make an alcove hidden from the audience. *Straightforward.*

Farther back, things got positively labyrinthine. That wasn't part of the architecture, only what happens when you have a million backdrops and no desire to throw them out. Apparently, Sid was a packrat, but not as bad as the folks on that show about hoarding.

The green room was literally painted green and large enough to accommodate maybe fifty people. It was a nice change after the cramped spaces on the way in. There were no dressing rooms, only two unisex restrooms with a toilet and sink in each.

"Guess modesty's not a thing in Drama Club," I mumbled.

"We use glamour bracelets." Sid pulled one off a pegboard on one wall and slipped it over his wrist.

"Whoa!" Jaxon took a step back as the stagehand's clothing transformed from cargo shorts and a Salem t-shirt into a tuxedo.

"Epic." I smiled.

"Tell me about it." Kiara reached for one. It turned her sundress into a suit of armor.

"My turn!" Jaxon's jeans and muscle shirt became a zoot suit, complete with fedora.

"Go on, Mavis." Sid nodded. "Give it a try."

The idea of glamour bracelets had me so excited I didn't even worry about where this guy had heard of me. I reached for one and put it on, checking the result in the mirror.

A garment of black fabric draped me in loose folds from my shoulders to my ankles. Attached to my back was a pair of black wings. I swallowed, struck by a sense of impending punishment, as though I'd done something wrong.

"Let's get this on Photogram," Kiara pulled out her phone. "Everybody say save the bees!"

"Save the bees!" We repeated. Jaxon and Sid beamed. I managed a grimace.

There wasn't a chill-out chamber back here, so I glanced at the bathroom as I briefly considered hiding in it. When Kiara showed me the pic, I relaxed. A few moments later, our selfie was done and posted.

I cut more of a tragic figure than the villain I'd feared. Especially next to Jaxon, who looked downright dangerous in his zoot suit. Up on stage, I'd be playing a role. Dressed up to look and act like someone I wasn't.

A costume and script couldn't change what anybody else thought of me. Still, what if I could avoid being the last in a long line of Merlinis who'd left nothing but pain at this school?

Maybe Drama Club could give me something I couldn't get anywhere else. A break from being myself. Trying to keep a low profile hadn't worked. Going to the opposite extreme and putting myself literally on display might work out in my favor.

Sid returned his bracelet to the wall. Kiara and Jaxon followed suit right away. I lingered, sneaking one long last look in the mirror before taking the bracelet off. I gazed until the last vestige of magical costuming faded before hanging the bangle back on its peg.

"I think I like it here," I said to no one in particular. As I closed the door, I thought I heard a barely-there voice reply, "good." That had to be my imagination.

I found out later that it wasn't.

After Mr. Hickson read aloud the list of show ideas, he said we'd vote on which to do soon. One of them made me scratch my head.

"Pirates of Penzance has a huge chorus."

"Well, that's a topic for another day." He tucked the paper into a folder. "You've got twenty more minutes of R&R. Use them amusingly. You're all dismissed."

I hurried out, making a beeline for the library, not wanting company on the way. Jaxon went into the gym. Kiara wandered toward snacks in the courtyard. The upperclassmen had gone out the door at the other end of the auditorium, which gave me an unobstructed path.

Library was a misnomer. There were bookshelves, most of them inside protective chambers because the tomes and scrolls on them would degrade or disenchant without special environmental controls.

Media Center might have made more sense, but Gallows Hill was founded right after the Great Reveal. Magipsychic tablets didn't exist back then, and some extrahumans caused technical issues with the old CRT televisions and computers in the early 1990s.

Don't get the wrong idea and start thinking the library was an open floor-plan sort of place. Shifters and changelings like their hidey-holes, which explained the chill-out chambers on this campus among other things. Also, the school used several teaching methods. It only made sense for the library to incorporate them too.

Instead of stacks, folding screens broke the space into sections. Some of these were newer and in the same art nouveau style as the rooming house décor. Several others were carved from wood and painted in geometric designs. A handful were rattan, with designs woven into the sides using a variety of stained fibers. These appeared to be the oldest.

They were all magically enhanced. Not only the sight-blocking screens but displays as well. Signs hung from the ceiling told me so. They were enchanted to interact with our tablets, giving us magical access to extrahuman-focused resource books and periodicals.

Activating the nearest one revealed a list of ebooks on different types of magic. The display was clear like my tablet, an overlay that blocked the paisley fabric when powered on. Curious about how it worked, I tapped the book list with my tablet. A chime signaled download completion.

I wandered around and through the other sections, not stopping, only intending to get a general idea of what was there. The sound of a conversation at low volume stopped me.

CHAPTER EIGHT

"Cos will insist it's her on his turn, Hope."

"What's wrong with that?"

"You saw her birth certificate. She's not the one." Saya sighed. "It's nobody's fault. Maybe you could change the agreement and exclude him for poor judgment."

"Olivia's birth certificate says Boston, but we all know that's not true," Hope pointed out.

"It was way easier to fake that sort of thing back in the 90s." Saya sniffed.

"Didn't you get chills when you saw her with those wings, though?" Hope asked.

"It's a magical costume. It's designed to have an emotional impact."

They were talking about me—the selfie with the glamour bracelet.

"Or maybe it's fate. One way to find out."

"Maybe Ed found the right person over at Messing, and all this is a moot point."

"That's too convenient."

"You know every small detail about how inconvenient that particular mantle is, I suppose." Saya snorted.

"Not everything, but more than you. I think Cos is onto something here. He said so before we even saw that Photogram."

"Cosmo's thinking with his lion brain again. Chasing laser pointers."

"Well, what about Ed, then? You of all people can't say that about him."

"Don't start with that." Saya sighed. "I tried to let him down easy."

"You broke his heart."

"It was that way long before he wanted me in it."

Someone cleared his throat behind me. I turned to discover Ramon.

"Mavis, I'm sorry."

"Huh?" I blinked. "For what? I mean, whatever it was, forget about it."

I wanted to get him out of there, continue listening in on whatever Saya and Hope were talking about because it had something to do with me and wasn't automatically bad.

"That's impossible." Ramon crossed his arms and planted his feet. He wasn't going anywhere.

I took a good long look at my friend's face. This was important to him. Mom wouldn't give someone who'd crossed her a chance. I didn't want to be like her, so I tried the opposite.

"Go on. I'm listening."

"That question I asked in Forum ended up making things worse. Now Wyatt's messing with you."

"Not if Captain Dunstable's got anything to do with it." I shrugged. "She said no fighting, and we're all pretty much bound to follow her orders. So it's all good."

"Okay, I'll buy that on the campus safety front." Ramon nodded but didn't ease his stance. "All summer, you hung out in our store. Helped us, said you felt comfortable there. I've got an idea about why. My parents are vamps, raising a dhampyr son. People make assumptions about us the same way they do about you. None of them are true. There's no way you're New Order."

"Ramon, it's different. My family did all those things. I'm the only one who hasn't…how did Wyatt put it? Gone feral." *Yet,* I added in my head where he couldn't hear.

"I know." He nodded. "That's why I brought it up. So you could declare it in class on the first day, in front of everyone. If I'd known you'd get derailed and run over like that, I would have kept my mouth shut. Can you forgive me?"

"Already done, Ramon. Thanks for believing me."

I offered him my hand. He shook it, lingeringly. The bell rang, and we walked to Lab together, in an easy sort of silence.

Once again, the seating in class was three tables. I recognized these as lab benches by their black resin tops. Unlike in middle school, these benches didn't have gas jets for Bunsen burners, electrical outlets, or water spouts.

I got the one in the front this time. Being early had its benefits. Ramon sat with me, and a few moments later, Fiona joined us.

"Hi," Ramon greeted her. "Didn't introduce myself earlier. I'm Ramon."

"Fiona." She tucked a lock of hair behind her ear and glanced at me. "You two are okay?"

"Yeah, it was a misunderstanding." I shrugged. "No hard feelings. And you?"

"Plenty." She leaned one dimpled elbow on the table. "But not about Forum or anyone at this table."

I put two and two together and figured she'd been at tryouts, and it hadn't gone well. I nodded, unable to frame a reply.

"Come by Tropica Mart after school." Ramon offered. "We have slushies."

"Maybe too many slushies is part of her problem."

I knew exactly what to say about that.

"Shut up, Wyatt."

"It's true." He shrugged. "But you weren't at tryouts so maybe you don't understand the, uh, gravity of Fiona's problems."

"Oh, right." Fiona narrowed her eyes. "Telling the ogre she's fat is so original."

"Wow, I'm totally excited." I smiled until my face hurt, doing my best imitation of Kiara in our room the night before. "I've never met an ogre. Are you from around here? Do the rest of your family have that mantle too or are you the only one? Is it true ogres can get taller than a building on demand?"

"Um, not until recently, we moved over the summer from Fall River. Dad's an ogre but Mom's Sidhe. Yeah, we can get up to thirty feet tall. It's temporary though. I can only stay that big for five minutes."

"Are you sitting or not?" Ramon pointed at Wyatt and the empty stool.

"Not!" He turned and stalked toward the back of the room.

I watched him stop in the middle, doing a double-take as he found the rear bench full. Kiara and Brandon sat with Jillian and Jaxon, and Cosmo had plunked his bag down beside the last seat there.

Muttering under his breath, face reddening, Wyatt took the furthest stool from where Hope and Saya sat, giggling over something on their phones. Hope looked up briefly.

"Behaving yourself, Wy?"

"It's Wyatt."

"It's Wyatt what?" Hope batted her eyelashes.

"Captain."

"Thanks, Wyatt!" She grinned.

Our teacher chose that moment to enter the room, giving us a bright smile. The prescription in her spectacles was so strong it distorted her eyes until the pupils appeared black. She seemed to have no trouble glancing at each of us. She smiled and spoke.

"I'm Doctor Aranha. Welcome to Lab."

Instead of a lab coat, Dr. Aranha wore a stiff gray apron with three large pockets on the front. It tied around her neck and waist, giving her an hourglass shape that reminded me of the old Victorian photographs in Salem's antique shops.

She wore her dark brown hair up in bantu knots, arranged in a pattern that made her parts resemble a spider's web.

"Today, I'm giving you an overview of the emergency equipment, which we'll hopefully never need. It shouldn't take long. After that, we'll do some hands-on learning about some of the basics and your individual powers. Any questions?"

"Thank God," Fiona said under her breath. Then she raised her hand. "Yeah, I have a question."

"Of course, Miss Connolly."

"I read the class description on my tablet, and it said we practice our powers in here. I don't think there's room for me."

"I understand." She nodded. "You're an ogre. We've also got a dragon shifter among others, so don't worry. All the laboratory rooms here have flexible capacity. We'll cover this more in the safety features. Anyone else?"

"What do you mean, we're using our powers?" Wyatt blinked. "We already know how they work."

"I'm confident the Claytons raised you with knowledge of all things redcap, Wyatt. However, first-year lab is about getting comfortable with your peers' abilities and discovering how you might work together."

"Why?" Ramon inquired.

"Magi and psychics have a much easier time. Elements are predictable, well-researched, and relatively limited. So, much of the research out there involves their elements along with psychic talents, in large part because of the meticulous records magi keep, which stayed secret thanks to their space and wood masters. But before the Reveal, faeries made enchanted items out of materials shifters gathered. Can anyone tell me who kept the records for them?"

"Dragons." Saya spoke without raising her hand. "Vampires, too. Because it wasn't easy to make or safely keep records. And the Under used to be an unreliable place for them before the monarchs reunited."

"I understand your brother is a doctoral candidate in extrahuman archaeology, Miss Harcourt. Do you share his interests?"

"No, I just have to listen to them all the time."

"That knowledge will serve you well in here, at any rate. Please feel free to share what you've overheard again in the future. For now, let's move on to the safety overview."

As promised, the room's dimensions expanded to accommodate the different shapes and sizes of a diverse group of extrahumans. Along with that incredibly reassuring feature, the lab equipment contained an eyewash station, fire blanket, chemical extinguisher, and first aid kit. The tension went out of the room. Well, almost.

Hope Dunstable was not okay. I couldn't figure out why due to only having met her that morning. I also realized neither Saya nor Cosmo seemed to notice. Or maybe they ignored her thinly-veiled distress to draw anyone else's attention away from it.

Dr. Aranha had us line up at a locked cabinet behind her desk. I was in front of the line, so I got to see her open it. Inside were pendants, similar to mine but made from blown glass instead of shell. Each glowed faintly white even in the bright classroom light.

"Please, take one." She gestured at the rows of necklaces.

"What are they for, exactly?" I put my hand over the small lump under my shirt.

"In your case, to retain your clothing when shifting."

"Oh, I'm all set." I showed her my shell necklace.

"Hmm." She nodded. "You're not the first student I've seen with an amulet. But I don't like to assume."

I stepped aside and let Ramon take my place.

"What does it do for me?"

"Dhampyr aren't particularly resilient, so it gives you protective warding."

"Like goggles in a mundane lab?"

She nodded. He reached out and took one. Its glow turned pink. He joined me on the other side of the teacher's bench.

"How dangerous is this class, anyway?"

I shrugged, watching Fiona take hers, which glowed moss green. She didn't ask what it did, as though she'd used one before. Maybe Fall River's middle schools had better accommodations for changelings than the ones in Salem.

Jillian's, Jaxon's, and Cosmo's amulets all glowed yellow, but Brandon's was blue. Saya's was seafoam green. Kiara's was amber and Wyatt's magenta.

"Miss Dunstable?" Dr. Aranha glanced around the room. But Hope wasn't in it.

"Um, Doc?" I jerked my thumb at the red door in the back of the lab. "I think she went in there."

"Let me handle this." Saya strode halfway across the room before Cosmo stopped her.

"You can't mess with the chill-out rooms, remember?"

"I don't care about the rules. She's my best friend."

"Miss Harcourt, perhaps you've got the wrong idea. It's not a rule but a function of how they work. After a period of calming exercises, students in chill-out chambers get a brief counseling session or visit with the nurse. Once that's done, Miss Dunstable will emerge."

"Come on, Saya. Let's do science." Cosmo patted her shoulder.

"Yeah, sure, fine." She sniffed. "Whatever."

We proceeded to show off and have fun, mostly. For once, I felt comfortable and went first, shifting into raven form and wheeling around overhead. The closer I got to the ceiling, the more it expanded upward. It was fun, and I stayed airborne observing my classmates until I almost wore myself out.

Down below, Wyatt rummaged through a box of broken glassware. His glamour dropped to reveal his sharklike gray skin as he crunched old beakers and flasks to bits between his pointy teeth. Kiara could have been playing a game of "the floor is lava," leaping lightly between benches and stools, eventually alighting on a windowsill.

Cosmo paced between the benches in his lion form, making a game of pouncing over the ones Kiara had visited. Jillian and Jaxon struck up a wildly melodic call-and-response, trying to see which of them could howl the longest. Brandon was in his seal form, barking and clapping his flippers to cheer them on.

Fiona and Saya played tag. Even from my vantage point, their game wasn't easy to track, partly because the color of ogre skin and water dragon scales nearly matched. I looked around for Ramon and didn't see him until I took a spin over the teacher's bench. He sat on the floor with Dr. Aranha, taking notes on his tablet without a view of the room.

"Now that you've written down what you think their abilities are and what they'll do with them, stand up and have a look at the reality, Mr. DelSangre."

I landed on the bench as he rose, so I was the first thing he saw.

"Caw!" I tilted my head, then hopped from one foot to the other.

Ramon blinked at me, then looked over my head and around the room behind me. After that, he threw his head back and laughed.

"Caw?" I asked. Which meant what's so funny, but he had no way of understanding that.

"They're playing, Doc!" He shook his head and made more notes on his tablet. "I guessed it all wrong."

"Of course, they're playing." Dr. Aranha smiled. "They might have unusual powers, but they're all still kids. So are you. Go." She waved him away. "Have fun while you learn some more."

I hopped on top of the tablet before Ramon could get it.

"Caw." I stared at Ramon, then at his shoulder.

"Sure, why not?"

I spent the last hour of Lab with my friend, listening to his questions and the answers our classmates gave him. The doorknob on the chill-out chamber stayed red up to the last minute before the bell rang, ending my first day at Gallows Hill.

Later that night, a message came through on my tablet, addressed to every student in section two along with their parents.

Apparently, Hope's classification in the national registry was a "magical faerie avian shifter, type undisclosed." The letter apologized for any stress or misunderstanding caused by the delayed disclosure, then offered to allow any student who felt uncomfortable to transfer to a different first-year section.

The next day, I found all our classmates still in attendance—even Wyatt.

CHAPTER NINE

John Clayton was right outside the lab when we emerged. He spoke in a low voice to his brother, Wyatt.

"You're in for it, kid."

"I didn't do nothing."

"Aunt D saw what you pulled in the hall and ratted you out." John shook his head. "You know how Dad feels about bullies."

"Oh no."

"Oh yeah. It's Mom's ghost pepper dinner."

"Isn't that a waste of food at the dorm?" Wyatt gulped. "How am I getting to Worcester and back?"

"Mom called the matron with her recipe. No escape, my dude. Might as well get it over with." John jerked a thumb at the magic door.

Everyone else decided to walk mundanely home from school. The Thornes lived out by Salem State so they turned left after leaving the building when the rest of us took a right. As promised, Ramon brought Fiona to Tropica Mart for slushies. Brandon, Kiara, and Cosmo tagged along with them.

Hope and Saya had gone directly into the bathroom together after the bell rang. I lingered outside on the school steps before remembering my orders. Talk to Ed Redford about the ghost in my satchel.

Messing Academy got out later than Gallows Hill, so for old time's sake, I passed the rooming house and took a walk through Salem Common. After one look at the playground, where I stopped my brother from attacking two Hawthorn Academy magi, I knew I couldn't stay.

It was only the scene of an attempted crime, but that was the first night I knew that Crow needed help. I'd done everything I could think of that year to pull him back from the line before he crossed it. Nothing had worked. I'd been too late.

The last thing I needed after my terrible, no good, very bad day was reliving my past failures. So I went to the only place that reminded me of triumphs instead.

Irzyk Park had a soccer field, a baseball diamond, and a basketball court. The section I cared about was barely the size of a median strip and should have been insignificant. Except it wasn't.

A child born to Polish immigrants in Salem commanded the 8th Tank Battalion of the 4th Armored Division in the US Army in World War Two. He wasn't extrahuman, but his division liberated the camp at Ohrdruf. Shifter and faerie survivors were among those freed, and some of them came here to settle after the war.

In 1999, the town of Salem dedicated the park to Brigadier General Albin F. Irzyk, and put a decommissioned M60 in one corner. The park had been a hangout for changelings and young shifters ever since. I was no exception.

I took my first steps picnicking at Irzyk park, according to Branwen. My first flight in raven form may have started and ended at my bedroom window, but the turn-back point was that old tank. I spent countless hours, days of all seasons, tagging along after Crow, Bar, and the other older kids I idolized in its shadow.

Once there, I sat on the pavement, back against the tank and facing away from the street. I had time to kill with my eyes closed, enjoying the breeze off the water even if my brain wouldn't entirely shut off. As I got around to thinking it might be time to go, try and meet Ed outside of Messing as he left, I heard a cry of pain coming from behind me.

I sprang up in an instant, dashing around toward the Fort Street side of the tank. Two boys and three girls about my age stood in a ring, holding hands and chanting something. They wore royal blue blazers, slacks, and skirts with white shirts and ties underneath—Messing Academy's uniform.

"Grim Reaper, Grim Reaper, come collect this creature!"

Something fluttered on the ground nearby, a notebook, pages turning in the breeze between an outline with geometric doodles and a sketched portrait I couldn't make out at first. A Providence Paranormal College backpack with a Night Creatures patch stitched on. I'd seen it before.

"Grim Reaper, Grim Reaper, he grows ever weaker!"

A pale hand reached out between two of the chanters. Slim, pale, with fingernails polished black.

These Messing jerks were bullying Ed Redford.

"Get off my turf, losers." I put my hands on my hips.

"Who says?" The tallest, a girl with blonde hair and brown eyes, snorted.

"Wait." The red-haired boy blinked at the tank. "This is Irzyk Park." He laid eyes on me, and they widened. "Shit, she's a Merlini! Run!"

He dashed toward the sidewalk, the shortest girl following on his heels. Then there were three.

"You broke the circle, Peg!" the tall girl stepped on Ed's tie, preventing his escape. "Gia, close it up."

"Sorry, Donna." Gia dropped the hand of the remaining boy beside her and backed away. "I'm out too."

"Same." The last boy looked over his shoulder and dropped Donna's hand.

"Diego?" I blinked at my ex-boyfriend, then looked him in the eyes. "What the hell?"

"Sorry, Mavis. Lost track of where we were." He backed up two steps, still locking gazes with me.

"That's all?" I tapped my foot and jerked a thumb at Ed. "An empath like you should know better. Apologize to *him*. And convince blondie to let him go."

"Uh, Donna—" Diego started.

"You mean this is *your* pet creep?" Donna snorted. "Should have known."

She lifted her foot and Ed scrambled across dusty grass to reach the pavement behind me. I heard his hasty breaths, his rapid heart beating in counterpoint. Along with the sourness of sweat, I caught a whiff of tears. Not fresh, from hours earlier.

However bad my day was, his could only have been worse.

I scowled, taking my hands off my hips and making fists as I took a step toward Donna and Diego.

"Get lost."

"Why should I?" Donna bared her teeth.

"I've never felt her this angry." Diego swallowed. "Not even when we broke up. Let's beat feet already."

"Have fun with your edgelady, Edweird."

Donna sauntered away down the sidewalk, swinging her hips as if she wore a designer ballgown instead of a school uniform. Diego tore his gaze away, staring at the ground as he turned and followed her.

"Sorry," Ed murmured behind me.

"Not your fault." I collected his backpack and notebook, tucked them under one arm, and headed toward the park side of the tank. "Come on."

I sat in the same spot as before and patted the span of pavement beside me. After he joined me, I handed his things over. As he took them, the notebook flopped open to the sketch.

"That's Saya."

He unzipped his backpack, got his inhaler, and took two puffs. "I'm no DaVinci."

"Better than my stick figures."

"Stop."

"What?"

"The self-deprecation." He shook his head. "You saved my miserable life. Why?"

"I know what it's like, ending up attacked unexpectedly." I got the uneaten apple out of my satchel and held it out to him.

"Touché."

"This isn't a duel."

"If it were, you'd win."

"But it's not." I wiggled the apple. "Go on. It's yours. Could barely eat a bite at school after Lecture."

"Oh no." His nostrils flared, eyes narrowed. "They didn't." He looked up. "Rob—" He blinked.

He listened to someone I couldn't see. I let them speak their piece.

"Okay, my friends are off the hook. Wyatt's a tool. But what's Horace saying about the captain giving you an order?"

I told him about the altercation in the hall.

"So, I have to ask you about the satchel."

"Fewmets." He deflated. "Well, the first thing you have to know is Horace, along with his satchel, is only on loan."

"What do you mean?"

"We weren't allowed to bring Horace out of Rhode Island, had to smuggle his satchel in Hertha's donation box. You ended up with him by accident."

"Who's he supposed to be helping then?"

"I can't say exactly." Ed peered into his backpack longer than he had to before stowing his notebook and inhaler inside, then zipped it closed. "Nobody, yet."

I had a million questions. Answers were the mental equivalent of shiny objects. I craved them, especially after overhearing Hope and Saya mention that Ed was on a mission at Messing Academy. That had ended in the epic bullying I'd witnessed.

He hadn't said I couldn't ask about that, so I did.

"They don't like mediums at Messing. There hasn't been a student like me attending since before I was born, so nobody thought to warn me. Apparently, asking too many personal questions is against the student handbook, which makes it worse."

"Personal? About what?"

"Families in town. I couldn't find any genealogies in the library."

"What about yearbooks?"

"No surnames in any of them, only talents." He rolled his eyes.

"Some counter-cultural effort where they record everything differently from magi. So I did the logical thing and started querying my classmates about their families."

"Big mistake?"

"Of epic proportions." He took a bite of the apple, blinked, then chewed it and swallowed. "They're a bunch of hypocrites. Allen the all-seeing sure had no problem dropping your surname like it was radioactive."

"All my siblings got expelled from Gallows Hill. Everybody knows my name. Can we switch? Being called Mavis the Birdbrain feels like a walk in the park right about now." I laughed. He didn't.

"It's not funny. Having an infamously damaged family member."

"I know." I leaned back against the tank and gazed at the sky, suddenly unable to face Ed's anguish. It looked too much like everything I kept inside. "But laughing's better than the alternative."

"Not my decision to make," he mumbled.

"Hmm?"

"Talking to Rob."

"What's he like, anyway? You never mentioned. And Horace?"

As he spoke, his tone of voice brightened so profoundly I couldn't stop staring at him. His face was still tear-stained and smudged with dirt, but his eyes glittered like blue diamonds.

"Well, Rob's the oldest ghost in New England because the rest have all moved on. He says he was Roger William's butler, but his manners don't match that story. He knows I think he was actually a privateer. He's always wearing a coat with shiny buttons and a tricorn hat but changes the color to keep things interesting. I've known him almost my whole life."

"Wait." I blinked. "Oh. Oh no."

"I always forget how shocked people get when I say that."

"Because mediums don't start seeing ghosts unless they have a near-death experience. If you've known Rob almost your whole life—"

"Mom insists I was premature."

"You don't believe her, though."

"How do you do it?"

"Do what?"

"Bullseye guesses. And those Parthian shots."

"They're no such thing." I shrugged. "Instinct and a life of looking over my shoulder is all."

"You're a raven." He pressed his lips together, clutching his backpack.

"And?"

"Mavis." His voice cracked, so he swallowed before continuing. "Where were you born?"

"Mom insists I was born in Salem."

"Ouch, got me again."

Ed deflated, reminding me more of a centenarian than a teenager like me. Then, his stomach growled. He held the well-gnawed core up, gazing at it in intense contemplation.

"Alas, poor apple, I knew you well."

"There are study snacks in the lounge."

"Let's head back, then."

I stood and offered him my hand.

"Don't."

"Okay." I let it drop to my side and stepped back, squaring my shoulders. Mostly to hide the fact I was shaking. Because Ed sounded like Crow. He never wanted any help either, especially when he needed it most.

We walked along in silence together. Despite the deserted park and that I knew he was splitting firewood in the glamoured room at Danvers Sanitarium, I looked over my shoulder. Of course, he wasn't there. If only my concern last year had kicked in earlier.

I'd offered help, my birdbrained ideas, mostly. The one thing I'd never done was ask my brother what *he* needed. Because I thought he could handle everything. He'd always been larger than life to me. When he started high school, I simply assumed that was how everyone saw him.

Until I experienced one day as a Merlini on that campus for myself.

"Hey, Ed?"

"Yeah?"

"What were they doing? Donna and the rest?"

"She's a summoner." He stared straight ahead, hands twisted around the shoulder straps on his backpack. "Calling the Grim Reaper."

"Why?"

"I'm not giving you a litany of my sins."

"Whatever happened, I'm sure it got blown out of proportion. Donna's always been a terror."

"She's a devil you know. I'm the one you don't."

"Donna would summon pixies to water the daisies while her house was on fire. At least your give a damn's not busted. So, what happened?"

"Messing Academy should have been called Messed Up Academy."

"How do you mean?"

"All the signs in the building are astrological. I got lost. Ended up in the girl's bathroom."

"Oh no."

"Oh yes. And of course, I had an asthma attack. Donna summoned a Grim, and it dragged me out. Through a puddle."

I winced.

"It gets better."

"Go on."

"I dropped my inhaler in there. Peg the postcog picked it up. In the hallway, she threw it at my face, said she saw a memory of me. It was absolutely true, totally embarrassing, and something I promised a friend never to repeat. But Gia the telepath pulled it out of Peg's mind and acted it out for everybody all the same."

"Back in middle school, they called themselves the weird sisters."

"Hey."

"What?"

"Do you know their surnames? Or maybe their family relations?"

"I know you can't tell me what you ultimately need to find, but could you narrow it down?"

"Are any of them related to, uh, shifters?"

"Donna's an Ambersmith, no shifters there. Allen Arnold is from a family of mundanes and psychics. His brother's a tarot-reading vampire. Gia's his cousin on the mundane side. Nobody expected her to have a talent." I pointed across the street at Mendez Psychic Readings. "Diego's family owns that place. Seventeen generations of psychics, nothing else."

"Yeah Rob, she is." Ed nodded.

"What did he say?"

"That you're helpful."

"Just a busybody townie. Everyone's business is my business."

"There you go, putting yourself down again. Promise not to hit me with any more truth arrows."

"I'm all out of those. For now."

We walked the rest of the way in unexpectedly comfortable silence.

I expected the lounge to be either a threadbare afterthought or too new and shiny for comfort in décor. I was wrong. It straddled a middle ground with brand new floors, walls, and windows but cozy furnishings and window treatments.

A cart and a water cooler stood against the wall beside the door. As we walked past it, Ed paused to fill a bowl with trail mix. His hand hovered over a stack of oatmeal Power Bars, and he paused.

"I can't stomach one of those today, Horace. Sorry."

As he passed them, I felt a chill on my right shoulder and a wave of sadness, profoundly deep and stretching overhead like an ocean wave. As though my grief and anguish of losing everything got washed away for a moment by someone else's.

There was an old saying around town. That sometimes, inexplicable sadness overcame the living. Supposedly, it moved them to grieve for the unmourned dead. It had happened to me exactly once before when I was six and ended up kickstarting my ghost obsession.

Now, here it was again. Except I had clear proof from Ed that Horace was here, affecting him. Why not me?

Without thinking, I stepped up after Ed moved aside, grabbed one of the bars, and got water from the cooler.

I'd had them before and thought they were awful but couldn't shake the idea that eating one was a tribute.

Ed took one of the wingback chairs, kicking his shoes off and pulling his legs up under him. I sat in the one across from him, then tore the wrapper and took a bite of that Power Bar. It was somehow chewy and grainy at the same time, with a hint of cinnamon.

"What are you doing?"

"What feels like the right thing."

"I mean, how are you doing it?"

"In human form, I have these nifty things called opposable thumbs and teeth instead of a beak."

I continued devouring the mediocre snack, telling Ed about that old Salem saying between bites. Ed stared over my right shoulder until I took the last one.

"Thank you," he said.

"For what?"

"Helping Horace. We've both been a wreck for years, over the same thing."

"Over a Power Bar?"

"His old medium, Bianca, was my mentor. She died in the Under. He, uh. Well, they were in love."

"Oh." I looked up and to my right. "I'm so sorry, Horace."

"Of course she already knows ghosts can't cross the barrier." Ed let out a laugh that sounded like it hurt. "Almost all of it adds up. But I've got to stick to the plan."

Before I could ask what that meant, Saya leaned in the doorway, leaving just enough room for Hope to peek in over the top of her head.

"You're a mess, Ed," Saya said.

"Thanks." He rolled his eyes. "You look fresh as a daisy."

"What she means is maybe getting cleaned up is a good idea." Hope shrugged.

"I don't need an interpreter." Saya snorted. "Edward, we have an image to maintain."

"Yeah, okay." He hoisted his backpack over one shoulder, then grabbed his untouched trail mix. "But we're talking later, the four of us. About stuff."

"I'm super confused." I reached for my cup of water because my mouth suddenly felt like I'd been eating paste.

"That's by design, Mavis, though I mean you no offense by it," Hope said, patly.

"People have secrets. I get it." My upper lip curled. "I also keep mine by design."

"You weren't out." Ed grinned. "Nice shot."

He followed them away. I sat alone, wondering why I had the urge to get up and follow, help Ed and even the rest of them.

"Aren't feelings weird, Horace?"

He might have tried to answer, but it was beyond my power to hear him. I sat studying my lecture notes with more palatable snacks, wondering how tomorrow would go.

After a while, a more personal problem distracted me. I headed upstairs to make sure it wasn't a moot point. The dresser drawers and the closet stood empty except for the sweats and donated underthings.

"No luck in the wardrobe department, then." I sighed and headed back to the first floor to pace the lounge and think more.

I had nothing to wear. The clothes I stood in were old hand-me-downs for around the nest anyway. I had no money to get more even at the thrift store across town.

If I'd thought about it earlier, I might have gone down to the office and looked through the lost and found. But school had long since closed.

As tough and scary as my classmates and the Messing bullies thought I was, Mom was a million times worse. The stone-cold mask of intimidation I'd recently practiced wouldn't work on her.

I couldn't just fly through the window and grab some essentials even if she'd left it unlocked because I couldn't sneak in, even if I waited until she'd gone out. The nest was never empty, and none of my siblings ever risked crossing her to help me. Or each other.

Except Crow. Danvers Sanitarium wasn't home, but surely they had supplies. He'd worn entirely new clothes. Maybe the faeries running the place would let me borrow something.

That's how I ended up skipping dinner and flying off to visit him for the second time in as many days. At least I knew the drill this time, so getting in was easy. The magic dropped me by the woodpile instead, but I still recognized the place.

Crow wasn't outside the cabin this time, which was a good thing. It was raining. Either the most powerful and realistic manifestation of glamour I'd ever seen, or somehow pouring real water. I hurried toward the door and knocked.

"Come in." Crow sat whittling something. An empty bowl sat on his left and a broken spoon on his right.

"Hi." I hesitated to tell him about my problem or ask for help. If the sanitarium faeries had him making his dishware, maybe they didn't have a spare set of jeans and flannels.

"You got kicked out."

"Yeah. She knew somehow."

"I figure it's the amulets." His knife slipped, carving too deeply. He sighed and got another piece of wood. "If only that occurred to me last year. Anyway, why'd you come back? She won't change her mind if you keep visiting me."

"I don't want to go back."

"Odin's beard, Mavis." He dropped the knife and wood and stood with his hands flat on the table. "You can't sleep rough all year."

"I'm not. Matron Klein put me up at the new rooming house."

"You're missing dinner, then. Sorry, I broke all the spoons. But you can drink it." He stepped away from the table, scooped a bowl of soup, and set it in front of me. "So, I guess the paranoid principal made a major move. Wow."

"That's what I thought when it happened."

"What's it like? For you at school, I mean."

He paced back and forth in front of the hearth. I started describing the walls and halls, but he stopped me.

"No. The important stuff. Have you made any friends?"

"I think. Ramon's in my class. You know, the dhampyr from Tropica Mart. My roommate Kiara lent me a book."

"He's a decent sort. Sounds like the roommate's a keeper, too." He raised an eyebrow, which mystified me. But only for a moment.

"Not like that." My face felt warm. I couldn't bring myself to mention Ramon's name again.

Crow knew well enough not to try giving me relationship advice. So he changed the subject.

"First day at school?"

"Not so great but it could have been worse." I told him about Wyatt. Also, Hope's weird play to head off further physical altercations, including Ramon's and Fiona's reactions. Then I shook my head.

"Then, in Forum—"

"You got Hickson."

"How'd you know?"

"No such thing as stupid questions. Even from pups with something to prove."

"He's a redcap, though. Technically, the Thornes are the canines."

"You know what I mean." Crow shrugged. "Go on."

I told him everything they said, not softening the blow. He hung his head a few times but didn't interrupt. So, I continued through Cosmo's advice, Drama Club, and ended with Ramon's apology.

"Stick with DelSangre and your roommate. The Connolly girl sounds safe, too."

"What about Cosmo and his friends?"

"You mean Team Dragon? Stay away."

"Do you know something or is it your gut?" I sipped.

"Practically every extrahuman family in New England knows of the Harcourts. They're nothing nice. One of them was poking around at Hawthorn the year we had intramurals. Lion-o was with him." Crow shook his head. "I know he did you a solid after Forum, but be careful. The Harcourts and the Seelies go way back. Dunstable said she's Queen's Navy, so Cosmo lives in coercion city. That's no place you want to be."

"There's something else." I sighed.

"Spill it, then." He got me another bowl of soup and filled his.

We sat sipping as I told him about Ed at Irzyk Park.

"Use the old turf as home base if you need it again. Might give you an edge over those weird sisters."

"What about Ed?"

"He's Team Dragon?"

I nodded. He sat, studying my face for a long moment.

"White knight for him, but don't expect a squire out of it. He'll get stuck obeying Dunstable's orders, too."

"I'm not in it for *quid pro quo*. He's, well, acting like a real friend."

"I'm not going to lie, Mavis. Gallows Hill's a rough school for Merlinis. Your year's got three more sections of ten to fifteen students. And there are upperclassmen still pissed at us over last year. Wyatt's only the first in a long line of toughs wanting to look like a hero. You'll have to pay that piper eventually."

I swirled the dregs in my bowl, thinking. The last thing I wanted was a series of on-campus brawls and detentions.

"Did you go out for Bishop's Row?" he asked.

"No."

"Entertainment wrestling? Cheer squad?"

"Drama Club."

"Thank the gods. Stay as busy as you can with that. Make friends with Sid, offer to help him out. He's a handy guy to know. Whoever you've got for Lab, same deal. Or spend your free time in the library."

"Why?"

"Just do it. Stay busy away from the jocks. Kids in drama and band have nothing to prove. And the toughs avoid chores like the plague."

"Will it work?"

"If it doesn't, come back and see me. I've got a minimalist lifestyle to maintain but not much else in here. Now scram, this spoon won't whittle itself."

"Thanks, Crow."

He went back to his carving as I headed out into the cabin's yard. I asked to leave the moment before remembering my whole reason for coming.

"The clothes, Miss."

The voice was squeaky, creaky, and totally unexpected in the empty lobby.

"I'm confused." I looked down and around, thinking maybe I'd missed a gnome or pixie somewhere.

"Miss Merlini, the extra changes of clothes your incorporeal friend requested are on the bench in the vestibule." It came from the wall, which appeared to be bamboo. A brownie, then.

"But I haven't got—" I did though. I'd brought the satchel. Horace was with me. "Understood. Thanks to both of you."

I scooped the three stacks of clothes into the bag without looking at them. Because I'd seen the clock and I didn't want to miss dessert. Getting out the door was easier this time. No sneaking required.

Flying back took only a few minutes. I sat with Kiara and Brandon as a row of peach pies appeared on the table.

"Where's everyone else?"

"Done with dinner. The upperclassmen are like vacuum cleaners. Wyatt's upstairs, no dessert for him." Brandon answered. "Ghost pepper indigestion's a bummer."

"Captain Dunstable called a meeting, but not for us," Kiara said. "Family stuff to talk about with Ed. His first day wasn't so great, but I'm not sure how or why."

"Poor dude." Brandon shook his head. "Wish there was something we could do."

"Maybe we can."

"How?"

"Messing gets out later than us. We could go right there after school and be outside waiting."

"I still don't get it. Am I missing something?"

"Yeah." I told them about the after-school bullying.

"Sounds like a good idea," Kiara agreed. "We could hang out afterward too when the weather's nice."

Brandon nodded. "Go to the park, see some sights."

"Thanks."

An alarm *beeped* on Kiara's phone. "I've got to go upstairs, call my folks, then get ready for bed." She stood. "See you later."

"Yeah." Brandon grinned as he followed suit. "Later, Mavis."

I sat, pushing the remains of my dessert around the plate with the fork. Crow was right about Kiara. Technically, I'd be taking his advice, keeping away from Gallows Hill jocks by heading to another school directly after mine got out.

"Perhaps I made a wise choice."

I turned in my seat and gazed up at Matron Klein.

"Excuse me?"

"By giving you a place here." The corners of her mouth turned up. "It seems you're rather in demand."

"I wouldn't wager on that." I stood, then slung Horace's satchel over my shoulder. "You shouldn't, either."

"I'm no gambler." She glanced over my head. "That's an observation of someone else's opinion."

I turned my head to see what she was looking at. Behind me, Ed leaned in the doorway, Cosmo behind him.

"I believe they're waiting for you."

Had I been shaken entirely off the path of my convictions by the last twenty-four hours? Was my brother right about everything because he'd walked through the fire of Gallows Hill?

No. I wasn't him. The point was to break this cycle.

He meant well, but if I did everything Crow's way, I'd risk ending up where he was. Or worse.

No matter how strange Hope, Saya, and Cosmo were or how disconcertingly familiar Ed's problems were, I couldn't stay away. I nodded and walked toward the very people my brother had warned me to avoid.

CHAPTER ELEVEN

"Thanks for helping Ed today." Hope sat in the middle of the loveseat, which stood in the center of the lounge. Saya stood beside the armrest to her right, and Cosmo stepped over to mirror her on the left. "He forgets common courtesy sometimes, so I felt the need to make it clear."

"I don't fish for compliments, captain."

"So it's like that." She nodded, then beckoned to Cosmo. He whispered in her ear. "Playing hero to make up for sins of the father?"

"Grew up without one." I grinned. "You're wrong."

"So many words, so little information. We could do this for hours."

"Lights out is a thing, so no."

"True enough. Let's cut to the chase. Why the daring rescue?"

Beside me, Ed's face went crimson. So I lied.

"It wasn't daring. He didn't need much help against those kids. Basically, I startled some jerks and gave him an opening."

"That's not how he told it."

"I know all too well the pitfalls of self-depreciation."

"Drop the act, Mavis."

"Like attracts like." I shrugged. "You get what you give. What comes around goes around. Karma's a bitch, Captain Dunstable."

"Do you have an answer then, Ed?" The air around her shimmered slightly.

"She overheard you in the library." He slapped his hand over his mouth. Horace must have told him. I risked a question.

"Secrecy isn't the best policy when you're looking for something in a strange town. Maybe I can help."

"I'm on a Quest. And under a ban. I can't give you details."

Capital Q quest meant monarch involvement. The fact that she'd already tithed at sixteen backed that idea up. Hope was deeply mired in serious faerie business.

"One way you could though," Cosmo mumbled.

"Watch it, Cos."

"So this is a stalemate." I shrugged. "I'm trying to stay out of trouble on campus, keep my head down and graduate. Upperclassmen angrier and more dangerous than Wyatt hate my family. My well-being's tied to the entire section as your crew. Well, you can do that math, captain. You owe me respect, at least where the juniors and seniors can see."

"You think we owe you for being under a ban?" Saya snorted. "The nerve."

"We should be more careful where we discuss things anyway." Hope nodded. "Fine. We won't talk about you on campus. Is there a problem with that, fam?"

"Yeah." Saya narrowed her eyes. "I'll say whatever I choose whenever I want."

"You'll do no such thing." Hope looked her in the eye. "Be a good lieutenant, Say. Express yourself at school about anyone but Mavis."

"Fine." Saya rolled her eyes. "But this'll come back to bite us in the tail, mark my words."

"What say you, Cos? Can you refrain from Merlini-related gossip?"

"Gladly!" He smiled. "You worry too much, Saya."

Hope held out her hand. "We have an agreement."

"Not yet." I hesitated. "Ed? Is this okay with you?"

"Speak freely," Hope told him.

"Only nice things to say about my new pal Mavis, here." His lopsided grin relieved me. "To her face or otherwise."

"We're agreed, then." I shook hands with Captain Hope Dunstable, wondering when the other shoe would drop.

Faerie bargains always have a catch.

A note on the inside of the door said Kiara was in the shower when I got upstairs. I shoved the clothes from the sanitarium into a drawer without looking at them. I was there for school, not a fashion show. I got a clean sweatsuit then hung the satchel on the back of my chair before heading to the bathroom.

"Uh, stay here Horace."

I heard no answer but hoped I hadn't insulted him. A grieving ghost didn't seem like the creepy stalker type. Still, for all I knew, he was under Hope's thumb too. She'd said she could see ghosts after all. I thanked the gods she couldn't hear them.

Steam filled the ladies' room and my roommate hummed. At least the nicest person I'd met so far had a great first day. Maybe things could get better. She left the bathroom before I finished. On the way back to our room, I found some hair accessories in the bathroom closet.

Kiara was in front of our wall mirror, wrapping a scarf around the bottom of her hair.

"Good night?" I asked, then went about the business of putting my own still damp hair into two loose plaits, hoping it'd look less unkempt in the morning.

"Yeah! We missed you at Tropica Mart. Didn't get a chance to tell you over dessert, but Fiona says hi. Ramon, too. Bet they'd take a walk to Messing tomorrow too."

"He's good people." I glanced at her reflection as she tied the scarf at the back of her head. "So, Brandon?"

"We went for a stroll before dinner." She smiled. "He's a total gentleman."

"Awesome." I used a covered elastic to hold my plait in place, then started on the next one.

"We missed you at dinner. Where'd you go?"

"Visiting my brother. Don't worry. I had soup with him."

"Oh." She took a silk bonnet out of her dresser drawer. "How's he doing?"

"Therapy helps, he says. I believe that from what I've seen."

"Do you visit him every week?" She stretched the bonnet's elastic and covered her hair with it.

"Not exactly." I tied the second plait. "But it's a good idea to make it a regular thing now that I—"

The bell for lights out chimed before I said too much.

"Goodnight, Kiara."

"Good night, Mavis."

My roommate fell asleep practically before her head hit the pillow. I stayed up, reading *Stranger in a Strange Land* until I couldn't hold the book up anymore.

It wasn't until I'd set it aside that I realized I hadn't turned on the small book light in my headboard. But I was too exhausted to investigate.

"G'night Horace," I mumbled before falling asleep.

Thankfully, I woke up before Kiara's bee-adjacent phone alarm. One look at the clock by my bed and I almost rolled over to suffer through it later. However, the first fingers of dawn had touched the sky enough to keep that from working out.

Instead, I grabbed my satchel, scooped some undies and one of the sanitarium outfits into it, and headed downstairs. The dining room was brightly lit but empty, and when I approached a table, nothing appeared.

As I was about to scrounge for snacks in the lounge, Matron Klein pushed through the door from the kitchen. She nodded, stepped to one side to hold the door with her foot, then clapped three times.

A cart laden with carafes, cups, and coffee and tea fixings rolled past her, at first seeming to be on a collision course with your friendly neighborhood birdbrain.

It turned at the last second, nearly toppling a stack of paper cups and revealing the driver. Plural, actually. If you could call what they did driving.

They stood on each other's shoulders, three high in two columns. Their clothes matched the metallic sheen of the cart until it came to a screeching halt against the wall by the door and they toppled.

I watched, laughing as their silvery jumpsuits slowly took on the color of the parquet floor.

"Not funny!" The first one on their feet shook a tiny fist at me.

"Yeah, nice manners, angry bird." A second made a hand gesture his words might have described.

"Okay, okay. Thank you for the beverages, everybody."

"Freshman!" One giggled. "Don't know who we are."

"You're gremlins," Matron Klein said. "Under contract for pay to assist with breakfast and dinner. Snap to it!" She clapped again.

They scrambled back to the kitchen in a series of six indistinct streaks.

"Gremlins, huh? Never saw one before."

"None of this would be possible without them." She shook her head. "Even with the Harcourt's endowment and donated labor for renovations."

"I promise to pay you back."

"Whatever for?"

"Room and board." I shuffled my feet, suddenly feeling too awkward to fix coffee.

"The spare bed in Kiara's room would have remained empty. The food is all family style." Matron Klein filled a cup with coffee, handed it to me, then got one for herself. "I'm not a faerie. You owe me nothing."

"All the same, maybe you could hire help with one more paying resident."

"I tried. Nobody wanted the job." She blew on her beverage before sipping it.

"I didn't realize it was like that."

A metallic *clash* came from the kitchen.

"Breakfast will appear in ten minutes." She turned and headed back. As the door swung behind her, I heard, "So help me, Sid will hear about—"

"Met the gremlins, I guess." Ed stood there, pouring coffee.

"They always bring this cart out, then?"

"Same way every day since I got here." He drank some, then winced. "Can we, uh talk?"

"Just a sec." I put some milk in my cup, then followed him to an empty table. "Go on."

The coffee cooled enough to drink, and we'd finished half our cups by the time he got around to speaking. I didn't mind.

"You already know everything I can tell you about my setbacks at school yesterday. I don't want a repeat, so I thought a different setting might help."

"You mean finding more information about Messing folks?"

"Right. Most of them go to this all-ages night on Tuesdays. It's at Dodge Street Café."

"Folks from my school go there too." I nodded.

"Cool." He sighed. "I asked Saya if she'd go with me, you know for backup, so Donna and company wouldn't start anything."

"She said no. Sorry."

"Glad you said it so I didn't have to."

"Sometimes, my powers of observation get used for good inadvertently."

We didn't talk about why he hadn't asked Cosmo or Hope instead or gone to them first after she'd turned him down. I hadn't been in his shoes but watched Bar pine over Cadence for a couple of years. Their found family tree might be more like a wreath for all I knew—clearly a delicate subject.

Unrequited feelings needed time and space. Bar avoided Cadence for a few months, then ended up dating a magus from Hawthorn.

With whatever quest they were on, Ed could hardly begin to replicate that tactic.

"Well, the upperclassmen from Drama Club invited me, but they didn't say I had to come alone."

"You're in drama too? I signed up for the Messing version. It's microscopic."

"Ours is also not big. Mr. Hickson said clubs grow after they post sports teams. Maybe the same thing happens over there?"

"We'll see."

"Anyway, I'll go to Dodge Street tonight. Be a good townie and introduce you around."

"Thanks, Mavis."

The food appeared. Our classmates followed shortly after that. Breakfast progressed much as it had the previous day. Fortunately, without any stupid questions from Wyatt about Kiara, who sat giggling with Brandon over a collection of aquatic mammal memes on his phone.

I walked into my second day on alert but without the profound sense of anxiety from the first. Coach Tremain's Pilates routine wasn't too strenuous. Dressing for the rest of the day was, unfortunately, a challenge.

There's a saying about how everything comes back into style every twenty years or so. That is profoundly untrue. I'm no fan of wearing mini-dresses without leggings or at least thick tights under them, but pairing one with jeans is going too far.

Fortunately, said jeans weren't of the skinny variety. I tucked the dress's lacy hem in, bloused it out a bit, and went about my day. It must have worked because Saya made no comment on my wardrobe besides a single eye-roll.

CHAPTER TWELVE

Everybody behaved in Lecture. I hoped the trend would continue, but extrahuman teenagers are impatient, impulsive, and inconsistent. Often at the most inconvenient moment.

That means we're not much different from our mundane peers. Someone in section two would eventually put a toe out of line and do Lady Ambersmith the honor of ending up in detention someday. But not that day.

At snack, I practically inhaled the biggest navel orange I could find, along with a bag of trail mix. My hair stirred again in that same formerly unexplained breeze. Horace must have been the mom friend in his clique when he was corporeal because he always seemed to react positively to acts of self-care.

"You took care of Bianca." I realized aloud. "You must miss her terribly, Horace."

I looked up, half-expecting to see him standing there, though I had no idea what the ghost attached to my satchel looked like. Or even his last name, which presumably started with the letter L.

The bell rang, disrupting my thoughts on Horace's tragedy. However, they lingered all through Forum. Fortunately, our discussions weren't about my brother's fall from grace last year. This time, Saya sat in the hot seat.

"In Lecture, Lady A mentioned a few dragons from history," Jillian said. "One had a hatching date, but for the others she said birthdate. So which is it, do dragons hatch, or are they born?"

"Saya, would you like to answer that since it directly pertains to you?" Mr. Hickson nodded at her.

"Well, *I* certainly hatched." She somehow managed to look down her nose at the rest of us although our seats were the same height. "All the live-born dragons come from dalliances with inappropriate mates."

"Star-bellied sneeches." Cosmo rolled his eyes.

"You have something to add, Mr. Gitano?"

"Yeah." Cosmo nodded. "She's putting her sister-in-law down. Kim's not a dragon. Her baby's getting born. Your mother arranged the marriage herself. Blaine's madly in love with her, and she's been like a big sister to us. How could you call her inappropriate?"

"That's not what I meant. She arranged my brother's marriage for another reason entirely."

"This sounds complicated." Fiona tilted her head. "And like maybe you're not so happy about it. Are you okay, Saya?"

"Why wouldn't I be?"

"You sound kinda surly." Jillian shrugged. "I just don't want to be confused about all those dates and stuff."

"Listen up, Jillian, because this is the last time I'll discuss dragon biology in this Forum." Saya leaned forward. "Egg-bearing dragons only lay when they mate properly, with a sperm-bearing dragon who also hatched. That's happened consistently for the last sixteen centuries. Until the Reveal, that is."

Saya's grip tightened so much on her tablet that I feared she might break it. Hope took it from her, then replaced it with her hand. They sat like that for a moment.

"Lady Ambersmith doesn't give a detailed lecture on immediate consequences of the Reveal until after winter break." Mr. Hickson paused, the muscles in his jaw visibly tensing. "Let's just say, despite their fearsome skill and formidable magic, dragons were victims of extrahuman trafficking."

Saya let go of Hope's hand, retrieved her tablet, and continued.

"After a live birth, the ability to lay eggs is gone. Only hatchlings get an extended lifespan. My mother and I are the last two egg-bearing hatchlings left in the world."

"So you can't go out with who you want?" Jillian blinked. "Marry someone you fall for? Or decide you don't want kids? That totally sucks."

"I have a duty to my species."

"What about other dragons, though? Ones born live who, uh, bear eggs?" Jaxon asked. "They can't lay if they mate with someone like your brother?"

"No." She sighed. "Hatchlings come out of the egg in dragon form and the live-born as humanoids. That's got something to do with it, but I don't have that level of post-graduate knowledge."

"I'm acquainted with someone studying it." Mr. Hickson said. "If you're interested in extrahuman obstetrics, Mr. Thorne, I can put you in touch at a later date."

Jaxon looked a little green around the gills at the idea.

"I'll take you up on that," Jillian said.

We moved on to the much more comfortable topic of dragon hoards, which often weren't conventionally valuable items. Anything could be considered a hoard. The only criteria was the level of value an individual dragon placed on a particular item or category of same.

Lunch was salad with a choice of beans, chicken, or fish. I almost chose beans because I felt weird eating anything avian after Saya's revelations.

The last thing I wanted was a scoop of dubious tuna salad slopped atop my meal. Then Cosmo walked by with his food tray before I ordered, which was a good thing because otherwise, I'd have missed out on grilled salmon.

Brandon showed up at Drama Club, which had Kiara walking on air. He hadn't made the cut for cheer squad but had heard us talking about musicals and figured this was the place to be if he still wanted to dance.

Sid sat at a piano and had us all run scales while Mr. Hickson took notes. Afterward, Wanda said it was to think about casting future musicals. After that, he set a box on the stage's apron and told us to go up and borrow as many one-act plays as we wanted for the rest of the week.

"Why?" Kiara asked.

"You'll each start writing one next week. Our winter production each year is a set of three entirely student-produced one-acts. I'm not assigning something like that without giving you some good examples."

"What if we have ideas and have questions?" Kiara smiled.

"I'm around for an hour after the bell rings."

"Isn't there a performance during Fall Rec Week, though?" Brandon asked.

"Variety show!" Wanda bounced on her toes.

"You all have to audition for that." Mr. Hickson nodded. "It can be any type of performance piece you want."

I rummaged through the box without really looking at the titles, chose four, and tucked them into the satchel. They weren't long, and I read quickly. Once everyone had at least one script, Mr. Hickson dismissed us.

Like yesterday, I went directly to the library. This time, I made a beeline for a research terminal. Horace's tragic story still had me in its teeth. I knew from long experience that it wouldn't let me go until I learned more.

I did a Boolean search with the words Rhode Island, Horace, Bianca, and medium. It unearthed four news reports.

"Athletic Scholarship in Name of Missing Medium" was first. "Medium Prodigy Assists at Local College" included a thumbnail image of Ed himself, though years younger. "Promising Young Medium Reported Missing," the third headline read. "Memorial Service for Hero Student," said the fourth. I clicked on the first.

The barely-there brief only gave a link for Bishop's Row players to apply for the Bianca Brighton Scholarship, nothing about her besides the surname, which I noted on my tablet. I clicked on.

The one about Ed was a human interest piece, describing the youngest person ever employed at Providence Paranormal College. He was only nine, but also the only remaining medium able to manage the campus ghosts and prevent a full-scale haunting.

At that age, I was a spooky kid, totally fanatical about ghosts, hauntings, and mediums. Full-scale hauntings resulted in condemned buildings and severe injuries to bystanders.

He'd stepped in for his mother, Delilah. The article described how a chronic illness flare put her into the hospital and out of commission. A full-scale haunting had utterly destroyed the Redford home when Delilah fell ill.

The Law Offices of Ichiro and Dunstable immediately petitioned the state to allow Ed's employment in the interest of the greater good. The only Ivy League extrahuman college in the United States was too important to risk.

They put all that on the shoulders of one talented, homeless child while his mother ailed in the hospital. My eyes burned, anger clawing at my gut.

Ed was nine. How was that fair? I read on.

Apparently, he'd proven himself resilient and mature beyond his years at age seven when he'd been trapped in the Under by Richard Hopewell, an extramagus guilty of crimes against extrahumanity.

Ed was a victim, too. Targeted because Hopewell considered his big brother a threat.

I noted down all the names in the story. Ed, Fred, and Delilah Redford. Richard Hopewell. Ichiro. Dunstable. Like Hope.

I opened a new window and typed in Law Offices of Ichiro and Dunstable, Rhode Island, and clicked the first listing. A tastefully designed website gave a list of legal services beside a picture of the Providence skyline. I clicked the Staff tab and scrolled through a series of names and images.

At first, I thought neither Dunstable attorney resembled Hope. They were related to each other and could have been movie actors if they hadn't gone into law. The man would have had more success despite his spectacles. His face had a twinkle in the eye and a slight smile.

That's where I finally saw the resemblance. Hope inherited her mother's features, but smiled exactly like this guy.

I put Albert Dunstable's name on the list with the rest and closed the window.

There wasn't any more to the piece about Ed, which was a relief. If the reporter had been angry on Ed's behalf, her prose didn't show it. Or someone had edited it out. I moved on to the third listing, which predated Ed's by two years.

The missing young medium was Bianca Brighton, of course. The article said she'd last been seen stumbling through a portal to the Under. Her friends and family were extremely worried because she had diabetes and needed her medication. There was an email link and tip line for people to send information if they'd seen her.

I hesitated over the last link. If these went in order from newest to oldest, the dead student it mentioned wasn't Bianca. However, it had something to do with her. The entire reason for this research was learning a story Horace couldn't tell me.

Still, what was the point of that if Ed would only take the satchel away anyhow? Was I only falling back into my old spooky kid pattern of interest in all things ghostly?

It started that way, continuing as a distraction from my substantial problems. The truth at the heart of the matter had changed, especially after reading that fool's gold spin on Ed.

I cared. About Ed, unfairly burdened. About poor Bianca, who probably died undiscovered in the Under. And Horace, who as a ghost couldn't cross the barrier between worlds even with a portal. They'd remain separated forever.

So, I clicked the link and opened an entirely different can of worms along with the obituary. The dead college student had rescued two of his classmates from a burning building. His name was Tony, surname Gitano just like Cosmo. I kept reading.

He'd saved Bianca Brighton and a girl named Olivia Adler before leaping out the window himself. They'd been fine, but he died in the hospital. The memorial happened at Swan Point Cemetery in Providence only days before Bianca went missing.

The piece identified his father, Gino, as his only living relative. All that happened when I was eight. That meant Cosmo would have been somewhere between my age and Ed's. But there'd been no mention of a sibling surviving Tony at all, even without a name or gender as sometimes happens in news articles with younger children.

Cosmo talked about his brother like he was still alive. From what I'd seen so far of Hope and Saya, they'd say something to a friend in denial. They'd never corrected or coddled him over it. I could only conclude that Tony wasn't dead.

No. Cosmo's brother wasn't dead. For all I knew, there was more than one Gitano family in Rhode Island. Maybe this heroic Tony wasn't related to Cosmo at all, or only in a distant way.

I added Gino and Tony to the list of names, also Olivia Adler. Then, since she connected to Tony but not Cosmo, I searched her name next. I found an engagement announcement, complete with a full-color photo of the lovely couple.

Someone had spared no expense to get it in the paper. It took up an entire page in the *Providence Journal*. There wasn't a wedding date, but the announcement was only a week old.

Olivia and Tony were close to the same height in their picture, and they both smiled. Other than that, the pair were a study in opposites.

She clearly wore makeup. I would have thought she was an albino if her eyes weren't a rich amber color. He had deep beige skin and wavy black hair with hazel eyes. Her smile was fierce, forward, and infectious. His was gentle and guarded, yet genuine.

He was absolutely Cosmo's brother. They shared hair and eye color, a nose, and a hairline. Though Cosmo was paler than Tony, the resemblance was much stronger than Hope and Albert Dunstable's.

This one listed Daniel and Julia Adler as Olivia's parents and Albert Dunstable as Olivia's cousin. It also confirmed visual evidence, naming Cosmo Gitano and Duke Ismail as Tony's brother and great-grandfather but no mention of Gino.

The bell rang as I wrote the new names on the tablet. I saved the file and closed it.

I stowed the device, cleared the library search history, and shut the windows down. Rushing to Lab wasn't fun, but discovering a new trove of mysteries was priceless.

Not that I'd have time to research them until it was too late.

CHAPTER THIRTEEN

Kiara and Brandon stayed after school with Mr. Hickson to work on one-act plays. I'd asked Ramon to walk over to Messing with me instead, but he and Jillian promised to help Fiona with her belated entertainment wrestling tryout. They'd all meet us at Irzyk Park with snacks later.

Cosmo overheard and invited himself, dragging Saya along after Hope got called to run Bishop's Row drills with Wyatt. Cosmo was on one of the two first-year teams already, first defense, but the redcap's potential inclusion was still up in the air.

"Wow, they announced a field trip already. Three weeks from Friday. Can you believe it?" Cosmo chuckled.

"Thank goodness it's Dr. Aranha running it." I sighed. "Can you imagine going to a museum with Mrs. A? Nobody could ask questions."

"I know, right." Cosmo shrugged. "Luckily, we don't have to."

"Honestly, Cosmo. It's not as though you haven't been to twenty better museums already." Saya rolled her eyes. "I don't know why you're so excited about the Peabody Essex. It's tiny and not even that prestigious."

"Not everybody gets to visit the Louvre and the Vatican Museum in one summer, Say." Cosmo grimaced. "Besides, that flight across the Atlantic was a super squirrely experience. A walk across town to a smaller exhibit is fine."

"We didn't have to go on the plane." Saya snorted. "But *someone* couldn't handle dragonback."

"It's not Ed's fault he's got asthma." Cosmo blew a raspberry at her. "It wasn't only him. I couldn't have handled it either. Nothing but your wings between us and all that water for hours on end."

"Seriously, the sibling rivalry between you two is exhausting." I snorted. "I grew up with six older brothers and sisters, so I know what I'm talking about."

"Wait." Cosmo stopped and grabbed my elbow. "You never told us you're the seventh sibling. Leaping Luna! Are you hearing this, Say?"

"Wait your turn." She sighed. "Let's get this protection racket over with, already."

We kept walking until we reached Messing Academy. Waiting for Ed was non-negotiable after yesterday. None of us wanted him out in front of that place alone.

The school itself was a classic example of 1950s Brutalist architecture, which meant blocky, monochrome, and jarring beside the more ornate nineteenth century and older styles. Those were sometimes over-the-top elaborate, slightly spooky, but mostly pleasing to look at. The psychics' school looked like a truckload of bare cement blocks had come to life, fallen in love, and decided to procreate. The disdain on my face must've been obvious.

"Ed wasn't kidding when he said they should call it Messed Up Academy." Cosmo wrinkled his nose. "Who builds them like that anymore?"

"I'll have you know that this was a very important design style in the mid-twentieth century." Saya sniffed but didn't smile as she studied the building's façade.

"Don't go quoting Blaine at me." Cosmo shook his head but grinned. "Her brother's a total history nerd, Mavis. You should meet him sometime."

"I'll keep that in mind."

The entire conversation might have made me mildly uncomfortable because bickering like this usually led to knock-down drag-outs at the nest. After my misadventures in the library, it bothered me more for a different reason.

The information I'd found made me internally question even the simplest of Cosmo's statements, despite his chummy mannerisms and chatty disposition. It felt odd, being more comfortable around Saya, who I'd come to understand was honest at her own expense. The discussion in Forum gave context to her prickly behavior. I knew how it felt, stuck in an out-of-control destiny without any brakes.

The bell tolled at Messing Academy. Yes, I said tolled. The one at Gallows Hill trilled with brassy excitement, and the rooming house's brightly tinkling handbell echoed its gleaming comfort. The one here chimed hollow and haunted, like an ill-omened shout. At least from my perspective as a raven shifter, which wasn't optimistic to begin with.

We stood across the street, away from the line of cars standing at the curb directly in front of the school. Ed didn't see us right away.

I noticed him almost immediately as he squeezed his way out between the door frame and a teacher. He hurried, ducking, dipping, and skirting students in groups of all sizes. I recognized his attempt to escape his classmates as quickly as possible.

Since he was tallest and most visible, I elbowed Cosmo, who immediately began waving. Ed saw him after staring at nothing for a moment.

Ed ran headlong across the street toward us without checking for oncoming traffic. Saya opened her mouth as he skidded to a stop in front of us. He cut her off before she could emit a single sound.

"Rob told me it was safe to cross, so don't bother."

"I'm only trying to make sure you're—"

"Stop the sister act, Say." He looked at me. "Why are you here, Mavis? I don't remember us making plans. For the afternoon, anyway."

The force of his gaze silenced me. What could I say to an unsteady child prodigy, nearly crushed under the weight of adult responsibility? Especially when I'd done nothing important myself.

"Spontaneous field day." I pasted on a grin. "Let's move out."

I turned my back on the three of them, heading up the street toward Irzyk Park. I sniffled, eyes stinging. That unbidden anger clawed my middle, again on someone else's behalf. For whatever reason, I never could muster up that sort of rage when it was my well-being on the line.

Ed's unusual plight inspired something in me. An unknown emotion of mysterious origin. I couldn't grok what to do with it besides leave it on a slow burn. Maybe I'd talk to Crow about it sometime. Not that night. I'd booked myself too solidly.

Down in the park, Ramon, Jillian, and Fiona waited. I spotted Kiara and Brandon halfway up the other end of Fort Street, Jaxon in tow. Hope and Wyatt were nowhere in sight.

"Hey, I brought those snacks." Ramon unslung the rucksack from his shoulder and opened the drawstring at the top. He rummaged inside, producing a can of nutrient shake, which he knew I hated.

"Don't worry, Mavis. It's for Cosmo." He tossed it.

"Thanks." He caught it. "After all those conjuring drills at R&R, I need it. That was an intense workout, right?"

"I wouldn't know. I only watched from the other side of the gym." Ramon shrugged. "There's no conjuring for a dhampyr in entertainment wrestling."

"No crying either unless it's for kayfabe." Jillian chuckled. "But those bumps were rough. You got any jerky in there?" Ramon tossed her bag of the beef variety. She opened it and split it with her brother.

"Fruit for the singing and dancing ladies." Ramon handed a coconut to Fiona, who smiled broadly before cracking it with her bare hands.

Then, he pulled out an apple, an orange, and a banana, juggled them, then tossed the orange at Saya, the apple at Kiara, and the banana at me.

Unfortunately, I couldn't catch anything but a cold. It came at me too fast to deflect. The yellow tree finger hit me in the face.

"Ow!"

The sound of fruit *thunking* to the ground didn't follow.

"Fewmets!" Ed stood staring at the air in front of me. I couldn't blame him. I stared too.

The banana hung in the air in front of me, lower than eye level and well within my reach. I held out my hand, grasped, and pulled. Whatever force held it let go.

I applied my poker face liberally, making a show of taking the weirdest event of my day in stride. So of course my next move was peeling the banana as nonchalantly as possible.

"Did you see that?" Cosmo elbowed Saya.

"Of course I saw it, Cos." She scowled. "It means nothing."

"Thanks, Horace. Or Rob. Whichever one of you saved my snack from an inedible fate." I grinned.

"There are helpful ghosts here?" Jillian blinked. "No way."

"Way." Kiara smiled. "Ed's a medium."

"He has two ghosts?" Jill grinned. "Sick."

"Uh, what?" Ed blinked, face reddening. "But I don't—"

"That's epic level for mediums." Jillian clapped Ed's shoulder. "You rock."

"Yeah, because *you've* met so many mediums, Jill." Jaxon rolled his eyes. "Give me a break."

Jillian blushed a little. For the rest of the afternoon, I caught her stealing glances at Ed. That's a story for another time.

"So now what?" Jaxon asked.

"Just fun." I knelt on the park side of the tank and felt around by the treads. Moments later, I found the item left behind by Bar the day before he left for college. "Here it is."

My hand stopped short of the pavement because Bar's glamour had made the box invisible.

"A little help from a glamour-enabled friend would be awesome."

"Sure thing." Kiara joined me, the half-eaten apple held aloft in her left hand, pinkie extended. She reached over and put her right one beside mine. "Eureka."

Her nose wrinkled with concentration and soon a purple plastic tote appeared, the sort of thing people with extra clothes stored them in.

I opened it, finding exactly what I expected—a frisbee, soccer ball, plastic sand-weighted horseshoes with wooden stakes, and a badminton set. We spent the next hour playing on the otherwise empty field. As time passed, passersby turned into spectators. Fifteen minutes later, spectators became participants. Most were middle school kids.

At the edge of the park, still only watching, stood a tall, lanky figure wearing a hooded sweatshirt in Hawthorn Academy purple and gold. I elbowed Ramon, asked if he looked familiar. By the time we looked again, the mystery magus was gone.

After returning from the park, I read a play and did a lab worksheet on mass displacement and shifting. Since she'd done her homework at the library, Kiara spent time getting ready for our outing later. She deliberated between two outfits, took a quick shower, and changed her hair from the morning's cute afro puffs to a braided high pony. I stood watching as she applied makeup.

"You look nice." I smiled.

"Thanks! I wanted to look more sophisticated. Brandon and I agreed at the park. It's a date, for real!"

"Wow."

"I know!" She tilted her head. "Aren't you going to change?"

"Nah." I shook my head. "Should have been smart like you and done my homework earlier. At least I finished in time to grab a bite before we go."

We headed to Dodge Street Café directly after a brief pause at the dinner table. Brandon had gotten dressed up, too. I would have felt out of place, but Ed wore the same black jeans and hoodie he'd worn to Tropica Mart two days earlier.

Wyatt ended up tagging along after giving me a stumbling apology about Monday morning, which I figured was Hope's doing. Ed stood through it, watching with his arms crossed and eyes narrowed. He tugged my sleeve as we continued walking.

"I don't trust that guy."

"Already there."

"Good." He opened his mouth and closed it again. After a moment, he spoke. "You mentioned this morning some Gallows Hill upper-classmen invited you."

"Yeah." I nodded. "I'm still going so I can help you with the Messing mission. But I should thank Wanda for inviting me."

"Wait, Wanda? As in, Wanda Davis-LaMontaine?" He blinked.

"Yeah. Met her in Drama Club. Ramon wants to meet her, which can only help my school situation."

"The 'everybody knows your name' issue?"

"One and the same."

He breathed easier.

"How does Ramon help, though?"

"Everybody loves dhampyr. Besides, he's way better at talking to people than me."

"I, uh, wasn't expecting that."

"Because people drop the ball on you."

We kept walking in silence.

"No." He spoke softly. "You're wrong for once."

"Then how was it unexpected?"

"Don't know about other people, but I give Mavis talking to me five stars."

"Brings my overall rating up to one star."

Cosmo stepped in front of us and walked backward.

"Heyo, friendos!" He put his finger over his upper lip. "It's a-me, it's a-Cos-a-mo!"

"Uh, what?" I blinked.

"You've never heard of Mario? Like on Nintendo?"

"Please, no." Ed covered his face with his palm. "Tell me you're not on that kick again."

"It's not that bad."

Ed gave him a side-eye.

"It was only six months. Come on. Everyone plays video games!"

"Never heard of them." Busting up the impending sibling rivalry felt right. "Lived in a nest my whole life. Raised by birds. Tragic story." I put the back of my hand above my eyebrows. "Hand, staple, forehead."

Cosmo guffawed immediately, almost stumbling backward. Ed hesitated, glancing at me before finally letting out a chuckle.

"Leaping Luna, did you actually laugh at a joke, Ed?"

"Had to make sure it was a good one. Didn't want to waste my yearly allotment for expressions of mirth."

I leaned against a brick wall, laughing myself breathless. Clutching my sides didn't help me recover, but it stopped the sobs that threatened to escape afterward.

Pain is the evil twin of humor. Cosmo didn't seem to know that fact of life yet. I didn't want to be the one teaching it to him.

"Come on already." Wyatt beckoned from the door. "Or not, whatever."

"No, no." I finally caught my breath. "Let's go."

I walked in behind Cosmo but ahead of Ed. Kiara and Brandon were already at the coffee counter, ordering a beverage. Jillian and Jaxon stood at the other end, waiting for their order. I spotted Saya and Hope already in a corner with whipped-cream topped smoothies. Ramon walked over, holding two matcha frappes.

"Hi, Mavis." He held one out to me. It shook slightly. "You look nice."

CHAPTER FOURTEEN

"Real smooth, DelSangre." Wyatt rolled his eyes. "She looks the same as all day at school."

"The captain said no fighting." Cosmo wagged a finger.

"You gonna rat me out for something I'm not doing?"

"Glamour doesn't need my help."

"Whoa." Ed whistled. "She's got you all under pact."

"True story." Wyatt nodded. "Shoot your shot then, DelSangre." He turned his back on us, then looked back over his shoulder. "Don't be a third wheel, Gitano."

Cosmo only blinked until Ed grabbed him by the arm and led him toward the table with Hope and Saya.

"Ramon? What's going on?"

"Sorry." He drew a deep breath and glanced at Brandon and Kiara. "I thought maybe, uh. Well, this is awkward."

"Ramon, I'm an entire mess. Like, my whole life, not only stuff at school."

"I know your situation." He nodded. "That doesn't make *you* a mess."

"Huh?"

"You keep going, no matter what happens. I stayed quiet in middle school, but I saw you last year. Then all summer. Today, you brought everyone to play at the park after they griefed you at school the first day. You're a badass." He swallowed. "That's why I like you."

I blinked.

"It's cool if you don't want this drink. I'm still gonna be your friend if you don't like me that way."

"Wow, Ramon." I sighed. "It's been. Well, hard to describe the parts you didn't see. And busy."

"Right." He nodded. "You're staying at the principal's new rooming house. Something's been bugging you since before Monday. Dad said you were in the store Sunday night."

"So, what do we do?"

"Stick to the original plan. Introduce me to Wanda. I'll give her this." He waggled one of the drinks. "If you want to talk about *vida loca* stuff after that, I'm here until curfew."

I nodded, thanked Ramon, and led him to the tall stools at a counter where the upperclassmen sat. Introductions went fine, and I accompanied Ed to the other end of the café where the Messing group stood in a cluster.

Donna, Gia, and Peg weren't there. Allen and Diego were, but I recognized Allen's brother Jonah and immediately realized that they wouldn't be a problem. We'd caught Messing Academy's most well-known alumnus in the middle of dressing his sibling down.

"A bully almost killed me, Allen. Dad'll send you down to The Academy if you do anything like it again. Do you really want that?"

"You don't understand." Allen shook his head. "He's not normal."

"Yeah, and he started it." Diego actually pouted.

"Page of Swords Reversed says no, Diego." Jonah waved the card in their faces. "Nobody at Messing is normal. Learn to get along with each other. Be thankful you're not at Hawthorn, where friendship's literally a matter of life and death."

I stepped toward them. Ed kept tugging my sleeve.

"Mavis, no. We can avoid them. What are you doing? Stop," he chanted under his breath.

"Hi, Diego." I deadpanned.

Diego froze, Allen squirmed, and Jonah looked right past me to gaze at Ed.

"Mavis, would you mind introducing me to your friend?" Jonah asked. "I saw him at the assembly today but didn't get a formal introduction."

"Jonah Arnold, meet Edward Redford from Providence."

"This is auspicious." Jonah held his hand out. Ed shook it without hesitation.

"Hello, sir." Ed nodded. "Thanks for speaking at our school."

"Sir?" I asked.

"I joined the Coast Guard." Jonah grinned. "I'm only a petty officer but gave a talk at Messing today about it. And learned a few unsavory facts about my kid brother's first day in high school."

"Sorry, Jo." Allen hung his head.

"Don't apologize to me."

"Ed, I'm sorry." Diego stepped in. "Donna's scary, and I'm a coward. I won't mess with you again."

"Okay." Ed nodded with his hands in his pockets. "You're an empath but also a pianist, right?"

Ed handed him what looked like a cross between a bookmark and a postcard, with a woman in cosplay from an anime playing violin. A brawny man with a red ball cap stood behind her, directing an entire contingent of pixies in a dance routine. He looked vaguely familiar.

"Huh?" Diego stared down at it and read aloud. "Irina Kazynski's playing the common in October? She went to Berklee. This is a ticket."

"You know her, of course." Jonah flipped a card, then peered at the ticket. "She's like family, or close to joining it."

"Pretty much," Ed answered. "The guy with the faeries is my brother, Fred. They're platonic life partners. Anyway, that's a backstage pass."

"Really?" Diego looked at him, then glanced at me. "You probably don't want me as your plus one."

"That's mine." Ed shrugged. "Already gave the other to someone else. I've seen Irina play a hundred times, anyway. So, do you want it?"

"Sure." He nodded. "What do I have to do for it?"

"Just stop and think," Ed said. "Before you follow Donna into treating anyone else like that."

"That isn't easy for an empath." He sighed. "We feel a lot of things we don't want to.

"Which is why schools like Messing exist in the first place." Jonah nodded. "To help us sort it all out."

"Never been a good student."

"Just sit up front, ask tons of questions, and study your brains out." I patted his shoulder. "Donna's already got enough help from her weird sisters. Don't give her any more."

"Good advice." Diego nodded. "Thanks." He took out his wallet and tucked the ticket into the billfold section.

"Now, what about you, Allen?"

"Uh, sorry, Ed." He winced. "I mean, there's really no excuse for clairvoyants behaving badly. Should have checked my cards. Hey. Maybe I could give you a reading, make up for it that way."

"Uh, no thanks." Ed swallowed. "But you know, I'm kind of an introvert with corporeal people. So, if you'd maybe introduce me around to folks—"

"Are you sure you want that?" Allen raised an eyebrow. "The thing is, after the whole bathroom incident, they might not—"

"That's why I'm here." I grinned, waving. "Bad omen bird, remember?"

"Yeah, okay." He nodded. "That works. Come on, Ed. And, uh, intimidating corvid."

Ed followed, listening and watching as we circulated. He had one hand in his pocket the entire time but responded to everyone with otherwise impeccable manners. That made sense because he lived with the Harcourts after his house imploded.

He paid more attention to everything than I did. Mostly because Ed hadn't had someone declare their feelings unexpectedly. I wanted to talk to somebody about my family issues, and Ramon was the best choice. Still, I had to collect my thoughts and feelings on him first. It was only fair

Dating was the furthest thing from my thoughts just then. However, I'd learned one reasonable thing about romance by watching Crow and Cadence. It's never about one person. Ramon had his idea of timing. He'd never judged me by the rest of my family. And he valued honesty.

I could certainly trust him. I'd trusted Diego, too, and been wrong. Five minutes earlier, that would have been a mark in the don't give Ramon a chance column. His ill-fated question in Lecture was a mistake he apologized quickly for—much like Diego. Everybody liked Ramon. And he was way more than easy on the eyes.

I put my decision off for one more reason. I'd promised to help Ed through this outing. I had to be sure we'd finished meeting all the Messing students.

"Mission accomplished?" I asked.

"Yes and no." He shrugged. "My part in it still isn't done, but it'll be way easier now. Admitting to the overachievers that something's hard hasn't gone well in the past. So, thanks for helping me out. Being an actual friend."

"When will you be able to tell me what this is about?"

"You'll know after it happens. I'm sorry."

"It's not you. It's faerie business." I nodded. "So, what now?"

"I go hang out with the fam, I guess." He wrinkled his nose. "Sounds better when Cosmo says it."

"Nah. I give Ed talking to me five stars."

"One star overall for me too, I guess."

"Maybe it'll impress Saya?"

"She told me about Forum, you know. Jillian's question."

"You knew about that long before today, though."

"Bullseye. But I couldn't just, you know, shut my heart off instead of declaring my feelings. Remembering that is painfully embarrassing, even with the passage of time."

"My brother says the same thing about his ex."

"Does he have any advice?"

"Maybe you can ask him yourself sometime."

"Ramon's flagging you down."

"Yeah. See you later, Ed."

"Thanks, Mavis."

I set my jaw, squared my shoulders, and went to give Ramon the truth. And a chance.

"So you have nothing?" Ramon's nostrils flared.

"You're not asking why I don't go back?"

"That's obvious. We might have moved into this town last fall, but it's pretty clear she owns half of it."

"I don't know what to do. I've got a roof and three squares, but—"

"Getting through the year with borrowed outfits from the lost and found and 1999 doesn't work."

"Pretty much." I shrugged. "It's not only clothes. That's my whole life up in that room. You know?"

"What if you showed up at the nest with a posse?"

"You missed the part where nobody knows."

"Mavis, you're not nobody."

"How do you mean?"

"Spontaneous field day, remember?"

"Nobody's afraid of outdoor recreation and tasty snacks. My family's another story."

"Fair enough." His lips wore a slight grin. "What if it only looked like you came with an army? Could you get some of your stuff back, then?"

"How do you mean?"

"In entertainment wrestling, the first thing Coach Tremain taught us about was kayfabe. It's selling the story."

"Go on."

"We need to put you over, give you an intimidating promo so you look scarier than your siblings." Ramon grinned. "Your reputation's changing. You've got connections from out of town, and you're making nice with local psychics. All we have to do is take that and run with it."

"How? I don't want to dump my old drama on all the new folks."

"How many more people are you willing to tell about this?"

"Ideally, nobody. But I get it. How many do you think I need?"

"Three if they're shifters. Two if you can bring changelings. Or just one if it's Captain Dunstable over there."

I sat, pondering. Hope and I already had an agreement, but her motives were mysterious. I definitely didn't want to trust her with my homeless status after reading about Ed's exploitation. It might not have come from the Dunstables, but I couldn't be sure.

"Veto on Hope. Let me think some more."

Ramon nodded. It wouldn't take long to deliberate. Three shifters would mean including Cosmo or Saya, which had the same issues as Hope. I thought over the three changelings I knew, deciding between them.

Fiona would help, and we wouldn't have to explain the kayfabe thing to her since she joined entertainment wrestling. Hugh and Manny had a phobia about ogres, too. That'd go a long way toward protecting her from retaliation in the future.

Kiara was right out. I'd almost spilled these particular beans to her Monday night. She wasn't stupid. Probably she suspected I had serious family issues. Still, she wasn't from town, didn't understand the dynamic here. She'd probably offer to help, but I worried she wouldn't take future risks seriously. She could get hurt, and I didn't want that.

Then there was Wyatt Clayton. He was a sour, antagonistic dude-bro, but he wouldn't question my situation. Plus, he'd treat my family with the correct level of caution. Also, I'd seen him in Lab. His mantle was so strong he'd probably have to take a gap year in the Under after graduation.

"Fiona," I said. "And Wyatt, but I can't imagine how to ask him for help."

"That's who I would have picked. Don't worry about Wyatt. I think I know the right angle to use." Ramon nodded. "I'll talk to Fiona at gym tomorrow."

"How, though? With Wyatt, I mean."

"Kayfabe, remember?" Ramon smiled. "It'll work for us in more ways than one. But we need one more thing. The glamour bracelets from Drama Club."

"I can get them for you." I sighed. "During R&R."

"Perfect. I'll get us together at the Mart tomorrow after school to make the plan. Probably should do this on Thursday, so don't grab those bracelets until then."

"Thanks, Ramon."

Kiara waved at me from the exit. After I looked up, she tapped her watch.

"I gotta go if we want to make lights out."

"Sure. You're welcome."

He walked me down Washington Street to the rooming house. Before going in, I reached out, and we hugged.

I still wasn't sure exactly how I felt about Ramon DelSangre in a dating sense, but I wanted to find out.

"Door!" Ed wheezed. I noticed he'd come from the opposite direction as the rest of us.

"Inhaler, dude." I stepped aside and let him through.

He stepped inside before taking two puffs.

"Where were you?"

"Tomorrow." He shook his head, tapping his watch. "Was cool. But." He shrugged, gesturing at the space between us. "Ghostly."

"Honestly, Ed." Hope scooped him up as though he were a small child. "You'll get in trouble. Come on."

I followed as she took him up the stairs, three steps at a time. With less than a minute to spare, she set him down outside the room he shared with Cosmo.

We didn't have to be in bed at lights out, just in our rooms. But Kiara was already sleeping when I got in. There wasn't time to go to the bathroom, so I changed into sweats like I was in the locker room. Showering in the morning wouldn't be much trouble. Getting up early was a given anyway if I wanted time to hear Ed's ghost story.

I glanced at the satchel I'd left hanging on the chair.

"Night, Horace. Sorry for leaving you behind."

CHAPTER FIFTEEN

Dead Man's Party
Ed

Monarchal faerie magic had rules. We'd all sworn to follow them on the anchor of Hope's ship, *The Odyssey*. I had no choice, no matter how much all signs pointed toward Mavis Merlini.

Acting on instinct and jumping ahead of schedule would have dire consequences. I'd never feared risks like that before, but she'd get hurt too. Paying kindness back with curses was no way to treat a friend.

I'd already hurt enough of mine to last a lifetime and then some.

So, that's why I didn't just hand the Sirin's feather to Mavis right there at the Dodge Street Café. Or go back to sit with my foster siblings, either. Instead, I walked out the door. Alone time was hard to come by, and walking around town was the only way I could hear my thoughts over the busy noises of both the living and the dead.

Faces, some solid and others translucent, passed me on either side up and down the cobblestone and concrete blocks. I ignored them, trying to console myself with the idea that keeping promises is what my brother would've done.

The only blood family I cared about anymore was my brother

Fred. Mom was an addict, a direct result of being forcibly possessed for months on end by a ghost on the edge of going full poltergeist.

After she overdosed, her ghostly contingent panicked and blew down our house. Dad dropped her at Butler Hospital, me at Hertha Harcourt's mansion, and himself on the first flight out of town. He only paused to sign the demolished lot over to me and the contracting business to Fred.

All of his responsibilities fell to my brother. Mom's went to me. Trying to pick them up had almost ruined me. My brother handled it, somehow.

He was a knight in the Sidhe queen's court, a graduate of the magical engineering program at Providence Paranormal College. A talented musician, too. He did all that, switching proverbial hats without missing a beat. No sweat, he said.

Fred helped put the sundered faerie realm back together, along with Hope and her parents, Cosmo's brother and future sister-in-law, and Saya's entire family. Heroes, all.

They'd done it by keeping their word and following the rules, which I'd always done. Still, I was never a hero—only "good old Ed, working so hard. Give the kid a break. He's only a psychic. Make sure he's got his inhaler and doesn't get in our way."

I hated it.

That was sour but true. For my asthmatic medium self, keeping up with bigger, more powerful extrahumans was an exercise in frustration. One I'd done for years. The fact I was chronologically older than all three of them rankled even more. However, that's another story.

The three of them were on track to either fill or surpass their parents and siblings. I was their weak sauce mascot. Messing Academy only made it worse. Despite the emphasis on mentalist talents like clairvoyance and mnemonics, mediumship was considered iffy. Apparently, Salem had a long history of false mediums.

It didn't help that I lived at Matron Klein's rooming house. She'd lived for decades in town with fake papers declaring her an empath instead of a dhampyr. No wonder even some of my teachers doubted my talent.

The only people I'd met so far who didn't make me feel less than were Mavis and her roommate Kiara. Kiara, mostly by merit of just being an outgoing, friendly sort of person, seemed baffled by all the coddling. She ignored it, though.

Mavis was different.

On Monday afternoon, I felt like a damsel in one of those old fairytales, except without the rosy cheeks and long hair. She rescued me from Donna and company, which I'd have hated if she hadn't acted like that earlier Snapple recommendation was an enormous favor. Mavis's insight rivaled an empath's. Or maybe she just understood sibling problems on another level.

As far as family went, maybe I was stuck in a tower. Or a fortress painstakingly built by intimidating found family. How did it end up like this? I was a prodigy, destined for greatness according to an old set of predictions. Here I was, puffing on albuterol in a strange town alone on a Tuesday night.

"Cat got your lungs, Ed?"

Okay, so mediums are never really alone. The world's full of ghosts, even if most people can't see them. Especially in a town with a long and storied history like Salem. The mundanes up here like a good ghost story. They even give tours, ascribing spectral presences to particular locations.

But they're more numerous than that, actually everywhere. Sometimes on top of each other, which gets difficult even for me. Every single one has thoughts, feelings, and unfinished business. Many want to move on soon, while some wait decades for living people.

My companion Rob was neither. He wanted to move on but didn't know what he needed to get it done. At some point in his long history, the memory of that had vanished.

"This whole Sirin feather business is harder than I thought, Rob." I murmured so I didn't spook the solids. "I don't know what to do."

"You fulfilled your obligation. Give it back and wash your hands of it." Rob shrugged.

"I can't stop thinking I'm right, though. Hope's thinking about getting the Alkonost feather. It was pushed on her without warning.

Of course, she wants to give whoever's next a choice. Why we can't start by asking the most obvious person we've met so far is beyond me."

"You've suffered under the curse of common sense your whole life." Rob nodded. "Who's getting it next?"

"It's Hope's turn. She's convinced it should go to someone older than the rest of us. So she's starting with upperclassmen at Gallows Hill."

"She's probably tired of being in charge all the time."

"We're best friends. I keep offering to help, but she insists she's got it." I shook my head. "The kicker is, I *am* older than her."

"Not physically, Ed. Not anymore." Rob floated in front of me and moved backward, which reminded me of Cosmo. "You know none of them wanted to grow up as fast as they did."

"Yeah. But I've been eating their dust now for years. What do I do with that, even?"

"Why not go back to the rooming house then? Get a little home-work done? You've got them outstripped in the brains department by a long shot, you know."

"I want to be out, Rob. Living. Not shut up in a magical dollhouse designed by Hertha and built by my brother. Tiamat's scales, Salem's famous for ghost tours!"

A gaggle of kids my age, likely from another school, crossed the street, staring at me. I'd raised my voice to my ghost, right in front of folks totally clueless about how mediums worked. It didn't help that I swore like a dragon, either. I was on the road to being the weird kid around town, not only Messing Academy.

It was Tuesday night, so why did I hear the enticing thump of elec-tronic music? There was no way any of the restaurants around here had live music at this hour on weeknights. The Dodge Street Café was near the wharf, which had a nightlife through most of September and all October. But not the commuter rail end of Washington Street.

I leaned against the nearest yellow brick wall at my back and stared across the street at all the storefronts. Most of the shops were dark and empty. Only restaurants and places to grab adult beverages were open. Scratching my head, I searched for any sign of the sound's source.

My eyes remained clueless so I followed my ears instead. In the end, I had to turn and pace that block several times. Finally, I pinpointed it in front of an Asian fusion restaurant. When I peered through the plate-glass window, it looked mostly deserted.

One extremely elderly man sat at the far end of the bar inside. The music unmistakably originated from somewhere behind him. So I walked inside. It was against my better judgment, but curiosity and desire for an adventure of my own compelled me.

"Welcome to K's Place, dine in or take out?" The host bowed his head, showing off spiky dark hair.

"Um, I'm not sure?" I patted my pockets, realizing I didn't have any money with me.

"He's with me."

"Just so, Old Grandpa." The host nodded. "I'll get the barman."

The older man waved me over from the penultimate seat at the bar. As I approached, he patted the seat closest to the door instead of the empty one on his left.

Another man stepped through a curtain behind the bar and raised his eyebrow at Old Grandpa.

"I'm too young to drink, you know." I opened with that, hoping he wasn't a psychic trying to ply his trade on an unsuspecting mundane. I needn't have worried.

"You hear all that racket, right?"

"Yeah, the music. What is it?"

"Dead Man's Party." The wrinkles at the corners of his eyes deepened farther than I thought possible. "Every Tuesday night. Part of the rental agreement for this place is, they've got to let the dead cavort."

"You mean vampires?"

"No, I mean ghosts, of course." Old Grandpa chuckled. "Like your friend. Though I can't see him."

"You're not a medium?"

"Nah. That's my buddy Tommy. He gave me this so we could keep in touch." The fellow held his left hand up, showing off a golden horseshoe signet ring, studded in diamonds on his pinkie.

"An anchor." I nodded. "Clever."

"He passed on a few years back, but I'm here every Tuesday. We've got an appointment to use the old board. And Tom enjoys the music, too."

I looked down at the bar and saw a full Ouija board burned and stained into the wood under the varnish. The glass at Old Grandpa's right had an odd triangular shape. One point was longer than the other two, and it had an arrow fused into the thick glass base.

I realized it acted as a planchette when it started moving. It spelled out a greeting and asked me to introduce myself already.

"Hello, gentlemen. I'm Ed."

"Yes, the Redford boy." He chuckled. "Read about you in the Providence papers. Tommy mentioned earlier you're at Messing with his grandson Diego. More's the pity."

"Excuse me?"

"Diego's apple fell a bit farther from the tree than Tommy would've liked." Old Grandpa grinned. "Anyway, why not go back and have a look-see. I would if I could."

"How are you hearing the ghosts and not seeing them, exactly? Also, you don't look like the staff's grandfather. Who are you?"

"I'm the oldest Mr. Ambersmith, but there's quite a few of us in town with that name. So everyone calls me Old Grandpa or OGP for short. I can listen in on Dead Man's Party only while we've got the board and planchette."

"Okay, but how?" I blinked. "I've seen these boards before, but that's not how they work."

"He's not at liberty to say, young man. Goblin King's orders." The translucent face peering over OGP's head was equally wrinkled but with more lines of the sad variety. "I've got no such restriction. My friend here had a brush with an artifact back in our halcyon days."

"Is Tommy spilling the beans?" OGP wagged his finger. "Ask him to save it for another night, Ed. Because now is not the time for that old story."

"He's right." Tommy nodded. "Instead, you should take my friend's suggestion. Have a gander at what they're up to in the back room. Bring your friend."

"I don't want to be a bother. Solids like me don't exactly fit in with the translucent crowd."

"Mediums always fit in with ghosts," Tommy said as if he'd been in my shoes.

He had, according to OGP. I decided to take a chance. What else could go wrong?

As it turned out, not much.

Ghosts, I understood. The living were another matter. The former danced in the back room. At least a hundred of them packed between the white borders on the otherwise black linoleum floor, moving in pairs, groups, and sometimes singly to the music. Despite the fact that they all stepped in time, the shape of those movements varied.

This was not a random collection of ghosts. My talent gave me the impression they'd come to congregate with familiar faces. Despite this, no two appeared to have lived in the same era. Everything about each was different. Hair and clothes, mannerisms, dance moves, and the way they spoke all varied.

Although every last one was dead, the mood felt fun and festive. This was their time to be themselves, their presence accepted and expected—a rarity for most uncontracted ghosts out and about in a town.

I looked around for the music's source since that's what brought me there in the first place. A long table kitty-corner in the back on the left caught my eye. I moved around the edges of the room, careful to stay off the black linoleum in the middle.

This must've been the K's Place's function room, probably rented out for parties on other nights. Or live music, maybe even karaoke or a corporeal DJ for the living to dance to. Once I got across the room in my roundabout way, I had a look at the audio rig on the table. The entire setup was ghostly—another thing I'd rarely seen.

Ghosts can alter their appearance. They don't have to look the way they did when they died, though that's the default most start with. I'm unclear exactly how ghosts get their energy, the origin of it, or what makes some stronger than others.

Rob couldn't explain it, and he'd been dead for centuries.

Bianca said she thought it was practice and confidence. Mom believed there was more to it, something to do with their unfinished business and how close they were to moving on.

Part of being a medium meant coming up with your answer to that question from your observations and studies. Books written by mediums were few and far between. And none in existence were authored by ghosts themselves.

If only I could find Bianca in the Under. When the monarchs reunited, I expected her to come around to either the castle or Hope's ship. Although I'd asked for her every chance I got over the years, she hadn't shown up.

She'd always given me the best answers. Some of the best were questions that led me to my own. Bianca was a better teacher than my mother, and I missed her. The music matched that mood, but in a way that felt more healing than nostalgic.

"Hey, medium. Good to see you." The DJ nodded.

I returned the gesture, then leaned in to ask a question.

"Hey, what's the song?" I figured music would be a safe topic to discuss with a ghostly DJ. A smile rewarded me.

"It's VNV Nation. Came out after I passed, but I love it." He adjusted a dial on his rig. "I'm Christian. What's your name?"

"Ed."

"Do you lean more goth or industrial?"

"I'm not sure?" I grinned.

"That's okay. I'm still not sure either."

"It never gets any easier, does it?"

"Life, death, or music?"

"All of the above."

"Would be a boring world if we had all the answers from the get-go, right?"

"Maybe, but I'd like to feel." I sighed. "Maybe more productive. Accomplishing something, you know?"

"It's easy to get caught up in other people's opinions. I get that." He nodded. "Hold on a sec."

He reached out, turning dials and pushing buttons. A set of headphones appeared over his ears momentarily while the music transitioned to the next song. I got a better look at Christian now. He had long, shaggy green hair, which reminded me of Fred's best friend Lane.

His t-shirt said Bauhaus, which reminded me of Maddie and Henry Baxter. They played all 80s post-punk music at their wedding. I'd been stuck working at the college and missed it. Cosmo made me a playlist.

I was over missing out. Up here in Salem, there wasn't a college taking up forty hours of my week between managing ghosts and getting tutored. Plus, they had ghost culture. Someplace I might fit in.

"So, you spin on Tuesdays. I mean you playing the music, that is. I already know the Dead Man's Party schedule, thanks to Tommy out there."

"It's not always me. We take turns. Sometimes it's Mary, and all you hear is sea shanties all night. She was a privateer so what you expect?"

"I like those too."

"You spend a lot of time with faeries don't you?" He grinned. "You've got the art of making inquiries without asking questions down."

"Matter of survival." I sighed. "My dad and brother are redcaps."

"That's probably for the best. Faeries and shifters make up most of the living extrahumans here. Avoiding direct questions is a fact of life in this town." He jerked his chin at the dance floor. "They like my music for the most part, so I do end up having at least a set most weeks."

"I guess I'll be back then." I smiled.

"Don't make me twist your arm or anything." He chuckled.

"You don't have to. It feels like...I don't know, me. If you understand what I mean."

"You don't know any other mediums, do you?"

"No. The closest I've got is my friend Hope.

"If you don't mind my asking, what's close to a medium but not one? I didn't think that was possible."

"Hope's special. She's the Alkonost, a magical faerie bird who can see ghosts but not talk to them. I'm kind of avoiding her right now."

"Friend drama?"

"She's my best friend. Has been since we were little. But, well. She can do way more than see dead people. And me, I've got asthma."

"Ouch."

"Yeah, I met someone recently who would say the same thing if I was allowed to tell her."

"Anyone interesting? Like in a not friends way."

"My heart belongs to someone already. Mavis is cool though. She gets it."

"Mavis Merlini?" He blinked.

"Yeah, you got a problem with that?" My fists clenched, though I was unsure exactly what had me suddenly angry.

"No. No, not at all. Mavis is good people. All the ghosts around town know it because we see things the solids don't. Most of her family's another story. Where do you know her from?"

"I might be stuck going to Messing Academy, but I'm staying with a bunch of Gallows Hill folks in that new rooming house. She showed up there the night before school started with nothing but the clothes on her back. Never said a word about how or why."

"Keep an eye on her, okay?"

"What's it to you?"

"She doesn't know this, but there's another side of her family. Let's just say I'm tenuously connected to it."

"Okay. Why the secrecy?"

"It's the kind of thing she should find out for herself."

I couldn't argue with that, so I changed the subject.

"Do you think they'd mind if I had a go at dancing?"

"Looks like the guy you came in with is having fun out there."

"Yeah, Rob says he loves fun so much he married a barrel of it back in 1701."

"There's more fun in the world than just his barrel. Go out there and have some, kid." He pushed another button, and the headphones appeared again. "I gotta do my job. Talk to you later."

"Yeah, thanks, Christian."

I still didn't set foot on the floor, opting to follow the wall again until I got near the door. If any of the ghosts got angry at my presence or told me to get lost, I'd have a shorter distance to cross.

Finally, I just did it. I stepped on the edge of the dance floor and swayed to the music. I didn't move my feet, not at first. Only swayed the top of my body, copying some hand movements I saw the ghostly dancers doing.

I'm not sure if it was because I focused on the music or if Christian had turned the volume up, but the experience became more than sound. Instead of only listening as I been doing before, I began to feel the music with my body.

That's when the rest of me started following my hand, and I truly danced. I didn't realize it right away, but when I became aware of the fact that I'd reached the middle of the floor, my nerves kicked up.

What was I doing out there? Dancing in styles incompatible with life? Was it smart for a guy with asthma to traipse around a dance floor where nobody had corporeal lungs for rescue breaths? I had no doubt Old Grandpa would try assisting, but he seemed too frail to be any good at CPR. Then I realized there was nothing wrong with my breathing.

Although ghosts don't need air or food or water, they had habits. In fact, I suspected a lot of them had collections of old habits they'd had while alive. It turned out the movements I copied were all compatible with breath. Unlike the one time I tried to dance and shred on guitar like Lane Meyer and wound up on the floor with the worst asthma attack in two years.

I got through five songs in a row without having to stop. My feet hurt by then, so I headed off to the side and sat. I spotted Rob out in the middle again, an enormous smile on his face. When I came back the next Tuesday, it wouldn't only be for him. This was fun.

It was also exactly what I needed—an adventure uniquely mine.

CHAPTER SIXTEEN

Mavis

I managed to get a shower early, as the sun was coming up, without disturbing Kiara. The clothes from the sanitarium this time were ridiculous. I wasn't sure exactly who invented the hyper-color T-shirt, but I was the opposite of impressed.

I put it in my satchel, along with the otherwise fortunately plain though neon blue leggings. Hopefully, Saya wouldn't give the early 90s garb dirty looks in the locker room.

Nobody was in the hall or on the stairs, but I used caution heading into the dining room anyway. This time, the coffee cart was already in place so I didn't have to risk hazardous gremlin driving before taking my first sip of magical bean juice.

Ed was already at the table in the same seat he'd occupied the morning before. His feet kicked slightly under the chair, which I'd only now realized was slightly too high for him. I got my coffee and joined him.

"So, last night?" I grinned. "What took your breath away?"

"Dead Man's Party." He chuckled. "Ghosts, not vampires. I had more fun than a—well than I've had in what feels like ages. I'd say you should go, but it'd only be an empty room for a raven shifter."

"I wish I could see it."

"I don't." He shook his head. "I wouldn't want you going through anything like that."

The near-death experience. That likely happened for Ed before his first birthday. Right. I buried my *faux pas*.

"What was it like?" I wrapped my hands around my cup, warming them. "Tell me everything."

He did. The details of his tale were incredible anyway, but Ed knew how to piece them into a good story. My mind's eye conjured images of Christian the DJ and all the dancing ghosts. I'd seen Old Grandpa and Thomas Mendez around town, of course, but Ed's descriptions helped me place them at that Ouija bar.

I'd known Ed Redford witnessed an entire world nobody could see, but that fact's true impact didn't fully hit home until that morning. It must've been lonely, being the only psychic in a found family of shifters and faeries.

Even at his all-psychic school, Ed was the only medium. Staying at the rooming house with all of us probably wasn't doing him any favors. There wasn't much I could do about that since the nest was a death trap my mom had kicked me out of anyway.

Except maybe bring him to Danvers to visit Crow. Not without telling him, of course. He might be worried about places like the sanitarium, considering his mom had been in one for six or seven years. Not all of those facilities were as well-run as Crow's.

Upperclassmen trickled or staggered in, some grabbing two or even three cups of coffee. Ed watched them, scratching his head and wrinkling his brow.

"It's only halfway through the first week. I don't get it."

"Crow told me about this. In third-year, things get intense for seniors on the Bishop's Row team at Gallows Hill. I bet most of these poor sleep-deprived souls went overboard at practice after school yesterday."

"Well, Cosmo didn't. Neither did Hope. She's team captain, ironically enough. Cos is doing some kind of front-line thing. What's it called again?"

"First defense. It's actually the second defense player that has a harder time unless the other team's full of southpaws. But freshmen can't be on the varsity team, so that explains it."

"How do you know so much about the old sportsball?"

"My brother." I tried to smile but worried it looked like a wince. It did, judging by Ed's response.

"Not a good topic, sorry. What did Ramon say yesterday?"

"Well, he." I tugged my collar and cleared my throat. "Um, I—"

"So he asked you out." Ed nodded sagely. "What'd you say?"

"That we can see where it goes. We've known each other all summer, hanging around town. But I had a bad breakup last spring. And this whole beginning of high school thing is—" I waved at our surroundings. "Well, you know."

"A mess. Yeah. So, is that the deal with you and Diego? He's your ex?"

"Bullseye, Ed." I blinked. "You got one."

"Shoot enough arrows, and you hit the mark sooner or later."

We laughed. It was nice, merely chatting about the inevitable but relatively uncomplicated awkwardness of dating.

"Well, he'd better be good to you."

"Or you'll sic Rob on him?"

"Hey!" Ed smiled. "Thanks."

"Thanks? For what?"

"Not saying 'you'll do what, wheeze on him' like everybody else."

"No way." I shook my head. "My siblings always say never cross a medium."

"A nest of tough birds worries about people like little old me?"

"You forget most folks are scared of ghosts. Seems to me you treat them like they're regular people."

"I sort of grew up thinking the whole world was full of my imaginary friends."

"You see, Horace?" I glanced at my satchel, then pointed at Ed. "That. Right there. That's why you don't mess around with a medium."

"Oh, oh God!" Ed covered his giggle with one hand. "Horace says, especially not if he's from Texas."

"But you're from Rhode Island." I blinked. "Wait, was Horace from Texas?"

"He." Ed wrapped his arms around his middle, lips twitching with barely restrained mirth. "He says. He says no, he's just into Western Steampunk."

I coughed out a chuckle that broke some sort of seal, even though Horace's joke wasn't that funny. We needed to laugh right then. So we did, this time for much longer.

It went on so long we needed tissues from the pack in my bag. The upperclassman all sat at their table, staring and leaning away, despite the fact they were across the room from our table. Whoops.

"Bad omen bird strikes again, I guess."

"Ditto on scary small medium."

"Small medium?" I imagined a tag in a t-shirt.

"Yeah." He shrugged. "I'm so short, nobody notices me without a microscope."

We laughed less hysterically, without startling the zombie athletes in their natural habitat this time.

"Hopefully, those big jocks don't mess with you today at school."

"Our classes are all opposite each other so we don't spend much time with them. It's only lunch and our R&R activities, which isn't Drama Club for that lot. But yeah, hopefully, I don't have to watch my tailfeathers around them."

"If my frenemies at Messing Academy could only see how intimidating I am now." Ed rolled his eyes. "But I gotta go back there again, I guess."

"Maybe after last night, things will get better."

"All I really want is some time and space to learn something there." He shrugged. "Everything else is sauce."

"Hey, early birds." Cosmo sat next to me. "How are the worms?"

"Are you implying I eat those?" I rolled my eyes. "Because I do, but only the gummy kind."

"I don't know." Cosmo shrugged. "Someone I know eats voles."

"Olivia does no such thing." Ed shook his head. "I mean, does Tony eat rats? Do you eat zebras?"

"Hey, ixnay on the Onytay."

"Aren't they getting married?" I slapped my hand over my mouth immediately, but I'd made the mistake. There was nothing I could do to take back.

"I never mentioned my brother's name to you before." Cosmo blinked. "How did you know that?"

"Are you really asking that after Blaine took out a full-page ad in the *Providence Journal*?" Ed glared at Cosmo. "You think I didn't do an Internet search on any of *my* classmates?"

"Yeah, but yours attacked you. What did we do, Mavis?"

"Nothing. It's curiosity." I shrugged and pasted on my poker face. "I'm a raven. We like shiny things and mysteries. I unexpectedly had to live here with you guys. Figured it'd be smart to consult Dr. Google for advice."

"You could've asked, you know." I imagined what Cosmo would look like at that moment in lion form. Probably crouched with his tail flicking back and forth.

"It's not like we can tell her much of anything when she does, Cos." Ed clenched his jaw.

"Whose idea was that?" Cosmo tapped his cheek with one finger and said the last thing I expected. "You doodle her face all over your notebooks. Light of your heart, remember?"

Ed leaned back as if Cosmo had slapped him. "Leave her out of it."

"Oh, look, pancakes." I pointed at the plates that had appeared. "We all need breakfast. Djeet in Rhode Islandese, remember?"

"Yeah, but I'm gonna go sit over there." Cosmo got up and moved to the other side of the table.

I sat blinking. Ed didn't budge. "Sorry," I said.

"No." Ed shook his head. "No apologies. Cos is squirrely. All four of us are, but he's having the hardest time because—another thing I can't say. I promise it's not your fault."

"I'm fine. Nothing he said hurt me." I studied his face. "Are you okay, though?"

Ed took a minute to stack two pancakes on his plate and pour honey on them. When he offered me the tongs, I took them and did the same, but with syrup instead. We sat together, cutting the flapjacks.

"He was harsh, yes." He sighed. "It hurt. But he's my brother from another mother. All three of them are like extra siblings, along with Blaine and Tony. I should remember that more."

"I get it." I nodded, doing some mental math. We weren't all that different, Ed and I. "I'm the youngest of seven too, remember?"

"Mostly I feel like the oldest." Ed pushed pancake bits around the plate. "Checking over any potential external threats, reminding them to follow the rules so we don't get hurt."

"Yeah, but those were all people you couldn't walk up to and ask."

"I could have had Rob follow my classmates. What Hope pulled in the hall at your school was extra suspicious with a side of hinky sauce. I told her as much. So, I don't blame you for checking on her history."

"You need to know the truth, Ed. It wasn't about Hope. It started with Horace and Bianca, then followed them and Tony and Olivia down a rabbit hole. I saw that article about you."

"Oh." He sighed. "Well, I'm still not going anywhere."

"It doesn't bother you?"

"Oh, it does. Not that you read it, what they wrote in the first place." He finally took a bite of his breakfast and swallowed it with a grimace. "I'm not the kid in that story. Never was or will be. It was all spin. Cover. Mom's an addict."

"I grok having an inaccurate reputation." I set my fork down and patted his arm. "Still want to be your friend."

"Thanks for that." He nudged me. "Don't you have double PE? Shouldn't you eat more than two bites?"

"Is that you or Horace talking?"

"I'm half-Italian. Food doesn't fix everything, but it keeps you alive long enough to do a few small repairs. Yeah, Horace gave me a nudge too."

"He reminds me not to skip lunch at school. I'm not surprised. Turns out I like having him around."

"I'm sorry." Ed hung his head. "I think you'll have to give the satchel to Hope, eventually."

"I still need something to carry my stuff though." The pit of my stomach sank. I should've brought it with me the night before. I'd forgotten I only had limited time with Horace.

"Don't worry about that. I'll find you something. Already emailed someone back in Rhode Island about it."

"I'm sorry. Again."

"I should be apologizing. But I can't make things right just yet. So I'm sorry, also again." He clicked his tongue. "We're broken records over here."

"What did you break now, Ed?" Saya sat on my other side.

"Nothing, I— It's just a figure of speech. You didn't hatch yesterday. Haven't you heard that one before?"

"Just looking to get in on your little conversation." She rolled her eyes and turned her nose up at the food.

"Aren't you eating anything?" I blinked. "You'll need energy for gym and cheer, right?"

"I couldn't possibly. Pancakes are sad excuses for waffles. The syrup runs right off without those little squares to hold it in. I simply don't want to deal with any of that."

"That's why I use honey." Ed gestured at it. "Try it sometime. It's good. Feels like I'm in Rivendell eating honey cakes."

I reached for the plate of home fries, scooping a helping on my plate and Saya's. I gave her a pointed stare as I shoveled some into my mouth and chewed.

"See? So easy, a bird can do it. Piece of cake for a dragon, right?"

"I prefer julienne hash browns, actually. I suppose these will do." She stabbed one with her fork, put it in her mouth, and chewed fifty times before swallowing.

I know because I counted.

"Bacon?" I offered.

"Saya, get your own breakfast." Hope sat and heaped one of everything on her plate. "Enough with the dainty dragon princess bit. It's old. You're not her servant, Mavis. Ed, you should have warned her."

"Aye, captain," Ed mumbled.

"Good morning." Kiara beamed, sitting down on the other side of Ed. "Pancakes are my favorite! It's like a race between me and the syrup."

"There are two kinds of people in this world," I said under my breath.

***

Wednesday at Gallows Hill was practically normal. I sat in Lecture taking notes on different types of mundane shifters, got my snack, and ate it like a normal person. In Forum, I answered everyone's questions about where I put all the extra mass whenever I turned into a little birdie. That was actually fun.

"There's math about it, for real?" Jaxon snorted.

"Yeah, the Green Equation." I nodded. "It's pretty simple, actually."

"Simple and math are opposites." He sighed.

"Dr. Aranha has multiple methods of teaching it to you, Mr. Thorne. So don't fret."

"Where'd the Green Equation come from, anyway?" Fiona asked. "Does it apply to people like me?"

"Yes, you can use it for any mass-displacing ability done on either side of the barrier between here and the Under. It's the most brilliant thing to come out of the Dark Ages," Mr. Hickson answered. "There's a set of equations and statistics about shifters from back then, found in the lair of a green dragon deep in the Black Forest."

"Will we hear about it in Lecture?" Saya asked.

"Lady Ambersmith did postgraduate work on medieval dragons, so yes."

"What was yours on, Mr. Hickson?" Kiara asked.

The bell rang.

"That's a topic for another day, perhaps. I'll see some of you for R&R. Have fun!"

Hope was nowhere in sight during lunch. I hadn't seen her at snack time either, come to think of it. When I asked Cosmo about it, he stonewalled me.

"The captain's social life is none of your business."

"Sorry for asking. I only worried she was missing lunch."

"She's not," Saya interjected. "Hope and food are never separate for long. Why don't you go have a seat with your beau?" She waved a hand in Ramon's general direction.

I did and made it a point to have as much fun as possible, helping him, Fiona, and Jillian plan out their entertainment wrestling personas.

In Lab, Dr. Aranha had us practice using our powers again. We'd get to do that for the rest of the week, but broaden our interactions and try collaborating.

"We can get together with Fiona and Wyatt, see what might work on Thursday," Ramon said. "I already asked them, and they're cool with that."

"Good call." I nodded. "Thanks."

He smiled his answer. We spent lab period in a cluster motley enough to raise a few eyebrows. Dr. Aranha encouraged us.

"This is exactly what I mean. Get familiar with each other, discover ways to work together beyond what you read in the lab manual. It'll help with your recreational electives, as well. Ask your coaches and instructors for more ideas on what you can do."

As if I didn't already have enough to do, preparing for a raid on the house I grew up in the very next day. I walked to Messing and waited for Ed, but he didn't need me there. Diego walked out with him, chummily.

On the way back to the rooming house, I asked him to tell me again about Dead Man's Party. Listening helped take my mind off the impending stress. Cosmo dragged him off to meet with Hope about secret faerie stuff before we turned the corner, so I was free to go to the Mart.

Fortunately, Ramon's plan was reassuringly sensible. Both Wyatt and Fiona agreed to all of it, and we'd get our convoluted raid on the nest done before dinner—unless we failed miserably.

CHAPTER SEVENTEEN

On Thursday, the worst mishap I had was finding Wanda in the green room during Drama Club. I needed to get those glamour bracelets for Ramon later, but she was in there, peering at the closet with a checklist of supplies.

"Hello, Mavis."

"Hi, Wanda."

"What brings you back here?"

"I thought I'd have a look at these playbills. You know, see what other shows they've done here in the past." I gestured at the wall and the sort of collage that covered it. "I'm stumped on what to vote for. Kind of new to musical theater, actually."

"None of these are terribly recent. Two years ago, we did intramurals instead of a musical, so there's nothing there from then, and last year we had a problem with the playbill for *West Side Story.*"

"Was anyone I know in that?"

"Nobody but me. Bar's tone-deaf, so I was the only crossover. Chorus was all I could handle, but that show had great dance routines so I didn't mind."

"How far back do they go?"

"The year Gallows Hill opened. If anything's illegible, covered up, frayed, or too old to read, there are copies in the library. All you have to do is search Gallows Hill Drama Club, and you'll find them."

"Thanks, Wanda, that was helpful."

"You know, I was wondering which way you were going to vote. I mean on the musicals. Which one do you like?"

"I love the idea of *Pirates of Penzance*. But I read the list of roles, and it seems too big. We picked up Brandon, but I don't think we have enough cast members for all those daughters and police and pirates."

"We're getting some folks from Messing and at least one from Hawthorn this year. Plus, half of cheer squad ends up filling out the big dance numbers. Don't worry too much about that. So you're voting for Pirates?"

"Still not sure." I shrugged. "What about you?"

"*Kiss Me, Kate*." She smiled. "It's my favorite, such a fun show."

"I don't think I've heard of that one. Tell me about it."

"It's lighthearted, with great dances and comedic songs. " Wanda smiled. "Basically, it's a musical about people doing a musical of Shakespeare's *Taming of the Shrew*."

"Sounds meta. I like it. Go on."

"The leads are bickering because they're exes, but it's opening night, and they're stuck doing the show. In the process, they make up. There was a recent Broadway revival, so there's a chance for graduating seniors to audition for that, or maybe a touring production when they start one."

"That sounds cool." I understood what Wanda was doing, talking to me about the musicals. As a senior, she'd naturally want her last musical at Gallows Hill to be her favorite. "Listen, maybe I'll change my mind about that vote."

"Thanks!" She headed toward the door. "I guess I'll leave you to your playbills. Talk to you later, Mavis."

"Yeah, later." I gazed up at the wall, scanning the lists of roles and names, looking for one particular—my surname, of course.

None of the bygone students on any of the playbills matched mine. I was the first and only of my siblings ever in the Gallows Hill Drama Club.

I'd have to do some work on that one-act play. So much was going on outside of school that I could barely keep up with academic homework, let alone the R&R variety. Still, if I wanted to go whole-hog into drama Club, I had to at least turn something in. If nothing on Mr. Hickson's desk had my name on it, I'd look like a slacker. I didn't want to do that here.

A strong urge, maybe instinct, welled up within me. To break the Merlini family cycle, if only long enough to graduate. But here I was already, stuck playing out my family's bad reputation like someone scripted it. Telling myself that stealing from the auditorium was pure necessity felt like a cop-out.

The more things changed, sometimes the more they stayed the same

I'd heard those exact words from the beaks of my siblings too many times to count. I sighed, scooping the entire rack of glamour bracelets into the interior pocket of Horace's satchel. I barely noticed the extra weight in the bag as I left the green room.

My heart was another story.

I passed the bracelets to Ramon outside the library before lab. He bundled them into a clean bandanna.

"Thanks."

"Why do you need them now?"

"Walk with me, and you'll see."

I followed him down the hallway to the front entrance. A couple that appeared to be college-age sat on the bench, holding hands and smiling at each other. As we approached, they looked up. I recognized them immediately.

"That's Azrael Ambersmith and Grace DuBois."

"Yeah."

"What are they doing here?"

"A few small repairs on some entertainment wrestling equipment, among other things." He jiggled the handkerchief.

"Ramon, hi." Grace grinned.

"What are you up to, Mavis?" Az asked.

"Uh, going to school." I cleared my throat. "Not anything against the rules."

"Of course not." Ramon opened the bandanna and held it out to Azrael.

"Hmm." He peered at the bracelets nestled against the fabric. "What do you think, Grace?"

"Those look like they could use an enchantment booster." She nodded. "Add them to the other stuff in the box there."

"Tie them up in that first," Az suggested. "Don't want Drama Club stuff causing real-life drama by snagging someone's singlet."

"Wait, so this is legit?" I blinked. "I wasn't, uh, you know. Uh, stea—?"

"Don't say the s-word." Az shook his head. "Our family's had the maintenance contract on all the rec equipment since this school opened."

"But—"

"Glamour bracelets need a refresh every year, yeah." Ramon nodded. "Thanks for fetching them."

Last night, I'd gotten the impression that the need for the bracelets was a covert and illicit exercise. In the light of late afternoon, I realized the tones of twisted upbringing had colored our conversation.

Any previous attempt to cross my family had been an exercise in subterfuge, laced with a high probability of failure and dire consequence. So of course I'd assumed the current plan must bear the markings of delinquency, including stealing from school.

Why had I assumed Ramon's brain worked the same way mine did? He'd been honest and honorable to a fault. If anything, I was the bad influence here, despite my determination to keep aboveboard.

Had life at the nest made me like this, or was I born to be a menace? I wasn't sure what to make of that, so I watched Az and Grace pack everything up in the box and wheel it out the door on a dolly.

Grace paused in the doorway, looking over her shoulder. "We'll be by Tropica Mart later with four of those. And we'll need them back when you finish testing them." She looked at me and winked. The bell rang before I could say anything.

In Lab, Dr. Aranha sent us to a different equipment cabinet. Instead of the amulets, this one had gloves. They were a stretchy fabric that looked like scaly hide but felt like nylon tights, the shiny kind dance students wore.

"Only take one each, and for your non-dominant hand. You'll need the other hand free to take notes."

"Aww, actual work?" Wyatt pouted.

"Are these made with spider shifter silk?" Hope held hers up, pinched between two of her fingernails as though they were tweezers.

"Yes, mine." Dr. Aranha nodded.

"And dragon molt." Saya wrinkled her nose. "Why do I have to wear one when I can just do a partial shift?"

"For practice. These aren't only to detect magic or psychic energy in an item. They also protect delicate objects."

"We're using them on the museum field trip, aren't we?"

"Astute observation, Mavis." Dr. Aranha nodded. "You'll have two more weeks to practice with them."

"Oops." Cosmo held his glove out, hanging his head. It sat on his palm in tatters.

"Leave it at my desk and get another." She clucked over the torn garment. "Try the bottom row. Those are larger. Once you're all properly equipped, take a look at the items I've placed on the benches. They're only vaguely labeled. See what you can gather about their energy. Remember, only use your gloved hand for examination. I'll know if you try using magic elements for those of you who have them. So don't bother with that. You'll get a chance to use those later this year."

I put the glove on, which wasn't as easy as imagined. The sheen and luster of the fabric made it slippery. Plus, taking extra care felt like a must instead of a suggestion after Cosmo's mishap.

I managed it more quickly than some in the class. Jillian, Wyatt, Fiona, Hope, and Saya struggled right along with Cosmo, whose larger glove wasn't making much of a difference. Maybe lion shifters lacked fine motor skills.

"Easy-peasy." Jaxon showed me his hand. "Right?"

"Yeah." I grinned.

"We should be decent at putting on costumes." Kiara smiled. "We're Drama Club."

"Pretty much." Brandon nodded.

"Not a costume," Ramon said. "I'm a wrestler. But that's okay. Let's figure out how these work."

We moved around in a cluster, watching each other take turns with the objects at each of the stations. The instructions on the board told us not to compare notes until the end, so we worked quietly.

Eventually, the others caught up with us, except for Cosmo, who'd wrecked another glove. He sat glumly with Dr. Aranha as she made use of a sewing kit.

After taking notes on everything, we stood to the side and compared them. Toward the end of class, the doctor used her tablet to change the instructions on the board into something like an answer key.

I'd only gotten two of them correct.

"Will this be on a test later?" Cosmo blinked.

"Yes." She nodded. "At the end of the year, so don't worry. You'll have plenty of time to practice. I run identification practicals twice a week, with field trips along those lines each month. Remember, all the information you need is in Lecture. Compare these notes to what you learned there over the last few days, and you'll know exactly what to study."

We removed our gloves and put them away fifteen minutes before the bell, so we discussed the artifacts.

"It's all Greek to me." Fiona sighed.

"Same," Jaxon said.

"Look." I pointed at a section on gnomes. "It says they use shiny things for dentures. Do you think that's what the sea glass might have been?"

"I bet," Ramon said. "Fiona, did it feel like glamour to you?"

"You know, it did." She gave us a sheepish grin. "I didn't think I was right back there at the moment, you know."

"I guess we have to not panic," Kiara observed.

"Trust our instincts, yeah." Jaxon nodded.

"And ask better questions in Forum," I added. "Pure faeries are probably a big topic for us to learn this year."

"I'll make a list of some I'm curious about." Kiara shook her head. "I should know more, but that's what happens when you're the only Sidhe in a family of shifters."

The bell rang. The apprehension I'd been trying to keep at bay all day rose, threatening to pull me under into a sea of panic.

"I'm off to the library," Kiara announced. "It stays open for an hour after school. Anyone else want to come along?"

Brandon nodded immediately. Jillian and Jaxon left, saying they had chores to do at home.

"Hmm." Hope glanced at Saya and Cosmo. "We probably need that. Today was, uh, humbling."

"Sorry, gotta go." Ramon held the door open.

"Later, dude." Brandon waved. "And dudette."

Ramon and I left the school together, Fiona hurrying to catch up with us at the sidewalk with a grumbling Wyatt in tow.

"They're all gonna think we're dating now."

"They won't." Fiona turned her nose up at him. "I deserve better than a dudebro redcap, and I'm not afraid to tell anyone who'll listen."

Wyatt stepped back, blinking as though she'd slapped him. He still followed us along Lafayette Street and Palmer to Tropica Mart. Grace and Azrael stood outside, leaning against a stretch of clapboard siding.

"Here they are." Grace handed the bandanna with the newly-charged bracelets inside to Wyatt. "There's four in there. Az and I are testing another pair, so we're coming with."

"Oh." I swallowed. "Um, no."

Wyatt threw his head back and laughed.

"You don't want to bring the big guns?" He snorted. "To a party like this?"

I put my hands on my hips, raising an eyebrow at Ramon.

"You told them it was a party?"

"Of course he didn't." Fiona patted my shoulder. "He said exactly where we're going, what we're doing. And why."

"I wasn't asking for permission." Grace grinned like she wasn't five-foot-nothing and a tailor. "We're backing you up."

"Aren't you from Canada?" I blinked. "You don't know what you're getting into."

"I sure do." Azrael nodded. "And we share everything, so."

"But why?"

"Making up for lost time," Az answered.

"Getting mixed up in stuff like this is my idea of fun." Grace grinned.

"I'd want someone to help if it were me," Fiona added.

"I just want to look like a badass." Wyatt shrugged.

"So let's do this." Ramon smiled.

We walked together down Salem Street, stopping on Harbor. For our plan, we couldn't approach the nest from the front, so we walked up the driveway of the house behind it. The fence between yards had no gate, but I'd used the loose corner to get past it for years. My allies followed.

The neighbors gave us no trouble. All of them worked, and it was too early in the day for any to be home yet. My family was working class, but only on paper. Everyone kept odd hours, so I had no idea who'd be around when we got there. I feared the worst, of course— Mom herself.

Tidy blacktop once covered the postage-stamp yard, now cracked into shards where purselane, dandelions, and other flat flora struggled. I knew how they felt.

We arrayed ourselves in a "V" formation, like a migrating flock with me in the middle. That was my idea. We needed to activate the bracelets simultaneously, keeping the fearsome descriptions Ramon had given us in our minds' eyes. I held my hands above my head, the bracelet in my right. I waited through the rustle of clothing behind me, then slipped it on.

Shadows lengthened and bloomed from out of nowhere on the hardpan in front of me. Night fell on the small yard. Or at least a reasonable facsimile. Grace was an umbral magus, able to conjure shadow. I'd had no idea she was powerful enough to cover an area this large completely, though.

I glanced over my shoulder and saw beefed-up versions of my compatriots, along with a small army of snarling magical critters, the type kids at Hawthorn Academy had as familiars. That must have been Azrael, who'd apparently focused on classic goblin illusion magic during his education at Gallows Hill.

Wyatt and Fiona had dropped the glamour changelings routinely used to hide their fae attributes. Without it, both cut alarming figures in only their plain clothes. The bracelets had outfitted them with an equally intimidating wardrobe.

Fiona's green flesh bulged with enormous muscles, and she struck a warlike pose, clad in armor-grade leather and red and green tartan. Wyatt's crimson cap stained his sandpapery, sharklike skin with blood, making a horror of his serrated smile. The bracelet had turned his t-shirt and jeans into a gladiator's kit.

Ramon's costume was something straight out of a lucha libre ring, styled like a skeletal bat. The glamour effects bulked him up, so he looked as tall as Wyatt but shorter than Fiona.

I'd chosen the dark angel look from the first time I tried on a glamour bracelet but did my best to replace that air of sadness with wrath. I wanted to look vengeful, not mournful.

We'd achieved the effect, then. No more time to waste.

"I'm here for my things!" I called to the house.

For a moment, I imagined it answering me instead of a sibling. The world's a strange and magical place, but not quite that weird. Because Hugh and Manny emerged on the back steps, both armed with Louisville Sluggers, their weapon of choice.

As predicted, they took one look at Fiona and stumbled over each other, trying to get back through the door. Wyatt laughed immediately, but everyone joined in a breath later. Even me. Laughter had always been the best armor I could muster, facing them.

My bedroom window opened, and Branwen leaned out of it, eyes narrow at first. They widened a moment later, and I watched her jaw clench, practically hearing tactical calculations in her head.

"The Boss says you can't set foot in this house until further notice." The height amplified her voice enough that she didn't have to raise it.

The shadows over the pavement at my feet darkened. I knew immediately what that meant. Fiona called on her faerie magic, increasing in size until she stood as high as the house I grew up in.

"In through window, tiny bird!" Fiona's voice rumbled uncharacteristically, but she chuckled. She put her hand on the ground in front of me, palm up. I rode it up like an elevator, planting my feet to avoid falling off.

Branwen backed away from the open window, not enough for me to get inside without tangling with her. I didn't care about her at that point or about Mom's orders. I only wanted to get the essentials and get out. I tensed my legs, preparing to leap at her. Instead, something else happened.

My room was untouched since I'd last left it. The outfit I'd hung on the outside of my closet door lifted itself by the hanger. It floated past my utterly shocked sister and through the window. My satchel opened, and it tucked itself inside.

"What in blue blazes?"

"Don't mess with me, Bran." I smirked. "I'm worse than ten mediums."

"How?" She gestured at the steady stream of items removing themselves from my room. Thanks to Horace, I assumed. I wasn't saying a word about him.

"Nunya's helping me. Nunya Business."

"Not funny, Mavis."

"Oh, but it is." I chuckled. "You just need an outsider's perspective."

"I'm serious. It's against orders."

"Technically, I'm not setting foot in the house. So it's not."

"It's my ass on the line when the Boss comes home and sees all this."

"Am I supposed to care?" Even though I did. Another thing she didn't need to know.

Bran paled, then gradually turned slightly green as time and my belongings went by. Besides the first outfit in my satchel, I ended up with two sets of pajamas, my three least threadbare t-shirts, two dressier blouses, two skirts, the contents of my top drawer, two pairs of jeans, and five pairs of leggings. Horace even managed to get my boots, sneakers, a pair of ballet flats, my box of costume jewelry, and a small stash of makeup into a tote bag, which I slung over my other arm.

The flow of objects stopped after that. Horace was probably exhausted, and we were pretty much out of time by then. I took one last look at my shelf of secondhand paperbacks, hoping Mom wouldn't go ballistic enough to burn them.

"What do I tell her?" Branwen slumped against the wall by the window, voice tight with fear.

"Exactly what you saw here." I winked at her. "I'm ready to get down now, tall, green, and helpful."

Despite Grace's still hanging darkness, we stayed in our disguises until we'd gotten through the fence and stood in the lee of the neighbor's shed. After that, I made everyone wait until I heard the window close before dashing down the driveway and back toward Tropica Mart. We gave the bracelets back to Grace and Azrael, who I assumed headed back to the school to drop them off. I thanked everyone.

Ramon walked me back to the boarding house, where we hugged again. Instead of letting go right afterward, I held on, looking him in the eyes.

"You don't even know what a big deal this was."

"Well, we got it done." He smiled. "Like a bunch of heroes."

"Don't heroes get rewards, though?"

"I'm supposed to say something like my reward is justice."

"Well yeah. It's important, justice, I mean. But maybe there's something I could do to thank you? Personally."

"Oh, uh." He blinked. "I'm dense about stuff like this sometimes." Under my hands, I could feel his trembling.

"Kiss her already, damn!" Wyatt stood at the bottom of the steps. We'd been blocking his way in all that time.

Ramon flushed crimson. I let go of his shoulders, took him by the hand, and walked down the steps and around the building's corner. The rooming house had a small parking area, and we were in it, out of view. Wyatt hadn't followed. We both heard the front door slam shut behind him.

"Guess that was a 'cap block," he said.

As if on cue, we both doubled over laughing. After the giggles died down, we faced each other and tried again. The world didn't go away, but it brightened a little.

CHAPTER EIGHTEEN

I didn't wear the outfit I'd chosen for the first day on Friday. Somehow, that felt risky, like I'd be jinxing myself. Instead, I chose black leggings, a polka-dotted skirt, and a blue t-shirt with three owls staring at the moon on it.

"Are you trying to be ironic?" Saya raised an eyebrow in the hall outside Lecture.

"Maybe." I chuckled.

Her reaction to my attire was almost as vast an improvement as the clothes themselves.

Lecture felt less grueling, somehow, more like a least favorite part of school than a place I'd have to watch my back every second. Mrs. Ambersmith still ran the class the same way. So I'd either gotten used to the system or merely had more confidence after getting some of my stuff back. Maybe a little of both.

In Forum, I finally got to speak my piece about my brother, all because of Wyatt. He took his tablet out and asked Mr. Hickson a question about a couple of local court cases. Jonah Arnold's and Crow's.

"Why did they get arrested and locked up in the first place if the documents say they both acted under coercion? How come Jonah's a Coast Guard officer, but Merlini's still locked up for the year?"

"Time, evidence, and perspective," Mr. Hickson said. "Jonah's trial happened a year earlier. The magus coercing him did it directly. Plus, he had several witnesses, including his victim, who insisted he wasn't responsible."

"What about Crow's then?"

"I'll answer that if you don't mind, Mr. Hickson." I stood.

"Go on." He nodded.

"Crow wasn't coerced. He got brainwashed. So, he made an insanity plea. Danvers Sanitarium is working for him. Last time I visited, he said he'd stay in there as long as it takes to get better, even if that's past his sentence."

"It also says in here that the New Order magus went on the lam soon after the cruise," Wyatt added. "You think they're gonna be a problem still?"

"Groups like that always have been, throughout history, probably farther back than our records go." Mr. Hickson nodded.

"Well, that sucks." Wyatt wrinkled his nose.

"This is why school's important. So we don't keep on making the same mistakes."

"Seems like we never learn, though." Saya sighed. "Collectively, I mean. So why bother teaching, Mr. Hickson?"

"When I was almost twelve, we moved to Salem from Oklahoma. My parents took me to the beach for the first time, which I'd never seen. It was the morning after a storm. After a few minutes of being shocked at the ocean's size, I noticed its cruelty. So many tiny creatures washed up on the sand and dying in the sun. I walked over, picked one up, threw it back. And kept that up."

"Let me guess, some cynic told you to stop, that you couldn't make a difference." Hope sighed. "But you kept saving them anyway."

"No." Mr. Hickson shook his head. "I got lucky. When my parents saw what I was doing, they came and helped. So did a group of other kids and their families. Eventually, we cleared most of Fort Pickering Beach. Do any of you understand?"

"You can't make change alone." Ramon's warm eyes widened. "It's a team effort."

Mr. Hickson's smile didn't reach his eyes. He tapped his nose whimsically anyway.

In Drama Club, we ended up choosing *Kiss Me, Kate* as the musical for the spring. Wanda was ecstatic, and everyone else thought she was a shoo-in for the lead in the show. While we all celebrated the selection, the auditorium door creaked open.

My hands went ice cold, and my face blazed with my stomach in free-fall. I nearly jumped out of my skin, certain it was Mom, there to drag me out by the hair.

But no.

Instead, Ed and Diego from Messing Academy held the door for whoever was behind them. They both still wore their uniforms, though Diego had removed his tie and untucked his shirt. After them came a girl and a boy I didn't recognize, wearing their Hawthorn Academy blazers.

"Oh! Welcome." Mr. Hickson clapped his hands once then sauntered across the auditorium toward the newcomers.

"Nice auditorium." Diego smiled. "Messing's only got a tiny black box theater."

"I thought they didn't have Drama Club there," Kiara said.

"It's a theater without a program. The creative writing kids do poetry slams in there." Ed shrugged. "You could probably give that a go, Kiara. Considering all that talent with writing."

"Excuse me?" Kiara blinked.

Ed reached into his backpack and pulled out a stapled-together bunch of paper.

"I read your play. I'll bet you dollars to donuts that it'll be in the Performance Showcase."

"How did you even get it?"

"Mr. Hickson sent it to us as an example of what to do," Diego butted in. "Because the extramural students also have to write one."

"I didn't know they were due." I swallowed. "I haven't written a single word yet."

"They're not due. I just finished early." Kiara patted my shoulder. "You have time."

"More than three weeks early, though." I chuckled. "Wow, Kiara. You don't play around with the homework."

I heard a shuffle and rustle behind me, then turned to see one of the Hawthorn students hovering like an awkward hummingbird at the fringe of our conversation. She had thick wavy brown hair, brown eyes, and a hesitant grin.

"Hi, I'm Mavis. Sorry if we seemed a little antisocial there."

"Hi. I'm Rita, from Albuquerque."

As we shook hands, I wondered whether all the Hawthorn magi introduced themselves with where they came from. It made sense, considering they were an international school. But something was missing.

"Did they let you bring your familiar, Rita?"

"Oh, yes." She nodded. "Tiger, you can come out now."

The source of the rustling became clear after she spoke. A bewhiskered feline nose poked out from the partially unzipped main compartment of her backpack. It twitched but vanished almost as soon as it had appeared.

"I guess he's staying in there. Sorry about that. Tiger's awfully shy for a sand kitten."

"I don't blame him with all us shifters around."

I introduced Rita to everyone I knew, including Wendy and her friends in senior year. She followed me back to the freshmen, though.

"Crap! Duck!"

It was the guy from Hawthorn who'd shouted. He'd been right about "duck" because that's what precisely what divebombed us from the high acoustic ceiling. Everybody hit the deck except Diego, who stood staring at the creature.

I dragged him down to the floor with me. The angry albino waterfowl soared back and forth overhead, frantically flapping and quacking.

"Get down here, Howie." The magus waved freckled hands over his head. "You don't want us to end up in Familiar Bonding with all the newbies, do you?"

"Quack! Quack quack quack quack!"

"Oh come on, this is getting ridi—" Jaxon started.

"Hush. Kiara held a finger in front of her mouth. "He won't chill out until he thinks he's got us cowed. I know waterfowl. They're part of the museum grounds."

"Thank goodness somebody does." The magus shook his head. "See, Howie? The big bad shifters are all terrified of you. Just land already, okay?"

The duck alighted on the arm of the aisle seat nearest his magus. He fluttered his wings, raised his head, then gave us a surly glare with one baleful red eye. This wasn't an ordinary duck, of course. All Hawthorn familiars were magical critters, even the mundane-looking ones.

"All right. So that's settled." The exhausted-looking magus ran a hand through his sandy fauxhawk, then let out a deflated sigh. "I'm Hayden and the duck's Howard. We're from just over the town line in Peabody. Anyway, it's nice to meet you. I'd like to promise he won't be trouble anymore, but ducks are unpredictable. Sorry."

"Don't apologize."

"Why? Are you all used to trouble or something?"

"Might as well tell you, I'm Mavis Merlini." I shrugged to cover my horror at blurting that out without thinking. "Take my word for it. Your duck's a walk in the park as far as I'm concerned."

"Oh wow." Hayden blinked. "I'm from Peabody, and yeah. That's a family of toughs."

"Wait." Rita's eyes went wide. "You're the gal whose brother almost won a fight against Xan Onassis last year. He's one of our Security Magi now, for his work-study."

Hayden and Rita glanced at each other as though trying to decide whether to back away.

"Uh, well. I'm mostly harmless." I swallowed. "A poison magus on security is no joke."

"Are you both in first-year?" Kiara came to my rescue like an extroverted cavalry. "What are your elements? Did you both just bond with your familiars, or have you had them for a while? Had you met each other before high school? What was your middle school like? Are there really mostly international students over at Hawthorn? It must be so cool, making friends from all over the world."

She kept querying away as she led them to the front row and got them settled into seats near the piano.

"I got a headache just listening to that. How do you handle sharing a room with her?" Diego shook his head.

"Wow, that was rude with a side order of jerk sauce." I raised an eyebrow. "How do you share a brain with yourself?"

"Blunt is my jam, and yeah, it's not nice. I'm working on it, okay?" Diego shrugged.

"He doesn't hang out with Donna anymore if that's what you're worried about," Ed added.

"That's perfect," Brandon said. It surprised me since he was usually so quiet. "My dad says to steer clear of Donna."

I wondered what else Brandon knew about the girl who insisted on being my nemesis. At some point, I'd have to ask him.

"Okay, if we're all settled down now, let's get started."

Mr. Hickson's voice boomed through the entire auditorium. Which meant he'd used proper breathing, a lesson he'd let us try exactly once. It hadn't gone well for most of us.

"What are we doing?" Kiara asked.

"I'm gonna teach you how to project like I just did. Everybody up on the stage." He clapped his hands. "Move it now."

For the rest of the time, we lay on our backs on the stage with books on our stomachs. Supposedly that helped strengthen our diaphragms. He said we'd need it between speaking and singing. At the end, a thought occurred to me. So I raised my hand.

"Mr. Hickson?"

"Yes?"

"If we have enchanted things like glamour bracelets and microphone charms, why do we need all of these breathing exercises?"

"You never know when projecting your voice will come in handy.

Or when enchantments might wear off. Back in the prehistoric era, a null magus came to a matinee, and none of our mic charms worked. So, practice. It'll be easier the more you do."

The bell rang.

"You're all dismissed. Our guests could use an escort to the front office, where Sid will open portals to the other campuses."

We filed through the door and into the hall, walking with the new theater geeks.

"That's nice of the principal," Kiara said. "Mustering all that magical energy for only four students."

"There are even more here from Messing for entertainment wrestling," Diego said. "Some of ours went over there for art and writing."

"Oh, wow. I didn't know that." Kiara grinned. "It's cool, but I had no idea until now."

"It's a new development," Hayden added. "Just started this year."

"How about from Hawthorn?" I asked. "Are there more of you?"

"I'll answer that." Rita nodded. "Our student body is tiny. Headmaster Hawkins said they lost a certain sort of student after everything that happened last year. The changes are for the good, but familiar magic's always been pretty rare. Mom almost didn't let me come to Hawthorn, even though I've had Tiger for six years. Mostly because they don't do theater. The extramural exchange agreement with Gallows Hill changed her mind, though."

"I'm glad they're doing it." I grinned. "This will be fun."

"I think so, too. It was good meeting you all. See you tomorrow."

The group of us from section two headed to Lab, ready to meet up for whatever the rest of our day had in store. The extra time in the hall gave me space to consider how some things had changed for the better last year, despite my difficulties.

Working with kids from the other schools would help me remember that. I'd mention it to Crow next time I visited. What I overheard outside Dr. Aranha's classroom reminded me we still had our work cut out for us.

"I can't believe that Brett character." Jillian clenched her fists. "Giving Fiona grief about that suplex."

"I know." Ramon shook his head. "He's jealous because she's got a better gimmick."

"Damn straight. I mean, I'm a little jealous too." She opened her hands, stretching them out instead. "Her act's gonna be great. But she only weighs a few more pounds than him. It's just wrong."

"Where's she now?" I asked.

"Chill-out chamber because she ran off crying." Jillian's lips twisted into a scowl again. "The next time I get my hands on Brett, I'm gonna—"

"Settle down, Jill." Jaxon joined us outside Lab, then set his bag at his feet. Cosmo followed suit. "You do this every time some dudebro goes toxic waste. Don't get another ulcer."

"You sound like Ed." Cosmo nodded. "He always stops me from breaking my claws out when things get hairy."

"Are you two, uh, dating?" Jillian asked.

Cosmo threw his head back, laughter squeezing tears past the corners of his eyes. He flopped against the wall like a fish, holding his sides and gasping for air.

"Guess that's a no." Jillian grinned. "Got anyone waiting on him back in Providence?"

"No." Saya sniffed. "Ed's single. But I'm not sure if he's searching."

"That's okay," Hope added. "Not looking works better for that for some folks. No harm in asking next time you see him, Jill."

"Is anyone walking over to Messing later?" Jillian asked.

"I am. You can come with me." I nodded.

"Cool. Thanks." She smiled.

"Yes, yes." The door creaked open, and Dr. Aranha peeked out. "That's enough chatter in the halls for now, students. Come along. It's time to learn something more academic."

Fiona emerged from the chill-out chamber in time to follow us into Lab. Of course, we invited her for the walk after school, along with the rest of the class.

Ramon and Fiona also agreed to walk with us to Messing Academy later. Hope declined and dragged Cosmo away at the end of lab for some extra Bishops Row practice. Kiara and Brandon did too, but for a different reason.

"We've got a study date back at the boarding house lounge." She smiled.

"Good luck, Jill," Brandon said.

"See you back at the house for dinner." Saya waved. "I've got squad practice."

"Uh, Mavis?" Wyatt tugged my sleeve. "Do you mind if I go with?"

"Sure, the more, the merrier." I nodded.

"I don't want to be a problem." Wyatt stared at his shoes. "You all shouldn't like me much. With good reason."

"I'm cool with you now." Ramon shrugged. "How else are you gonna fix that if you don't come hang out sometimes?"

"Oh, right." Wyatt nodded. "Yeah. Even though I probably should be studying like my dude Brandon and his lady."

"Ditto." I chuckled. "That pop quiz in Forum was uncomfortable."

"Same." Jillian sighed. "I spent all my free time working on wrestling."

"Don't worry. We only do two per month. And we get them back corrected to help us study for winter exams."

"Reassuring. I don't want to talk about tests anymore." Jillian wrinkled her nose. "What musical did they end up picking, Jax?"

"*Kiss Me, Kate*," Jaxon answered. "There's a big tap number in that I'm itching to do."

"Good thing you got more actors from the other schools," Jillian noted.

"Yes, it is." Hope nodded. "Everything's different at Hawthorn after last year."

"Right," Jaxon said. "They're under a new Trustee Board, I heard."

"It's a major improvement," Jillian drawled. "Our great aunt's a magus, and she knows a few of them. They want us to collaborate. That way we'll all benefit from it."

By that point, we were already outside Messing Academy. When the students emerged, Ed saw us right away. He hung back, sneaking glances at the crowd of us. I realized too late how intimidating we probably looked. Without incident from Donna and the rest, Ed joined us.

"We're going to the park," I mentioned. "Wanna come?"

"Sure." Ed brightened up immediately. "Field day, cool beans."

"Cool beans?" Ramon chuckled. "You sound like *Tia* Marisol."

"What can I say? I hang around with a lot of dead people." Ed shrugged. "They're not exactly part of our generation."

"I think that's wicked cool," Jillian commented. "You must hear so many stories."

"Being a medium's definitely good for learning the way things actually were back in the day instead of how the living talk about them."

As we walked toward the park, Ramon brushed his hand against mine. I took it, thinking nothing of any risk despite my brother's warnings about Mom always watching. It didn't matter all that much if my friends saw us holding hands. They all knew we were an item.

Also, I thought it might give Jillian more courage. She still seemed a little nervous. Even with Saya's, Hope's, and Cosmo's encouragement, I couldn't blame her. Still, even if Ed wasn't interested, I doubted he'd be harsh about it.

In the park, we threw a frisbee around, then had drinks and snacks. After a while, I noticed a few students from Messing leaning against the chain-link fence on the sidewalk near the tank. I dropped what I was doing and jogged over.

On the way, I realized I could've asked Horace, but hiding behind a ghost wasn't practical. Especially when it came to mending fences with psychics, a group I partly belonged to.

Maybe it wasn't the best idea, cheerily greeting Donna's weird sisters minus Diego. Despite the lecture he'd been given, Allen the all-seeing was still hanging out with Gia, Peg, and Donna.

I plastered a smile on my face, told myself Allen might be a good influence, and spoke.

"Hello." No matter how hard I tried, that smile refused to touch my eyes. "Did you all want to play frisbee?"

"No." Donna wrinkled her nose. "As if I'd get sweaty doing something as banal as that."

She didn't have her Grim with her that day. Instead, the creature she'd summoned was a Spite. They were the Seelie equivalent of a hunting hound, bright and glowing but vaguely skeletal instead of looming and shadowy like the Grim. The faerie dog's tail wagged as they looked up at me.

"I think your pup wants to play." My smile warmed as I aimed it at the Spite. "Good doggie!"

"I don't. Besides, Lucius is under my contract and orders." Donna sniffed.

"You never let them have any fun, Donna," Gia said. "After being at school all day, the poor thing's stressed out."

"We just learned in class that Spites need exercise, or they get aggressive," Allen said, glancing at a card in his hand before putting it back in his bag. "The cards say playtime's a good idea."

"Fine. Don't blame me when your little friends run away screaming." Donna waved a hand at the field behind me. "Lucius, you may play if you wish. For five minutes, no less no more."

The Spite took off running toward the open gate, through it, then out into the field. Almost everyone scattered, running in fear.

Jillian stood her ground, shouldering out in front of Ed in a defensive crouch. Ed tapped her on the shoulder and shook his head. The wolf shifter stepped aside, and Ed picked up the frisbee. Clearly, this was not his first faerie hound rodeo.

Ed tossed the disk. It sailed through the air and Lucius chased after it like a lightning bolt. Moments later, the Spite leaped up at least seven feet in the air to catch it, then landed on all fours perfectly, more feline than canine. After that, Lucius took off running with it, chasing after Jaxon and Wyatt, who'd realized by then that they weren't in any danger.

Ramon guffawed at their antics. When Fiona intercepted the flying disc, he waved both hands in the air.

"Over here!"

She tossed, and Ramon caught it, then played tug-of-war with

Lucius. He lost at that, the hound tumbling over him and doggily licking his face. Dhampyr were like the capybaras of the extrahuman world. So of course the ferocious Spite acted like a big puppy, playing with him.

"That looks like too much fun. I'm going." Allen trotted past the tank, dropping his school bag beside it before dashing out across the field to play.

Gia followed him without a word or even a look back. Peg hesitated, remaining on my right. I paid too much attention to them, as it turned out.

"I hate you." Donna's voice sounded low yet harsh and way too close. "You and your gang of miscreants deserve everything you're going to get."

I turned, placing my hands on my hips and staring directly into her eyes. She hadn't expected that, considering how closely she'd stepped to whisper that threat in my ear. She took a step back and almost tripped over the curb behind her.

I was glad she hadn't fallen into the street and the oncoming traffic. If she had, I would have leaped the fence and rescued her, bullying be damned. Since she didn't, it denied my poetic justice. So instead, I satisfied myself with imitating the expression Mom always wore while entering the kitchen at the nest.

"I don't care about you hating me." I moved my hands to the fence's top rail. "But if you mess with my friends, you'll regret it."

Donna glanced to my right. Peg reached for my hand. I snatched it away.

"Don't you dare touch me."

"Afraid of what she might see, I bet."

"Not afraid. I just don't want your lackey's slimy hands on me."

"Slimy." Donna chuckled. "That's rich coming from a Merlini. Greasy Italians, without purpose."

At the edge of my vision, Peg beckoned someone over from the field behind me. A moment later, Gia returned, standing a few feet away at the gate.

"Say what you want, *Doña* Donna. They don't let you use it at

Messing, but I know your family name comes from northern Italy. I'm only still in your face to make sure you let the good doggie keep on playing nice."

"Gia, how fake is her bullshit?"

Finally back from her brief recreation, Gia couldn't avoid getting in the middle of this mess. As a telepath, she could only read my surface thoughts at this range. I didn't care if she read those or repeated them either.

"She thinks you're a hypocrite, Donna," Gia said. "And that it's funny. Are you surprised?"

"Yea, that you're lying to me." Donna's nostrils flared. "Don't make me summon up anything frightening now."

"I'm not lying," Gia insisted.

"Of course you are. She's about to run crying to her mommy, and you know it. Anyone would, facing me in a fight."

"You think this is a fight?" I snorted. "Don't make me take that laughter out where everyone and their grandma can hear it."

"All right, then. Fight me." Donna narrowed her eyes.

"No." I jerked my thumb over my shoulder. "I'm here at the park to have fun with my friends. You know what fun is, right? Or didn't your parents let you have any?"

"See, she's afraid. Read her again."

The whole situation was awful. Partly because Donna was right. By then, I was afraid. But not of the summoner's threats.

"Fine." Gia rolled her eyes, then flattened her voice like a robot's. "She does not want to fight you. I sense fear."

"That's what I said."

Gia glanced at me and away. I understood what she'd done, of course. Read my reluctance to fight because I feared getting expelled from school, then spun it another way.

"Well, it's been five minutes. Call your dog back," Peg said.

"Call Lucius a dog again, and you'll regret it at school tomorrow." Donna snorted.

"You'll look weak if you let him play any longer," Gia said quietly.

Donna put her hand in her pocket, and Lucius returned to her side. The hound blinked at me, tail wagging. When the Spite looked at her, the tail stilled.

"What about Allen?" Peg asked.

"I don't care about the all-knowing know-it-all, not anymore." Donna flipped a lock of hair over her shoulder. "Let's go."

They walked away in a strange single-file line. I was glad to see the back of them.

CHAPTER NINETEEN

We went to the park both days that weekend. The Messing mean squad didn't show, though. Allen and Diego joined us on Monday, walking with Ed out of the school. Things were different on Tuesday. Ed sent a message to Jillian during the day.

She said he'd asked if she'd meet him after school. Alone. I didn't mind getting that information secondhand. Or not going to the park because I had a mountain of homework to scale in the lounge.

Ed grabbed a sandwich at dinner and left early.

"Later," was all he said at the table. And "got somewhere to be" on his way out.

Kiara and Brandon watched a movie in our room after dinner, so I went back to the lounge to finish scaling Mount Homework. As I was about to pack up, I heard Ed saying goodnight to someone in the foyer. After the door closed, I peered out and grinned at him.

"Hey, where'd you go?"

"Hi, Mavis." He hurried to join me in the lounge. "I took Jill to Dead Man's Party."

"Oh wow." I swallowed my jealousy. Not about their date. I was totally into Ramon. Rather, it was because I still hadn't visited the ghostly dance hall. "Awesome. Did you guys have fun?"

"Yeah. Jill couldn't see the ghosts so OGP loaned her Tommy's ring. It let her hear the music. We danced the whole time."

"And?"

"If the Koto had a rug, it'd be in ribbons by now. She's an awesome dancer." Ed smiled. "And she didn't think it was weird, dancing in an apparently empty room. Plus, we liked all the same songs."

"Well that's amazing."

"If Tommy had more of those rings, I'd say you should bring Ramon next week. Like a double date."

"You know, I'd ask him, but you're right. It's sort of limiting. Maybe we could all meet at a regular place. Like the movie theater, the café, or something. Then Kiara and Brandon could go too."

"Well, you're the local. Pick a place, and we'll plan it."

"So are you two officially dating, or what?"

"We absolutely had a date. But we maybe need to go on another and have a chat before either of us answers a question like that."

"But you're into her."

"Of course. She's pretty, fun, likes adventure." He chuckled. "I'm just surprised she even noticed me."

"I'm not. She asked practically every day after seeing you at the Dodge Street Café how you were doing." I fist-bumped his shoulder like I used to do with Crow. "You should have seen her face when I suggested bringing you to the park."

"Wow." He blinked. "I had no idea. It's just that I'm used to being in the background. So far, Jill acts like I'm front and center."

"I'm really happy for you, Ed."

"Thanks Mavis. I'm not sure I'll get that response from everyone else."

"Wait, what?"

"My foster siblings are insular." He shook his head. "I didn't get their approval ahead of time. But you already know how that is."

"I hear you on that. They might surprise you." I told him about how Hope encouraged Jillian to ask him out. "Cosmo just laughed because Jill asked first if he was dating you."

Ed leaned against the wall, clutching his sides. His laughter wasn't as raucous as Cos's had been but just as intense.

"No. No, stuff like that always goes over Cos's head." He dabbed the corner of his eye. "Hope says we should all be free to figure that out on our own. Guess she's still mulling it over herself."

"Yeah, Hope seems to avoid dating like the plague. What about Saya?"

"She talks fashion, not crushes. Maybe because of the hatchling thing." His face fell. "Oh no. I hope she doesn't want to be celibate or something."

"That'd be awful."

"I always worried she'd start telling us not to date people. Because of going through that."

"There are two reactions to suffering. One is thinking everyone else should because they had to. The other's wanting to make sure nobody else goes through it, or at least not alone."

"You think Saya's the latter, then."

"It's a hunch. You know her better than I do."

Ed blinked, then shook his head. Maybe the four of them were too close for objectivity.

The lights dimmed three times.

"Well, that's lights out in a half-hour. Guess I'd better pack up my homework and head upstairs." I sighed. "At least I got it all done."

"You're a grade-making machine." Ed nodded. "See you tomorrow. We can set that date up."

"Yeah, tomorrow."

I messaged both Ramon and Jillian on the way upstairs. They both said it was a go, so I had a chat with Kiara as we put our hair up before bed.

"I'd love a triple date with you all!" She beamed.

"I was thinking the Arcade at the Willows on Thursday after dinner. It's good to go in September before it's crowded with Halloween tourists."

"That sounds awesome, can't wait."

I told Ed the good news about the outing over breakfast the next morning. However, his entire mood remained deflated.

"What's going on, Ed?"

"More like what isn't." He showed me a message on his phone from his brother, Fred.

"He canceled plans? But doesn't say why."

"He almost never does. We had a huge argument over the summer, where I told him to stop making excuses."

"Explanations and excuses are two entirely different things."

"I know that. Apparently either he doesn't or has no real reason. At least your brother lets you in when you go visit him in Danvers."

"Oh, Ed. I'm sorry. It must be horrible."

"All the more reason to put my nose to the grindstone with school." He sighed. "Maybe I have no business dating anybody if my brother can't be bothered with me."

I tried a little reverse psychology.

"Well, maybe I don't either."

"Wait, what?" He blinked. "After everything you've been through, of course, you—" He tilted his head. "Touché, Mavis. You got me again."

"I love to say I told you so."

"Duly noted. Anyway, we can't shirk school. This goes double for you, ever since you told me it's your ticket out of here with your brother."

"School is school. Both better and worse than I thought it'd be. But we need it, right?"

"It's a means to an end, for sure. All the extra stuff we're supposed to want to do seems frivolous. Not essential. I know fun is important. It makes existence into life. But I'm so tired of being where I am, at this age and in my grade. Stuck, almost."

"I hear you. I'm always looking over my shoulder. It doesn't feel like I should let go and have fun. Which might be why I keep on trying." I grinned. "Ramon says he likes that about me. That I don't quit. Maybe Jill likes seeing you smile."

"Things in Rhode Island are so serious." He shook his head, peering down at the rest of the group. "Cosmo's practically a rebel with all his corny jokes. Can't imagine that on me."

"I think he just up and refuses to think sometimes."

"Is that how you do it then, turn off the brain? If so, can you teach me? Hope and Saya could use some pointers, too."

"Look, I can't blame Saya after what she said in class about hatchling dragon shifters."

"I was at Messing, remember."

"You must know she's supposed to save the dragon race by getting with the right guy."

"Guys plural. Become an egg factory. Yeah, I'm painfully aware of that."

"It's the reason she gave you, isn't it?"

"No. She said I'm her brother. She can't think of me that way."

"Ouch." I winced. "Sorry."

"I'm not. I'm with Jill now, and she's way more appreciative." He blushed a bit with a dopey grin on his face. "Wasn't shy about getting her message across in more ways than one."

"Thank goodness for Jillian Thorne, then."

"And Ramon, from what I hear."

"Guess we're lucky, with folks like them." I took my turn grinning and blushing. "But there's a tiny chance we might actually deserve being happy."

"Thanks, Mavis. Especially for that last part. It's too easy to forget."

He was right about that.

Thursday came with its own set of problems, all self-inflicted because we'd gone overboard with the fun and games.

"Why'd I ever agree to another field day before this cockamamie date hydra?" I groaned at the mirror in the second-floor hallway. My hair was utterly unkempt. "I look like Medusa. Or a hydra."

"Date hydra is the new raid boss?" Ed wrinkled his nose at the chipped remains of his black nail polish. "Looks like I sowed soldiers with these hands. Smells like it, too."

"Dragon lady to the rescue." Saya hustled us toward our rooms. "Get cleaned up and leave the nails and hairdo to me."

I brought the clothes I wanted to wear into the bathroom and put them on as soon as I was dry. Ed stepped out of the guy's restroom wearing a flannel bathrobe.

Saya gussied us up using supplies from the cabinet. By the time dinner started, Ed had shiny black nails again, and my hair hung in soft waves, held back from my eyes by a couple of barrettes.

Ed hurried toward the door, presumably to his room to get changed. I moved to follow but paused and turned.

"Thanks, Saya. You're a lifesaver."

"Yeah, Saya," he echoed. "Thank you."

"You're welcome." She smiled, eyes twinkling.

I smiled and waved, then went to my room to stow my hairbrush. Wearing one of my few outfits meant one less for the week to come, but I didn't care. I wanted to go out and have fun. Wearing sweats for one day of classes was worth it.

On the first floor, Ramon waited with Jillian. They chuckled together over a cat meme on her phone. They looked up when they saw us on the stairs.

"Where are we going?" Ramon asked.

"The Arcade." I grinned. "Kiara and Brandon are already on their way."

"Wow, I overdressed." Ed gestured at his pinstripe slacks, suspenders, and wingtip shoes.

"They don't mind people getting fancy up at the Willows." I chuckled.

"Maybe I should go change."

"Nah, I think you look awesome." Jillian's grin was downright wolfish. "Let's head out."

Ramon offered me his arm, and we were off.

We walked toward downtown, then took a right and went all the way past the wharf and Irzyk Park. Farther up was the Willows, a place I hadn't visited frequently since before I started middle school.

Magi tended to congregate there, and they didn't mingle much with the Tanks, which was what my brother's friends called themselves back then.

On arrival, I discovered several figures in Hawthorn blazers milling about, a trend that continued. I tried to ignore them, worried about whether coming here was the wrong choice.

"Hey, look!"

The voice nearly drowned in the din of arcade machines and a quacking duck because Hayden was at the Arcade along with his familiar. Rita, too. They stood halfway in, waving at us.

"Hey, it's the Drama Club magi!" I waved. "You down for some Skee ball?"

"Absotively!" Kiara smiled. Brandon grinned right along with her.

"I'll try it." Ed shrugged. "Never played it before."

"You'll do great. It's fun." Jillian grinned. "Just get the ball up the ramp and aim for the five hundred. You'll hit lower, but that's cool."

"Are you sure?"

"After the way you danced last night, you can do this." Jillian took his hand. "I'll help with your form if you want."

Rita and I went to get a round of sodas after throwing a few games. Ed wasn't much good, but having fun with Jill's attempts to instruct him. Ramon and Hayden had hit it off, chattering away about Picstagrammer's flock of trash gryphons.

"Hey Mavis, are you all going to the Harvest Moon dance?" Rita asked. "It's taking the place of what used to be Parent's Night at Hawthorn."

"Well, I want to go." I sighed. "I'm not sure I'm welcome."

"Why?"

"I'm sure your third-years mentioned the cruise incident last spring."

"Oh." She sighed. "Yes, I've heard."

"So maybe I'll stay home."

"No, don't." She shook her head. "Headmaster Hawkins even has his parents helping expand the lobby so everyone will fit. I'm sure you're invited."

"Invited is different from welcome."

"I'll welcome you personally." Rita grinned. "You have more friends at my school than you think. So don't let that stop you."

"Thanks, Rita."

We brought the sodas back to a table near the Skee ball lanes. I handed one to Ramon, who sipped before speaking.

"Hey, let's go to that Harvest Moon dance together. What do you say?"

"I wouldn't go with anybody else. I mean, you're my boyfriend."

"I don't take that for granted."

"So, Jillian." Ed cleared his throat. "Want to go to that dance as my date?"

"Of course."

They chuckled, elbowing each other. A moment later, they were holding hands. Kiara already sat in Brandon's lap, giggling.

Rita glanced at Hayden, who'd rushed off to chase Howie. Before she could go after him, Diego Mendez stepped up.

"Hey, Rita. About that dance—"

"Oh. Right. I'm helping out with refreshments, so I wasn't entirely sure whether I should have a date." She tittered.

"Well, if we're both going stag, I'll see you there then." He shrugged.

"I'll save a dance for you."

"Oh." Diego grinned. "Yeah, that rocks. Thanks, Rita."

That's when I noticed Donna on the other side of the arcade, eyes narrowed as she stared at the exchange. Diego saw it too. He waved once, then headed away from us but not toward his classmate. I followed him, weaving through the crowd. Once we reached the relative safety of the ticket counter, I spoke.

"That does not bode well."

"Yeah, caught that," Diego said. "She's up to something, and I refuse to get roped in."

"Hope it doesn't get too drama-riffic."

"I know what you mean. The drama needs to stay on stage."

"Keep me in the loop."

"No." He shook his head. "She's already on guard against you. But I could use some help."

"Well, you've met most of my section. Pick one, and I'll ask them to give you an assist."

"The lion."

"Cosmo. Yeah, good choice. He's a goofball but thinks on his feet."

"Noticed that. Thanks, Mavis."

"No biggie."

I returned to the table, where Ramon sat guarding my drink. We sat together, watching Brandon rake in tickets while Ed improved with each throw. I told him about Diego's situation.

"Trouble from Donna at an extramural event is the last thing we need." He sighed.

"Cos has his work cut out for him. Anyway, it seems like Ed and Jill are hitting it off. They're outdoing us in the being a couple department, even." He chuckled.

"Maybe it's because we already knew each other." He gestured at the Skee ball lanes. "We've been here and done this."

"Well, I know we've skeed the ball together, Ramon. But I don't think we have any problems coupling up." I raised an eyebrow, leaning against him.

"Oh. Well, you know." He smiled with his eyes. "When a shifter and a dhampyr, uh, like each other very much. Sometimes, coupling happens."

"You two make me sick." Donna's voice was like a bucket of ice. "Get a room."

"Get a date." I sniffed, doing my best Saya impression. "If you haven't scared them all off with your attitude."

"Turns out all the Merlinis aren't thugs after all." Donna leered. "This one's a tramp instead."

"What did she just say?" Ramon blinked.

"Nothing unpredictable." I chuckled. "Donna here is just being herself, that's all."

"What the hell does that mean?" Her voice cracked like she was about to spit nails.

"It means I've got a lifetime of bad examples and managed to make friends." I grinned. "But you can't and don't even have bad parents as an excuse."

"You're nothing but vermin."

"That's a good one." I snorted. "Call me when you've got better insults than my mom in her sleep."

"If you're so tough, prove it."

"Whoa, Mavis." Ramon patted my shoulder. "She's goading you. Don't let her."

"Listen, I've got it a deal for you." I pointed at the Skee ball lanes. "If you win, I leave. If I win, you leave. Sound fair?"

"No. I don't play games with shifty ravens."

"You play." Jillian loomed over Donna. "Her or me. Or are wolves shifty too?"

"Screw this."

Donna's face flushed crimson. She snapped her fingers. A Grim appeared between her and the angry wolf shifter.

"Cover my exit." She turned on her heel and marched out of the arcade, the Grim pacing behind her, casting a few confused glances over their shoulder as they went. Jillian threw back her head and laughed.

"Did you see the look on her face?"

"I was facing her. I did." I grinned at Jillian. "Thanks, Jill."

"Hey, if she can't handle the kayfabe, she should get out of the kitchen."

"Donna smelled what the wolf was cooking." Ed nodded sagely.

"She's not the student who came over for entertainment wrestling is she?"

"Matter of fact she is." Ramon sighed. "All attitude, no teamwork."

"Wow."

"That's what I said." Ramon sighed. "She wants an excuse to bully people."

"She won't get much ring time." Jillian shook her head. "Not with how Fiona trounced her today."

"Wish I was there."

"You don't have to be." Ed grinned. "Jill recorded it."

"Check it out." Jillian whipped her phone out.

Fiona totally dominated Donna in the ring. It was refreshing to watch and all the more entertaining because of the ogre's newfound confidence. Entertainment wrestling was good for my friend. It suited her.

"You're right. Fiona's good. She's got real presence. She'd have done well in Drama Club too."

"Yeah, I guess she could've." Jillian grinned. "Then I'd be out a tag team partner."

"You guys must be amazing. I can't wait to see a match."

"It's coming. Rec Week, after that dance."

"I'll be there."

A pair of guys in Arcade aprons came out from behind the ticket counter. That never happened unless someone reported trouble. Apparently, Donna had called the manager.

"Hey Ramon, can we get out of here?"

"Okay. Sure. I can walk you home."

"Yeah, that'd be great."

"I'll let Kiara and Brandon know you guys are going," Jillian said.

"Oh?" I asked.

Ramon led me of the building and down the street. We walked in silence, holding hands most of the way. When we got to Washington Street, I let go.

"You want to get back to the boarding house by yourself now, I guess."

"No, it's just—"

He glanced down the street at a car with its parking lights on.

"You don't want your mom seeing."

"You're a genius. But yes. I'm sorry, you deserve better."

"What you're going through has nothing to do with what I deserve. I want to be with you, Mavis. I don't care if you want to hide it from your mother. If I had a family member like her, I'd do the same thing."

"Okay."

"I've got an idea. Let's go around the block, take Dodge Street."

We did and held hands the whole way. We stopped, taking a detour at the side of the building where we'd first kissed. We spent some time there. Eventually, we parted, and he left me at the bottom of the steps. I hoped our flushed faces didn't betray us too badly. I barely felt my feet touch the ground as I ascended the stairs.

In Drama Club on the third Wednesday in September, we had to choose acts for the variety show. Brandon and Jaxon practiced a tap routine together, already set.

We rummaged through a box of old librettos, searching in vain for something, anything to do. Because when you're under pressure, something's gotta give. I'd dropped the ball on rec a second time. Once again, my roommate wanted to help.

"How about *A Heart Full of Love*?" Kiara waved a copy of *Les Misérables*. "Three of us could do that one together. Oh, wait. That doesn't fit any of our vocal ranges."

"Don't look at me." Diego shrugged. "Gonna do Shakespeare anyway."

"Same." Hayden nodded.

"What about—Ow!" Ed tossed *Little Shop of Horrors* back in the box and pouted at a paper cut. "It bit me!"

"Everybody does those." I shook my head. In a fit of impatience, I took my tablet out instead and ran a search on underrated musicals.

I came up with *Peter Pan*. Most of the songs from the original show felt a little too simple or saccharine. I tapped on the song list from a revival a while back. A song title exclusive to that version caught my eye. *When I Went Home.*

One look at the lyrics, and I had to try it out. I found music on the tablet, then set it on the piano's music stand.

"That's interesting." Sid raised his eyebrows.

"What's interesting?" I blinked.

"Never had someone bring me music on a tablet before. I'm not sure I've ever heard this one. But if you want to give it a try, I'm game."

"Thanks, Sid."

Fortunately, I could sight-read. My aptitude in music theory was entirely self-taught after the big let-down about not being a medium. Plus, a direct result of boredom back in grade school.

When I Went Home felt too close to home. I reached for the tablet, about to ask Sid to stop. Then I noticed something that gave me pause.

The room, filled with chatter before, was silent. I couldn't imagine why until I glanced across it during the chorus.

Brandon and Jaxon stopped dancing, one foot still in the air. Kiara sniffled. Diego's eyes widened. Hayden hugged Howie. Rita had one hand on her cheek. Ed tugged at something on a chain around his neck, staring at something nobody else could see.

Wanda paced toward the apron, put her hands on it, and gazed up at me.

Once I finished, breaking the song off on the last word without finishing the sentence as the script required, she took her hands off the stage and clapped. Everybody joined in. Even Hayden's duck flapped his wings.

"Wow." Kiara shook her head. "I'm totally inspired now."

She hurried to the piano, tugged Sid's sleeve, and asked if he knew *Only Pretend* from the same show. He didn't, so I brought it up on my tablet.

As she warmed up, Ed whispered at one or both ghosts, glancing at me occasionally.

"We have a wire system, but there's no flying during that number,"

Wanda said. "Maybe add some if you do this song. You'd definitely spice things up in the show."

"Thanks, Wanda. I'm not sure I want to do this one, though." I shook my head. "It's intense, maybe too heavy for a first-year like me."

"Don't let your grade stop you, Mavis. The main thing here is to have fun. If it's not, maybe choose a different number from the same show. You'd be an amazing Peter Pan."

"Thanks. Yeah, the fun factor is pretty much it."

"You'd better do that song or something like it." Ed grinned. "Rob says he'll throw rotten tomatoes if you sell yourself short. Because that was awesome."

"It sure was. You started a trend, too." Diego jerked his thumb at Kiara.

"Looks like I'd better suggest Peter Pan to Mr. Hickson for next year." Wanda winked at me. "There's your Wendy. Now, if only we had a Hook."

"Wow, Horace. You're right." Ed nodded.

When Kiara finished, he practically dragged me back over to the piano and co-opted my tablet. After a moment, he put it back.

"Can you play it *allegro* please, Sid?"

"Yeah, sure. I know this one!" Sid cracked his knuckles. "Get ready."

I managed to sight-read fast enough, but it was a near thing. All the jabs and taunts in the lyrics helped me imagine what the number could be in full performance mode with all the blocking. And the flying rig Wanda had mentioned.

"Think you found your number." Mr. Hickson clapped slowly. "No flying without extra practice, Mavis. But we've got some nice foils if you two know how to use them."

"Helped, uh, Bar Micello with *Fifteen Minute Hamlet* stuff." I cleared my throat, ashamed at omitting Crow. "Ed?"

"Fencing lessons." He nodded. "Finally get to use them for something."

"Costuming is optional but super easy with the glamour bracelets." Wanda smiled.

"That's one more act chosen." Mr. Hickson clapped at the end of the song. "Is anybody doing a monologue, by chance?"

"I am." Diego raised his hand.

"Awesome. Let's hear it."

He got up on the stage and began Mercutio's Queen Mab speech from *Romeo and Juliet*. It was one of my favorites, and it helped that Diego rocked Shakespeare pretty much constantly.

"Hey, I was gonna do that one." Hayden snorted. "But not anymore. You're too good."

"If you've got it memorized, why not let us hear it anyway?" Mr. Hickson gestured at the stage.

His interpretation was utterly over the top physically. Hayden also emphasized the meter more than Diego.

"Like, you're good." Diego punched his shoulder. "That's high praise, my dude. I won prizes for this back in middle school."

"Should have thought about that harder. That was you last spring, *As You Like It*." Hayden glanced at me. "With Mavis, no less. It rocked."

"And I saw your Androcles." Diego nodded. "Back at you. But Willy Shakes is forever my jam. I'm not picking something else."

"Maybe you could team up then?" I suggested. "Like, do the whole duel between Tybalt and Mercutio or something."

"And fight over who gets which part? Nah. It's okay." Hayden sat on the apron, then hopped down from the stage. "I've got another trick up my sleeve. But it's a surprise."

"Even if the scary bird lady wants a scene out of us?" Diego raised an eyebrow.

His sarcasm was like a neon sign from my perspective. Not all of my other friends saw it.

"She's not scary." Kiara blinked. "How could you say that?"

"Diego's seen me angry." I dropped her an enormous wink to be sure she understood I was kidding. "That's extra scary. With a side of scary sauce."

"Is this over that whole Merlini thing?" Rita drawled. "Because all the third-years over at Hawthorn say—"

"I'd like us to all lay off the whole Merlini family reputation for now." Mr. Hickson inserted himself in our conversation. "Especially since the bell's about to ring."

It did. On the way out, I caught up with Kiara.

"Diego and I are chill now. He's just sarcastic."

"I don't grok that most of the time."

"I noticed just now. Do you want help with it?"

"If it can be maybe a gesture or something." She shrugged. "Not like a call-out. Those get embarrassing."

"Okay, how about a wink like earlier?"

"Yeah, that works. Thanks, Mavis. You're absolutely unscary."

The rest of the way to Lab, she chattered about the song she decided on. *Popular* from *Wicked*. Which, looking back on that first night in the dorm, suited her perfectly.

⁂

Our third Thursday at Gallows Hill started uneventfully, except that Hope's still inexplicable obsession with the upperclassmen had ended.

Instead, Saya turned nosy, asking faculty and staff, including Sid, all sorts of questions. I cornered him after gym.

"What did Saya want, Sid?"

"Dunno, exactly." He shrugged. "Bunch of questions about magi. How many you'd be seeing at the museum tomorrow."

"Okay, thanks."

Was this part of the mission that led Ed to investigate his Messing classmates? I already knew asking Saya herself would be fruitless, if so.

Her new behavior extended into Forum.

"Why don't we have magi at our school?" Saya asked. "They can't all go in for familiars around here, and there must be more of them our age in Salem than the thirty at Hawthorn."

"That's a good question, Miss Harcourt, if unrelated to our course-work. Do any locals have a brief answer?"

"Only some magi send their kids away for school, the ones keeping traditions from before the Reveal," I said.

"That's mostly correct." Mr. Hickson nodded. "There's a general public school for magi in Massachusetts, but it's in Northampton. So, Salem magi your age who aren't at Hawthorn go out there and stay in a dorm."

"Thank you." Saya nodded. "I'll keep my next question on topic with pure faeries. How are gremlins different from gnomes?"

Mr. Hickson told us that, while both had communities, gremlins worked together and pooled their resources. Gnomes tended more toward solitary foraging, gathering back together to brag about their finds and trade.

Gremlins were also creatures of crafting, breaking things down to their base components then making something new. Gnomes were more concerned with time, though how and what they did with that remained mysterious.

In Drama, we learned a short dance. Sid played the piano while Wanda taught it to us. I managed not to trip over my own feet, but it was a near thing. If I wanted a part in the spring musical, I'd need help. That was a long way off so I didn't let it get to me.

I stayed to practice so long that there wasn't time for snooping in the library. Still, I finally spied Hope on her way out of there, hovering at the edge of a cluster of upperclassmen. It baffled me because her behavior appeared to be pure popularity-seeking.

Wasn't she the queen bee of our entire class section? Had she been trying to ingratiate herself to juniors and seniors all day? It made no sense even with the information I'd dug up on her before, so I added that to the notes on my tablet and went on with my day.

In Lab, Dr. Aranha gave us a pamphlet from the Peabody Essex Museum about the exhibit we'd see on Friday. Even though I'd been in there every year on field trips, this one looked more exciting. It focused on extrahuman privateers in early Salem. Pirates were always cool. At the end, she gave us even more compelling information.

"Students from Hawthorn and Messing will be touring with us." She smiled. "Be sure to bring your questions and be prepared to answer any of theirs."

"Wow, I thought we only mixed for rec stuff." Wyatt glanced over his shoulder at me. "After, uh, the Hawthorn Trustees made a rule?"

"The new board members changed several things. Messing Academy never implemented such a ban. So be prepared to engage in a collaborative experience, as I said."

Over breakfast, everybody seemed nervous about the field trip. Finally wearing the outfit I'd chosen for the first day of school had me in a good mood. I'd expected Mom to mess with me or call the school after I raided the nest. She hadn't. Even if the mysterious Hawthorn hoodie magus from the park was there on her orders, nothing came of that.

My head insisted this was it. I was out of the woods with my family. A rational idea. My gut disagreed. I couldn't find it in my heart to let my guard down. Another shoe could drop eventually. Still, I managed to convince myself it wouldn't be that day, at least.

That changed in the hall as I headed toward the magic door to campus. I overheard Matron Klein on the phone. Her tone and words stopped me in my tracks and reduced my earlier enthusiasm to sub-zero.

"You'll do no such thing without contacting Campus Security. I don't care how many alums are in your family." Her voice sounded more closely clipped than a surgeon's fingernails. "I said good day!"

Immediate dialing followed the sharp clatter of the handset on the hook. I stood there, praying she'd been on the phone with the Ambersmiths, Claytons, or Micellos. Anyone but my mom. But there was no way of knowing unless I kept listening.

"Sid, it's Steph. Give your gremlins fortress protocol and alert Buttons Goldfarb." She paused. "No, it's preemptive. But only at the school until R&R. After that, I want them all through the magic door to—"

An arm interlaced with mine, and I found myself dragged toward and through the magic door to the gym. One glance down at the brawny trench coat-clad forearm identified my surprise escort. Cosmo Gitano.

"Eavesdropping is a dick move, Mavis."

"Are we doing this again?" I sighed.

"I don't know. Are we?"

"I didn't much like it the last time."

"Tough."

"What's your problem?"

"You." He clenched his jaw. "You're always snooping and spying, but you're clueless."

"You're harping on me now instead of Saya because you can't or won't step up to Hope yourself. Is that it?"

"No. Look, if you want to go kick up trouble in town with your other friends, that's fine. But my family lives here with you. If they get hurt because of your hijinks—"

I planted my feet and yanked my arm from his grip.

"So you're an eavesdropper too."

"No. Wyatt told me." Cosmo's nostrils flared. "About that shindig at a certain nest a few weeks back."

"What did he say?"

"Mostly, he talked about Fiona dissing him. I'm better at reading between the lines than you."

"We're not talking about this here." I waved my hand at the open gym.

"That's fair. Library. Snack time."

"Fine."

"You'd better show."

"I said fine, Cosmo. What do you want from me?"

"Just that chat. For now."

He stalked away, heading for the most distant stack of exercise mats. Once equipped, he went to Coach Tremain, who was leading yoga that morning. It relieved me in no small measure that he'd chosen a grounding activity for morning gym. Also, yoga was one of the only athletic things I could do.

"Well, that's disappointing but not totally surprising." Kiara put her hand on my shoulder. "Are you okay?"

"Wait, what? Not surprising?"

"Well, maybe he has a crush on you. And now you're seeing Ramon."

"If that's what it's about, never date him." Fiona handed me a mat. "Nobody needs a jealous partner."

"You're right." I nodded, unrolling the mat. "I don't think that's Cosmo's problem."

I followed Coach Tremain's routine, doing the challenge versions of each pose. It wasn't often I had to use exercise to tire myself out of anxiety, but it was a given after all that.

All through Lecture, nightmarish daydreams of my mother barging in had me looking at the door frequently. I hoped nobody noticed but had no such luck.

"Strike one for today, Merlini," Mrs. A said.

Kiara tapped my foot with hers and stared intently at my tablet's empty screen. I nodded, then put the stylus against it and took notes.

Mrs. A made two columns on the board, one Unseelie and the other Seelie. Then, she listed the names of pure faeries. These weren't the sort that got born, grew a mantle as changelings, then had to tithe to a monarch eventually. The pure were part of the Under's ecology but sapient. They each had different attributes, magic abilities, and preferred habitats.

Fortunately, this topic intrigued me. My hand cramped from the frantic notes I took, not only copying down Mrs. A's information but adding questions I wanted to ask in Forum later. There were lots of them, which made the meeting with Cosmo much less intense than it could have gone.

"Mavis, you can't possibly understand the danger here."

"Try me."

"We're in a vulnerable position right now. I can't tell you the exact details. We can't be at risk. Not when we're so close to—well. The thing I can't mention. Saya needs to do her part before me. But your mom's a threat. Here and now."

"We're going on that field trip soon, though." I sniffed. "After that, she can stomp around the office and yell at the principal all she wants."

"Matron Klein's going all-in on security. Don't you know who Buttons Goldfarb is?"

"A guidance counselor? Saw the name on a door in the office. Licensed social worker. Never met him."

"Them. Hope says Buttons is nonbinary. They're also a veteran. Extrahuman Marines. I overheard more than you did, too. The principal wants them at the museum with us, along with Hawthorn's security magus. Your consequences are about to end up on all of our heads."

"I never meant for that to happen, I swear." I sighed.

"So what did you mean, then? When you went over there looking armed to the teeth?"

"Thought we were all clear, considering she didn't do anything right afterward."

"I get that." He nodded. "But your mom sounds like my bio dad. The long road to vengeance type. So, why did you do it?"

"I only wanted my stuff. Hasn't Ed told you I'm homeless?"

"No." Cosmo's eyes widened. "He hasn't. I didn't know. And I got all up in your face. I thought it was a play to look tough, deter future bullies. Or even your siblings."

"That'd be a nice side-effect. Mostly, I had no clothes besides what Klein gave me. Even after that raid, I had to make do with a few fashion-backward pieces from the lost and found."

"Why didn't you buy some, though?"

"Asshole parents don't kick you out with money. She never even let me open a bank account."

"Oh." He winced. "Sorry. Saya's brother throws money at problems like this, so I don't really know any other way. What'll she do if she gets to you, do you think?"

"Nothing overt. She'll act concerned or angry in a normal parent way. But she'll probably take me out of school."

"There are laws. She can't."

"She's threatened me with homeschooling for years. Which she made clear will be an education on confinement in my room until I'm eighteen."

"Look, I'm not mad at you. I just wish things were different. But what will you do if she shows up?"

"I haven't been able to grok it. At the same time, it's all I can think about this morning."

"What about those pure faeries, though?" He grinned. "Saw you taking notes like your stylus was on fire."

Before I could answer, the bell rang. We hurried out into the hall and down toward Forum. Halfway there, Hope gave Cosmo a dirty look. He hung his head, apologized, then followed them.

At least he'd returned the momentum of my curiosity in time for Mr. Hickson's class. I put it to good use.

"Are they really all genderless, though?" My arm ached from holding it up. "What if they want to present one way or another? They're sentient and sapient, Mrs. A said."

"Pure faeries are all agender, yes." Mr. Hickson nodded. "Treat them as such unless one tells you otherwise, or you risk their extreme displeasure."

"Where do they come from, then?" I asked. "I mean, I know pixies emerge from water and brownies grow in fields. But I mean, how do they reproduce? Or do they? Do the monarchs make them? Or can, like, a gnome decide they're lonely and want company, and another one comes out of a geode one day?"

"We've got gnomes in our garden." Wyatt wrinkled his nose. "You see one, and the next day you find four. So I bet you're right, Mavis.

It's hard to get information out of them, though. Because you ask too many questions, you end up owing your life."

"That applies to them, too?" Ramon blinked. "I had no idea."

"Good thing you learned it now, then." Jillian snorted. "Pretending to owe a pure faerie might make a good storyline for entertainment wrestling."

I let them drive the discussion for a while, listening, watching, and taking notes. It wasn't until the end of class that I realized that Hope, Saya, and Cosmo stayed silent throughout the entire topic. My guess that they were hiding what they knew turned out to be right later.

The courtyard had bagged lunches for us, which we brought with us to the Peabody Essex Museum. I thought we'd be walking since it wasn't far, but instead, Dr. Aranha escorted us to the magic door. A throng of gremlins stood on either side of it, with Sid the jack of all trades holding it open.

"Thanks, Mr. Muscat," Dr. Aranha said.

"Wait for me!" A person wearing a set of sparkly cat ears, a black gold-trimmed blazer, striped capris, and a red collar complete with a bell jogged down the hall toward us.

"Counselor Goldfarb?" Jaxon blinked. "What are they doing here?"

"Huh?" I asked.

"Right, it's weird," Hope said. "Why do we need a guidance counselor at the museum?"

"I'm Guard Goldfarb at the moment." They pointed at the red collar. "Blue for therapy, red for security."

"Gods, not security." I wrapped my arms around my midsection.

"Shh." Cosmo nudged me.

"Leave her alone." Saya dragged him back toward where she and Hope stood. He leaned down and whispered in her ear. The dragon shifter's eyes went wide.

"Why didn't you tell—"

"Class, we're heading through now," Dr. Aranha interrupted.

I paced along, eyes on the back of Jaxon's head, hands gripping the thick leather strap on Horace's satchel. Maybe he'd help if something went wrong. The way he had at the nest. That idea gave me some small measure of comfort as I entered the museum. Seeing a familiar face gave me more.

Ed stood in the lobby, turning to face me. He smiled before Hope and Cosmo ushered him into a corner. His eyes grew wide as they spoke. Then, I heard my name and turned away.

"Hey Lena, look." The round-faced guy with messy brown hair pointed. "It's Mavis. Hi!" He jogged over, dragging the slightly-built, mousy magus behind him.

"Hi, Arick." I grinned. "How's things?"

"Awesome! I'm playing out pretty much every weekend with Piercing Whispers. Why haven't we seen you at any gigs?"

"Oh, you know." I sighed. "Busy summer, starting high school. How about you, Lena?"

"Okay." She jerked a thumb at my satchel. "Nice."

"Thanks, I'm only borrowing that, though."

"Ahem. Introductions, please."

I turned to find Saya at my elbow, so I made them quickly. Mostly out of shock, but partly because Ramon beckoned.

"See you guys later." I waved at Cadence's friends. No. Mine, I realized. They'd been wondering where I was all that time, apparently. That made me feel bad, but imagined scenarios of impending doom took up too much of my head and heart space. I realized something. Ramon had no idea. Neither did Fiona or Wyatt. I gathered them together.

"Guys, we might have a problem."

"Yeah, I know." Wyatt jerked a thumb at Buttons. "Nobody brings Goldfarb to a field trip unless they expect trouble."

"So, the guidance counselor's a badass." Fiona nodded. "Bear or dragon shifter? Or maybe crocodile? I've heard you don't want to tangle with those."

I let them woolgather. They didn't need to know my mother wasn't the sort of dangerous brute force could handle.

"Neither," Wyatt said. "Cat."

"Like, a tiger?"

"Nope, like a tabby."

"It's your mom, isn't it?" Ramon asked. "The security problem?"

"Yeah, pretty sure. Sorry I didn't tell you."

"I figured." He sighed. "Don't worry. Dr. Aranha's no slouch either. Spider shifters are good at de-escalation. They just web the troublemaker."

"She'd be stupid to come in here." Wyatt bared his teeth. "I feel like chicken tonight."

"Gross." Fiona rolled her eyes.

"Hey, the group's moving on without you." Kiara waved from a doorway on the other side of the room. I saw the banner over her head with the exhibit's name—The Wonder of the Under.

"Come on, let's go."

In the exhibition hall, we found the same gloves we'd used in Lab. Cosmo practically sobbed when he saw them. The curator said we had to use them if we wanted the full benefit of the interactive display. Plus, that feature gave us an extra five points on our first Lab exam.

Everyone put them on. Students from all three schools milled around, testing the interactive displays and chattering excitedly. I headed toward my friends, who peered at a collection of yellowed twigs and leaves.

"Brownie molt!" Kiara clapped her hands. "I've never seen them before. Check out what happens when I use the glove."

I turned at a tug on my satchel strap but didn't see anyone. Horace must have pulled it, so I looked up.

Saya turned her nose up at the pair of magi I'd introduced her to and was in the process of striding toward another. I recognized him too, but as one she shouldn't talk to in such a forward manner even if he wore purple Hawthorn sweats under his blazer.

Xan Onassis was a poison magus. Also, some sort of minor nobility from overseas, though possibly disowned. He'd also fought Crow hand-to-hand without any powers on the cruise last year, preventing whatever disaster had embroiled my brother.

Saya probably shouldn't approach him, especially if there were any chance he'd seen her talking to me. I had no idea what motivated her to do it in the first place. Probably that mysterious mission nobody could tell me about. Still, she couldn't know how formidable Xan was. Somebody should warn her. Not me, but I was the only one who knew any better.

Fortunately, I had a friendly ghost even if I couldn't see him.

"Horace, tell Ed that Saya needs to back off. Now."

I felt a rush of air at my left, saw the puzzled expression on Kiara's face, and opened my mouth to explain. Plus apologize for not telling her there'd been a ghost in our room all month.

That's when I heard the commotion from the lobby.

"Mavis." Cosmo stepped between me and my roommate, his face an odd shade of green. "Help."

"Are you okay?" I touched his forehead. It was clammy, not feverish. "Don't tell me you tried to eat the science."

"Yeah." He shook his head. "But no." He pulled open one side of his trench coat, eyes cutting toward the door between us and the lobby.

Something gleamed there, faintly. His mouth opened and closed three times, like a fish. Finally, he managed to get something out.

"Do you wanna buy a letter F?"

"F?" I blinked.

"F is a failing grade. Who'd want that?" Kiara shook her head. "But seriously. We're worried about you, Cos. What happened?"

"Mavis. Yes or no?" He flapped the fabric like a bird with one wing. "Do you want it or not? Because you're—" He swallowed, grimacing. The sickly sweat at his brow intensified. "You—" He cleared his throat, but it still came out raspy. "Take it, you should."

"Is this some kind of prank?" I studied his face.

"No." He shook his head, then wiped his mouth with the back of his free hand. "Look. In here. Carefully." He flapped the coat again.

An object attached to the inside of the black broadcloth shimmered and glittered darkly, like a puddle of oil in sunlight with a pile of diamonds underneath. It was shiny and intriguing and shaped like my raven form's seventh pinion feather.

Something within it called to me.

Something inside me answered, setting all my nerves tingling.

The commotion from the lobby sharpened into the strident call of

Mom's voice. She was here, coming for me. Exactly as I'd feared. Guard Goldfarb dashed toward the slowly opening door. The Hawthorn headmaster blew a whistle. A purple dragonet dove after Goldfarb from the rafters, and Xan took off running after them.

Shit was about to hit the fan, and it was all my fault.

"Choose." Cosmo's voice came out stretched as though something strangled him. But nothing was around his neck. "Please." He rasped, swaying dizzily.

More light caught the object, revealing its shape—a feather, glowing and thrumming. I pointed at it with the enchanted glove, which told me the artifact was magical, extremely powerful, and utterly unknown.

I reached with my other hand, the bare one.

"No, Mavis!" Hope called from across the room. "Don't!"

It was too late. My fingertips had already brushed the feather's slick surface.

The feather hidden on the inside of Cosmo's coat began bonding with my hand, sending its power coursing through my body.

No matter how much force of will Captain Dunstable put into her command, there was no way to stop it.

I heard more than saw my mother burst through the door from the lobby, partly due to her small stature. Buttons and Xan blocked her slight frame from view.

It was also because of all the other people in the room—translucent ones. I hadn't seen them up until the moment I touched the feather.

Ghosts.

Most walked like the rest of us, but some floated, one even above my head. I recognized him instantly by his tri-corn hat and the shiny-buttoned red coat. I stared up at him, hardly able to believe my own eyes.

It was Rob, Ed's Colonial-era ghost friend.

"You've gone and done it now, Mavis." The ghost threw back his head and laughed uproariously. The sound and energy behind this expression of emotion were so strong that other ghosts joined in. But not the one to my left.

"It's not funny." Horace put his hands on his hips. His voice was as familiar to me as any of my classmates. That's how I knew who he was, though Ed hadn't given me a description.

I hadn't imagined him accurately. The cut of his suit was more modern than my mind's eye had made for him. The bowler hat and sepia tones weren't a surprise, but his full beard was.

"It's hilarious." Rob grinned. "Haven't you been listening to her all month, agonizing over an escape from her parental predicament?"

"She managed that already, brilliantly, I might add. Haven't you been paying attention?"

"Well, what about her desire to see ghosts? She got her wish. She didn't even have to almost die to do it. This is a good thing, Porous Horace. Won't Ed be happy?"

"I am no such thing." The medium himself stood before me, glaring up at his ghostly partner. "This all happened in the wrong order, with a broken ban. Who knows what kind of consequences we'll all face now? Yourself included Rob."

"Ed, I'm—"

"No apologies, Mavis." Ed shook his head. "This is on Cosmo's head, not yours."

I looked down, finding the guy in question on the floor. And in his lion form, unexpectedly. He'd have to shift back soon. The museum could press charges if this were a public event.

Cosmo was a tawny lion, complete with a mane. His old trench coat lay on the floor beside him. Probably enchanted.

Kiara grabbed the garment and threw it over him.

"Cos." She shook his shoulder. "You've got to change back. Dr. Aranha hasn't noticed yet. Come on. You don't want to be in this kind of trouble."

She must've seen someone pay the price for shifting at the wrong time before. A classic expression of alarm graced Kiara's face, genuine and intimate. In a family full of shifters, perhaps she'd worn it too often.

"Yeah, Cosmo. Come on, buddy." I held out my hand, stunned to see nothing in it. I was even more surprised at the sensation on my back, itching and stretching, something writhing over my shoulder blades.

Shifting had always come with its own set of small discomforts. But whatever happened that time hurt.

My eyes stung in response. The pain amped up, steadily increasing until it matched the road burn on my back the first time Mom hit me with the car.

It didn't stop there. I gasped, clutching my chest because I couldn't reach the spots on my back. They felt aflame now, like getting the belt but over bone.

Except this time, *she* hadn't done the number on me. *I* owned this anguish. In another moment, it'd envelop my world and own me.

"Fewmets! Shut her up!" Saya dashed to my side with her hand raised as if she wanted to slap me. Instead, she tried to cover my mouth.

Too late. I opened it, desperate to scream.

The tearing on my back was flesh. It ripped asunder, air blowing hair over my face as feathered wings danced at the edges of my vision.

Who was singing? Was I hearing things? Why wasn't I screaming? Because I couldn't.

Instead of that strident and stereotypical sound, something else poured forth from my throat. A sick, tangy smell wafted up from the floor.

No, I didn't vomit. That was poor Cosmo, right after he shifted back to human form. He wasn't naked like he should have been. The explanation for that was obvious. He wore one of the glass amulets, clearly filched from the lab cabinet.

The wordless melody I sang by rote was utterly and heartbreakingly beautiful, all in a minor key. I'd never made such fluid and musical sounds in my life. Not even while singing *When I Went Home* in the auditorium.

At my left, Ramon stood blinking, clearly shocked. Fiona took a step back. Brandon's mouth dropped open. But it didn't surprise everybody.

Across the room, Hope Dunstable wept, red-faced with racking sobs. Her eyes were out of focus, as though she'd stood in my shoes before. Still stood in them, couldn't take them off even if she wanted to.

I only remembered meeting my maternal grandmother in the

courtyard at the sanitarium a handful of times before she died. She'd been on a barge during the Boston Internment and watched Slayers take my uncle. The dementia meant she couldn't avoid triggering her PTSD flashbacks.

Mom set them off. So I knew them when I saw them.

Here was good old Captain Dunstable, having one of her own.

Her damage had something to do with this strange experience. Did that mean I'd end up like her?

By then, my mother had gotten past Buttons Goldfarb and Xan Onassis, which was a feat nobody in the room besides me expected. Most people underestimated Morgan Merlini, but her physical prowess was unstoppable. Now everyone in the room with me, ghosts included, knew that firsthand.

"Mavis Merlini, I'm withdrawing you from school. Move your things out of that dorm the moment we leave this building. You stay in the nest unless I give you direct permission to leave it. Do you understand me?"

I grinned, feeling a strange but unmistakable magical tingle through the rapidly fading pain on my back.

Faerie magic and wings. Like Hope in the hallway.

The corners of my mouth tilted up. I flapped the wings there, watching with pure satisfaction as my mother blinked and took a step back.

"It's probably not a good idea to ask me too many questions, Mom. I've got faerie powers. Somehow."

"You liar."

"She's not." Ed stepped between my mother and me. "Mavis is the Sirin now, for better or worse. Do you know what that is, ma'am?"

"I don't need an undersized medium telling me faerie lore." Her lip curled up in a sneer. "I probably know more about those three feathers than you do."

"Good." Ed nodded. "So you also understand what comes next."

His back was to me, so I couldn't see the expression on his face. But I knew a bluff call when I heard one.

Ed had no idea who he was messing with, though. No matter what magical mess I'd stepped in, my monster of a mother would exert any power she had over me, including harming my friends and allies.

"You're sixteen, Mavis. Still one year out from legal responsibility for your education. Sirin or not, the decision to withdraw you is mine alone."

"It's not."

"Who do you think you are?"

"I'm Guard Goldfarb." Buttons shrugged. "Only an administrator at Gallows Hill. But as it happens, Mavis won't qualify for home-schooling after this. She'll have to be enrolled somewhere with proper accommodations, according to protocol."

"How would you know?"

"Because we've already got the Alkonost at our school, staying in the same boardinghouse as your daughter, ma'am. We sent a letter home about that. Surely you've read that." Buttons glanced at Hope, who Saya now had her arm around.

I had no idea what an Alkonost was, but if it was anything like what I'd just become, no wonder the Providence kids hadn't wanted to talk about it.

"I'll just go down to town hall and have a little chat with the mayor then." My mother sniffed.

"I'm afraid that's by order of the Extrahuman Education Board." Buttons shook their head. "National."

"Magical shifters must attend approved schools," Ed chimed in. "Hope's dad researched extensively. Almost everyone on that side of her family is a lawyer."

Hope didn't speak up because she still struggled in the flashback's grip. I thought back to that overheard conversation in the library, the one between her and Saya. Had Hope mentioned something awful happening? Yes. Probably how she'd become the Alkonost. It must've been more traumatic than this day at the museum.

"Don't look now, but it's about to get more interesting," Horace said. "In the ancient Greek sort of sense."

Horace was right. I saw Principal Klein walking with the Hawthorn headmaster and the Messing director striding toward us.

"What's the meaning of this?" Principal Klein raised an eyebrow and looked down her nose at my mother. Which was easy, considering she had more than half a foot of height on Mom.

"I'm merely stating how my daughter doesn't belong at your school, *Ms.* Klein."

"Your opinion is misinformed, *Mrs.* Merlini." Principal Klein shook her head.

"Honestly, I'm surprised you aren't expelling her yourself." Mom waved a hand at my wings. "Absorbing a priceless artifact without permission. Aiding and abetting underage shifting in public." She tilted her head at Cosmo. "This boy was a lion a moment ago, in case you weren't aware."

"We pay the event rate, so this field trip is a private affair." The principal's grin glittered like ice. "One to which we didn't invite you, I might add."

"I'll leave when I'm assured my daughter's not endangering anybody. Including herself."

Horace stared at her with his mouth wide open.

"Gaslighters are horrid." Rob made a fist and aimed a ghostly haymaker at her. Which, of course, had no effect whatsoever on my corporeal mother.

A touch on my hand, light as a feather, made me glance to my right. Ramon stood beside me, the back of his hand brushing against mine. An offer of support I couldn't take without putting my boyfriend in danger.

When she couldn't control someone, the next best thing in life, according to Morgan Merlini, was controlling what everyone else thought of them.

If I didn't do something, she'd own this narrative and destroy the little life I'd tried carving out for myself outside her orbit.

I had no choice but to act. That's why I stepped forward, making a triangle between me, Mom, and Principal Klein.

"I'm fine, Mom." I tried on an impression of Cadence, tilting my head and batting my eyes in a simper I hoped wasn't too much of a caricature. "So are my new friends. I know I complained about starting high school. But I like it there, honest."

Three of the five adults in the room bought my act. The two who didn't know the truth already anyway. Still, having Headmaster Hawkins, Guard Goldfarb, and Messing's director on my side tipped the scales in Stephanie Klein's favor. The slowly growing warmth in her expression told me as much.

"Mavis's conduct at my school has been nothing short of admirable, and I expect that trend to continue. I believe it's in her best interest to remain at Gallows Hill, residing at the boarding house as her studies continue."

"I disagree." Mom narrowed her eyes. "She'll be more than you can handle before long."

"You'll have to bring that to the Extrahuman Education Board."

"You can count on that." My mother turned on her heel and stalked out of the exhibition room. I watched her go, knowing she meant every word she'd said.

"Later, Karen." Rob blew a raspberry after her.

"Mrs. Klein?" Kiara had her hand up, staring at the principal from where she knelt beside the still ill Cosmo. "I think he needs the nurse."

"Sid's on top of that already. Nurse Wilson's en route to the boarding house now."

"He'll need a faerie practitioner," Ed cautioned. "He's breached a ban."

"Don't worry. She's a goblin." Principal Klein maintained a mask of stoicism.

From my proximity, I knew better. She understood the entire scope of this situation and its specific gravity but refused to alarm the rest of her students over it.

"I'll get Hope and Saya." Ed lifted one foot, about to walk away.

"You'll do no such thing, Mr. Redford." Principal Klein shook her head. "Miss Knight, will you escort Mr. Gitano through the magic door?" She held up a key carved from what looked like black stone.

"Yes." Kiara took it without hesitation.

Sid Muscat joined Guard Goldfarb at Cosmo's side. Together, the adults supported him, following Kiara toward a door marked "Staff Only." She put the key in the lock and turned the handle.

It opened on the first-floor hallway in the boarding house, where a chalky-skinned woman in scrubs with long green hair waited. Guard Goldfarb let Kiara take their place supporting Cosmo and held the door. Once through, they kept their foot in it, leaving it slightly ajar.

"Excellent. I'll see the five of you in my office at the boardinghouse. Immediately after Nurse Wilson treats Cosmo."

"What about my school?" Ed asked. "I have to check back in with my teacher."

"Everything's arranged." The Messing director nodded. "As foretold."

"What's that supposed to mean?" I blinked.

"It's Messing. What do you expect?" Ed shrugged.

"Don't think you're off the hook with me, Mr. Redford," Principal Klein warned. "The four of you have an awful lot to answer for."

"Four?" I blinked. "Why do you want to see me then?"

"I believe you might have some missing pieces of this puzzle, Mavis. Don't worry. As I told your mother, you're in no trouble. I merely need more information. Miss Dunstable and Miss Harcourt, on the other hand, are another matter."

"What do I do with these?" Saya held up the museum-issue magipsychic gloves.

"Dr. Aranha will get them later, as well as Cosmo's. Come along now."

She walked to the door with Hope, Saya, and Ed following. I turned toward Ramon before I went.

"Sorry."

"See you later, I hope."

"Yeah, definitely." I patted my satchel, where I kept my phone. "Call me."

Guard Goldfarb had gone back to the class by the time I reached the door. Principal Klein held it for us as we filed inside one by one, Horace and Rob between Ed and me. After stepping through, she closed the door behind her, then locked it with the same key.

CHANCE FOR JOY

PART TWO

CHAPTER ONE

Nobody was really in trouble. I got the impression that Matron Klein only wanted the whole story from us. Which, at least, she knew I didn't have on my own.

In the relatively safe confines of her office, she got Hope's parents, Saya's mother, and Cosmo's brother on the phone. She tried Ed's, but nobody answered. Of course, Matron Klein didn't bother calling my mom.

Horace and Rob sat with Ed and me the entire time, Horace on an end table and Rob in the air. Of course, nobody else could see them besides us. Hope kept glancing in their general directions. I remembered what Ed had told me. She could see ghosts but not hear them.

I stayed quiet until directly questioned, a relative walk in the park compared to what I was used to. I'd grown up keeping my head down when adults asked incriminating questions.

Whether that was a deliberately cultivated trait born of self-preservation or one my mother hoped I'd naturally gravitate to while living in the nest, I might never know. Since I was somehow a faerie creature, it might serve me well in other situations.

"So what you're saying is, somehow a medium, a lion, and the Alkonost smuggled the Sirin's feather out of my vault without the security system alerting me or anyone else in the family." Hertha Harcourt sounded almost exactly like Saya. I imagined they looked similar as well.

"It wasn't them at all, Mother," Saya said. "That part was all me. It was too easy, actually. Don't you remember last summer?"

"Yes, you spent all that time with Kim, asking a million questions about cybersecurity. The poor girl had no idea you'd use her lessons to steal from me."

"Probably she did, though." Rob snorted. "Kimiko met Blaine while breaking into that vault, you know."

I locked down my poker face so I wouldn't burst out laughing. Nearby, Ed covered a suspiciously shallow cough.

"It wasn't stealing, Lady Harcourt," Hope insisted. "The queen gave me a quest. I couldn't tell anybody about it except my siblings."

"You have no siblings, child."

"Blaine says otherwise. That I'm like a second daughter to you and Ed and Cosmo like sons."

"What I don't understand is, why bring the boys into this at all?" Matron Klein raised an eyebrow.

"I volunteered," Ed informed her.

"I got a quest too," Cosmo said. "But from the king."

"Be silent!" Hope stood. "You're already sick enough."

"It's okay." Cosmo coughed. "I never broke his ban, only yours. The long-term effects might pop up for kicks, but all the short-term stuff's over."

"You'd better be right." Hope shook her head. "I mean, seriously, what were you thinking?"

"Took the easy way out, actually." Cosmo shrugged.

"By picking my pocket?" Saya blinked. "By going against the plan?"

"Matron Klein?"

"Yes, Cosmo?"

"If Mavis hadn't got that feather today, would you have let her mom withdraw her?"

"I'd have had little choice."

"So, that's why, Saya." Cosmo sighed. "I'm not apologizing because I did the right thing, and you all know it."

"How?" The voice on the phone sounded like a deeper version of Cosmo's. Even the snort matched. "And don't bother trying to lie. Olivia's listening."

"No need for the extrahuman lie detector, Tony." Cosmo chuckled. "The second I met Mavis, I knew she was the right person. Ed and I wanted to vote on abandoning the plan and offering her the feather. Hope vetoed that. If she hadn't, I wouldn't have had to step in."

"It was her decision to make, Cos." Ed sighed. "I'm not an equal partner in all this."

"He's right. I'm the one with the rank and fancy title." Hope nodded. "Abandoning my plan would have meant broken ban backlash for all of us. If you weren't a lion shifter, you'd be in intensive care. Are you saying I should have made a decision that harmful? Ed could have died."

"None of them will admit that Ed can handle himself." Rob glared at Hope. "I could have helped him soak that damage via possession. But nobody can hear me, and Ed's too proud speak up."

"Say something, Mavis," Horace urged.

I paraphrased Rob's lament, then made my admission for good measure.

"When it comes down to it, I'm the responsible party. I took the feather even though Hope said not to."

"And I'm the one who stole it for her in the first place," Cosmo added. "So can we get off Ed's case?"

"I don't need more shifters fighting my battles." Ed jerked his thumb at Hope and Saya. "Those two are more than enough."

"Edward Redford, if you insult my daughter again—" The anger in Hertha's voice was palpable.

"Sorry," Ed said.

"I figured it out." I sighed, leaning my elbow on Matron Klein's desk and resting my chin in my hand. "It's nobody's fault. Ed brought the feather to Messing. The first day didn't go well, so he kept trying on Tuesday. Then it was Hope's turn to find someone, and she chose upperclassmen at our school. But there are so many it took her Wednesday and Thursday. Saya was supposed to check the magi, right?" I glanced at her. She nodded. "So Cosmo would've gotten his turn tomorrow. Hawthorn Academy only has thirty students, who were all at the museum today. She would've gotten it done." I sighed. "I ended up hurting you all by pissing off my mother. Cosmo could have waited if she hadn't busted in there. I angered her over what? A couple of bags of clothes?"

"I'm not letting you take responsibility for that, Mavis," Matron Klein said. "Parents should provide for their children, and your mother did the opposite."

Beside me, Ed sniffed. Only a moment after, I did. I didn't dare glance over to see if he was also on the verge of tears. I wouldn't want to be caught out like that and figured Ed wouldn't either.

"It all turned out okay, though," Cosmo insisted. "Because I know Mavis is the right person. The one we were seeking the whole time. I still can't believe none of you guys saw it. Do you all have no faith or something?"

"Let's not start attacking each other, Mr. Gitano." Matron Klein shook her head. "It's past the point where that will do any good, for one thing. For the other, I've received word you'll need to work together for the time being."

"What's this about a time being?" Rob nudged Ed. He glanced up, grinning with his cheeks still wet.

"Technically, gnomes are time beings." Horace studied his fingernails. "But that's none of my business."

I grinned too. Having ghost friends was as cool as I'd imagined so far. Since nobody else could hear them, the tense conversation continued. At least Ed and I got a little respite.

"What? How?" Saya blinked. "I'll work with whomever I choose, thank you very much."

"I was afraid you'd say something like that." The voice coming through over the phone line was Mr. Dunstable's. "I've got an official summons here that says otherwise. I'm sorry, kids. It looks like you'll have to do more than just get along. According to the monarchs, you're a team now."

"No way." Hope glared at the phone. "You gave up your Sidhe mantle, Dad. There's no way you know more about this than I do. Working with Mavis is going to put us on hard mode in this town. So we can't. Her mother's horrible—"

My hands clamped down on the edge of my seat. I sat there convinced I was about to get judged and kicked out again.

"You can and you will." That alto voice was Hope's mother. "Take a good long look around that office. At your friends, the ones you consider family, Hope. We didn't raise you to treat people this way. Or quit when things get challenging."

Hope locked gazes with Cosmo and opened her mouth.

"I'm a lion. I can take it." He shrugged and jerked a thumb at Ed with one hand and patted my arm with the other. "Besides, I grew up not knowing the jerk, unlike them. But that guy there's your best friend forever, and you just met poor Mavis last week. Work it out with them, not me."

"Sorry." Hope sighed. "I owe you both. I still want to know how Dad heard about this before us."

"Your grandfather's still the king's admiral," Hope's dad said. "His Majesty expects an audience with the new Sirin at her earliest convenience. I'm sure Mavis can tell us when that is."

For a moment, I sat silent, not realizing he'd addressed me at first.

"Mavis." Horace waved one translucent hand in front of my face. "He's asking you something, in a roundabout way."

"Oh. Right. I'm sorry." I let out a nervous chuckle. "Um, I mean, I've got a bunch of homework, but as long as it doesn't take the entire weekend, I'm free. I'd kind of like to get out of town if it's all the same to you. Things have gotten a little hairy around here."

"Well, I like this Sirin," Tony said. "She's got humility, which the rest of you tend to lack. Ed excluded, of course."

"You see what I mean." Horace grinned. "You're going to be fine."

"Yeah, Horace." I nodded. "Maybe I am."

"She hears ghosts, too." Hope sighed. "Totally unfair."

"Your voice is a weapon, also unfair," I said. "Besides, you're a captain, with a ship and everything."

"Don't be surprised if you end up tithed." Hope narrowed her eyes. "Because the king wants to see you, and that happened with the queen when I got my feather. So good luck with that."

"You know we each have our own set of powers." The new lilting, feminine voice reminded me a little of Hope's father's. "Fair is relative."

"Yeah, Olivia. I know. But it feels limiting."

"That's by design," she said. "Trust the process, Hope. You too, Mavis."

"It'd be easier if I knew anything about the mystic birds."

"Don't worry. We'll take care of that." Hertha's voice made a crisp contrast with the others. "But after you meet with the monarchy. We'll have a better idea of time frames then."

"I'll need a time for his Majesty," Hope's father said. "He's waiting to hear from me."

"Thank goodness the monarchs are reunited," Tony said. "You've got no idea the danger we all went through. They didn't look concerned at all back then. This time, they seem...I dunno, troubled."

"That's an excellent point, Tony," Mrs. Harcourt said. "No need to make extra issues. Be decent to each other from now on, children. Or you'll answer to me."

Saya rolled her eyes while Hope pretended to snore. Cosmo hammed up his shrug. Ed covered his face with his palm. All appeared less disturbed by her declaration than me. Maybe I'd developed a phobia of mothers in general.

"My schedule's free, Mr. Dunstable." I cut to the chase, wishing I could go upstairs and change out of my torn shirt. "It's up to the rest of you. Maybe someone has a planner we can use to hammer out a schedule. Matron Klein, do our tablets work in the Under? As I said, I am getting behind on my homework, so bringing it might be a good idea."

"I'll ask his Majesty," Hope's father said.

"I appreciate it."

"I suggest we discuss that schedule so Mavis doesn't have to bring the tablet," the matron said. "The Under has many distractions, and she's there on business. However, she may need help to finish it expediently."

"I'm not much use, sorry." Ed sighed. "We're not studying the same things at all. Once we get on to history and stuff, let me know."

"I'll help," Saya said. "We've got loads of Green Equation questions to do, but I've got that down."

"Thanks, Saya."

Matron Klein didn't have a planner. Instead, she used her tablet to get our schedule sorted. It took her less than five minutes and resolved everything brilliantly. I'd work with Wyatt and Saya tonight to catch up on the pure faerie lecture and Green Equation practice problems. In the morning, I'd have time to work on my one-act play.

We'd leave on Saturday after lunch when homework was clear. Hopefully, I'd also have a little time to get my heart and mind in order before heading off to the Under to meet royalty. For what I thought was the first time in my life.

Much like several details concerning the Under, my mother had misinformed me about that.

CHAPTER TWO

"Why can't I find anything about the Sirin feather in this damn thing?" Wyatt smacked the side of his tablet.

"Would you cut that out?" I wagged my finger at him. "It's mine, and if it breaks, I can't finish my homework."

"Oops. Sorry, Mavis. Picked up the wrong one, I guess."

I didn't like how Wyatt cringed. It bothered me because scary was the opposite of who I wanted to be. Instead, there I was, stuck in the first-floor lounge intimidating a redcap to the point of flinching. Maybe I shouldn't have felt bad since he'd tried to bully me after all. My head and my heart couldn't agree.

After handing the tablet back, Wyatt sifted through the loose papers on the table until he uncovered his. Then, he entered the same search he'd done on mine, with the same results of course.

"Try a Boolean," I suggested.

"A what now?" He scratched his head.

"It's when you use keywords with and, or, not, quotation marks, or parentheses to make search engines spit out more relevant results. Put it in quotes, and you'll only get results with those two words together. Give it a try."

"Why are you helping me?" Wyatt slapped his hand over his mouth. "Crap."

"Just because you owe me something doesn't mean I have to call it in, I think." I shrugged. "I'm still fuzzy on how all of it works. I never expected to end up with faerie magic."

"I've already got some, but debt by questions won't be one of my issues until I tithe." Wyatt shook his head, sighing. "I should seriously know better. It's like being bad with faces or names, though. Once you've got something down about a person, it's kind of hard to change tracks midstream, you know?" His face fell. "I did it again."

"That one doesn't count, I could tell."

He raised an eyebrow instead of using words, but I understood what he wanted to know. How.

"I didn't feel a thing. Maybe because it's rhetorical or something."

"Thank God." Wyatt snorted. "Although I don't know what He has to do with any of it. The monarchs are kind of ambivalent to stuff like religion."

"Have you met them before? Either of them, I mean. I'm a bit nervous."

"Saw the king from far away once. That's about it. Most of the time, they don't get involved with changeling business, for most of us with lower-ranking family members. Until it comes to tithing. I'm not looking forward to that."

"The year and a day thing should sound like it sucks." I nodded.

"Yeah. I think I know now why Hope already has a rank and everything." He jerked his thumb at my shoulders, even though I'd put my wings away hours ago and hadn't unleashed them again since. "She's like you."

"Well, if I have to go live in the Under for a year, at least my mom can't bother me."

"That's another thing." He sighed. "Your mom sucks, and I had no idea. Sorry for ragging on you the first day."

"I bet you say that all the magic shifters." I waved my hand at him dismissively but with a jokey smirk on my face.

"No, really. My parents are strict, but nothing like that. After being at school with you for a week, I know she was talking trash. You don't seem like the rowdy type. I mean, you're in Drama Club. You talk like a book. And Ramon likes you."

I deflected with banter, wondering what Wyatt the would-be bully thought of our other classmates.

"So Ramon is the class trendsetter, I guess."

"Well, Brandon sure isn't. And Cosmo, no way."

"What about Jaxon?"

"He's too quiet. I can't figure out why."

"His sister's not."

"Yeah, Jillian's something."

"Don't you dare insult her."

"I wouldn't dream of it. She'd rip me in two. That is totally a compliment."

"Good."

"Was thinking of asking her out, but she's with Ed now."

"Don't you dare make that ship into a triangle."

"No way I'd harsh Ed's mellow, don't worry."

"Good."

"John says you were always tagging along after your brother. It was really Bar, wasn't it?"

"Yeah, that's right." I nodded.

"Had it bad, didn't you?"

"For a little while. Honestly, that's old news."

"He was the man, from what I heard. Salt of the earth kind of guy. Give you the shirt off his back."

"You're talking about him like he's dead, not in college."

"Well, it's sort of like they're on another planet when they go away, I think."

"You're not looking forward to your brother's impending college career. Or tithing, either, huh?"

"Bingo." He tapped his nose with his forefinger. "I see why that spooky kid likes you around."

"What, Ed?"

"Yeah, nobody gets him. But you. You get everyone."

"I don't think so."

"You had me pegged from the get-go."

"Lucky guess. On the other hand, I had no idea Ramon was asking me out."

"Maybe your brain just guesses right about other people most of the time. Like the way mundanes used to fake being psychic."

"Thanks for helping me study by the way, Wyatt."

"Nobody knows gnomes teeth and pixie toenails like me." He chuckled. "I get faerie stuff like you get people stuff. I'm still gonna try looking up all the Sirin, Alkonost, and Gamayun stuff. At the library. This tablet's useless for any of that."

"I heard they didn't even have books on it at the college. Ed says he was in there every day after school, looking it up. When it happened to Olivia, I mean."

"I wonder why."

"I was hoping she could resurrect Tony, of course." Ed strode into the room, two paper bags in his hands. "I got you both hamburgers. Hope you don't mind. You didn't show at dinner. This was the only thing I could grab before they cleared the plates."

"Hamburgers are cool." Wyatt nodded. " I hope both of those bags are mine."

"Oh, no way." My stomach rumbled.

"Just kidding. I won't force you to eat all those Power Bars."

"Oh, that reminds me." I got up, headed to the snack cart, and grabbed one. I set it beside the brown bag Ed had placed next to my tablet. "For Horace, later."

"Nice of you." Rob popped his head above Ed's, grinning. "Nobody's noticed a thing about good old Porous Horace for almost ten years."

"You're a jerk, Rob." Horace sailed past him, turning his head to glare over his shoulder at the colonial ghost. "Everyone's noticed that about you for centuries."

"Cut it out, guys." Ed shook his head. "Last thing we need is you bickering. Mavis needs to get her homework done. Leave her in peace."

"Ghosts?" Wyatt raised his eyebrow at Ed. "How many?"

"Just two," Ed answered. "But only one in a minute or so."

"You're not sticking around?"

"Nah." Ed shook his head. "I've got nothing to add to your faerie studies. The only thing I know about are Grims, and that's because the mean girl happens to summon one."

"Donna's still making problems?" I raised my eyebrow.

"Nothing I can't handle since Allen and Diego defected. But thanks for asking."

"Donna? Wyatt blinked. "The summoner?"

Ed nodded.

"John says if I see her in town, steer clear. Sounds like he had a good reason."

"Yeah, she's nothing nice." Ed shrugged. "I've met one exception. But apparently, antisocial behavior is common with summoners."

"Well, folks say the same thing about mediums." Wyatt shook his head. "So far, only one of those generalities seems to be true."

We stared at Wyatt. Rob and Horace blinked at him right along with Ed and me. They didn't care that the redcap couldn't see them.

"Just because I'm a jock, I can't have a big vocabulary?" He hung his head. "Dammit."

"No, you're good," I assured him. "No magic goosebumps."

"That was a general to the room question, and it applied to four people." Ed indicated Horace and Rob. "Since I told you they were here."

"It seems like there's a pattern." I sighed. "It doesn't make sense to me yet, though. These rules might take more study than my actual homework."

"You'll get the hang of it, don't worry," Ed said. "Just try not to speak until spoken to tomorrow afternoon with his Majesty. It should go smoothly, I think."

"Thanks for the vote of confidence, Ed. But I think it runs counter to my typical luck."

"Do I have to kick you in the shin for insulting yourself again?" Ed grinned. "Yes, I know I asked you a question. One is safe."

"See, that takes balls, man." Wyatt laughed. "Better listen to him, Mavis."

"Okay, okay." I shrugged. "I'll stop putting myself down if you stop asking me questions. Go do your homework, Ed. The king wants to see you too."

"Easy-peasy. See you later." Ed waved as he walked out of the room.

I spent the next hour eating hamburgers and the Power Bar while Wyatt pointed out ways to tell different pure faerie castoffs apart. It wasn't anything I couldn't have looked up on my own. But if I wanted to get caught up, having somebody to verify my educated guesses helped. Studying with other people helped me stay focused instead of falling through off-topic rabbit holes or having brain death spirals about Mom.

Before he left, I thanked him and stayed in the room. It took only a few minutes to tidy up after my meal. Horace thanked me for choking that Power Bar down. I stretched, then got a cup of tea. By the time Saya showed up, I was back at the table, flipping through a list of ancient dragon customs instead of reviewing my notes on large shifters.

"Let's get on with it already." She sighed.

"I'm already comfy with the Green Equation about displacement so it won't take long."

"Good." She woke up her tablet, then opened a file and flipped through a few pages. Once she found the one she was looking for, Saya turned it to show me an illustration.

"This is how my mother explained it to me."

She showed me a dragon diagram, the vast bulk of it contained within the space between the mundane realm and the Under. Only a section the size of the dragon's right foreleg remained outside. It looked humanoid.

"Is this why dragons are stronger than mundanes, magi, or psychics when they're in human form?" I asked. "Because they can decide how brawny they want to be when shifting?"

"That's part of it." Saya nodded. "The other piece of the puzzle is that we can choose what parts to bring. That's how we can have our wings out or scales over our bodies. After reaching full maturity, we can even use our breath weapon to a small extent. Blaine hasn't quite gotten that part down, so of course, I'm not there yet."

"I thought he was already married, though?"

"That's right. But it takes a while for us to reach full maturity in dragon form, a bit longer than our human forms."

"You don't have to answer if you don't want to, but I was wondering about the egg-bearing thing since you're not at full dragon maturity. Couldn't you put off deciding who to marry?"

I hoped Saya would have a chance to keep growing up for a while. It seemed absurd to me, seeking a husband when she couldn't even start laying eggs immediately after high school.

"We've been worrying about it since I hatched, actually. Mother's got a list a mile long, names of families to research, mostly. We've got to be very careful with genetics."

"So it's a big process then."

"Exactly. I'm able to lay eggs now, but my doctor would rather I not start until I'm about Blaine's age. Mother thinks he's playing it too safe, and I hope she's right."

"Hope what now? Did you need anything?" She stuck her head in the door and peered at Saya.

"No, we weren't talking about proper noun Hope." Saya grinned. "Just the conceptual kind."

"Okay." Hope shrugged. "Let me know if you do. I'm around."

"Thanks," Saya replied brightly. Then, she leaned close and lowered her voice. "I hatched prematurely. Hope saved my life."

"Oh. I had no idea." I winced. "I'm sorry."

"Nothing to be sorry for, just a fact of my life. One of the better ones, to be fair."

"Okay."

"As I was saying, we hope I can start laying eggs sooner rather than later. But it's no guarantee because of a little hiccup."

"What kind of hiccup?"

"To save me, Hope made a deal. Not with a faerie, but someone the queen has imprisoned. A different sort of creature. Let's just say I am both less and more advanced than my brother was at this age."

"That sounds unusual." Curiosity burned through my brain. "How'd it happen?"

"It's not my story to tell. So I'll say no more on this particular subject.

"Whose?"

"I'm not under a ban, but there are some promises I refuse to break. Dragon's honor."

"Okay." I nodded. "So, let's get back to shifting. Is there a limit on what you can bring with you in human form?"

"We have a bit more control than you smaller types when it comes to shifting. But yes, we're limited. Scales are denser than skin, so we bring thinner versions with less color. Wings are easiest because they weigh less."

"That makes sense." I nodded. "I don't get to pick and choose in human form. But when I change into a raven, everything gets squeezed out, and I have to pick things based on bird biology and physics. Heavy birds can't fly, after all. My oldest sister does this creepy thing with her eye color. It scares all the kids on Halloween."

"Exactly. Cosmo's brother also changes the color and texture of his fur. But he has to keep the other things so he can still function, and he loses bulk and strength."

"Aren't lions about the same size as some humans?"

"Tony's a cat. Felis catus, as in a house cat."

"Wow. I would never have guessed."

"Even after all those articles you read in the paper?"

"Yeah, awkward." I let out a nervous chuckle. "It just said cat. So I assumed—"

"Assume nothing about the four of us or our family members. An open mind will serve you better, especially in the Under."

"I'll keep that in mind, Saya. Thanks."

She stared, silent, face inscrutable.

"I said thank you." I blinked. "Was that the wrong thing to do?"

"I'm not used to it." She pressed her lips into a thin line. "I'm not entirely sure why."

"I have a hard time getting my brain around why people treat me the way they do, too. Maybe it's something to do with your family."

"No, it's likely my attitude." She sighed.

"You mean your confidence."

"No wonder my younger brothers advocated so heavily for you." She sniffed. "You're unexpectedly easy to talk to. In our odd little family, that's rare."

Family. She'd meant Hope, Cosmo, and Ed. Growing up with them, knowing she'd have to mate with or marry whoever her mother told her to, of course, she wanted their places in her heart to remain fraternal.

"Hey, I've got something to say." I gave her a big dopey smile and elbowed her. "Thanks. Thankity thank thanks!"

She surprised me by laughing. In short order, Saya returned to the topic of large shifters and how they managed the composition of their smaller forms. I might have been envious before when my abilities were less complicated.

We were uninterrupted by any offers of help from Hope or our other classmates. My hour with her was over all too soon.

"It's almost lights out. Time to abandon the lounge." I gathered up my things, checking my phone without unlocking it.

"What's the problem?"

"No message from Ramon."

"Maybe he figured you'd be busy."

"I'm not sure." I sighed, then told her about not holding his hand back at the museum.

"Hmm." She raised an eyebrow. "I'm no romance expert, but considering how he helped you get your stuff back, something like that shouldn't flap him."

"I hope you're right." I nodded. "My gut says there's a problem."

"Follow it then, perhaps." Saya tucked her tablet into her handbag. "I likely won't see much of you tomorrow afternoon as Hope and I visit the queen. But best of luck to you in all your pursuits."

"Thanks, Saya."

We headed up the stairs together in companionable silence. In my room, I found Kiara reading. Not from a paperback or her tablet. A spiral notebook.

"Is that your one-act play?"

"Yeah, it is." Kiara smiled. "Are you ready to start going over yours tomorrow morning?"

"I would be if I had a draft."

"Don't worry. We can do that instead."

"Thanks, Kiara. I appreciate it."

"I'm going to go brush my teeth. Come with?"

We headed into the bathroom together after gathering our things. Kiara stayed to have a shower while I opted to wait until the next morning.

Finally alone, I got cozy in my bed where I finished reading *Stranger in a Strange Land.* I'd known the story could only end in disaster for Michael Smith, so I didn't expect a happy ending.

I predicted the show he'd made of his death. I hadn't imagined the depth of Jubal's guilt. Or that tag-end, where he replaced Foster.

The implications, hints, and widening impact of the story chased each other around my brain as I fell asleep.

CHAPTER THREE

I didn't write an entire play on Saturday morning, of course. Though I rose early, as I had the last few days of school, I used that time to take an extra long shower and even more on finding a top that would work. In the Under, my wings might decide to put in a surprise appearance.

I wondered how Hope handled that inconvenience. Besides her and Olivia, only dragon shifters could wing out. That made clothes to accommodate extra shoulder anatomy rare and therefore an issue. I'd never seen any available off the rack at clothing stores.

Probably, her lawyer dad had enough money for tailoring. Saya's blood was even richer than that. Maybe the Harcourts had a family designer who made everything in their closets.

It finally made sense now why shifters in that social strata had come here. That quest was serious business. The one that awaited me either matched or surpassed it. If only I had resources like the rest of them.

Everything I'd managed to steal back from the nest would get torn to shreds on the back like my dearly departed favorite shirt. In the end, I did laundry and ended up wearing the dress from the sanitarium. Yes, the decades-old throwback I'd tucked into jeans.

Perhaps faerie monarchs weren't up with the latest mundane fashions anyway. Since it was a dress, it felt more formal than the gray plaid pants I selected earlier. Thanks to Horace, my wardrobe had expanded enough to wear it with something that still gave coverage.

My drawer contained a decent pair of tights, which weren't quite as opaque as I wanted with a minidress. I put a slightly longer skirt in a darker gray under the short, frilly hemline. It gave my outfit a gradient effect, which I liked.

The spaghetti straps meant wearing a slightly pinchy strapless bra. But that and the dress left my shoulder blades free—plenty of room for wings to pop out without any fabric tearing. The last thing I wanted was a wardrobe malfunction in front of the faerie royalty.

If only I had one of those glamour bracelets from the auditorium. Maybe I could ask Mr. Hickson to borrow one next time. Still, for all I knew, things like that didn't work in the Under.

Kiara waited in the lounge, where she sat with two lattes and a pair of scones from the Witch's Brew on Essex Street. I thanked her profusely. Their coffee was amazing, but I hadn't dared show my face in there after the night of the displeasure cruise.

There was no way to make a complete draft before breakfast, but our efforts weren't fruitless. With her help, I managed to write a full outline with a beginning, middle, and end and a list of dramatis personae. It was about a princess in a tower who'd lost all her hair. Kiara was excited at the prospect of us exchanging drafts in the future.

"We can do it like a table read. It'll be fun!"

"Yeah, that sounds like a blast." I nodded. "Thanks for all your help."

"You're welcome. I'm just so happy you're not getting withdrawn. It'd be lonely without you here to geek out over books and plays."

"Ditto." I smiled back.

We hugged, and I said I'd see her later.

In the dining room, I was surprised to find food on the table still. I had intended to beg leftover breakfast scraps from Matron Klein or Sid or whoever was in the kitchen. Instead, it seemed brunch was a thing in the boarding house on Saturdays.

Instead of food appearing on each round table, it was on the sideboard along the back of the room, buffet-style. I toasted a bagel, grabbed some fruit, and took a few packs of peanut butter. Once equipped, I sat with them and started slathering half the bagel with nutty protein.

"You must be nervous." Cosmo sat beside me. "I am."

"Well, you should be." I put jelly on top of the peanut butter. "You broke a ban after all. Even if it wasn't the king's."

"Yeah, I expect some form of punishment." He grinned. "It was worth it."

"How do you figure?"

"Like I said to Matron Klein yesterday. I don't think you could've waited for today if I hadn't. Unless you wanted a lion jumping up through your window early this morning." He shrugged. "Because that's what I would've done when Saya didn't find any of those Hawthorn magi eligible."

"Eligible how?" I blinked. "I thought it was something weird, like the feather picking someone."

"Nah. There are rules but nothing as wonky as that. The hardest part though is finding someone who was born in the Under."

"I wasn't born in the Under." I blinked.

"Ed says you left that a little shaky with him." Cosmo smirked.

"That's because I don't know for sure where it happened. Only that Crow says the certificate was wrong. I wasn't born in Salem Hospital."

"Well, you were Under-born, or it wouldn't have worked." He chuckled. "So tell your brother he was right."

"The next moment I see him, he'll hear about it."

"I hope it helps him get better, knowing he was right."

"He'd be the first one to say it'll take time and work. I'm worried about you, Cosmo. You already got sick. I hope you don't get punished on top of all that."

"Whatever happens to me, I'd do it a million times again so you're out of that house." He shuddered. "Freedom from a place like that is important."

"You shouldn't trivialize such an enormous risk, Cos." Saya sat beside him, a plate of lox, eggs, and onions in front of her.

"Where'd you get that? I want some!" Cosmo stood so fast he almost toppled his chair.

"You're getting off the subject. You ought to exhibit more contrition when you meet with his majesty."

"Oh, I know." Cosmo nodded. "That's why I'm getting all the trivialwhatsis out of my system now. So where do I get some eggs?"

"The grill window." She inclined her head toward the far corner of the room.

I'd seen the window before but hadn't wanted to be a bother. I wasn't all that hungry after the scones earlier anyway. Bread and fruit felt like the best choice for an anxious stomach.

That didn't stop Cosmo Gitano. Maybe he needed extra calories after all the shifting and sickness the day before. Whatever it was made him saunter up toward that window and order at least seven items. I wasn't sure exactly what from that distance.

"He's acting like it's his last meal or something." I shook my head. "Why, Saya?"

"Don't worry. It won't be."

"How do you know?"

"The king will be happy you've got the feather, even if Cosmo broke the rules in the process. That's part and parcel of Unseelie magic."

"What about you? Aren't you mad at Cos?"

"Honestly, I was hoping it wasn't one of those boring magi." She took a bite of her meal.

"Really?" I blinked. "No offense, but I thought you were against me as a matter of course."

"None taken. I wasn't *against* you, per se. Mostly, Hope and I originally wished for someone older than us, with more faerie experience than you've got."

"Upperclassmen here are so busy though. Plus, there aren't many at Hawthorn to begin with."

"Once the reality set in, we might have considered changing

course." She sighed. "That wasn't possible with a ban in place. Messing doesn't do much in the way of faerie education. And every magus at Hawthorn Academy has a familiar. Let's just say, it might have been difficult to carry out the Sirin's duties while burdened with another living being to care for."

"Time was, I looked up to the magi with critters. It's a lot of responsibility and builds empathy." I pushed cantaloupe around on my plate.

"Perhaps such skills would've dovetailed with your new duties. That's all moot speculation at this point."

"What if there was one? A magus born in the Under, who fit the bill. Did Cosmo rob that person of a chance?"

"It doesn't matter if he did. Besides, their campus between worlds makes mediumship nigh impossible.

"Yeah, I'm still unclear on how I'm supposed to learn that."

"The king likely has a plan in mind. You'll certainly know more after meeting him."

"You're more upset because Cosmo got hurt, then. Not angry I didn't come by the feather properly?"

"I'm not bound to doing things by the book. Just as long as they get done."

"So you're an 'ends justify the means' sort of gal."

"Not entirely. But for matters of this much importance, yes. It makes for an interesting dynamic, considering Hope's Seelie."

"Philosophical discussions for breakfast?" Ed grinned from over Saya's shoulder.

"Eat something, Edward. You're practically a skeleton, for Tiamat's sake. I swear you've lost five entire pounds since we got here. Your body needs food if you ever want that growth spurt."

"Oh. Right. I'll go do that." He hurried toward Cosmo at the window.

"Maybe that was a little harsh, Saya."

"He needs it. Ed gets too caught up with ghostly matters. He'll waste away to nothing if we don't remind him he's corporeal."

"I get what you're saying."

I didn't really. I'd made an awful lot of progress, getting Saya to talk about anything at all, let alone stuff that bothered her. Throwing all that under the bus seemed like a waste. Working with the kids from Providence was a fact of life now. I couldn't afford to alienate any of them.

So instead of protesting, I sat and ate the entire bagel and all my fruit. Classmates came and went, along with a steady stream of upperclassmen, some of whom got their meals to go. Apparently, Bishop's Row practice on Saturday mornings was a thing.

At eleven-thirty, Matron Klein beckoned to us from the doorway. We discarded our dirty plates and followed her into the hall. Near the stairs was a door we'd never seen open. She held it for us, and we descended another set of stairs, all made of stone but not polished marble like the ones upstairs.

Instead, it was granite, worn in places but never polished or even given a finish. The entire stairwell and corridor at the bottom of it were similarly unfinished. The rough-hewn stone had a rustic look, reminding me of Crow's cabin at the sanitarium.

I missed him, but we'd agreed I shouldn't go to see him every day. Next time I visited, there'd be loads to tell him. I wondered for a moment what he'd make of it all. I derailed that train of thought. I didn't have enough specifics to finish that line.

One glance over at Hope told me maybe all the specifics were impossible to get even with a lifetime of living as a faerie shifter. Perhaps nobody had all the answers. That bothered a curious gal like me because a teenage faerie was one thing.

The monarchs were practically gods.

The queen had Hope on a quest, one so important that the most influential dragon in the world and a handful of heroes who'd unified the faerie kingdoms bent over backward to send their youngest relatives to Salem.

I'd done some digging. Troutbook Academy was right there in Rhode Island. It was prestigious, older than dirt, and a private school. Both of Hope's parents, Ed's mom and brother, and Saya's Ph.D. candidate older brother were alumni there.

Hope, Saya, Cosmo, and Ed were here at Gallows Hill, a charter school that might have closed if Hertha Harcourt hadn't made a donation enormous enough to have this boarding house named after her.

But wait, there's more.

The king had enlisted Cosmo on a quest behind everyone's back. Clearly, even the monarchs didn't have everything figured out. For better or worse, this adventure was only beginning. If someone taking up the Sirin's feather was important enough for redundant capital Q quests, something big was coming. I'd be in the middle of it with them.

At the end of the hall, one level directly below the door that led to the school from the boardinghouse on weekdays stood a gray stone archway. It was bricked over in red, the hastily applied mortar reminding me of the old Poe story with the drunkard behind the wall.

That spooky idea vanished when Matron Klein held her watch to it. The stone of the archway lightened, then began to glow with an inner light. Soon the bricks over its middle shimmered like a heat mirage.

With a brief flash of light, they faded to transparency. No old bones or empty casks met my gaze. Instead, it was the Under on the other side. Sid stepped past me a moment later, put his hand on the arch, and held it open. Impossibly, a dhampyr had opened it. Another curiosity I didn't have time to investigate.

Hope strode directly through like it was any other doorway. She might've been going to Lecture for all the concern she displayed. Saya pulled a necklace from her handbag, then slipped it over her head. It was a bauble, similar to the one we wore in Lab but set in a wire cage. Once it settled, she walked through.

On the other side, she retained her human shape. Saya looked back, raising her eyebrow at the rest of us. Hope kept walking. I saw her brightly colored wings folded over her back. At least I had some idea what to expect before venturing forth. I hesitated too long.

Cosmo glanced at Ed and me, held his nose, and winked.

"Last one in's a rotten egg." He dashed through, shifting into his lion form as he crossed the barrier between worlds. He shook his mane, which looked in much better shape than at the museum the day before. Of course, he wasn't vomiting all over it, which made an enormous difference.

Ed lingered, but not because of nerves.

"Guess I'll see you later, Rob."

"Yeah, kid. Tell Kasa I said hi." The ghost blew a raspberry. "Not."

"I won't tell her, then." Ed chuckled. He didn't saunter like Hope or walk with confidence like Saya. Still, he headed through the portal as if he'd done it a million times. Maybe he had.

"I guess I'll see you later too, Horace." I looked up at my ghostly friend.

"Yeah. If you happen to see a dreamy lady ghost with purple hair, about yea high." He held his hand a little bit above my head.

"Bianca." I nodded. "Yes, I'll tell her you miss her immensely. Anything else I should know?"

"I wish I could tell you." Horace shrugged. "But I hadn't been to the Under when I was still corporeal. Now I'll never get to go. That's how it is."

"But why, though?"

"Nobody knows, ladybird," Rob answered. "But you should head in. Sid Vicious here can't hold the door open forever."

"Thanks, Sid."

"You're welcome?" He blinked.

"I figure it's a good habit to be in. Thanking people."

"Okay." He nodded, smirking. "Looks good on you. Have fun."

I stepped through, utterly unprepared for what was in store.

CHAPTER FOUR

Yes, my wings came out when we crossed. Hope's did too, so it wasn't awkward. She grinned at them, then nodded at me. I copied her and got myself dazzled in the process. They were gorgeous.

Looking at her Alkonost wings was like staring at a stained glass window with the sun shining directly through it. I'd take tiny jealousy over awkwardness any day. Or having to be in animal form like Cosmo. His capering across the sand was a clear indication he didn't mind that, though.

Under my feet was the biggest stretch of beach I'd seen in my life. That's saying something since I grew up on the coast.

I was wrong about the shore's size relative to the ocean it bordered that day. I had some inkling that my sense of scope was off. I just didn't know by how much.

That's all part of what we all learned for certain later. Here's a hint: it put the Atlantic and Pacific combined to shame. My companions didn't even comprehend its total scope, and they'd lived part-time in it. None of us would, not for a while.

One thing was clear immediately. The sand to the east on my right brightened to off-white. On my left to the west in the opposite direction, it deepened inkily.

We straddled the divide between each monarchy's domain. Although the king and queen had reunited as allies and spouses recently, the nature of faerie meant they still ruled separately yet as peers.

Where the water met the sand stood two dinghies, one painted gold and white, and the other green and indigo. Beside them stood similar figures, both with diaphanous wings, slender and longer in the limb than mundane realm denizens.

In coloring, dress, and comportment, the two were opposites. I sensed a theme there, of course—Seelie and Unseelie.

The Seelie had gleaming butterfly wings, clearly a naval uniform yet as varied in color as Hope's wings. They stepped out of the dinghy, put one hand over their heart, and bowed from the waist before speaking.

"Captain Dunstable, I give you greeting."

"Hail, boatswain." Hope smiled. "I appreciate your offer of conveyance, good sprite. I have one companion, Miss Saya Harcourt."

"As expected, captain." The boatswain nodded. "Step forward. The lieutenant will greet you aboard."

"A thousand thanks." Hope stepped into the dinghy, then turned and reached out to Saya. She took it lightly, reminding me for some reason of a young woman invited to dance. Of course, she did no such thing after stepping aboard. I thought the boat would have tipped.

Apparently not because Saya managed a deep curtsey to Hope and a half-bow to the sprite in the tiny space. After that, she sat on the bench in the middle of the boat. As the boatswain pushed the small craft into the water, Hope turned, waving at the three of us still ashore.

"See you later!" she called.

Ed, Cosmo, and I waved, saying nothing. I was about to ask Ed what all that was about but didn't get a chance.

"Ahoy, Redford the Youngest." The Unseelie boatswain had shadowy wings, but they stole light instead of catching it. Instead of a uniform, they wore rugged yet lightweight clothes.

"Hey." He nodded. "I'm here with Gitano the Younger and the Sirin. This is Mavis. She's new."

"Hi." I held my hand up and wiggled my fingers.

"Yo, old shade!" Cosmo brushed past us, doing the complicated handshake he'd subjected me to the first day of school.

"Yo yourself, mane man." The shade chuckled.

"This is different," I murmured to Ed. "From how it went with Hope, I mean. All those manners."

"The Navy's like that." He grinned. "This is the Fleet, and yeah. It's different but in a good way." He walked toward the boat.

I stood there, wondering where we'd end up. I could see Hope's dinghy approaching a tall golden ship, but whatever craft the king had sent, I couldn't see it on the water.

"Yo!" The shade stood by the dinghy, waving.

"Yeah, I said hi." I blinked but waved back.

"I know you're new, but have sense and get in already."

"Oh. Right. Sorry about that."

I got in, which was harder than Saya made it look. My wings stretched and flapped behind me, helping with my otherwise uneasy balance. Once seated with Ed beside me, the shade pushed the small boat out. It moved on its own with no rowing toward what looked like an oily spot on the water.

It turned out to be a shadow, which belonged to the ship I hadn't been able to see until a rope dropped over its side made contact with the dinghy. The shade tugged it, and the boat levitated until it rested in a cradle attached to the side of the ship.

An elderly yet still hale and hearty man in similar garb to the shade's but more accessorized strode toward us.

"Youngest Redford, Young Gitano, welcome aboard."

The man turned to me. He had a bushy white beard laced through with red here and there. Those streaks matched the hair on Hope's head almost exactly. What I could see of his face was weathered and crinkled. The lines implied a life of mirth and good nature for the most part.

I couldn't help but stare at his tusks. I knew a few troll changelings and their family members, but they took great pains to hide those attributes with glamour in public, even in a town as supernatural as Salem. Too many mundanes, even so long after the Reveal, found a troll's natural appearance frightful. Ogres were the only others who went to greater lengths in the camouflage department.

"Ahoy, Young Sirin, and well met." The man smiled, his eyes sparkling. "Not long ago, I conveyed the Gamayun herself across these waters to his majesty's lodge. It is my privilege to do the same honor for you."

Then he gave me a flourishing bow, including the removal of his plumed hat.

"That seems a bit much." I let out a nervous titter. "I'm not a big deal."

"Mayhap you weren't once upon a time. That's not true now."

"I can't imagine how that's possible."

"His Majesty's waited long and long for someone to take up the feather you now possess," the troll said. "Come, I'll make that knavish lion show you to the galley below for refreshment."

"I'd rather stay out here if it's all the same to you." I swallowed against an unfortunate rise of bile. "I tend to get a little seasick."

"Ah, another airborne landlubber, I see." He chuckled. "Much like Miss Olivia. We'll find you a tonic for this voyage. Perhaps an amulet for future journeys. You ought to get used to seafaring."

"You seem to know who I am. But I've never heard you mentioned before. Or recall an introduction, good sir." It felt all too easy, using the Under's odd speech patterns. Familiar, almost. And absolutely natural.

"I'm Admiral Tolland. Captain Dunstable's maternal grandfather. Also known as the scalawag responsible for the King's Fleet."

"Another name for a Navy, I suppose."

"Nay, young Sirin." He shook his head. "We're a Fleet, not a Navy. His Majesty would have it no other way. And I'd be reluctant to serve in such an outfit. We're pirates, one and all."

"Hope was a pirate here as a kid before we were friends." Ed grinned. "We met right in the middle of her career change."

"Aye, you'll have to tell Miss Mavis the story one of these nights," the admiral said. "You'll have lots of time, after all."

"We've got school on top of our duties here, sir. Homework, tests, lab." I sighed. "I'm not sure we'll have time for that much chatter along with voyaging."

"You'll make time."

I didn't like the sound of that. But I didn't dare protest any more than I already had. Not with Ed shaking his head and putting his finger over his lips behind the admiral.

I'd agreed to keep quiet on this visit, but that wasn't exactly in my nature. The admiral, despite his size and bluster, seemed more chummy than anything else. If the king wasn't intimidating, I might have trouble keeping my trap shut.

I managed on board, mostly because the shade brought me lozenges instead of a tonic. They were like one of those enormous jawbreakers purchased with tickets down at Salem Willows. They tasted of mint, honey, and lemon and prohibited conversation handily.

The voyage wasn't long, thank goodness. Night fell as we sailed, which was a strange thing considering our time on board was shorter than Lecture. I knew because I checked my watch, one of those wind-up affairs instead of a digital timepiece. At least I knew for sure it worked in the Under.

My phone was another matter entirely. It resembled a shiny glass brick and only functioned as a mirror. I hastily put it away because I looked like a hamster with the lozenges stuffing my cheeks.

The boat docked and we disembarked, heading up along the pier. A carriage waited, the roofed sort with a driver up top and doors on the side. Instead of horses, lions, tigers, and bears drew it. Cosmo headed toward an empty spot and let the shade attendants harness him in.

"After you." Ed gestured at the carriage's open door.

"Thanks," I managed around the lozenges, which thankfully were much smaller.

I stepped inside to find it small but cushioned thickly in a cozy way. With only one seat on either side, Ed and I faced each other. Our knees bumped a few times during the ride, but not hard enough to bruise. Neither of us minded.

"Why haven't I seen a ghost here yet?"

"If it's anything like the last time I visited the king, they're all waiting at the hunting lodge. They have more fun up there."

"I can't imagine ghosts having fun in the Under. Isn't a major part of this whole realm being your truest self? Ghosts can already do that, I thought."

"That's right, but the ghosts are kind of stuck. I'm not sure if Horace mentioned anything after we talked about Bianca that one night. But she's not alone. None of them can leave the Under if they died here. The reverse is also true."

"No, we didn't talk about it. We should. It's so tragic."

"It is for every ghost I've met here. Which is why the king—" He sighed, but with a smile. "Well, you'll see when we get there."

"How long do you think this will take?" I peered at my watch again. "I still have homework."

"I understand. Time's weird between the realms. Inconsistent. I don't think you'll have a problem. Usually more passes here than there. Having twenty-six hours every day is part of it."

"It can be thirteen o'clock then?" I snickered.

"It's not that funny." He wrinkled his nose. "Okay, maybe it is but try to remember that's not an auspicious hour. It's associated with ultimatums."

"That's good to know." I swallowed the last of the lozenges. "Oh. Does that mean the admiral was right? I'll be on a boat for a long time."

"Probably, sorry. But we'll be on Hope's ship, *The Odyssey*. It's got motion magic, cuts down on seasickness. We can stock up on Dramamine anyway, though. Just in case."

"You sound like you've done this before."

"Too many times." Ed sighed. "Part and parcel with having an actual captain for a best friend."

"Exactly how long ago did you meet her, anyway?"

"It feels like forever."

"Listen, I was fine with the whole evasive game before. Since I'm all mixed up in this now, a little less obfuscation would be nice, you know?"

"I get it. I really do." Ed sighed. "The best I can say is something happened to them. An ordeal I wasn't forced to endure. It's not my story to tell. It's up to each of them."

I wondered if this had anything to do with what Saya said the night before about her age and development as a dragon. Probably, it did. It made sense when I considered the articles about some of my new friends in that search.

None of them mentioned Cosmo and Saya at all. All the years for certain events didn't match up with their ages. Only Ed's chronology aligned, which he'd come out and said.

Maybe the Under's time instability had something to do with that. Or maybe not, since Saya mentioned a creature, someone imprisoned here. I pulled the notebook out of my satchel and wrote myself a note.

"Don't tell me you're doing school stuff in here." Ed blinked.

"No, it's Sirin business. Just making sure I don't space and lose track of everything. It seems complicated already."

"Makes sense. It's a good idea, one I should borrow for myself."

"Yep, I'm a bona fide genius. Too bad I haven't got the looks to go along with it."

"Oh, come on." Ed rolled his eyes but grinned. "You've got a boyfriend already."

"Yeah, I'm not sure. I haven't heard from Ramon, and he said he'd call last night."

"Could your mother have shut your phone off?"

The pit of my stomach dropped more than any time during the entire voyage at sea.

"What's that word you say, Ed? When something goes wrong."

"Fewmets."

"Fewmets!" I sighed. "Hadn't even thought of that. So much for the genius bit. You want the job? I think I just got fired."

"No thanks. Been there, done that, got the trauma to prove it."

"You two are a regular laugh riot. You know that?" Cosmo stood at the door to the carriage, swinging it open. An amulet similar to Saya's gleamed over his solar plexus. His clothing was intact despite all the shifting this time, thank goodness.

"Thanks." Ed winked at Cosmo.

"Come on, Ed. Get out already." Cosmo jerked his chin at my seat. "She can't with your scrawny ass in the way."

"What's with going people-shaped, Cos?"

"Shades made me wear it." He gestured at the amulet. "Easier to answer questions this way. I like being a lion here better, but this is a business trip."

"Maybe we should watch our manners, Cosmo." I raised an eyebrow.

"At the king's court, nah." He shook his head. "As long as you call him majesty, he's not picky. Or terribly formal, either."

"That's sort of right." Ed nodded. "You'll get the hang of it, but he does have some rules. Mostly, he's concerned with being a good host whose guests have fun. But like I said before about the ghosts—"

"Right. I'll see it when I get there."

CHAPTER FIVE

Once outside the carriage, we walked up and through the gate in the stockade fence. Past that was an unpaved courtyard. The gravel covering it shimmered in the torchlight. On the other side stood an enormous log cabin, which turned out to be more like a log mansion.

I'd expected a fortress, stony and intimidating. This was much more interesting than anything my imagination had conjured. Along the way, Ed explained that his majesty had recently remodeled.

Carved statues flanked the wide double doors, a pair of bears on their hind legs on either side of the threshold. They faced each other so that to cross the threshold, you had to pass their gazes. It would have been disconcerting, except they were so obviously made of wood. Then I remembered.

"Brownies are wood."

"That's right, we are."

"Call the new one Captain Obvious," the bear on the right said.

"There's already a Captain Obvious. Don't be a downer," the bear on the left chided.

"I'm not down. If anything, you are slightly shorter than I am."

"That's enough, comrades."

The squeaky voice came from somewhere near my feet. I looked down to find a gnome grinning up at us, a tall pointy hat perched on top of his head. He wore his small shirt open, displaying a series of scars on his chest, most of which resembled peppercorns.

"Yup, you're the Sirin all right." The gnome tilted his head, squinting at my wings and then my face. "You'll do. Come along, his majesty's waiting."

"Gee Nome! Buddy!" Cosmo chuckled and clapped. "Great to see you."

"That's my name, don't wear it out." The gnome chortled. "Like I said, follow me. Do it quickly because the king hates ketchup. And cat soup."

"Splat cat tomato." Cosmo punctuated his next bout of laughter by slapping his knee.

"Stop with all those 'you had to be there' jokes," Ed asked. "It's not fair to Mavis."

"Oh, sorry." Cosmo looked over his shoulder, wincing at me. "Didn't mean to leave you out."

"Don't worry. I grok it." I waved a hand. "I'm from a big family too so I know that drill."

"Don't know this one!" A drill, the old-fashioned hand-crank kind, appeared in the gnome's hand.

We all laughed at that before continuing up three sets of ramps before coming to a room with cathedral ceilings, clearly located at the top of the building. It was cavernous and filled with ghosts.

Most of them took full advantage of the overhead area, soaring and wheeling through the air. Many of them danced, but some played a game with what I first took for a ball. It turned out to be the ghost of an armadillo shifter who uncurled herself for a moment to wave at me.

I waved back. My initial grin bloomed into a smile as I noticed how diverse the ghosts were. Many were faeries, but I counted plenty of shifters as well. Initially, I thought it'd be difficult to discern the ghostly psychics from the magi, but in the Under, that was easier than in the mundane realm.

The magi's hands glowed with representations of their elements.

Some had more than one. The psychics had auras in a variety of colors I didn't recognize. I got my notebook out and made a note to look auras up at the library next week.

After I put it away, we crossed the room together, almost resembling a scene from the *Wizard of Oz*. Except there were only three of us, no dog, and I didn't want to go home.

We didn't approach a talking head, either. Instead, it was almost a man, but not quite. Goblins didn't look entirely human with their pointed ears and spun crystal hair. Their skin tones were as varied as types of quartz.

The king's was like pale chalcedony, the blue enhanced by a crowd of wisps lighting the room. He wore silver-gilt hunting attire, sitting sideways in an armed chair with a tall back. Almost a throne, but not quite.

That was a good way to describe just about everything I'd seen so far in the king's demesne. Almost but not quite. His Fleet was almost a Navy, but actually not. His lodge was almost a castle, but not exactly. And his throne room, including the seat of the monarch himself, was almost royal but just slightly short of anything I'd seen, read, or heard of.

A little like me, if I wanted to be honest with myself.

"Cosmo Gitano, step forward," the king drawled from his seat.

"Yes, Your Majesty." Cosmo paced forward, using measured steps but at his usual brisk pace. He dropped to one knee and bowed his head.

"No need for that." The king waved his hand, then turned his head to look directly at my friend. "Well done, young lion."

"Thank you, Your Majesty." Cosmo rose to his feet and bowed his head, then stepped back and to my right.

"Make me an introduction, Redford the Youngest."

"Your Majesty." Ed stepped forward, bowing at the waist more gracefully than Cosmo had managed. "I present Miss Mavis Merlini, of Salem, Massachusetts. Formerly a raven shifter, and in most recent times, your new Sirin."

"Miss Merlini, well met." The king swung his legs over the arm of his chair and put his feet in their proper place on the floor. He leaned forward as if to stand but didn't. At least not yet.

"Well met, Your Majesty." I nodded.

"This isn't the first time we've met, you know." He gave me a half-grin. "However, back then, you hadn't even been named yet. So there's no way formal introductions could happen until now. I give you greeting, and welcome to my demesne."

"Thank you, Majesty."

He shook his head and sighed, but with a grin.

"Which one of you told her not to speak unless spoken to?" He looked at my companions.

"I did, Your Majesty," Ed confessed.

"Wisely done." The king chuckled. "This does make my task slightly more interesting, however."

Everything paused, including the cavorting ghosts overhead. None of us dared ask the king a direct question although it seemed he waited for us to do so. I certainly wasn't about to start owing him any more than the feather I'd picked up merited.

Suddenly, my brain birthed infinite questions about a million different things. Beginning with how he'd met me before I was named. How had I been born in the Under? When had we met, and under what circumstances? Had he known the father that my mother raised my siblings and me to fear? Did the king know when he'd return?

I couldn't afford any of those questions. Owing the Goblin King my life several times over would only decrease its worth.

I swallowed all my curiosity. I had the same powers as a medium, and the Under was as haunted as Salem seemed to be. Ghosts, as long as they weren't faerie ones, were safe to ask if I could keep patience enough to find one later.

Surely the king knew this too. Probably he'd been testing us. No. He didn't need to measure Cosmo or Ed. He was testing me, specifically. However, I could sit around without a straight answer from authority figures all day.

Life in the nest had been good for something, then.

"I can't stay cross at such a talented trio of youngsters." He clapped his hands and called, "Refreshments for the mortals, if you please."

The room erupted into chaos as pure faeries of all types bounded through the space. Some I simply hadn't noticed until they responded to his majesty's orders. Myriad others entered any which way through doors and windows, of course. Also, from cracks in the floor, from behind canvas paintings, down the chimney, up from the grate, and literally from off the wall.

Gnomes, including Gee himself, marched in lines like oversized ants. Shades swooped below ghostly feet. Brownies creaked and cracked, making their way stiffly across the room. Gremlins tottered around on each other's shoulders, in towers three high. Grims capered through all the chaos, some with smaller fae riding on their backs. One stopped in front of me and let out a long, wild howl. A moment later, a shadowy portal opened, and a ghostly hand held a steaming mug out to me.

"To the new Sirin's health."

The aroma wafting from it wasn't light or heady as I'd always imagined regarding faerie victuals. It wouldn't have remotely tempted me if so. Instead, it smelled earthy, dark, and decadent like espresso from my best-ever dreams, the ones where Crow and I had escaped to Italy and lunched al fresco at a mountainside café. So of course I took it.

I sipped the beverage, which was just south of scalding and every bit as grounding to my senses as my nose had promised.

"Thanks."

All the chaotic activity in the room ceased the instant I spoke. I stood blinking, unsure if I'd made a grave mistake.

I hadn't, as it turned out.

"*She* said thanks? She said *thanks*! She *said* thanks. She said it! *Thanks*!"

The reaction in the room was less frantic this time, more celebratory. As though I'd gained some modicum of approval from the pure faeries.

"Nice." Cosmo elbowed me. "They're a tough crowd."

"Him too," Ed added.

The king himself stood on his dais, clapping. He applauded, stepping down from the best seat in the house and crossing the distance between us in only three steps.

"You chose well, though I expected as much." He grinned at the guys. "Both of you. Which is auspicious since any mishap is on your heads, gentlemen."

"Begging Your Majesty's pardon." I cleared my throat, unsure how to curtsy or even bow while holding a nearly full beverage. "I made the final decision to touch the feather, sir. So any responsibility, in case something goes wrong later, is mine."

"This is amazing." The king smiled and clapped me on the shoulder. "Truly, destiny had a hand in this, absolutely. However, fate's grasp is wider than mortals ever imagine. No one thing is ever a single person's responsibility, young Mavis. Remember that."

"I will, Your Majesty."

I hadn't imagined the Goblin King would seem like a mentor, despite Cosmo's and Ed's hints. I had expected something else. Not more formality. More like something congenial on the surface but turbulent underneath. Like family dinners at the nest.

Instead, it seemed the natural order here was largely unstructured but equitable accountability. The king was welcoming, even playful. Like Mr. Hickson but with an air of authority turned up past eleven to a degree I'd never experienced.

Which is just a fancy way of saying I felt entirely out of my depth. Up was down, and down was up.

"Now, we've unfortunately got serious business to discuss." The king beckoned the three of us and headed toward a door to the left of his throne. "Do keep up."

We followed him out onto a widow's walk. If you can properly call something so rustic as a scaffold made from branches and logs one of those. He paced toward the sea-side of the building, then stopped and turned to face us.

"Out there." The king gestured toward the ocean, his finger in line with the horizon. "Across that vast ocean, at the uncharted and frayed edges of the Under's oldest map, is where you'll go."

"I can't imagine why I'd take a cruise like that." Cosmo shrugged. "Cats, water, you know."

"I do." His majesty put a hand on my friends' shoulders. "But you will. For there lies the objective of your quest."

"I just finished the last one, your majesty." Cosmo blinked.

"Yes. This new one is my reward for such faithful service." The king winked. "You'll have help. And a fine vessel to sail in. Her Majesty is giving a similar charge to your Alkonost counterpart as we speak."

He paused again as though waiting for one or all of us to ask him a direct question. It was tempting, I'll admit. Still, he was one of only two faerie monarchs. The Sirin feather tied me to him. And we stood at the seat of his power.

The last thing I wanted was to lock horns or get into debt with him. But what hope did I have when I hadn't even entirely escaped my mother's clutches.

"It does him no good to withhold information. Blink twice if you understand."

I put on my poker face as I gazed at the ghostly woman in front of me. She reminded me of someone vaguely, with the blood-stained leather vest over a checkered shirt, threadbare denim pants, and a long braid snaked over her left shoulder.

Should I trust a strange ghost in the Under? Especially when Ed's face was as blank as mine felt. Nobody else offered me advice, so I blinked twice and heeded hers.

"He wants your success, so he isn't likely to lie. Phrase your questions as statements."

"Please tell me about my first quest, Your Majesty." I smiled.

"Very good then." He nodded. "The balance has been restored with the arrival of the Sirin. Unfortunately, conditions conducive to a certain, shall we say, hmm. Monarchal pursuit remain too far from ideal for comfort. Making things right will come in three stages." The king dropped his arm, then looked me in the eyes.

No other gaze I'd experienced had ever felt this piercing. The

Goblin King resembled any other faerie I'd met like a candle resembled the sun. He and the queen were godlike figures, on a level that no mortal extrahuman could match. An ancient dragon might have come close. But said hypothetical creature would have had to hatch before the common era to get anywhere near as powerful.

Somehow, he needed my help. The only possible reason my service could matter to someone like him would be the Sirin's feather. It must have conferred some small measure of his power in a form meant to be carried by somebody else, at an amount he could afford to risk losing for a time.

"You must understand the gravity here, Sirin."

"Yes. I'm ready to hear more, my king."

"You're charged with the discovery of a certain anchor. The archipelago it hides in has already been marked on that map I mentioned earlier. You must reach it. It lies at the edge of the ocean. While her majesty has her Alkonost along with the most talented dowser in several centuries assist in plotting a course, I've had no suitable proxy to send. Until now."

"I'll need a boat, your majesty."

"The queen will supply that, along with the captain and crew. Your charge is to make the voyage, discover the object, and devise a means to retrieve it. There are islands to search, and as you are more formidable in the air, I'll send Cosmo to cover the ground."

"I suppose my job's staying in school and studying hard then, your majesty." Ed's eyes twinkled. He knew that wasn't the king's intention.

"Quite the contrary, Mr. Redford. None of my vassals has knowledge of how far the ghostly unrest situation stretches. However, I've sensed dissonance in that area despite being unable to do more than read the lips of spirits in my presence." He grinned up at the ghost woman who'd helped me. "Miss Kasa insisted it needs investigation, but with a more authoritative touch than she can manage."

"I understand, Your Majesty."

"Well then. I suppose that concludes all of the boring stuff. You're welcome to admire the view from here or gravely contemplate the future."

The king sauntered past us back the way we'd come. He pushed through the door and back into his throne room. The three of us stood outside, blinking in the moonlight. His majesty poked his head back through the doorway.

"I almost forgot to mention. There's a celebration in the new Sirin's honor. Perhaps you'd like to attend it."

"Of course!" Cosmo chuckled and dashed through the door after the king.

Ed and I followed more slowly.

"Why do I get the idea that thing he's looking for and the ghostly unrest problem have more in common than he said?" I asked.

"Because they do. Hal said as much."

"Hal Hawkins?" I blinked. "Son of the Hawthorn headmaster? That Hal?"

"So you do know him." Ed gave me a half-smile.

"I met him a couple of times. Looked up to him even more. The guy's a genius with enchanted inventions."

"Also a space magus, with affinity. He's the dowser the king mentioned."

"You'll have to tell me more about him sometime."

"From the sound of things, we'll have time. At sea."

"Mouth full of lozenges on my part, then."

"Captive audience, you mean."

We chuckled.

"I know the time difference is on our side. Is there a portal on board or what? Because I can't imagine how we'll get across the ocean if we have to start on that beach every time."

"It won't be easy. The capital-Q quests never are. But there's always a device or a pure faerie helper. Sometimes both."

"How many have you been on?"

"I'm not even sure." He shrugged. "I've been kind of a sidekick on several, but just as many directly charged. It doesn't make any more sense the longer I do them, though."

"Well, I guess I'll follow your lead then." I held the door open for him.

"Follow Hope's. Or Saya's." He made a face Rob would have been proud of. "I'm just a medium."

I already knew better than to take that seriously. There was no 'just' anything about Ed Redford. I followed him back into the almost throne room.

We celebrated for what felt like hours but turned out to be much shorter. I was footsore from dancing when we walked back through a door the king opened for us. The clock on the wall told me only fifty minutes had passed.

CHAPTER SIX

I grabbed a sandwich to go from the table in the dining room, then headed out of the boarding house. I had to find Ramon, either explain why I'd been out of touch or learn he'd stood me up. Eating the sandwich forced me to slow down instead of hurtling toward Tropica Mart.

The way was familiar, but not this strange new instinct to assume he was in danger and run. I didn't trust it. Ed was probably right about Mom canceling my phone. He didn't know how awful she was, but that was a moot point. She didn't do things by halves but only struck one blow at a time.

So that's why I loitered with Horace on Palmer Street to inhale my lunch. I pulled my phone from my satchel, tapping it to wake it up. But it didn't have a charge.

"It must've been on the Under, looking for a signal. Batteries drain pretty quickly in there," Horace said.

"Yeah, I should've shut it off before I went in." I sighed. "What was I thinking?"

"You weren't. You've never been in the Under. Who could expect you to think ahead about something like this?"

"No, not the Under. My Mom. Bran probably stalled over telling her to save her skin. The twins wouldn't let that ride. The second she knew I made off with some of my stuff, she'd have shut it off. She's predictable, and I usually don't make mistakes like this about her."

"Yeah, I hear what you're saying. But after a moment of triumph like that, it's easy to forget being cautious."

"I bet your mother wasn't a monster, though."

"No, she wasn't. My father wasn't either. He was a happy drunk. Anyway, you have an awful lot in common with Tony."

"Tony Gitano? You mean Cosmo's brother?"

"Yeah, his dad's from hell. Fortunately, he's out of both his sons' hair for probably the rest of his life."

"How, if you don't mind my asking?"

"Witness protection. Olivia shot him with a truth arrow. It felt like a major victory until Richard Hopewell showed up and sent everything sideways. We tried to fight him, but." He hung his head, unable to continue.

That must have been the night Bianca got trapped in the Under without her medication.

"I'm sorry. By the way, I saw an entire ballroom full of ghosts at the king's lodge. Bianca wasn't with them. I'm sorry. Should've told you immediately."

"I expected as much." Horace shrugged. "Ed's looked every time he's been there for almost a decade, but nobody seems to have seen her. Even the ghosts he knows well are worried."

"With good reason." I told him about Ed's orders. "It sounds like we're going on a voyage. Barely charted territory, some islands way out at the edge of the ocean. I'll keep my eyes open for your, um, lady friend."

"Love of my afterlife."

"You're destined." There was no need to ask him something so obvious.

"Yes."

Destined loves were only for pure hearts and true heroes. He'd already told me Bianca died seeking justice and saving her friends.

Horace must have done something as selfless, too. There was only one thing to say to that.

"I'll do everything in my power to reunite you two."

"Thanks Mavis. It's good to know one more medium's looking for Bianca down in the Under. Ed's the only one they've allowed in for a long time."

"I guess I am sort of a medium now."

"I don't know much about the Sirin's feather except for the fact that its bearer gains that talent. And flight, like all the mystic birds."

"I know there are only three birds. Are mediums that rare?"

"Not until fairly recently. Modern medicine, especially after mundane doctors joined forces with the extrahuman types, has decreased the number of mediums significantly. I mean, there are still all kinds of accidents. Not too many people have near-death experiences anymore."

I chewed on that for a while, but not too long. I'd started walking during our conversation and was across the street from Tropica Mart all too soon. It felt strange, the shift in focus. I never used to be so easily distracted.

Maybe it had something to do with the magic feather, but it could as easily have been normal teenage hormones. Through the window, I saw Ramon's aunt at the register. That meant he might be there, working in the stockroom. I looked both ways, then crossed the street and headed inside.

The bell jingled, a sprightly chime. Aunt Marisol looked up and waved, smiling broadly.

"Hello, Mavis. Nice to see you. Ramon's in the back stocking the cooler. You can wait around or go see him there if you don't mind the refrigerator."

Thanks, Marisol." The benefits of being a summer denizen at the Mart had given me certain privileges. Being allowed into the cooler was one of them. It was much nicer on the days pushing one hundred degrees Fahrenheit than on that balmy September afternoon but tolerable in the current circumstance.

I don't know why I got a twinge of guilt, watching Ramon restock bottles of Snapple from the back of the shelves. I'd spent almost as much time with Ed, Saya, and Cosmo as my boyfriend. I didn't think of them that way. I guess you could say I had a type;—tall, dark, and extrahuman.

"Hey Ramon, I'm sorry."

"Can't imagine why." Ramon didn't even look at me.

"You said you'd call, and I didn't even think. My phone—"

"Got a disconnected message. Figured it was your mom. Don't worry. Let me finish with these, they're glass, and I don't want that kind of mess in here with you."

"Want help?"

"Yeah, if you don't mind."

Helping him restock the narrow shelves meant stepping into his personal space before we'd seriously talked about the communication issue. That made me wary because Diego had always sulked after stuff like that. At the nest, it meant punishment.

I expected awkwardness. There wasn't any. Ramon didn't create drama, which was one of the reasons I liked him. He looked up at me a few times, grinning whenever our hands touched as we handled bottles together. Flirty, not frightening. Once through with our task, he led me out of the cooler into the small employees-only hallway.

"So I was thinking, don't our school tablets have messaging?" He blinked. "Whoops."

"Yeah, that's going to take getting used to. Technically I don't have a rank, so I'm not sure any debt owed me is even real. Don't worry. I won't press you into service as a cabin boy or anything."

"Nobody wants to break a ban and end up in a fetal position losing his lunch." He let out a nervous chuckle. "I'll be careful with the questions until we know more."

"Good. We can practice together and ace any exams Hickson gives us on faerie phrasing. Yes, I think there is a chat function. Haven't checked that out yet."

"Let's tinker with school property, then."

"Sure. I'd rather be doing something more fun, though." I sighed. "This whole business has been kind of a downer."

"I guess you're in trouble with Principal Klein."

"I'm not. Hope and Saya are, though. Cosmo too."

"And Ed, I bet."

"No, he's the only one with zero blame. Even in my book. He got vetoed every time he wanted to do the right thing, and the ban kept him from going to Klein behind their backs."

"Lucky dude."

"In that department, you're right."

"So are you. Because you can see ghosts now."

"Yeah, it's kind of awesome." I grinned. "I've got a buddy, Horace. He was a medium before he died so it's super helpful having him around."

"Tell me more about Horace."

I did, looking up from time to time to make sure the ghost in question was okay with everything I said. Ramon sat listening, fascinated.

"The king probably did more than just say hi." Ramon shook his head. "Dang, this no questions thing is harder than I thought it'd be."

"Sorry."

"You're worth it, Mavis."

"Well then, I guess you deserve to know that he put me on a quest already."

"Bet there's a ban on talking about it."

"No, I can say what I'm doing and where I'm going, but not what I find or what I'm looking for."

"That's cool. So tell me about it."

I gave him all the info I had, except that we were seeking some kind of anchor. He sat with our tablets, finding and adjusting the chat function on both of them. Luckily, my boyfriend was cute, supportive, and technologically inclined.

Having a boyfriend felt like a miracle in my chaotic life. Plus, things were different than they'd been with Diego. For one thing, we lacked that sense of a forbidden relationship.

Diego's family was closely aligned with the Morgensterns, making them Mom's de facto enemies. The DelSangres were new enough in town to be under her radar. Also, we were at the same school in the same class section, so we'd see each other frequently. The only thing I worried about now that we figured out a way to text was my new status as the Sirin.

If I was still a garden-variety raven, I couldn't endanger him much, even with the toxic Merlini family weighing me down. All that changed for me the day before. What sort of effect could that have? Mom always said she didn't put up with men who couldn't abide her power. I generally trusted the adages she applied only to herself even if she espoused those ideas for the wrong reasons.

I could talk to Crow. Maybe I could visit on Sunday night if I got my one-act play done in time. That was a tall order, all things considered.

"Okay. We're all set up to text each other with tablets. Nothing too sensitive, though. We don't know how the school monitors these things. Or if we've got other genius classmates hacking them for fun. But it's better than no phone."

"Absolutely." I nodded. "You're awesome, genius classmate hacker."

"You're not too shabby, either." He chuckled. "By which I mean you're a goddess, of course."

We grinned at each other, glanced at the still-closed door from the store, then stole a few more moments alone together.

On Sunday, I visited my brother. All the sanitarium faeries must have been used to me by then. Or maybe their newfound sense of deference had more to do with my status as the Sirin. How they knew about that was anyone's guess. Had a formal announcement gone out, or did they have a rumor mill? Perhaps their strange eyes saw it plain as the nose on my face. But my treatment as a guest was entirely different from my last visits.

"Welcome, esteemed Sirin," the voice intoned from overhead. "Miss Mavis Merlini, sister of Cornelius. Please state the purpose of your visit."

"Yes, I'm here to visit my brother. He prefers Crow, though. Even I can't get away with calling him Cornelius."

"Pondside accommodations are available."

"I've never heard of pondside."

"It's a more pleasant, shall we say, venue for visiting with our residents in the aggression wing."

"That sounds interesting. You've never offered that before. I wonder why."

"True. The reason will be clear once your visit begins regardless of how you choose. Please make a selection."

"Let Crow decide. I'd rather meet him where he's most comfortable."

"As you wish."

I waited a moment, pacing three times before finding myself relocated. Unlike my previous visits, this wasn't as jarring. Instead of an abrupt transfer of space, I faded gradually, as though they were taking their time with me this go-round. I didn't exactly appreciate it though. Abrupt transfers had their benefits. The gradual thing made me a little queasy, which I hadn't expected.

"So this is pondside." Crow stood with his back to me, hands in the side pockets of an orange checkered quilted flannel jacket. "Swanky."

"Hi. I like the orange."

"It's an upgrade. They clothe us like DEFCON levels. I'm out of red now, so I get a woodstove and metal flatware. And meetings here."

"What's after orange, then?"

"Yellow. The weather in there gets nicer, and I start group therapy. When I get to green, it gets even better. But I'm unclear how at this point."

"So then you're doing well."

"Improving, they say." He glanced at me over his shoulder, eyebrows raised. "I don't feel any less awful about everything, though. Mainly, I'm learning to wrangle the anger. That's different, I guess. So are you, I hear."

"Aside from seeing ghosts everywhere and winging out in the Under, no. Not really. It's a little odd, but mostly I'm still me."

"I remember when you were about eight, you went over every book about mediums that you could find. You got a card at every library within walking distance, looking for evidence that shifters could be mediums. You never found a thing."

He shook his head, and his lips twisted wistfully. I smiled, hoping to coax one from him.

"Right. I even hogged the nest computer, looking online. What a silly phase."

"Not so much. Ghosts were your world back then. You came to my room one night crying. Because you wanted to see them so badly. Befriend them."

"Yeah, Mom said it was foolish. Stupid of me."

"I never thought so. I even argued with her over it. But you don't remember."

"No." My eyes stung. "I do. Those rare bouts of kindness were crucial."

"We both needed those when we were little." He sniffled. "You returned them in kind. It's not like we got that from anyone else in the family."

He pulled his hands from his pockets and opened his arms. I paused, staring at my brother's work-worn hands as though seeing them for the first time. In a way, I was. They were that different now.

I stepped closer, and we hugged. That's an understatement. We clung together, a present-tense manifestation of that support from years ago.

"Part of the wreckage, bits and pieces are all we have to hold on to. Maybe I should be in here with you. It might do me some good."

"No way." He patted my shoulder. "I did this to myself. You wouldn't be with me. The trauma wing has much more comfortable accommodations than my old hut."

That was the first time anyone called how we grew up trauma. I swallowed the rest of my tears. Crow didn't need that, and I didn't have time for it, either. So I changed the subject.

"From what I understand, even that's better than anything at Butler."

We let go of each other and walked along the shore. I told him about Ed's mother.

"Yeah, I heard about that old place down in Providence. There's been a lot of reform since the Reveal, but Rhode Island's full of influential mundane holdouts. They didn't have a mistake like the Boston Internment to learn from like we did here."

"What's with the sudden interest in history?"

"History books, old news stories, crosswords, and sudoku are most of what we're allowed for reading in here."

"You're reading?" I chuckled. "Remember when you said I'd end up with a bookwyrm form?"

"Yeah, I do." He smirked. "I was jealous. Most of the time, words jumbled up on the page when I tried to read them. Turns out, I'm dyslexic, so they gave me enchanted glasses to help with it. I found out after getting here that Mr. Hickson wanted me evaluated for it. The Bo— well, you know who I mean. She wouldn't send me."

"Which set you up to fail."

"She's a lousy parent. She started way too young. And she gave up a lot, getting married to cancel her father's debt."

"Don't parrot her excuses. She had five other kids before us and should have known better by the time we showed up. We never met Grandpa before he died. Dad's out doing whatever so much I barely remember what he looks like. So I don't understand how any of that matters."

"Maybe I just want a tidy explanation. Like, a reason she treats us like employees instead of kids. Caring hurts when you lose someone. Wouldn't she want to avoid more pain?"

He shook his head, rolled his eyes, and pointed at his mouth. "What a stupid way to waste a question."

"You get three per day before you owe me anything."

"Right." He nodded. "I remember that from school. Anyway, I missed you all week."

"I missed you too. But I'm going to kind of have less time. Even though I'd like to visit more often than I do now."

"Is it less time because of the Sirin stuff?" Crow pointed at his mouth again. "Don't worry, I know I've only got one left."

"More like don't ask another one. But yeah, it's the Sirin thing. I'm on a quest."

"Tell me whatever you're allowed to about that, then."

I did.

"Sounds like serious business. I wish I could help. But, you know." He waved his hand vaguely above his head. "Stuck in here. Do the crime, do the time."

"It's a hospital, not a prison."

"Right. But my stay is court-ordered."

"I know." I nodded. "I'm also stuck a little under the king's orders."

"Same storm, different boat for you and me, I guess."

"Wish I could navigate it as easily as Hope."

"Bet you're butting heads with the other magical bird by now. Wasn't long ago I thought you'd have more trouble with the dragon princess."

"You said they'd both be trouble before."

"Yeah. Maybe they'll be a cakewalk compared to the rest of our family. We learned a lot of unhealthy stuff in the nest. Some of it's worth keeping because it helped us survive. Figuring out what to toss is the hard part. They've got counselors at school. Use them and do that work. We do it here, and it's totally worth it."

"I will." I nodded. The sunlight changed, which meant our time was almost up. There was one piece of news he still needed, though. "By the way, I have a boyfriend now."

"Oh no." Crow wrinkled his nose, then put one hand to his throat and faked a gag. "Barf! My kid sister's hooking up with somebody."

"We're dating, not hooking up." I didn't say yet. That wasn't his business. "It's Ramon, by the way. In case you were wondering."

"I figured as much. He's a good kid."

"He's not good. He's awesome. I really like him."

"You don't want *her* knowing you've got someone special."

"I'm doing everything I can to keep Mom out of the loop on that."

"It's more important than you think. You don't want her stalking him or messing with Tropica Mart. She did that to the DelMars. Things went south with Cadence after that."

"She stalked Cadence?" I took a step back.

"Yeah. Sent nastygrams to her parents, too. It sucked. Unless you start dating someone she'd be afraid of, best hope she never finds out about Ramon."

"I'll remember that." I sighed, then put my hand on his shoulder. "I didn't say this before, but I should have. Thank you."

"You're thanking me, but you're the one who visits. Weirdo kid."

"It's not, though. You're only a little older than me so you must have been scared. You stood out in front anyway. Looked ahead but never left me behind." I sighed. "Now you're in here to work on yourself but still giving me advice. I want you to know how much that means to me."

"Least I could do with all the visits. But you're welcome."

The faeries announced my departure. Right before he faded from view, Crow smiled. That was rare and precious as diamonds. And twice as hard to see without weeping. Fortunately, the trip back gave me enough time to compose myself.

CHAPTER SEVEN

On Monday, I went back to school. All of us did, acting like every-thing was normal, exactly as it was in the weeks before. It wasn't. Nobody at the school besides our class section saw anything, but somehow everyone knew about what went down at the museum.

Someone had said something. Maybe a student from another school, or even a pure faerie. I shook off the grip of that speculation. Slacking at school wasn't part of my plan. Besides, nobody bothered me much over the new revelations. Hope, on the other hand, had a harder time.

A dragon shifter named Brett was sour because his eagle shifter buddy shooed Hope away when investigating upperclassmen about the feather. I stood outside Lab with Kiara one day, listening to Hope, Jillian, Saya, and Fiona talk about it.

"He ranted at me for almost five minutes," Hope said. "Because I didn't give Lance enough information or whatever. Not that he was even Under-born in the first place."

"Brett's got sand in his shorts." Jillian snorted. "Making you step out of practice just to give you grief right during conjure drills. I hope I see his birdbrained friend in the ring soon. Open a can of whoop-ass on his tail feathers."

"I'd rather you not." Hope shook her head. "Brett might take it out on someone in our crew. I don't want an all-out brawl between us and the second-years."

"Regardless of what you may want, you won't get it in regard to Brett." Saya rolled her eyes. "I won't have the luxury of not seeing him. He sent a letter to Mother. A formal one. About me."

"Don't tell me he's a hatchling." Fiona gaped, one hand on her cheek. "I don't want to know."

"He says he is." Saya leaned against the wall behind her. "I'll have no choice but to do as Mother says with him in the future."

"You mean you have to date that arrogant bastard?" Jillian snarled. "Say the word, and I'll give dragon mom a piece of my mind."

"It won't do any good, Jill." Fiona patted her shoulder. "Hertha Harcourt's centuries old. She's not intimidated by wolf shifters, no matter how fierce."

"I guess you're right. Still doesn't change how I feel."

"We'll have duties in the Under right after that dance," Hope reminded us. "So Saya has every excuse to bail on him."

I made relieved noises right along with the rest of them at that until Dr. Aranha ushered us into her classroom. Still, I suspected we'd have issues with Brett eventually, no matter how many legitimate excuses our captain came up with.

I managed to keep up with homework for once that week. Hope worked overtime to get ahead. She said it was because she never knew when the monarchs would call for help or even a meeting. I couldn't get ahead, even with extra solo study time. Maybe it was stress.

Saya seemed determined to match or outdo her brother Blaine's academic achievements. He'd been valedictorian at his academy down in Rhode Island and gone on to graduate salutatorian at Providence Paranormal while halfway done with his Master's. She wanted to follow in his footsteps and study extrahuman anthropology. But his

Ph.D. program only accepted two applicants per year. That was a tall order, but competition gave her drive and purpose.

Ed wanted to learn as much as possible. Messing's system meant he only needed to study for daily quizzes and weekly tests. It fit his academic style perfectly.

Cosmo slacked in his studies, often asking to look at my notes out in the hall before class started. I didn't know any other feline shifters, but they didn't seem much different from the corvid variety. Easily distracted and prone to bouts of procrastination.

I didn't think he was mailing it in academically. He seemed genuinely interested in the work but missing some very basic information. He mentioned how someday he'd join Tony's freelance extrahuman services company. Go into a different sort of family business than the one his father had intended for him.

"There's no way I want to get involved in a bunch of Cosa Nostra stuff like my dad." Cosmo rolled his eyes. "That kind of work freaks me out."

"I know what you mean." I nodded.

"How?" He wrinkled his nose. "Oops."

"One strike is all good. Anyway, all my siblings call our mom Boss except for me."

"No way." Cosmo put his hands flat on the courier table where we sat with the remains of our lunch. "You're from one of those families too. I can't freaking believe it." He ran the sentence on so it wouldn't turn into a question.

"Yes. Like you, I don't want any of that. Neither did Crow, but he couldn't avoid it. Mom took him out of town for a weekend in his senior year, and his entire attitude changed."

"Thank God you got that feather." He shook his head. "That's what she would have dragged you back to. I can't believe I didn't see that before. Oh wait, I can." He cleared his throat and mimicked a green alien. "Opposite of mafioso material, I am."

"I should've told you. Including the fact that my mother had some kind of beef with your dad back in the day. Maybe still does."

"Yes, you should have. What kind of beef was it?" He sighed. "Oops again."

"It's only number two. You're good. I don't know what it was over. She never told me anything and never will. Plus, I'm no longer in a position to eavesdrop on dear old Mom."

"Maybe your brother knows."

"I could ask about that. They started giving him more freedom in there. He's been progressing well. But that might make it difficult for him to answer."

"If he's doing so well, maybe he'll be allowed out soon."

"Maybe. I really want to introduce him to everyone. He believes me about the feather and the Under and all that. He's a skeptic when it comes to you and your family."

"Well, I'm good with that. We're a pretty outlandish bunch. I wouldn't believe the youngest medium in recorded history, two mystic birds, and the last dragon princess were my crew if I wasn't living it, either. Anyway, good lunch. But—" He waved his hand at the silent bell on the wall above us.

A breath later, it rang at a frequency I could hear. I realized he must have always heard it moments before everyone else. I silently thanked the gods for his amazing cat ears.

***

Drama Club went normally, with some vocal and dance practice. I'd left right at the bell to walk my friends from the other schools to the office for their portals.

On the way back, I took my time. We ended up waiting a minute before Lab sometimes if it was messy after the section before us. As I approached the end of the line outside the door to Dr. Aranha's lab, Mr. Hickson stopped me.

"We need to talk, Mavis."

"Why?" I blinked. "Did I do something wrong?"

"No. Unfortunately, it seems like you might have trouble soon. I want to help you get ahead of it."

"It's my mom, isn't it?"

"Yes. I'm not sure whether your schedule's free after school today."

"I'll make time. I'm supposed to go to the park, but my friends can handle a field day without me for once."

"It's probably better if you refrain from those unless you're in a large group."

"Fewmets, it's worse than I thought."

"Maybe. One thing's certain. It won't get better without preparation. For now, head on into Lab before the good doctor scolds us for loitering in her hall."

"Sure thing."

Lab was diverting, almost to the point where I forgot about Mr. Hickson's serious talk. We worked on partial shifting, which only three of us could do. The rest of the class observed and took notes, using the Green Equation to figure out how much body mass moved in and out of the space between the mundane and the Under. After about the fifteenth time popping out my wings, I got bored.

"I wonder if you magic bird chicks can shift anything besides wings." Wyatt tapped his tablet with his stylus. "I keep getting the same answer for both of you."

"I've never tried that, but I guess there's a first time for everything." Hope sat on one of the benches, held up her legs, and stared at her feet.

"Let's see if this is a eureka moment or a big mistake." Cosmo rubbed his hands together.

I figured Hope wanted to shift her feet into talons. Instead, those rainbow wings sprang forth from her back once more. She continued exerting her will on her body, glaring at the toes of her sneakers. Eventually, they shimmered with something. I wasn't sure what. It looked more like magic than actual shapeshifting.

Hope's shoes turned a nearly blinding shade of neon pink.

"Guess you just glamoured them." Cosmo shrugged.

"Huh." She waved her hands over the sneakers. "Yeah. That's not going back to the way it was."

"Oh well." Saya shrugged. "At least it's a stylish color for athletic wear."

"Looks like I'm a one-trick partial shift pony unless we go to the Under." Hope got down from the table. "Maybe Mavis could give it a try."

"I guess so." I took her place and gave it a go.

The exact same thing happened with my wings. I left them folded against my back and continued trying to concentrate. Instead of color or anything about the rest of me changing, something else happened.

I felt it, a strain at my temples and a drain on my energy. At first, I had no idea what happened besides my classmates going silent. I looked up from my battered ballet flats. Hope shared my confusion, brow furrowed.

Kiara studied my face, then moved on to Hope's. We were the only unalarmed students in the room.

The rest of them stared past my right shoulder, on the defensive. Saya stepped in front of Hope, covered with scales with one eyebrow raised. Wyatt guarded Ramon, teeth bared. Fiona and Jillian stood side by side in a grappling stance, Jaxon snarling behind them. Cosmo got out in front and spoke to somebody behind me.

"You'll regret coming in here."

"Stand down, guys." Hope's voice carried command. "He's a friendly ghost, not dangerous."

"Oh!" Kiara grinned. "You must be Horace. I'm Kiara Knight, but you probably know that already. Mavis told me you'd been around all month. I never thought I'd get a chance to see you in the, er, ectoplasm. So nice to finally meet you!"

Sure enough, I turned my head and saw Horace leaning in the corner of the room as usual.

"So I guess I reveal ghosts instead of glamouring things." I winced. "Sorry."

"Bro, you scared the crap out of me. But I gotta say, Horace. Your steampunk game is strong." Wyatt tapped two fingers against his temple in some kind of salute. "Props to you, my man."

"Um, thanks?" Horace blinked.

"I can't hear him." Wyatt poked my shoulder. "Turn the sound on, maybe."

"Don't know if I can." I chuckled. "Didn't think I could do this, even."

"The monarchs never said anything about this." Hope scratched her head. "Or my glamouring thing, either. And I don't dare ask them."

"This is certainly a set of interesting developments. But the topic of mystic birds is rather advanced for first-year students." Dr. Aranha said. "We all need more practice with the Green Equation. I can request some university libraries, ask for access to literature on the mystic birds. Anyone who turns in an essay with findings and proper citations can earn extra credit."

The rest of my classmates cheered and made generally positive noises except for Hope, who seemed wary about being the subject of a school assignment.

There was no way keeping her true nature a secret for most of her life had been easy. Old habits die hard, and though our identities were out to the school and maybe Salem's extrahuman community at this point, she wasn't used to it.

I understood not wanting too much attention. However, she made herself scarce before I could talk to her about it. I couldn't chase her, either. Not with that meeting looming over me.

I had time for a snack but didn't want one. So I spent five minutes in the restroom, convincing myself that I'd survive whatever happened.

CHAPTER EIGHT

The door to the auditorium near the stage's apron creaked open, as always. I wondered when they'd get around to fixing it but soon derailed that train of thought because Mr. Hickson wasn't the only person in the auditorium waiting to talk to me.

All of my teachers were there, along with Principal Klein. I stood frozen in front of the apron, wondering what kind of trouble I was in with my mother, which was worse than any detention Mrs. Ambersmith could imagine.

"Mavis, please come up here with us," Mr. Hickson said.

Instead of vaulting up on my hands as usual, I took the steps at the side. A table with folding chairs stood at center stage. The faculty were all around it, and there was no available chair for me. So I stood in front of it, back to the seats while they all stared at me. That sounds harsher than it was.

Coach Tremain gazed mildly at me instead. Mr. Hickson leaned back in his chair, hands folded over his stomach with his eyes on a folder in front of Principal Klein. Dr. Aranha sat on the edge of her seat, eyes melting with sympathy. The only true stare came from Mrs. Ambersmith, whose expression reminded me of Saya's more than anything else.

"Don't be alarmed, Mavis. We're only here to discuss your future lesson plan and schedule." Principal Klein opened the folder. "It seems you'll need extra instruction."

"That's my idea, by the way," Dr. Aranha said. "The revelation of your ghostly companion in Lab is proof you'll benefit from extra instruction."

I breathed a sigh of relief, hoping I'd only need a tutor. Why bring in my entire set of instructors, then?

"Let her out of my lecture." Mrs. Ambersmith sniffed. "She can always get the notes from someone else."

"That's true." Mr. Hickson shook his head. "But she uploads all her notes to the class database. Some of the other students download those. They might suffer if she misses time in your classroom, Mrs. Ambersmith. It seems your teaching style and her study methods mesh well."

"I'd never have dreamed such a thing possible on the first day." She sighed. "But I must agree. I've seen her tab stamp up there with Miss Knight's. Three students in particular favor Mavis's notes. Their first sets of grades support that idea."

"Considering what I see at the boardinghouse, how she gathers to study with others in the lounge, I'm not all that surprised," Principal Klein added. "We want to encourage collaboration."

"I know I'm new to this school's system, but maybe we should explain to Mavis what's going on," Coach Tremain said. "She's nervous. Look at all the tension in her shoulders."

"Quite correct." Principal Klein flipped the paper over. "Your mother is aware that the Sirin feather confers mediumship upon its bearer, among other things. Because of this, I think it's best we carve some time out in your day to receive certified psychic instruction at Messing Academy. You'll be in class with Ed Redford and Diego Mendez, two familiar faces."

"How will I keep up with everything here?"

"I doubt you'll get into academic trouble, Miss Merlini," Mrs. Ambersmith said. "Concern yourself more with what you're willing to give up."

"How about morning gym?" Coach Tremain directed his question at Principal Klein. "She's one of the best yogis in there, but I'd rather let her go than see her withdrawn from school."

"That's quite impossible, I'm afraid." Principal Klein shook her head. "She chose Drama Club as her elective but still needs a physical outlet. Otherwise, the Extrahuman Board of Education will deem her program here inadequate for her shifter side."

"Oh. Hadn't thought of that."

"I wouldn't have either my first year teaching." Dr. Aranha nodded. "Don't be too hard on yourself, Bobby."

"That said, she can't be excused from Lab. It's essential."

"I suppose she could give up research since she's studying with other students at the boarding house." Mr. Hickson suggested. "She'll need access to snacks at Messing if permitted. Maybe that's our solution."

"I can speak with their director about that." Principal Klein said. "It's up to you, Mavis. You've been in the library every day. You're the only one who can say how much it contributes to your academic success overall."

"If there were some way I could access library resources from off-campus, I think I could manage it." I nodded.

"What about testing time?" Mrs. Ambersmith asked. "Their courses are an hour, but they give twenty to fifty-minute tests afterward. How can she meet Messing's standards if she's rushing back here every day?"

"I'm afraid there isn't much room in anyone's schedule here. That's by design and usually with good reason."

"What about the Under?" Coach Tremain suggested. "Time runs differently there. It'd get her enough extra time for quizzes and tests."

"While I'm well aware of the time differences in our realms, I'm not sure that would be amenable to the mediumship instructor over at Messing," Principal Klein said. "That is something I'll have to address. The Under itself has its own set of challenges."

"I thought the mystic birds had the right to cross realms at will," Coach Tremain said.

"His Majesty is the only one who can answer that question," Mrs. Ambersmith said.

"And me." I raised my hand. "Uh, I kind of know."

"Pretend we're in Forum," Mr. Hickson said. "Say anything."

"Okay, I do know." I nodded. "I met His Majesty over the weekend. He said to consider myself welcome in his domain."

"Then he didn't bar your entry. Which is a passable invitation in Unseelie terms." Principal Klein made a note in her folder. "It's a good idea to announce your arrival each time and use the same location. I'll write the messages and have Sid send them every school day. Perhaps this concludes our business."

"We should talk more about her mother," Mr. Hickson said. "I know it's a bit grave and not exactly an academic topic. It's still important."

"Most of us have had run-ins with Mrs. Merlini." Principal Klein glanced at Mrs. Ambersmith. "Or Mavis's older siblings. Or all of the above. That merits discussion, but an informal one. If you have access to information Mavis needs, Mr. Hickson, I'll leave you to it." Principal Klein closed her folder and rose, tucking it into the crook of her arm.

"Stick around for five more minutes if you can, Mavis."

"Yeah, I'll do that." I nodded.

"You mind if I stay?" Coach Tremain asked.

"I suppose not, but why?" Mr. Hickson asked.

"I don't know anything at all about Morgan Merlini. Research is important."

"I'm staying too." Mrs. Ambersmith sniffed. "If there's Merlini-related danger on this campus, I want to be informed."

"I'm amenable to both of you remaining here. It's also up to Mavis," Mr. Hickson said.

"I don't mind." I swallowed my annoyance at my Lecture teacher. According to Crow, trauma got toxic the longer it sat ignored. If Mrs. Ambersmith wanted to work through things, I wouldn't stop her. Letting her stay was what he'd want me to do.

Dr. Aranha and Principal Klein headed out of the auditorium. I took the seat previously occupied by my Lab instructor and waited for whatever Mr. Hickson had to say.

"I'm the one who informed the principal about your mother's likely tactics, Mavis," he said. "Which I'm predicting based on our history together here. And advice from a psychic friend."

"Wasn't Gallows Hill different when you went here?"

"Right. We started as a tiny private day school for Salem residents only, but we were one of the first schools for extrahumans in Massachusetts to get our charter. Hawthorn Academy was still something of a secret, and Messing still pretended to be mundane."

"Wow, I never knew." Bobby shook his head. "I mean, I went to Providence Paranormal. It hid in plain sight and went public immediately after the Reveal. But it wasn't integrated until a few years before I got there. Magi and a few well-connected psychics. Not like Gallows Hill."

"We admitted everybody before the Reveal, even magi and psychics. That ended the year before I started. Anyway, Morgan Merlini and I used to be friends. Part of the same pack, actually."

"She never mentioned a pack." I shook my head. "She tells me nobody needs those. All you need is your family. It's been that way for as long my oldest sister remembers, anyway."

"Yeah, I know about the Merlini family way. Morgan Canto was our alpha. None of us wanted her to marry Owen Merlini. We all tried to stop it seven different ways. In the end, they got hitched, and he made her drop out."

"So she's bitter?" Mrs. Ambersmith blinked.

"I can't answer that." Mr. Hickson sighed. "The night before she got married, Paolo challenged her to a duel on the beach. They left the rest of us at Winter Island Park, but after a while, I got antsy and followed them. Morgan was gone, and we had to take Paolo to the hospital. "

"Wow. Underhanded move for an alpha." Bobby's eyes narrowed. "Glad you saw the back of her."

"Technically, she's still alpha. She won that challenge, so we couldn't dissolve the pack and move on. It hinders all of us." Mr.

Hickson sighed. "The big take here is that Morgan looks at all the angles, then attacks unexpectedly. If she misses, she tries again."

"So I can't trust you, Mr. Hickson." I blinked. "She'll see you as an angle eventually."

"Which is why I promised on the first day not to let you fail." His hands pressed flat against the table. "She can't make me go against a vow to protect her child. It worked for your brother. Ask him."

I already knew he hadn't sabotaged Crow academically. I'd also seen firsthand that Mom pushed him over the edge outside of school.

"I'll borrow a phone and call the second I'm out of here."

"Good." He nodded. "That pack bond goes both ways."

"Is that where your information comes from? Schrodinger's pack?" Bobby blinked. "But how?"

"Trade secret, sorry." Mr. Hickson shrugged. "Trickster packs work in mysterious ways. It's not like your Tinfoil Hat. Yes, I've heard of you, first wolf-led pack with a vamp beta since the Reveal."

"That's your pack, Coach?" Mrs. Ambersmith blinked. "Color me impressed."

"Hey, I don't know the differences between the types of packs."

"I'm lecturing on that in two weeks," Mrs. Ambersmith said. "Be sure to pay attention since your section's practically a pack already. And trouble follows you, Miss Merlini."

"Listen, Mrs. Ambersmith. I know you don't like having me in your class, but I'm stuck there. This trouble's not my fault, any more than it's yours."

"From the mouths of babes." Mr. Hickson laughed. Coach Tremain joined in.

"I don't understand why that's funny." She sniffed. "I'm correct, although I don't blame you for it. Trouble follows you, Miss Merlini. It's not bound to stop anytime soon, either."

"The last time I checked, redcaps aren't clairvoyant." I raised an eyebrow. "Or at least that's what you told us in Lecture just the other day."

"Your admirable memory of a single fact may earn some respect. Knowledge may be power, but attitude swings its balance. In the

Under, you'll find beings far more particular than I, so consider this interaction instructional."

"Okay. I get it." Everything was a lesson to Mrs. Ambersmith. "Is there anything else I need to know, Mr. Hickson?"

"Only that getting you into mediumship class will work as far as the school board's concerned. It'll foil your mom because she's using the concerned parent angle. But she'll come up with a different counter later on. Maybe something to do with your abilities testing. We've got to stay one step ahead of her. Or at least in step, as a worst-case scenario."

"What happens if we end up a step behind?"

"I don't even want to contemplate that." He shook his head. "You're not helpless. You've got your whole section on your side. Plus ghosts, which she can't see. Stay cunning and full of tricks."

"Sounds exhausting." Coach Tremain shook his head. "And way too familiar. Mavis, would you mind if I talk to my fiancée about some of this? She's the smartest person I know."

"Sure. Go right ahead. I need all the help I can get."

"Well, I've got work to do." Mr. Hickson said. "It's time to close up the theater for now. Mavis, I'd keep a low profile in town for the next few days if I were you."

"Any particular reason why?"

"Just a gut feeling. If you do go anywhere, bring friends. As many as possible."

"I've always got a friend with me, right Horace?" I patted the strap on my satchel as I slung it over my shoulder.

Coach Tremain blinked, sniffed, and blinked again. I didn't think much of it until I was halfway back to the boarding house and Horace spoke.

"Bianca was his packmate, you know. Bobby Tremain's. Before she died."

"I'm so sorry."

"Technically, maybe I'm still a Tinfoil Hatter. They never dissolved. I'm sure they continue on better terms than poor Mr. Hickson's pack."

"You must miss them almost as much as you miss her."

"I do. But knowing they're well, for now, it's enough."

"I hear that." I spent the rest of the walk home thinking about my brother in the sanitarium and wondering whether this new history lesson would do him more harm than good.

When I called, they didn't let me speak with him. However, they relayed my question and his one-word answer about trusting Mr. Hickson.

Yes.

CHAPTER NINE

The moment I stepped through the portal into Messing Academy, I understood why Ed hated it there. I almost turned and went back, just because of its aesthetics.

Bright lights with the type of fluorescence that hummed and flickered at frequencies that disturbed pretty much everyone filled the entire place. The interior matched that brutal architecture exterior perfectly. All the rooms, halls, doorways, windowsills, and all, were boxy, blocky, and utilitarian.

There was no color, only a bleached-out whitewashed monochrome nightmare, the proverbial white rabbit in a snowstorm. The students themselves stood out dark and somehow dull in their royal blue uniforms against all of that. At least it was easy to know whether you were alone or not as far as anybody corporeal went, anyway.

The ghosts were another story entirely. Most ghosts were translucent. Their appearances varied in terms of color, with pastel ruling everything. Most of the ones at Messing had those same blue uniforms but pastelized. They blended somewhere between that awful lighting and the stark paint.

Ghosts with warmer colors appeared just fine. I spotted Horace easily, in his brown suit. And Rob, with his colonial red coat.

Although I sensed ghostly presences, looking at them wasn't easy. No wonder Ed couldn't focus on his surroundings during his first day.

"Welcome to Mediumship, Miss Merlini."

There at the head of the classroom stood the last person I expected. Old Grandpa Ambersmith. I'd expected a medium from out of town, perhaps. But a magus who could hear a medium's ghost wasn't a bad alternative.

"Have a seat."

It was easier said than done. Although the seating and table arrangements we had at Gallows Hill seemed rigid while I had been there, Messing's were another matter entirely. Like the walls, ceilings, and floors, the desks and chairs were also white.

Some of them bore dings and dents, scars from students past. But they didn't differ much in color. The desks and chairs were stuck to each other and also the floor, which didn't allow flexibility for people of diverse sizes and shapes.

That wasn't as big of a deal at Messing as it was in Gallows Hill. Shifters needed room to breathe and move around if we got cagey. Psychics couldn't be shifters and resembled mundanes more closely than any other extrahumans.

So I fit in like a sore thumb. It wasn't rocket surgery to figure out that the seating wouldn't easily accommodate me.

I wasn't significantly bigger than them. We all had arms, legs, curves, and planes. However, the one-piece desks boxed me in, without a way to get out quickly or easily. My constant worry was my wings popping out in front of the entire class of psychics. And that somehow I'd hit the student behind me and get in trouble.

It wasn't only the furniture, either. Their positioning appeared to be a certain ideal measure, the spaces between them done with specific proportions in mind. It was almost like someone had done a mathematical equation to figure out the average size of a teenage psychic, then welded the desks in rows the ideal length and width of that hypothetical person.

Of course, nobody else in the room was an actual medium besides Ed and me. I didn't make the mistake of considering that an automatic advantage. Everybody knew I was there due to gaining new powers. That was so unheard of in extrahuman society it made folks uncomfortable.

As I discussed at the meeting with my faculty yesterday, news of my change was all over town. Maybe the most reclusive extrahuman in Salem city limits didn't know the youngest Merlini was the Sirin. Then again, maybe not. It was a small world.

"Let's get started." Old Grandpa Ambersmith pushed a button on his desk. A magipsychic display lit up behind him, embedded in the wall. Or maybe the entire school was enchanted, and that's why the walls looked so uniform. Regardless of how he managed it, the result was that his entire lecture, including notes, photos, and even music, played out behind him as he taught.

The slideshow had photos of actual ghosts. I could tell they were authentic because I'd seen the real thing before. The other students regarded them all as a facsimile. Except for Ed, of course.

"You know it too," he murmured. I nodded back, not wanting to get either of us in trouble.

It'd be easy to mistake the pictures for illustrations, perhaps digitally rendered by an actual medium well-versed in graphic arts computing programs. But no, that wasn't it at all.

"These were all done with Kirlian photography," Old Grandpa explained. "Enhanced by means beyond the sort of thing that brought in the big bucks in pre-Reveal Salem during Haunted Happenings. Some of which I made myself." He winked.

I already knew the inventors of Kirlian photography designed it to take photos of auras. I hadn't seen it used on ghosts, even in my bygone extensive Internet searches.

"My late friend, Mr. Thomas Mendez, modified his Kirlian camera to take pictures of ghosts." Old Grandpa Ambersmith grinned. "All of these are his work. He left me his camera."

I raised my hand. Everybody stared. He nodded.

"Why aren't any of the pics yours then, sir?"

"Unfortunately, mine don't come out quite right. I can't see the ghost while shooting, so most of the time I miss 'em, or they're halfway out of the frame. And some of the local ones know what I'm doing, see. They make some—" he chuckled. "Colorful gestures the muckety-mucks in charge here don't want me showing at their school. That was a good question, but not what this lecture is about. You'll have to bear with this old coot for now."

Nobody laughed, but Ed grinned. It was hard to fathom the Messing Academy students' clinical attentiveness. They were almost like a hive mind. Maybe I wasn't far off about that. Telepathy was possible at a psychic school, and maybe they didn't want the shifter exchange student in on it.

I sat through the lecture, learning a few things about ghosts I hadn't known before, including that they needed a purpose to keep from turning into wraiths or poltergeists before they finished their business and moved on. Because mediums could interact with ghosts, they helped prevent hauntings and kept the spiritual ecology in balance.

Most locales within the United States employed at least one medium in the municipality but usually more. Since mediums were rare and the pay at or below average, those positions often went unfilled.

Instead, networks of freelance mediums traveled the country, sometimes the world, helping just enough of the ghosts to avert disaster before continuing elsewhere. It was an old tradition, and one carried on for ages before the Reveal by mediums in nomadic societies. Ed could end up with an extremely lucrative future if he wanted. Or an averagely compensated but immensely stable one. And stay extremely busy either way.

"So that's all for today." Old Grandpa grinned. "I hope you all paid attention because it's time for your quiz. You have thirty minutes, but you can go to the library if you finish early."

My time at Messing was almost up. So I raised my hand again.

"Yes, Miss Merlini?"

"I don't have time." Hadn't he gotten the message? "Uh, or I need my accommodations."

"Certainly." Old Grandpa chuckled. "Right this way." He led me to the far corner of the room. I didn't notice the door there until he opened it.

"Step through here, and you'll find yourself inside the simplest room at His Majesty's lodge." He handed me two sheets of paper printed with questions. "You bring that test in there, and you've got an hour before I fetch you, which is two minutes for me. If you finish early, come back and put your paper on my desk. You'll have time to get to the office portal and return to your campus."

"Thank you, sir."

"It's no bother."

I went through the door, and it was exactly as he described. A simple room with a desk, an hourglass with purple sand from the king's end of the beach, and a cup of pencils. I sat down and got to work.

All the questions were things he'd gone over in the class. This was easy stuff, too. Very basic but numerous questions. They were essential facts, even if I'd known half of them before going to class that day. Taking a test before ten other things could distract me also helped. It took me only ten minutes before I set my pencil down.

I followed Old Grandpa's instructions to the letter and was back at Gallows Hill right before the bell rang, ending the research period. I headed to Forum, feeling optimistic about the new coursework. At least with the constant testing, I'd never have homework.

During Drama, Ed followed me to the props room to look for foils.

"Hope that wasn't too bad. Medium class, I mean."

"Oh, the test was easy." I sorted through a bucket of fake flowers. "Long, but everything on it was practical. Like, common sense, you know?"

"I know. I could test out of most of this. I couldn't have handled being in second-year. Donna's got a cousin in there who's as bad as her, and he's almost twice my size. That would've been utterly brutal."

"Glad you're first-year. It's good to see a friendly face in there. Is it true there's no homework at all?"

"Most of the classes don't give homework unless there's a field trip."

"I go through my school for those." I sighed. "That's a relief. The last thing I need is more homework."

"The academics are the only thing I like at Messing," Ed said.

"Why's everybody so serious in there? I didn't like the vibe."

"Our grades are cumulative by year, not class. Half our score comes from the four quizzes each week and the other half is the longer tests every Friday. It's a brutal system for folks with test anxiety."

"I thought they were using telepathy or something."

"Mostly, they're worried about their grades. They have dampeners to prevent cheating, but it covers telepaths only, not devices because some people need magipsychic tech for accommodations. If I were a devious villain, that's how I'd take over that school. Buy and rig telepathic gadgets, sell them as study aids, then hive mind the entire place during a boring class like Numerology. Nobody would notice until it was too late."

"Is this a supervillain conversation?" Kiara held up the pair of foils we'd been looking for. "Because that sounds totally like Lex Luthor."

"Don't ever say that in front of Donna." Ed shook his head. "She loves that guy."

"Don't let her hear you talk about that hypothetical plan, either." I sighed. "It's bad enough she summons and controls ferocious beasts. We don't need to give Donna ideas about an army of zombie psychics."

"Sounds like Messing's a mess." Kiara clicked her tongue. "Glad I don't have to go there. And sorry you two do."

Messing Academy was certainly a strange place. Not too difficult, but unfortunately, the opposite of fun. Maybe it wasn't the best environment for Ed or me. Still, we didn't have any other choice.

At least we'd found the foils. We spent the rest of our Drama Club time getting used to them and going over the blocking for our routine.

CHAPTER TEN

"It's not about Lecture, Mr. Hickson. I have a question anyway," I said at the end of Forum.

"Go on." He nodded.

"We do a variety show on Rec Week. Then there's the performance showcase with our one-act play. I'm a little unclear on the differences there."

"The variety show is for individual acts, short ones under five minutes. The performance showcase is different. The play is part of an extramural event at Hawthorn Academy, where each school gets thirty minutes. Messing's is split between a poetry slam and interpretive dance. Hawthorn does creatives and a familiar's parade. We share our time with band. It's a way to showcase our performance artists where everybody can see them."

"What about entertainment wrestling?" Fiona spoke with her hand up. "Why don't we get part of the thirty minutes?"

"I helped Coach Tremain work that out. There isn't room for a ring in the Hawthorn auditorium, which is why you're doing an elimination match in their gym at intermission. Headmaster Hawkins came up with that to include you all. It's clunky, but it's also the first year we're doing this."

"Wow, I didn't realize that match was going on tour." Fiona smiled. "I'm excited, aren't you, Jill?"

"Absolutely. Can't wait."

"Remember, we've still got a boatload of academic work along with the Harvest Moon Dance and Rec Week coming up. Exams are after that but before Yule Ball and the showcase, though. So don't fall behind on studying."

"Thanks, Mr. Hickson." I tucked my tablet into my satchel and didn't say one word about everything else hanging over my head after Rec Week because I had no place to go for Thanksgiving or winter break.

All through lunch, I reacted to my friends' jokes and conversations with a series of auto-piloted nods, smiles, and chuckles. Because all I could think of was how Principal Klein surely had room for me at the boardinghouse.

Of course, I'd be the only student there, rattling around like the last bean in the can, as Kiara put it. Both holidays were a big deal at the nest, but probably not in a nearly empty Art Nouveau dorm, no matter how palatial.

At Drama, the first two rows in the auditorium were blocked off for the auditions. Mr. Hickson sat there, and so did Mrs. Ambersmith along with three other teachers I didn't recognize. They must have been teachers for other sections or years. I didn't know, and it wasn't the time to ask.

We set our bags down in a row halfway up, all too nervous to chatter. Once our guest students from Messing and Hawthorn arrived, the auditions began. No matter how the act went, we all applauded whoever was up on stage. It helped morale, and we'd all formed a bond.

By the time it was my turn to get up there with Ed, I'd achieved an odd sort of calm. The butterflies in my stomach and the anxiety that sang through my veins for the half-hour I'd waited went on ice. I wasn't sure what it was like for Ed, and it was too late to ask him.

We got up and did our song, using the fencing routine as practiced before everything went down at the museum and after that with the foils. No flying rig because we didn't have time to practice with it.

But everything had changed since then. Toward the end of the song, right before my big dodge away from Ed-as-Hook's sword, I popped wings and lifted myself into the air instead of simply jumping back.

Oohs and *aahs* erupted from the front of the house, which I couldn't place because of the lights. Were those the judges or our friends? I had no idea, and at that point, I didn't care. We'd done something incredibly cool. If Ed had been shocked, he didn't show it. Instead, he'd played off my improv in his way.

On the stage below, he and Rob merged, making Hook's last angry scream as startling as my impromptu flight.

I fluttered back down to the stage, put my wings away, and took a bow with Ed, who flourished as though he wore an invisible hat. That met with more positive responses.

We stepped down from the stage and got back to our seats, where Kiara clutched my arm.

"That was so awesome. You guys are totally in. I never would've thought of using wings like that or a ghost, either. It was amazing."

"Wait a minute. You saw Rob?"

"I don't know about Rob, but Ed got larger-than-life all of a sudden there. I figured it was a ghostly something-or-other."

"That's right. We did a hecking possession." Ed chuckled. "It's fun, but taxing and you need a ghostly partner you can truly trust."

"Well, however you did it, everyone loved it," Diego added. "I'm totally jealous."

"Don't be. You really do rock that Willy Shakes," I said.

"True." Diego elbowed me. "Always had a feeling you could sing. But I had no idea Edweird here carried a tune like that."

"What did I say about calling me that?" Ed shook his head.

"Sorry, my dude. Whack me on the nose next time with a rolled-up newspaper or something, and it'll stick."

"I know this is Drama Club, but seriously." Rita raised an eyebrow. "Chill, Diego."

The next auditions consisted of people from elsewhere in the school. We had a string quartet from some third-years in band, performing a medley of songs, a modern dance routine from Saya, and John Clayton doing a stand-up comedy bit he called "Ten Things I Hate About Worcester."

"We'll post the list of acts tomorrow before the Rec period," Mr. Hickson announced. "Thank you all for auditioning. I can't wait to see what you do next."

Lab went by with little trouble. The only issue I had was another incident where everyone saw Horace. I'd been holding a metal tube while Hope infused it with glamour, and I revealed my ghostly pal entirely by accident. I wasn't even sure how to keep from doing that again, either. At the end of the class, I apologized to Dr. Aranha.

"You're still learning, of course. I don't expect you to have full control of brand-new powers after all."

"Well, I don't want it to happen again. My mediumship class doesn't cover this. Or even mention anything like it happening. It's a bit embarrassing, being out of control, you know?"

"I understand." Dr. Aranha nodded. "It's easy to feel self-conscious in high school. Spider shifters like me have silk accidents for a couple of years after our first change. It's not the same thing, but unintentionally webbing classmates in Lab was embarrassing too."

"I had no idea."

"It's not something we advertise. Ask Mr. Hickson about it tomorrow in Forum if you're curious."

"He got webbed? You were in the same year?"

"Yes and yes." She smirked. "When it happened, it mortified me, but we've laughed about it for years now."

"So, what did you do to control it?"

"Practice. And time. With some abilities, that's the only way. At any rate, your ghostly friend is welcome here, of course. I don't mind seeing him. Perhaps the other students will grow accustomed to seeing a ghost now and then."

"Thanks for understanding, Doc."

"It's really no trouble. Part of my job here in Lab is helping with discovery, self and otherwise."

"Is that only for stuff we do in school, or outside it too?"

"As long as it relates to your abilities, yes. It sounds like you've got a specific reason for asking that."

"I do. You see, I'm supposed to discover something. On a quest, with companions who've got a lot more experience. I'm not sure I know enough to keep up with them."

"Lab is a safe place to practice. Feel free to do so more deliberately once you've finished assigned work. I'll announce that generally tomorrow. Some of your classmates might have similar concerns without the courage to speak up."

"You're a great teacher. You know that?"

"I don't often hear that from students, and despite my doctorate, impostor syndrome is my constant companion. So thank you."

I wave goodbye as I headed out. Practicing in Lab every day would let me hone the ghost-revealing power. Maybe I'd even find a way to make them audible.

Along the hall to the doors, Horace walked beside me in silence. When I got there, he stopped me.

"Good thing you're practicing here and not in the Under."

"What? Why?"

"Your teacher's right about time and patience. You need more practice when it comes to dangers you'll face on your quest. There are things hidden there and beyond the veil of death that you can't even imagine. Learn everything you can. Get intimate with your powers. You'll need them."

"Wow, that's intense, Horace."

"The best warnings usually are."

"I grew up in danger, though. You saw my sister. Mom is like her to the hundredth power. I'm so used to it, my first reaction to almost anything is considering it a threat."

"That's changing. I've watched you letting your guard down all month at school. The park. The boarding house. You can't let that soften you at the wrong time, and I can't come to the Under to remind you. You should have someone there. An ally not bound by the monarchs."

"You're probably right. But who?"

"Ask your brother."

"Yeah, hearing his take on this will help. Thanks, Horace."

"Hmm."

I headed out into the golden afternoon, too much on my mind to do anything but let it wander. I was almost asleep before I realized what Horace meant. That I needed Crow's help, not only his advice. However, he was locked in Danvers Sanitarium.

Unless he fully recovered. Or asked for judgment from a different authority.

CHAPTER ELEVEN

I found myself at the bus stop, the one that went to Danvers. I wasn't exactly waiting for it, or sure I'd stay long enough for it to arrive. Then Ramon showed up.

"You're going to see Crow."

"Maybe. I don't know. I want to."

"Then do it. I'll take the bus with you for buddy system reasons."

"Is that what the teachers call it?"

"No, Hickson asked us to be your escorts."

"Wyatt must have had a field day with that."

"He didn't. Ended up explaining to Cosmo what that meant and why he laughed. *El lion* is naïve."

"Nothing wrong with that. He's like a big kid or something. Anyway, I'm not worried about Mom."

"I know. I was thinking more about the monarchs and your lack of phone. I'm your boyfriend, so the captain will call me if she can't reach you."

"You've got a plan for everything, don't you, Ramon?"

"Not usually." He grinned. "Guess you inspire me to think about the future."

"Danvers Sanitarium is run by pure fae. I'll get the message."

"Hadn't thought of that. Anyway, I've got an ulterior motive."

"Might as well tell it to me, then."

"Always wanted a romantic date on public transit." He chuckled. "Really, I just like spending time with you."

"You're awesome, Ramon DelSangre. I want you around. Even if we end up riding the bus until it turns around and comes back."

"Bet you a kiss you'll go in and visit."

"You win. You're always so good to me about this."

"Crow gives you perspective. And has good taste. I mean, you said he told you to hang out with me."

"He was right. I'm glad you don't think he's some malign influence."

"Look, he's your real blood. That's huge." He winced. "Didn't mean it to sound like that. The rest are only important because they're blocking you. Crow's the family in your heart, thicker than the waters of birth."

"No, I get it. It sometimes feels like the rest aren't actual siblings. But Crow's my brother for real. And he's alone. I go so he isn't, more than for advice. Even if it's scary."

"You're afraid your mother might do something."

My breath caught in my throat. Ramon got it, even though he hadn't been in the thick of dysfunction like mine. I couldn't speak, so I tapped my nose instead.

The bus pulled up. I got on and gave fare borrowed from Matron Klein to the driver. Ramon held up a pass. It was another indication of how different our families were. He was right. Relatives were significant even if you didn't want them to be.

The bus was only half full, but we left the seats in front open in case less abled folks needed them. But mostly because, as a teenage couple, we wanted to sit in back. The bus bounced and hitched as it started up again, part of the fun.

It made stops, though only a handful of people got on. Everybody besides us got out at the Danvers Mall. The driver glanced back at us, eyebrow raised. She looked relieved when we got out at the Sanitarium.

We went to the entrance and through the doors. When the brownie spoke, my heart sank.

"Mr. DelSangre is not an authorized visitor."

"That's okay, Mavis." He unslung his backpack. "I'll wait in here with my Lecture notes. If your friends call for you, I'll tell the brownies."

"Are you sure?"

"No problem."

"Thanks again, Ramon."

I went to the wall. Pressing my hand against it felt routine by then. A moment later, I was back at the pond where Crow sat cross-legged, skipping stones across its surface.

I approached and sat beside him, wrapping my arms around my knees.

"They sent me to Messing for mediumship class."

"Whoever came up with that idea is a freaking genius."

"I'm pretty sure that was Mr. Hickson's brainchild to counter Mom."

"Yeah. Judging by that phone question, you know she was tight with him back in the day."

"Did you hear it from him?"

"No. Rumor mill. I knew before I even set foot in his classroom. Because of Bar."

"Oh yeah. Right. I bet you didn't know this part."

I told him about how they hadn't dissolved their old pack.

"I figured, from the way she went on about Paolo's entire family being inferior to her in every way even though they barely crossed paths."

"Probably hates him with a passion like a thousand fiery suns now that he helped me. At least things between her and Mr. Hickson are more like a copacetic cold war."

"My sister, the walking dictionary." He smirked. "I think you're wrong. Mr. Hickson just knows how to put on a good show. He's not the drama teacher for nothing."

"He got ultra-serious in that meeting."

"Makes sense if the pack's unbroken and she's still alpha."

"We haven't talked about pack types yet, let alone the energy involved. How dangerous is that going to make her?"

"It'd take a lot out of her to exert any authority unless she's in regular contact with the packmates. Enough to not make it worth her while except as a last resort."

I mulled that over. Mundane attempts at coercion were more likely than pulling pack rank.

"You're probably right. Hickson said Mom left them all hanging since the night before her wedding."

"Yeah, our old dad probably liked that. He plays that same game she does, turning people against each other. At least according to Branwen."

"I remember her rants. But I always had my nose in a book."

"What I should've done. We wouldn't be here now. Then again, you wouldn't have gotten that magic feather."

"Maybe, maybe not. The king implied fate's involved."

"Interesting. Thought you said *she* mentioned those feathers at the museum."

"She did. Something about knowing all the facts." I shrugged. "Didn't learn much myself. Except that you've got to be Under-born and have enough bird shifter blood to bond with one."

"Heading to the Under while pregnant is dangerous. You have to prepare, have an amulet if your animal form's small like ours. So she planned it. She wanted you Under-born. Probably wanted you to get that feather, too. Just, not while having friends and a place to go that wasn't under her thumb."

"Wish I knew what was in her head. Unfortunately, my psychic friend's not a telepath. But they're only good for surface thoughts. I'd need a mind magus, too."

"That'll be a cold day in hell." Crow chuckled. "Telepaths are a dime a dozen, but mind magi are rarer than hen's teeth. Then, there's finding one of each who'll work together."

"It can't be that uncommon for magi and psychics to be friends." I told him about the Rec exchange students, even though I was thinking about Thomas Mendez and Old Grandpa Ambersmith.

"Your exchange students are offshoots of extramurals. Definitely a better way, making it collaborative. The competition screwed things up big time."

"I don't remember it being that bad."

"It was worse than you remember. Bar and I kept our mouths shut in front of you. That youngest Fairbanks girl terrified me. And you know who raised me."

"Wow." I blinked.

"She was all set to murder Jonah Arnold and Noah Morgenstern, but she didn't get her way. Don't you remember, she killed a te—"

I interrupted him before he could finish his accidental question.

"Heard that on the news." I shook my head. "Always alleged everything."

"I met the girl, and I'm sure she did it. You don't have to take my word for it. Ask Arick. Or Onassis, he knows more."

"They're not at our school." I peered at him. "Wait, Onassis? From the boat? You want me to talk to him?"

"You've got a common enemy. He runs security for all the functions. So you might see him around."

"Isn't he your enemy too, though?"

"If you asked him, he might say yes. I'm glad he tried to stop me. I was wrong." He hung his head, sniffling. "No matter what would've happened to me for refusing to follow orders."

"Hey. Hey." I put my arm around him. "It's okay. You're my brother, and I'm always gonna love you."

"Maybe you'd be better off if you didn't. But that's the way it goes. Love you too, kid."

We sat like that for a while. After his eyes were dry, he shook my arm off then turned to face me.

"You have to be on guard. She'll mess with you. There's no way to predict how she'll do it either. Maybe academic, but don't be surprised to find her stamp in unexpected places. On other extrahumans from town, even."

"Horace gave me a similar warning, but about being careful in the Under," I explained.

"Wish I could meet this Horace ghost. Sounds like a cool dude."

"I like him. He doesn't ever say I'm paranoid when I worry. You're both probably right. I need to be on the alert, even if I don't ultimately escape whatever Mom's got in store for me. It's better to shore up my defenses and be ready to react."

"Sounds like you got your head on straight about it then. Her biggest strength is when she hits you out of nowhere. If you can't see her coming, the next best thing is being as prepared as possible."

"The same thing goes for you."

"She can't visit here. She's not on the list. I'm an adult, and I wrote her down as a prohibited individual."

"What about when you get out of here?"

"That's probably not happening anytime soon. I'm doing better, but you get plateaus and setbacks with mental health. Just like working out. I'm not ready to go out anyway."

"Into the mundane, yeah." I tapped my chin with a finger.

"Something's got your brain moving."

"Thinking about his majesty."

"The Goblin King. We're talking about my sentence, and you think about the Goblin King." Crow blinked and swallowed. "You don't have, like, a crush on him I hope."

"No. You're not ready to go back to mundane extrahuman society. The Under is different. Anyone who goes there becomes their truest self. A trip there might do you good if you go at the right time. That's up to the monarchs and your treatment plan, but I'm connected there. What do you think?"

"I'm not sure if you should even ask him. I mean, he's stuck with you because of that feather. Asking him to let me into his domain seems like an imposition to me. Or bad etiquette. Or maybe something I don't deserve. And I've got no idea about my counselors here."

"Well, I won't ask again unless you bring it up. But that quest they've got us on is huge. We might need help."

"Yeah. That's sounds rough. And you can't give me details unless I'm on it with you." He sighed. "I'll bring it up in therapy. If it's good by them, I'll let you know. Might be a bit before I have that answer, though."

"Take your time."

"I gotta go put the soup on the fire if I want any dinner tonight." He rolled his eyes.

"They still got you in that cabin, huh?"

"It's rustic, but I kind of like it. Cozy, almost. Even if I wish I had some beef or bacon instead of fish and rabbit." He stared up at the sky as he spoke that last part. Probably hoping the pure faeries would hear him. "I'm not vegan, you know."

"I'll leave you to it. Hey, don't forget to think about the Under."

"Yeah, yeah." He nodded. "I'm already thinking. Bet you can see the hamster running on my brain wheel. Thanks for the visit."

"You're welcome."

The fae sent me back to the lobby, where I joined Ramon on the bench by the door.

"I'm all set. We can go now."

"That's cool. I got my entire promo written."

"For entertainment wrestling?"

"Yeah. We were supposed to write one for our persona, and I figured it out while you were in there."

We went out to the bus stop and stood waiting. All the way back, he talked about his wrestling persona and the promo he'd written. He was afraid it was too generic or not intimidating enough.

"I think it's great. I'm not sure about using your actual name, though."

"I'm bad at titles, I guess. Everyone else has one."

"What are they?"

"Jillian's the She-Wolf. Fiona's going with Tiny. Wyatt's Big Red. Even Donna's got a decent one with Houndmaster. DelSangre, well, that's just me."

"It sounds like a stage name, though. Even if it's regular for you, the audience might not see it that way."

"That's a good point. I'll try it out tomorrow and see."

He walked me back to the boarding house from the bus. I meant to get homework done but ended up going to bed early. My brain felt overloaded, and I couldn't focus.

On Monday morning, I got called to the office. Fortunately, it was only during gym and not Lecture. Unfortunately, Principal Klein had bad news.

"Your mother wants an inquiry into your eligibility. For studying here, I mean. It's a delicate situation, and I've already had a conversation with a friend who works for the state."

"We expected this, though." I sat in a seat in front of her desk. "Mr. Hickson did, anyway. That's why I'm at Messing, in the mediumship course. Right?"

"Mr. Hickson knows how to handle complicated students, which is one reason you and Hope are together in section two. We got lucky that their director allowed you on campus."

"So what's the problem now?"

"For some inscrutable reason, your mother vehemently denies you are the Sirin. She's called into question the veracity of several witnesses, including Peabody Essex Museum staff, who witnessed your receipt of the feather. So she's demanded a full investigation into your abilities. Which means a visit from the Director-General, I'm afraid."

"I'm not an extramagus." I gripped the armrests on the chair.

"They're changing regulations about them anyway. Also, Hope's here, and she's not getting tested."

"Hope's family had tests done and documents drawn up years ago, verifying her abilities in the Registry. You don't have that. Since you're a minor, your mother has the right to request the same thing."

"I know my rights. Mental and reproductive health. How did Hope's parents do it? Maybe your friend at the state board can arrange another way."

"I'd love to hear your reasoning on that."

"Those tests are basically torture. I saw Aliyah's video last year. I'll refuse it on the grounds of mental health."

"You can't." Principal Klein shook her head. "Rest assured that this test isn't traumatic. They won't subject you to extramagus standards because you're not one. They'll photograph your aura, check for magic elements, check psychic ability, and have you demonstrate a partial shift."

"What about that extrahuman blood typing test?"

"I'll ask. It's still experimental, and I'm afraid even if they authorize it in your case, your mother can refuse. Unless you get legally emancipated."

"I know." I sighed. "Maybe I should get on that."

"You wouldn't receive that judgment in time. But I agree, you should. For now, I'll note in your record that you're cooperating and keeping things as simple as possible."

"Principal Klein, thank you. You've already done so much to help just by believing me that first night. Most people don't understand unless they see it firsthand, exactly how my mother is."

"You forget I was principal during all three of Crow's years here. Marge, Hugh, and Manny were students in my classroom. So I've seen plenty of Morgan's ersatz parenting."

"So why all the paperwork?"

"I'm a firm believer in following CYA protocol."

"I've never heard of that."

"It would be massively unprofessional of me to spell out what that means. I'd wager you've used it yourself. Ask your brother what that means next time you visit him."

"I'll do that." I nodded. "Thanks."

"One more thing before I send you to Lecture, Mavis."

"What's that?"

"You must have some idea about your mother's reasoning. Why she's gone to all this trouble, putting you through this ordeal. It's not just the hassle on our side, you see."

"I'll do my best to explain, even though the only example I have of normal comes from books and TV. Regular parents are helpful, mostly. They go out of their way to make things better for their kids. My mom's the opposite. She spends her time putting things in my way."

"So it's an act of sabotage, perhaps."

"Sabotage is how it looks, but a little off. Deprivation is better. Coming home hungry, opening the fridge, and finding nothing but water in there and a note that she's dining five-star. She finally brings stale bread at midnight, and you have to scrape the mold off before eating it."

"That's figurative, I hope."

"You'd hope." Echoing a person was easier than lying to them.

"I could make you an appointment with Counselor Goldfarb if you want one."

"Yes. If we can carve out some time."

"That won't be easy, but there are inquiries I can make. If you're not comfortable with Counselor Goldfarb, I'll try to arrange someone else for you."

"No. That's who I want. Goldfarb saw the whole confrontation, so I don't have to explain that."

I stood. She did too, stepping out from behind the desk and escorting me to the door.

"Good. You'll get through this, Mavis. And anything else she throws in your way."

"Why do you say that?" I blinked.

"You're flexible. The tree that bends in the storm lives through it.

When things go wrong, remember that. Now, head to Lecture before you're late."

In Lecture, I had too much on my mind to focus. Fortunately, note-taking by that point was practically automatic. After Mrs. Ambersmith let us out, I met Sid to get the portal to Messing Academy. Saya tugged my sleeve.

"You're coming with me after school today."

"Why? What did I do?"

"Nothing a little fashion intervention won't fix. The dance is coming up, and I already know you haven't got a thing to wear. Kiara let me look in your closet."

"I'll get by."

"Call it a late birthday gift."

"I was born in March."

"Half-birthday, then."

"I'm not particularly comfortable with other people choosing clothes for me."

"I promise the place we're going will let you choose."

"No budget for anything that fancy."

"My brother went overboard because it's my first high school dance. He gave me enough to outfit the entire first-year class if I want. So I'm doing this for the entire section and their dates. Shopping is happening. That's final." She turned on her heel and took three steps before adding, "See you on the steps after the bell."

I thanked Sid for the portal before stepping through to Messing.

Old Grandpa had us pair up for an activity. One of us pretended to be a psychic, the other a person asking questions about a deceased loved one. It didn't make much sense, and I'd missed the introductory explanation. But I got partnered with Allen, who was enough of an overachiever to repeat the rules.

"Psychics get uninformed requests from mundanes so often that they teach us what to do if we don't have the talent they think we do. In some ways, it's a safety lesson."

"You're clairvoyant, though. Why wouldn't they want a card reading instead?"

"That's not how grief works," Allen said. "Psychics are like a lighthouse in a storm to people in need. They want help so badly sometimes that you can't reason with them."

"This is something you do in the other classes, I bet."

"That's right." He nodded. "Much like our surroundings, our coursework is also utilitarian. Jonah liked that, but not everybody does." He glanced across the room where Diego sat with Ed, arms crossed over his chest.

"He's got a different idea of practicality, is all." I shrugged.

"It makes them stand out, not a good way. I'm not sure why it doesn't work for Diego, because it made his sister Miss Popularity."

"I think I get it. In a school full of folks intent on being as avant-garde as possible, someone actively bucking the norm would seem ideal. Diego's prickly, so it's not the same for him. I don't get why Ed has such a hard time. Rare talent and all."

"Ed's first day messed that up for him. He got unlucky."

"It's not just that. It's her." I glanced at Donna.

"Yeah, she's scary. And all her dogs too. There's not much we can do about that. Despite all the academic structure, discipline in here is like a Montessori sort of thing."

"I thought nobody used that past preschool for obvious *Lord of the Flies*-type reasons." I blinked.

"It's unconventional." Allen gestured vaguely at the room. "But that's this school in a nutshell."

"Thanks for the explanation. Let's get started on the assignment."

"Okay. I'll be the mundane."

Allen proceeded to barrage me with tearful questions about a fictitious deceased family member. Horace gave me a hand, mentioning more than one tactic Bianca had used during his time as her partner. Old Grandpa stood by, watching and listening.

"It sounds as though you're a natural, Miss Merlini."

"Not so much. Horace is probably the most helpful ghost in Salem. And Allen's a good partner."

"Yes, Mr. Arnold's doing great. I'm surprised he didn't also join the Drama Club. Help or no, using your particular psychic talent is the best practice. As you can see, Gia's making a passable effort with her telepathy."

"Wow. So she's reading surface thoughts to understand what the client wants instead of mediumship?"

"That's right." Old Grandpa nodded. "With telepathy, she can discover what they need, give them some measure of comfort. Most mundanes don't stick around as ghosts. If that were the case, we'd have massive hauntings worldwide, on a catastrophic level."

"I always wondered why Salem isn't one of those places," Allen said.

"That's a very interesting question and not something covered in first-year." Old Grandpa shrugged. "I can't give any more than the most rudimentary explanation, anyway. You'll have to wait until second-year when we've got a medium on staff."

"So there'll be one next year?" I raised an eyebrow. "Why not now?"

"It takes time. Mediums work under contracts and are already rare as you learned the first week. Scarcer still are those who happen to be teachers. Generally, they're on the elderly side. They've been looking for my old friend Tommy Mendez's replacement since he passed last year."

"If we get one next year, that means there's a contract already."

"You're too clever by half, Miss Merlini." Old Grandpa smiled, showing off his missing two front teeth. "Yes. But we can't disclose their identity until their current contract has expired."

"You're a fun teacher, but I'm glad we'll have an actual medium next year," Allen said.

"That's fine and well. I'll be no stranger. I'm a Trustee at Hawthorn. You'll see me coming here and going there at all the extramurals."

"Can't wait." I grinned.

"Well, I ought to go see how Donna's doing over there with Peg. Poor thing."

We continued practicing, feeling more comfortable after praise from the teacher. Sometimes, knowing you're heading in the right direction makes all the difference.

"I don't know if I should ditch her," I said to Fiona at Lab. "It feels awkward."

"She said the same thing to me at lunch, and I'm going." Fiona chuckled. "It's not every day you get to go shopping for formal wear with a dragon princess, after all."

"I guess it's just not my sort of thing. In general, I mean."

"I hear you." She shrugged. "I probably won't find anything in my size anyway."

"Oh yes, you will."

I turned. Saya was behind us, of course. Probably listening the whole time.

"Fewmets," I said under my breath.

"Don't worry about sizing, Fiona. We've got an appointment at State of Grace. They do everything custom, so whatever you order will fit."

"Wow." Fiona blinked. "That's amazing, Saya. If it weren't for you, I'd be stuck wearing one of Mom's old vintage numbers from the 90s."

"Everyone who wants to should look pretty at the school dances." Saya glanced at Hope. "Some don't care much about that, though."

"Yeah, yeah. She's a tomboy." I shrugged. "I'm not far off that myself."

"Hope prefers looking dapper. Possibly handsome. But pretty, no. She's already been to her appointment and happy with the results, I might add."

"Okay, then I'll go. Thanks to both of you." I chuckled. "For including a miscreant like me."

"You're the nicest miscreant I've ever met." Saya sniffed. " I really should get back to tidying my station. I don't want Dr. Aranha docking points."

We went about the business of sorting and stowing the pure faerie artifacts. Dr. Aranha let us out five minutes before the bell since we'd been diligent tidying, which left us time to hit the library.

"Just a sec, I've got to upload a few things to my tablet. Old Grandpa recommended them in Mediumship."

"You're really taking that seriously," Fiona said.

"Well, you saw what happened last week and all the practice I do revealing Horace."

"Yeah, it's unique. But I can't imagine how an old magus can help with ghost stuff."

"Hence the books. Remember, his best friend and brother-in-law was the only medium in Salem for a very long time."

"That's right. I forgot. Some of the old family histories go over my head still. I didn't have the entire summer like Ramon to explore this place."

"Yeah, Kiara's in the same boat."

"And having an easier time of it. She's lucky, so outgoing. Being the prettiest girl in our year helps too, I bet."

"Mostly, she's kind. It's like her superpower. She helped me with it that first night in the dorm."

"I bet I could come up with pretend superpowers for everybody in section two."

"That'd be fun. If you do it, show me."

"I will. It might help me refine my persona. I've got a gimmick, but it's supposed to grow with us. Entertainment wrestling is no joke. I thought you guys in Drama Club had it rough, memorizing lines. We build an entire character, then play it impromptu while doing suplexes and stuff."

"Is it really important to nail down every detail?"

"Coach Tremain says the other wrestlers will always play along for the kayfabe. But when you talk to fans, especially the younger ones, you need it. They're meeting superheroes. You need to be the persona."

"Hickson says improv is the hardest form of theater." I nodded.

The bell rang. I shut my tablet off after confirming it uploaded the three books I wanted. "Time to go meet Saya."

We headed out of the library and through the doors. When we looked around, neither of us saw our friend on the steps. A moment later, Fiona pointed at the curb. A long black car rolled to a stop there. Saya waved from the open window.

"Come on, get in."

We did, though I wished Fiona would hurry up and move faster. Out of the corner of my eye, I'd seen something black and feathery in the tree nearby. Of course, that made me uneasy. Especially after the news from Principal Klein that morning

The car rolled a few yards down the street. We passed that same figure in the Hawthorn hooded sweatshirt from the park. The bird flew away from them instead of following us.

Thank the gods for strange magi and small favors.

State of Grace wasn't a dress shop. Instead, we entered a small office over a restaurant on Washington Street. We rang the bell at the street level, got buzzed in, and followed Saya up a flight of stairs and down a narrow hallway. The door opened, and we stepped inside.

Instead of clothing on racks or samples on mannequins, State of Grace had an entire wall of magipsychic displays, showing images of finished dresses and suits with customers wearing them. Some of these had familiar faces.

"Almost forgot she did three years of formal wear for her class at Hawthorn."

"That's right."

Grace Dubois grinned from her seat behind the sewing machine. Instead of holding the fabric taut and coaxing it through, she held her hands beside it, a steady stream of violet magical energy flowing between her hands and the garment in progress.

"Hope mentioned you had a 3D display." Saya raised an eyebrow.

"We do, one moment."

Azrael Ambersmith stepped out from between two racks of fabric squares. He pointed a wand at the display wall. The figure on the screen shimmered, then bulged. Instead of watching Grace's portfolio like a movie, enchanted holograms stood beside the wall. It was almost like being in the room with Hawthorn Academy's graduating class from last year. And then some.

"Handy magic," Horace said. "These models look almost ectoplasmic. Tell them I'm impressed."

I did. Azrael blushed.

"Thanks, that's high praise coming from a ghost." Grace nodded.

"Wow." Fiona gasped. "I love that blush and green on Faith Fairbanks."

"Was it the color or the design that caught your eye?" Azrael asked.

"Oh, the colors. I could never wear a mermaid cut like that," she said.

"You never know, Fiona." I elbowed her. "Maybe you could try something like that on."

"We've got glamour bracelets here. You can try a variety of silhouettes that way." He went to a drawer, opened it, and set a tray on a table in front of us. "Just put them back in the corresponding boxes when you finish."

"No problem," I said. I didn't bother with any of the bracelets. Instead, I watched Saya and Fiona cycle through the lengths and shapes.

"We can measure you while they're doing that," Grace said.

"I thought you were busy."

"I'm done now. I was just putting trim on the end of the sleeve."

"Well, okay then."

Grace whistled three times, then clicked her tongue once. Something long and sinuous slithered through the air. At first, I thought it was dragonet, or maybe a bookwyrm. But no, it wasn't a magic critter or anything else alive.

An enchanted tape measure hovered in the air, waiting until I got a good look at it before wrapping itself around my natural waist, then my hips. Of course, a magical dress shop used magical tools with good manners.

"Now put your arms out and your feet shoulder-width apart. The tape measure will do the rest," Grace said.

I let it go about its work measuring the rest of my body, even when it tickled. I noticed something.

"Why doesn't it have numbers?"

"It does, but you don't see them," Grace said. "Those go right on our enchanted pattern paper. Once I apply the style you want, the lines appear."

"Wow." Fiona smiled, eyes misty. "That sounds heavenly."

"Your friend Hope said the same thing when she was here."

Fiona blinked but didn't speak. I thought I grokked her mindset anyway. Hope Dunstable was in peak physical condition. Yet she still wasn't any more comfortable with her size and shape than the rest of us.

"How'd she decide on a style?" I asked.

"I'm not sure." Grace shrugged. "She did that before coming here. Had a few magazine clippings."

I had no idea what I wanted to wear. Unsurprising, considering how much had changed.

By the time the tape measure finished with me, Saya had finished her structure selections. The measuring device moved on, running along and around her as she moved through all the appropriate postures without guidance.

She'd done stuff like that all her life, probably.

"I want the neckline plunging. Sleeves three-quarter length, fitted at the top and flowing at the ends. In seafoam green, of course. Silver accents. I suppose you could add turquoise embell-ishments."

"Like this?" Grace held up a tablet that visually represented every-thing Saya had said, including her hair color and skin tone.

"That's beautiful." She smiled. "Though I've changed my mind about the seafoam. It's a bit much now that I see it next to my face. What do you recommend?"

"Hey, Mavis." Fiona whispered.

"What's up?"

"I'm clueless. Saya told me I could pick colors and ask Grace to pick the shape and length. But I'm worried."

"Yeah, me too. At least there's loads of evidence she knows what she's doing."

"Yes." Fiona nodded. "But. Well, these other girls in the portfolio. None of them is bigger than a size eight."

"I see what you mean," I said.

Technically, Hal Hawkins' first two suits had a fuller cut. He'd been a husky kid who grew out of it later. But Fiona didn't need me whatabouting.

"Would it help if I did the same thing? Left most of it up to her?"

"You'd do that?" She blinked. "For me?" Fiona was so distraught that she didn't even correct herself about asking me two questions.

"I'm not far off the size of those Hawthorn gals. But I've worn hand-me-downs and thrift clothes my whole life. I don't know the first thing about formal wear."

"Tale as old as time." Fiona rolled her eyes. "The poor girl and the fat girl, baffled by ballgowns."

"Under the circumstances, we're coping reasonably well." I gave her a half-smile. "Stole that one from Counselor Goldfarb."

"That's smart. And right, I think." She grinned. "Thanks."

"That tape measure will be over here any minute now. Do you want me to go tell Grace what we decided?"

"Yeah." Fiona nodded. " I'm ready for whatever the tape measure throws at me, too."

Before long, we were all set at State of Grace. Azrael told us to expect a call in a few days to make an appointment for fittings.

"Thanks, Saya," Fiona said. "I really appreciate this."

"I wish I could do more."

Down in the street, we got back in the car. I glanced toward the front, but the partition didn't let me see who the driver was.

"Please thank your brother for me," I said.

"I will. But it would've been a lonely endeavor, doing this alone. And strange, not sharing my good fortune with our section. When I was still in my egg, my father told me friendship is more precious than any metal or stone. I strive to follow his example."

Beside me, Horace sniffled. I'd seen ghosts emote before, but not like this. When I asked him later what had happened, he only told me he was proud of Saya, that she was a credit to her family legacy.

I didn't find out until much later what happened to Wilfred Harcourt. Or that Saya's family legacy was perhaps more abnormal than mine.

CHAPTER THIRTEEN

On Friday night, we left for the Under again. The message instructed us to bring an overnight bag. Through the doorway, we ended up on the beach again. Only one boat waited in the water this time—a different one than the two from my first visit.

This ship was smaller than either but somehow more sturdily built. It also flew the colors of both courts, with sails to match. The figurehead was a gryphon with its eagle head painted amber with the hindquarters blue-black like a panther's instead of a lion.

Once aboard, I noticed that the queen's naval officers mingled with His Majesty's fleet personnel. Everything about the voyage mingled Seelie and Unseelie. Something impossible less than ten years ago.

I was pleased to find no need for enchanted lozenges. The boat's special magical attributes included a calm-water stabilization system. Plus, his majesty had supplied me with an amulet to stave off motion sickness in case of choppier waters or foul weather.

"If it's an overnight trip, I want to see my bunk. Take me to my quarters, ensign." Cosmo said to the nearest crewmember of that rank.

"Aye, sir."

The shade nodded instead of giving a snappy salute like the sprite we met at the door to the cabin. Below decks, I discovered a brightly lit area. It reminded me of his majesty's lodge but without any actual fire. The monarchs had probably supplied wisps to light it, which I appreciated, even if Hope blinked and scratched her head.

"I didn't think there'd be this much light." Hope shook her head. "It's not what I expected. Even though it's my command, I don't have final say in the decor."

"You must have wanted something more like where you grew up." Saya patted her shoulder. "But this is your ship, not your grandfather's. I think it suits you."

"It's different." Ed nodded. "But yeah, you'll get used to it. It's more practical for all of us. Especially with all the homework."

I instantly recognized the ghostly woman floating near a porthole at the far end of the room.

"Hi, Kasa." I waved.

"Kasa's here!" Cosmo looked around. "Can't see her, of course. Ask her what she's doing here."

I had a brief conversation with the ghost.

"She's pointing out our quarters. Looks like Hope, Saya, and I are in the captain's quarters. The aft cabin is for the guys." I grinned. "Kasa says she hopes you don't mind sharing with the fellow she's guarding."

"Wait. Nobody got word there's a prisoner on board." Ed blinked. "Staying with me, no less."

"I did," Hope said. "We're transporting the Tsuchigomo."

"That's either a bunch of bandits or a yokai." I gulped. "Not sure which is worse."

"He's the latter." Saya sniffed. "I've made his acquaintance before."

"With any luck, he won't be on board for long." Cosmo shuddered. "Gives me the creeps, that guy."

"He's not so bad," Saya said.

"You're only saying that because you don't have to share a room with him."

"Relax," a voice said behind me. "I've been in there with him from the queen's harbor. He's restrained. And pretty chill."

"Hal Hawkins?" I turned. It was true.

Hal had been in an enchanted chair last time I saw him, too thin and with an ashen face, suffering from a horrible magical disease. The Under's magic-rich environment had him functioning at near-normal.

His bronze skin glowed with good health, and he stood upright, looking crisp in the queen's naval uniform. The insignia meant he was the first mate. One hand gripped a brownie I almost mistook for a walking stick.

"It's me." He grinned. "I didn't think I'd see anybody from Salem for the whole year. But there you are. I'm the dowser his majesty mentioned. Turns out I have space affinity."

"You look different."

"I am, a little. You're going into uncharted territory, and all we've got to go by is energy. Fortunately, I can map it once we get farther out. So I'm helping with some of this quest."

"What I really want help with is someplace else to sleep." Cosmo crossed his arms over his chest.

"Her majesty prepared me for that eventuality." He gestured at what looked like an enormous cat basket in one corner. "That's your alternative, Cosmo. In lion form, of course."

"Holy wow!" Cosmo clapped his hands. "That's amazeballs with awesomesauce! I'm writing her majesty a thank you note when I get back to Salem."

"You're like a big kid. You know that Cos?" Ed chuckled.

"Totally. How else should I be?" He winked at me. "Next time, request a nest. I keep telling Hope she should try that out, but she's not as fun as you, Mavis."

I pondered that, not sure what to make of it. Cosmo acted like the youngest in any given group but looked older than most of us. Once again, I wondered exactly what happened in the ordeal Ed mentioned.

I followed Hope and Saya to the captain's quarters and put my bag down. There were two bunks on one side and a hammock on the other. I took the hammock. I told myself it was a way of thanking Saya for her generosity, not Cosmo's comments about nests.

Saya and Hope began unpacking things and going over notes on Hope's desk. I decided to make myself scarce. And satiate my curiosity at the same time.

"I'm going to visit Ed, see what the big deal is with this yokai."

"Have fun," Hope said.

Out in the main hold, I strode toward the aft cabin door and pushed it open. Inside I found a trio of bunks along the left-hand side. Ed set his bag on the middle one, and the lower already held what I assumed was Hal's bedroll.

On the right wall hung something out of a nightmare.

"Hello there."

The voice was lighter and airier than I'd expected. Especially from such an old man. Or yokai. Because man didn't entirely apply to him. Only his upper half was humanoid complete with arms, like a merman. His lower half was an oblong abdomen, with what I assumed were six legs for a total of eight limbs. But he was trussed up from the waist down against the cabin wall, so I only made out the vaguest outline of spindly legs.

In addition to the cocoon on the lower half of his body, this fellow also had alternating chains of black and gold wrapped around it for good measure. What I at first thought was a lengthy mustache and beard turned out to be mandibles and stiff whiskers. And his hair, though mostly gray, appeared more bristly than anything else.

"Relax, Mavis. This is the Tsuchigomo. Sir, this is Mavis Merlini, the new Sirin."

"How'd you end up on this voyage?" I asked.

"You're a sharp one, Miss Mavis. I'm to live out what remains of my days on some remote island, in more freedom than I'm accustomed to in the queen's castle." He nodded. "Worry not, young Sirin. I'll only be on board for as long as it takes to find a suitable one."

"What did you do?"

"I've stolen the most precious resources over the course of ages. Getting into specifics would bore you and go against the terms allowing me more freedom."

"They went to a lot of effort in restraining you." I raised an eyebrow. "How do we know you won't escape?"

"Wow, Mavis." Ed shrugged. "Good point. Back when I met him, proximity to her majesty was the only way to keep him confined."

"With the monarchs reunited, their power has doubled. Now, merely their chains are sufficient. As well as my word. Since you've no inkling and young master Redford may appreciate a reminder, I've never broken it."

"Right." Ed nodded. "He doesn't go back on promises. Ever, no matter what kind. So we're safe, even if Cosmo's jumpy."

I didn't want to mention the issue in front of the Tsuchigomo. That he hadn't made us any promises about our safety. But we had time for that later, so I changed the subject.

"I wonder if we could get a tour of the whole ship."

"Yeah, it'd be good to know where the galley is, among other things. See you later, Tsuchigomo."

"Enjoy your tour."

Hal escorted us above deck. He tried making small talk about school. Ed kept mum, so I answered.

"It's not easy. I won't lie. My brother's reputation precedes me. I wish he'd turned things around." I sighed. "Crow's the hardest worker I know. And he did a lot of things to protect me."

"Faith keeps me updated, so I know how his trial went. And where he ended up. Cycles are hard to break, but he's in the right place to keep trying."

"He says he's making progress. That he likes it there. I've noticed a difference."

"Everyone I know has nothing but nice things to say about Danvers Sanitarium." Hal nodded. "I wish him well."

I wasn't sure what to say to that. An uncomfortable silence stretched. Luckily, a whistle broke it.

"That's my time at the helm," Hal said. "I'll see you at mess, or maybe below decks later."

"Later, Hal." Ed waved.

Hope called the crew together with another blast on the whistle. It warbled almost like a bird call. She announced the start of our voyage and gave the order to set sail.

The boat moved away from the shore, and I watched it recede from sight. I wasn't used to all the naval terminology, despite growing up in a seaside town. Learning that might be a good distraction if my thoughts wandered into dangerous waters.

I could tell time by the sun in the mundane realm. In the Under, on the ocean at the border between Seelie and Unseelie, that was impossible.

Fortunately, each deck had a clock. I noticed the hour stood at noon, so no wonder my stomach rumbled. The sprites and shades served us mugs of hearty white chowder. The hunk of bread with it was hard and crusty, without much fluff in the middle.

I finished the entire meal. Aside from Cosmo, I was the only one who did. Ed sat chattering with Kasa, mostly ignoring his stew until it got cold. Saya wrinkled her nose at the bread and picked clams out of the broth. Hope got frequent interruptions from the crew.

"I think we need either distraction or discussion, Mavis."

"Let's practice our variety show number, then."

"Are we getting a concert, Ed?" Cosmo asked.

"Only if you show us some Bishop's Row moves." Ed rolled his eyes.

"Right after your song." Cosmo grinned.

"You're playing not it." I chuckled.

"Pretty much." Cosmo tapped his nose. "Not it!"

"Fine, we're singing, Mavis. Come on."

Ed took his tablet out of a half-sized messenger bag and set it up to play the music without lyrics. We sang it a few times, then let it play and worked on combat choreography.

I borrowed heavily from that I'd seen Crow and Bar practice over the years. Ed didn't have experience with stage combat, but I could tell he'd done the real thing, along with the fencing lessons he mentioned at school.

Some new fact about one or more of the Rhode Island kids seemed to reveal itself every day. At least they weren't boring.

After about an hour, we took a break. Ed took a few puffs from his inhaler, then headed to the galley for some tea.

"It's coming together," Cosmo said. "Never thought I'd see duels in a musical. It's pretty cool."

"Thanks."

"Thank me by checking my orbs."

"If you have an extra set of ballistae, I'll try blocking you. Did some drills with Crow for a few years."

"Yet you didn't try out for the team." He handed me a set from the bag he had on deck.

"The theater bug bit me in middle school."

"Just like Ed." He nodded. "Let's do this."

Cosmo tried conjuring orbs of shifter energy, but they didn't come out right. Hal came by to adjust Cosmo's amulet. After that, his ballistae worked the same as in gym.

"I'll adjust it back when you finish. Have fun!" Hal continued making his rounds on deck.

Blocking Cosmo wasn't easy. He was faster than me for one thing. For another, his orbs had big energy. His playing style reminded me of Bar on his best days. No wonder he'd made the team. Hope joined after a while. I dropped out to sit with Ed, who Hal had joined. Something had been on my mind as we played.

"How are we getting back to the boat instead of ending up on that same beach with no boat?" I asked.

"I'm holding the portal's position," Hal said. "It's space magic. But after my year's up, you'll need someone else to make that connection."

"Space magi are super rare, though," Ed said.

"We are. Fortunately, the same effect happens with mystic birds if they've got the right set of circumstances."

"I'm too clueless about my powers. Just got them last week."

"Don't worry. The monarchs consulted a clairvoyant. They say they've got a plan to help you manage the portals."

Hope and Cosmo came over for a water break.

"Not sure how those even work. Some faerie I am."

"You're not supposed to make portals before your eighteenth birthday. It's illegal."

"They teach it at school," Hope said. "Don't worry. You'll get the hang of it."

"You probably learned it before even setting foot in Salem."

"No practice though. Only watched Olivia do it."

"She had her feather before you. And you've had yours nine years longer me."

"Yeah, that's true. But again, my dad's a lawyer. He made sure I stayed aboveboard with my powers. Living on the Harcourt estate with Hertha's crazy security system meant if I tried anything, everyone knew."

"Everyone knows everything in that house," Saya said. "But we're practically family. We'll help you."

"The blood of the covenant is thicker than the waters of birth," Ed added.

"That's how it goes?" I shook my head. "My mom likes to tell it the other way around."

"Nobody has to worry about mothers here," Ed said.

Ed probably worried about his mother constantly in an entirely different way. I envied and mourned for him at the same time, but only on the inside.

***

"Thank goodness I handled everyone's makeovers before the voyage this time," Saya said the next morning.

"Wait, she's done this before?" I blinked.

"Oh yeah." Cosmo sighed. "First day of middle school. She had me in skinny jeans, and it was awful. I couldn't feel my feet the entire day."

"I don't know, Cos." Hope shrugged. "I thought it was cute."

"Come on. Look at these quads!" He gestured at his athletic thighs.

"I still wear mine." Ed snorted. "But I don't have ripped lion paws like you."

"Gave mine away." Cosmo shrugged. "Maybe I won't wear the suit she ordered for the dance. Tony wouldn't stop laughing about those skinny jeans for six entire months."

"He's been freer to laugh without your dad around."

Cosmo turned, staring out at sea. I sauntered over and leaned against the railing with him.

"That's harsh." I patted his shoulder. "I never even had a conversation with my dad. Only seen him from a distance."

"Mine's in witness protection."

"Mine's just separated from Mom. Workaholic, she says. I don't know which of her lies about him to believe. She says he only ever cared about my sisters. They're the oldest."

"He should have cared about you," Cosmo said. "Sounds to me like you're the brains in your family."

"Crow wants nothing to do with him." I grinned. "And he's the only one of them who feels like my actual brother. Is that how it is for you and Tony?"

"Tony is my only brother, though. I'm pretty much an orphan with no family. Was lucky Hertha took me in."

"So Ed's pretty much your brother too. And Hope and Saya are like sisters. And Blaine, I guess. Your found family's bigger than your biological one."

"You have a point. Don't leave Fred out either. He's not around much, but he never forgets I love anchovies on my pizza."

"Are you going to wear it, then? Have I changed your mind?"

"The what now who?" Cosmo smacked his forehead with his hand. "Dangit. Asked a stupid question."

"Chill, if you end up in debt, I'll ask you to bring me a bagel in the dining room or something."

"You're too much of a softie with the faerie debt, Mavis. It's part of your powers. Not using it properly is like me refusing to shift. Yeah, I guess I'll wear the suit."

"Does she want to be a designer or something?"

"Ask her yourself. Say's always been like this about clothes. She has a good eye. Hertha has a shopper for her wardrobe. Saya never needed one."

"That's good to know. I hope she doesn't go nuts with my entire wardrobe."

"I don't see why not. You've got a week's worth of clothes, according to Ramon. It must get boring."

"If I can convince Matron Klein to let me do work-study I'll be all set. With mundane money, at least. I'm the queen of thrifty shopping."

"Ed's like that too."

"Sometimes, it feels like he's my brother from another mother."

"So I guess we're sibs from another crib then." Cosmo elbowed me.

"I like that. It rhymes and everything."

"Oh, I rhyme all the time. I'm a poet, and I don't even know it."

"Oh, but you do." Hope wrinkled her nose, tapping her foot with her arms crossed over her chest in mock disapproval. "And you never forget to remind us, either. Next thing you know, Ed will come over and start quoting that—"

"You've a great gift for rhyme," Ed said with a light Castilian Spanish accent. I recognized it immediately from *The Princess Bride*.

"Don't you dare, Cos." Saya sniffed.

"Yes, yes." Cosmo recited. "Some of the time."

"What, you don't want any more rhymes now? You mean it?" I blinked, feigning innocence.

"I told you she belonged." Ed chuckled.

"Right." Cosmo nodded. "She even knows our old movie."

"I can't believe you two." Saya sighed. "That movie's so old that it doesn't even need a fake ID to buy alcohol."

"It's a masterpiece."

"You're right. It's old enough to be my mom." Cosmo stepped back, dropping his hands.

"Oh no, Cos." Saya reached out. "I'll get Hope."

"Come on, Mavis." Ed tugged my sleeve.

"What just happened?" I followed him along the deck.

"His mom passed when he was still a baby. He forgets sometimes. When he remembers, Hope's best at handling it."

"Oh."

I looked over my shoulder, watching Hope shift into her full bird form, which wasn't anything so mundane as a raven. Her plumage was as bright as a scarlet macaw's, though her song warbled like a nightingale. Cosmo handed his amulet to Saya, then chased her around the deck in lion form.

"But I had another reason, or motive really." Ed jerked his chin up toward the top of the mid mast. "You see that up there."

"Yeah, it's the crow's nest."

"That's not all."

"Yeah I see something. Is that a ghost?"

"Part of one, actually. Come and see." Ed stepped toward the rope ladder leading up there. "Think of it as a mediumship lesson."

"Hold on a sec. We don't have to climb that."

I popped my wings out, stepped behind him, then caught him around the waist. I lifted us both easily off the deck and flapped toward the round platform overhead. I immediately sensed ghostly energy. And saw something totally new to me.

"What's that silver line, Ed?"

"A soul tether. Astral projection psychics have them when they're out of body. They can also tether ghosts to an object, like Tommy's ring. This one's got glamour reinforcing it, but I can barely see that part."

"Whose is it?"

"Kasa's. She's acting as lookout."

"How's that work if only we can hear her?"

"Hope sees her. They use sign language to communicate."

"Is this something all mediums can do? See soul tethers?"

"Every medium I've ever known." Ed nodded. "But that's not a very wide sample. I'm waiting to learn more at school. It's slow."

"Can all ghosts do this?"

"It takes practice, so that depends on how they apply themselves. Kasa's been around a while, so she's got skills. She was in my dad's first pack, their scout back in the day. Anyway, I wanted to show this to you. Yesterday, you mentioned wanting to know more about your powers. Putting you in the class at Messing was a good idea. But it's slow."

"I bet you could teach our class, almost."

"Feels like that some days." Ed sighed. "It's frustrating. Like, I'm at college-level with my talent. But I've got to get through high school for all the other subjects, even if it feels like I'm dying in the slow lane sometimes."

"I hear you. I wish high school was behind me already, too. Thanks, Ed."

"You ready to go back down there again?"

"Yeah, I'm good.

"I'm glad your seasickness amulet is working."

"Oh, me too. It's almost as awesome as Ramon."

We chuckled at that. Then I ferried us back down to the deck. By the time we got there, Hope and Cosmo were through playing animal friends, and she'd gone back to her captaining duties.

We went to the galley and had breakfast, then practiced our variety show routine followed by Bishop's Row again.

After a few hours, Kasa returned. Ed brought me with him as he followed her to Hope and Hal. I watched him translate her information so Hope wouldn't have to. Hal pointed his magic at a mostly blank parchment, and a map appeared, fitting Kasa's description of distance. And also terrain.

"We'll see land sometime after lunch," she said. "The island looks deserted, but I spotted some ruins."

"Is it close enough to drop anchor and make a portal by supper?" Hope asked. "We've got to get back in time for school."

"Should be." Kasa nodded. "But you'll have to land and explore on your next visit."

Saya and I coerced Cosmo into doing some homework, even though he wanted to slack off. After that, I read one of the books Old Grandpa had recommended, *Beyond Solid*, by Sam Endor Ph.D. I had time before the winter exams to pursue other topics. Borrowed time in the Under might end up being good for my grades and playing catch up for mediumship.

Cosmo and Saya went back over the material from earlier with Hope. That made me think she would eventually end up grasping it better than the rest of us. I asked Ed why he didn't have any school work.

"That's Messing for you. The quizzes at the end of every period take the place of homework. They give us books to read about our talents, but it's optional. They'd rather have us practice our talents outside of school. I wish there were more ghosts on board so we could do that here."

"Maybe we'll meet some ghosts on the island. Kasa said there are ruins. Someone must have built them, maybe lived there."

"Keep me appraised if you do," Hope said.

"Of course I will. You're the captain," I said.

"Not only for me. That's the sort of thing the monarchs need to know. We're emissaries."

"Right." Saya nodded. "Hope has to report the same things to the queen as you do to the king. We don't want them at odds again."

"Makes sense when you put it that way." I grinned.

"That's my little-big sister." Cosmo smiled. "Super smart."

Hope made a zipping gesture over her lips. I didn't think anything of it, assuming Cosmo's "little-big" thing was only a joke about much more physically developed he was than the rest of us.

I found out much later that I was entirely wrong about that.

"Can't believe you're going with Brett." Hope scowled, nearly smudging her eyeliner in the mirror.

"It's what Mother wants." Saya kept her face still, managing to apply the perfect line. She'd used navy blue instead of black to complement the cornflower blue with gunmetal accents she and Grace ultimately agreed on for her dress. "If she tells me to date Brett, then date him I shall."

"I'm so sorry," Kiara said. "Unfortunately, he's not all talk. Wanda says he really is that much of a jerk."

"I wish she could've gone stag like most of section two." I shook my head, failing to coax my too-long bangs out of my eyes with a round brush.

"Here, try a headband." Saya passed one to me from the box of supplies in front of her. "Bought it before Grace and I decided on a different metallic accent."

It was still in the package and silver like the accents on my dress.

"Oh, thanks." I breathed a sigh of relief as I used the headband to sweep the unruly hair away from my still unfinished eye makeup. "That's so much better."

"I kind of like the long bangs on you." Hope shrugged. "But it must get annoying."

"Did anyone hear from Fiona?" Saya asked. "I wanted to see how her dress came out."

"Yeah, she's getting ready at Jillian's," I answered. "They'll meet us at Hawthorn, along with Jaxon."

"This is exciting! Rita says Hawthorn hasn't had a dance like this ever." Kiara beamed. "I mean, they had the one during extramurals two years ago. But it was in winter. Their fall dance used to be Parents Night, and now Hawthorn does the parent tour thing on Saturday. But it's Harvest Moon from now on. Magi, breaking traditions. Isn't that interesting?"

"What's even better in my book is that they don't allow any parents in unless they're faculty or staff at one of the schools." I dug through my makeup bag, trying to find the lip gunk I wanted. "Anyway, there's no parent anything at Gallows Hill."

"Well, my folks came to town anyway. They're here for a week, doing the tourist thing and taking in the history. And as many pictures as possible out on Essex Street," Kiara said. "You're welcome to join us for that if you'd like."

"That would be great Kiara, thanks. I bet Ramon will appreciate it too."

"All the parents got a memo inviting them to take pictures," Hope added. "Mine couldn't make it, but Bobb— I mean Coach Tremain's chaperoning so he'll send some to our folks. Anyway, Principal Klein probably didn't notify your mom, Mavis."

"She's banned from the premises and all our school functions." I nodded. "Including the ones that aren't on our campus."

"Essex Street is a public place," Saya said. "But we're all with you. She won't bother the entire lot of us."

There was no way to tell my friends the truth without bringing them all down. That Mom was wily, underhanded, and wouldn't hesitate to use a cat's paw to harass our group. So, I left all that out.

"I'll try and make it quick."

"Phones can take pics at Hawthorn." Kiara nodded. "Rita says they don't get any network in there, but cameras work fine. Airplane mode is how they handle it. But we can't post them until we're back." She grinned.

"That's good to know." Hope smiled. "Otherwise, my plan to light up Fred's notifications with a million adorable Jillward posts will utterly fail."

"Fred?" Kiara tapped a glittering gold fingernail against her chin. "Oh, right! He's the only redcap knight in the queen's court if I remember correctly. So, he's Ed's brother."

"That's right. He's also on tour with his partner Irina. Which is why he's not around much."

"Ed never mentioned that to me," Kiara said.

"That's how Fred pays the bills. He couldn't run the business side of Redford Construction after his dad took off and ended up dissolving it."

"What about Ed's job at Providence Paranormal? I asked.

"All that money's in a trust until he's eighteen. Ask him yourself if you want to know more."

"That really sucks."

"Well, that's why Mother fostered him. And Cosmo too, though mostly that came from Tony and Olivia only being able to afford a studio apartment."

"You know, your mom sounds like an awfully generous lady," Kiara said. "The social papers make her seem totally aloof, but from what you all say, they're leaving a lot out."

"She's abrasive, doesn't sugarcoat much of anything." Saya shrugged. "But my mom's got a big old heart. Most people don't notice."

There was a knock at the door.

"You're taking longer than the third-year girls, you know."

"Can it, shabby lion boy." Saya sniffed. "Enter only if you're prepared to wash your face."

"Ed beat you to that. But I refused to wear guyliner without a dual monarch request."

"We're all decent, right?" I asked.

An affirmative chorus answered my question. So I pushed the door open to let our buddy in.

"Damn." Kiara clicked her tongue. "New leaf lion looking like he belongs on the catwalk over here."

I managed to keep my jaw off the floor, but only barely because Cosmo Gitano looked almost like a different person.

Instead of that threadbare old trench coat and the well-worn jeans and t-shirts forever underneath, Cosmo wore a three-piece suit in a coppery velvet that shimmered under the hallway lights.

The riotously frizzy curls at his crown were defined and glossy. As promised, he'd washed his face for once.

"Quit blocking the door, Cosmo. I need to use the—"

Wyatt shouldered between the door and the shiny lion shifter. A moment later, he stopped in his tracks.

"Oh, never mind." Wyatt stood there shuffling his feet. "I'll go up and ask to use John's restroom. You all look wicked awesome."

He hurried away. But before that, I caught a glimpse of his outfit. Instead of the usual baggy cargo shorts and t-shirt, Wyatt wore a suit in brick red. His outfit epitomized Hollywood's golden age. He'd glamoured the eponymous red cap of his fae side into a fedora to match it.

"Redcap right behind that lion, Kiara." I chuckled.

"I don't know who picked that out for Wyatt, but they have a good eye," Saya said.

"Yeah, it was Ed. Who's responsible for this." Cosmo gestured at his suit. "He went back with Wyatt and Ramon to see that enchanted tailor Saya dragged us to."

"Well, you look cute, Cos," Hope said.

"Thanks, but you should see the other dudes," Cosmo said. "Thought I'd look ridiculous, compared to them."

"Look, no," I said. "Act, that's a different story."

Cosmo stopped bouncing on his toes and gazed at me.

"Called you gorgeous the first day we met, Mavis. I was wrong. You look downright celestial now."

"Don't flirt with Ramon's girlfriend, Cos." Hope rolled her eyes. "Be a good crewmate and lay off."

"I'm not flirting, just being honest. Don't pretend you're not thinking the same thing, Hope."

"Yes, yes. State of Grace did an even more impressive job with everyone than I'd imagined. Section two will be the best-dressed folks from our school."

"Everybody got their custom clothes, then." I grinned.

"Yeah, I had my appointment before you did. And brought Kiara and Jillian over there after you." Hope grinned.

"Your outfit came out great, Hope."

Pantsuit was not a fitting name for the garment Hope wore. Yes, it featured trousers with pockets, and yes, a jacket went with them.

But the styling was frothy and graceful, like the prow of *The Odyssey* gliding across the Under's purple sea. Diaphanous fabric shimmered in a range of rainbow hues, flattering her athletic frame. A net and feather fascinator sat jauntily on the left side of her head, completing the look.

"I know mine looks like something you'd find at my dad's museum." Kiara twirled. "I just love 1920s style. Grace did everything I wanted and then some. And I got to go with Brandon so we match."

Her dress was emerald green with golden accents that matched the undertones of her skin. The front of her hair was in finger waves, with a pair of looped braids in back. She looked like she could have stepped out of a juke joint or jazz hall over a hundred years before.

"Well, I'm all set." I shrugged. "Now that I have real eye definition and don't look like a sheepdog shifter, thanks to Saya."

"Don't mention it." She grinned. "I'm ready too. Let's stow our makeup back in our rooms, and we'll be off."

Once we did that, we met up in the lobby.

Brandon stepped up immediately to offer his arm to Kiara. His outfit was reminiscent of the same era but more reserved than hers, done in charcoal gray with sea glass green accents.

For a moment, I missed Ed because he resembled Horace so much despite his lack of facial hair. His maroon brocade suit coat was short in the front and had tails with two rows of silver gear-shaped buttons on the front. Jaxon wore something similar but in a blush color with brass accents. They both had bowler hats, just like my ghost friend.

Jillian stood between her brother and Ed in a crimson satin knee-length cocktail dress with a pencil skirt and corset top. Strapless of course, to show off her defined arms.

Ramon practically took my breath away. He wore the same colors as me, but instead of chiffon silk, his suit was shantung, with a color block effect in silver. His hazel eyes almost seemed gray until I joined him at the foot of the stairs, which is where I finally saw Fiona.

Grace had decided on a tea-length empire waist dress with a circle skirt to show off Fiona's dainty ankles. A lace-up bodice and draped cap sleeves flattered her figure. The terracotta color complemented her sometimes ruddy skin. Bronze accents made the highlights in her hair pop.

"Like your dress." Cosmo grinned. "You look like Cinderella but in pink."

"Thanks!" She blushed.

The entire contingent from the boarding house walked over from Washington Street to Essex together. I felt no fear, sensed no danger as we went. The presence of the upperclassman helped with that. So did the size of the group. I positioned myself in the middle, confident that my flowing silver and black gown wouldn't draw too much attention under the streetlights.

Once on Essex Street, Kiara's parents waved. They stood right outside the door to the CVS, which as it happened, was beside the entrance to Hawthorn Academy that night. It moved about Essex Street at random.

After snapping several pictures of me with Kiara and Kiara with Brandon, they exchanged pleasantries with me. I hadn't met them before and had been Kiara's room roommate for just over a month. So it was good to meet them finally.

"Kiara talks so much about you it feels as if I know you," her mother said. "Is it true you two exchange books all the time?"

"It's true. You might want to watch out about asking questions. I've sort of got a tithed faerie thing going on."

"Ah, yes. I remember the memo from your school now. Thank you for the reminder." She glanced at Kiara. "Well, I won't keep you any longer. The dance will start any minute now."

"It was nice meeting you, Mrs. Knight." I smiled.

"Likewise. I'm sure we'll see you again."

We headed into the hallway that connected the outer door to the lobby at Hawthorn Academy. I'd been inside the magic school only once to attend a talent show for Crow's extramurals. It was no less impressive this time.

The entire place was wood, from floor to ceiling. All of it appeared ornately carved. I knew better, though. It was wood magic combined with space, a tandem enchantment. Solar magic fueled all the lights, their intensity set to resemble a full autumn moon, in keeping with the dance's theme.

Ramon and I stopped at the refreshments table, where we got a quick drink of water before hitting the dance floor. I asked how he managed to order a suit that matched my dress when I hadn't even known what it'd look like.

"I told Grace we were going together," he said. "She said what the colors were to be sure I'd like them. I had no idea you'd end up looking like a moon goddess."

"I don't know what to say."

The music started.

"You don't have to say anything. Dance with me?"

"Of course." We headed toward the dance floor, but we weren't the first ones out. There was another couple there, one I recognized immediately.

I noticed Xan Onassis and his boyfriend. Dorian was away at college but had come back to escort his fellow to the dance. Seeing them together gave me hope because Xan's mother was at least as bad as mine. If his romance could survive, maybe mine and Ramon's could too.

Hawthorn Academy's DJ played waltzes for every song, a long-term tradition there. Every one of them was in three-quarter time or its close cousin, six-eights. We got through four of them before wanting a break.

Ramon went to get water while I sat down and kicked off the fancy shoes Grace paired with my dress. They had heels, of course. The straps at the back were the real problem. I leaned down to check for damage to my heels. They weren't bleeding as I'd feared, only blistered a bit.

Ramon came and sat with me. After a moment, Ed and Jillian did, too.

"Beware of dress shoes. They bite," Ramon said. "Or pinch like a hermit crab, in my case."

"Wish you warned me earlier."

"You need a bandage? Hawthorn's nurse is around here somewhere."

"Nah, it's just a couple of blisters." I examined my heels again. "Shifter healing took care of them after I took the shoes off."

"Lucky." Ed chuckled. "That explains why Jill has no trouble with her shoes, then."

"Sorry." Jillian hung her head and made puppy dog eyes at Ed, the corners of her mouth twitching. Neither of them could keep a straight face and ended up giggling together at her mock chagrin.

"Looks like Ed's lucky, too." I elbowed Ramon. "Brought the right person to the dance."

"Yeah, but not as lucky as me." He winked at me.

Ramon and I went back to dancing. This time, the place was pretty packed. Even most of the Messing kids were out there cutting a rug by then. Allen danced by us with Fiona. She beamed at me, lifting a hand and waving. He looked away.

Off in the corner, I saw Donna, a cruel grin twisting her lips.

"Uh oh." I stepped on Ramon's foot.

"My foot's fine," Ramon said.

"No, I think Donna's using Allen to grief Fiona."

He turned his head to glance in their direction, then turned back, about to whisper in my ear. For a moment, he froze, then relaxed.

"Don't worry."

"Hmm?"

"Watch, you've got the perfect view."

I was amazed to see both Wyatt and Hugh pass us. They stood by Fiona and Allen, both trying to cut in. Fiona blushed so deeply her cheeks almost matched the terra-cotta color of her dress.

"Mind if I duck in?" Hugh winked at her.

"Or maybe have a nightcap instead?" Wyatt bowed with a flourish.

"Whatever." Allen shrugged and backed off.

As he walked by me, I put a hand out, but that didn't stop him. Ramon and I turned together, following Allen the all-seeing off the dance floor. Ed sauntered over from the punch bowl.

"What gives, dude?" I persisted.

"Donna put me up to it." He turned to face me at the end of a row of chairs, putting his back to the bully in question.

"What, exactly?" I sat beside him.

"Humiliating the ogre to make her bulk up. Cause a ruckus at Hawthorn. As if they haven't had enough of those in here. But it wasn't in the cards."

"So you knew it wouldn't work?" Ramon blinked. "Whatever plan she had?"

"Yeah. Told her so, too. Donna only believes what she wants no matter what I say."

"Hey, could you tell me what'll happen if she doesn't wake up and deal with reality the way it is?"

"Sure, but you have to make it look like we're arguing from across the room. I'm already in enough trouble with her."

"Okay." I nodded.

Allen reached into his pocket and pulled out a card. He frowned, then pulled another.

"Slow burn on a long fuse." He held up the Knight of Pentacles reversed. "And then eventually—"

He turned the card and showed it to us. Ramon's eyes went wide. Ed let out a low whistle. I planted my feet, determined to make a good show and keep my word. With one hand on my hip, I wagged my finger before speaking.

"That's scary but helpful, Allen." I stamped my foot loudly even though Donna couldn't hear it.

Ed joined in, stepping between his classmate and me. Ramon grabbed him under the armpits, making a charade of hold-me-back.

"Tower came up for her at school last month. Bad omen city." Ed bared his teeth and shook his fist. "Tell me if it happens a third time."

"Will do." Allen put his arms out, pushing a path between Ed and me.

"Thanks for the reading." I gave him the two bird salute.

As he walked away, I turned and glared at Donna. Partly to keep up the act, but also out of true anger. Her smile made the pit of my stomach sink.

How could she do this to herself? Get so out of touch that she couldn't even take a requested reading at face value? It baffled me. Because her delusion was so enormous, all her cronies noticed it. But none of them thought they could stop it.

Like Crow's descent into New Order madness last year.

After the incident on the cruise, people talked about how nobody saw the signs. Cornelius Merlini was always mysterious, enigmatic, unpredictable. His cries for help hadn't been loud enough, such a tragedy. I realized something.

They only said those things to comfort themselves after the fact.

The truth was, they'd known. Not even deep down, either. They'd been stuck, cowed by self-doubt the same way Allen was tonight. So, nobody preempted his attack. After the dust settled, not a single one of them dared to admit they'd been wrong.

"Mavis?"

"Hey, you okay?"

I wound up escorted toward a chair by Ramon on my right, Ed on the left, and Jillian behind me. I must have been in a state for two of them to risk asking me a direct question.

"No, no." I shook my head. "I mean yes. I'm okay now. Just gathering too much wool off a fence that turned out to be electric, I guess."

"Maybe punch or water is a good idea," Ed suggested. "Helps when I get a case of the morbs."

"I'll get that myself, thanks guys." I turned to go but slowly so I could listen in on their banter for a moment.

"Nice slang, Redford." Ramon chuckled. "Fits the steampunk garb. Did you lose a bet with your bro, Cos, or something?"

"Nah, he's the one who lost the bet. I promised Horace I'd give this a try instead of pure goth tonight."

"That's Mavis's ghost, right? Bummer ghosts can't get in on this campus."

"Right, I think he'd like it here. Rob wouldn't, but he'd deal."

I really wanted to know why but needed that drink more. So, I moved out of earshot, albeit regretfully.

On the way to the refreshment table, I spotted an unmistakably familiar face.

I took off like a Spite chasing a frisbee. When I tackled my old friend, he barely budged despite my new and improved powers. My unconventional greeting still had the intended effect of taking his breath away, even if it felt like I'd run into a brick wall.

"Oof." He turned, gazing out as though expecting someone his height.

"Bar!"

"Mavis." He looked down, blinking.

"Exactly! You're here with Lena?"

"She's, uh, powdering her nose. But yeah."

"How's school?" I grabbed a cup and ladled some punch into it.

"Could ask you the same but shouldn't."

"So you already know." I shrugged. "Bummer."

"Word travels. Your ma must be pissed."

"She is, and I don't care."

"Watch out, though."

"Crow says the same thing."

"You visited him, then."

I filled him in as his girlfriend Lena returned. She scooped a small furry creature up from the floor, which turned out to be her opossum familiar. Ramon stood nearby, sipping punch. When I finished, Bar let out a low whistle.

"That's a story and a half."

"Oh, way more has happened. By the way, this is Ramon DelSangre, my boyfriend. Ramon, this is Bartholomew Micello, but everyone calls him Bar."

"They talk about you in the gym all the time, man." Ramon held his hand out. "Nice to meet you."

"Likewise." They shook. "This is Lena Zanelli. She's the best first defense I've ever shared a court with."

"Hi." Lena blushed but looked each of us in the eye. She ended with me. "Unseelie. Good going."

"Yeah." Bar nodded. "King's court's a good place for someone like Mavis."

"You think?" Ramon asked.

"If he and the queen were pants, he's cargo, and she's skinny jeans. Hickson explains it better than me. Dunno who your Lecture teacher is. Ours retired last year."

"Dana Ambersmith," I said.

"Ouch." He winced. "Major Merlini grudge on that one."

"We found that out right away." Ramon nodded.

"She's chilled out since the first day."

"And since the museum," Ramon agreed. "When your mom went ballistic."

"Kosher, then." Lena grinned. The opossum climbed down from her to curl up on one of the chairs. "Gonna dance." She headed toward the now crowded floor.

"Good idea." Bar took a step to follow her. "Later, Mavis."

"We should, too." I reached for Ramon's hand.

"Right, because you turn into a pumpkin at midnight." He took it.

At no previous point in the evening had anything felt magical despite the fact that Hawthorn Academy's campus occupied space between the mundane world and the Under. After everything that had happened during my first month of school, that was a relief.

Instead, it was normal. Time with Ramon was like that since the first day we met outside Tropica Mart. No pressure, no drama, and a sense of welcome. That time flew faster than I thought it could although I wasn't aware at first. It dawned on me at the end. As we danced to the last song, the night's figurative magic finally happened.

My entire body warmed as if I'd been out in the sun instead of a dimly lit dance hall. I tensed, every nerve thrumming. His hand brushed my cheek, tilted it up. We locked gazes, then lips.

The world went away.

Near the door to the hallway, I saw Hope. She caught my eye, then pointed at the clock. The hour stood at five to midnight.

"Hey, thanks." I hugged him. "For the best last dance ever."

"Time's up already, then." He murmured in my ear, hugging back. "But we'll have more dances. First and last."

Right then, the last thing I wanted was to leave Ramon there. But I had no choice.

"King's business." I sighed, leaning my head on his shoulder. "Wish I was leaving with you instead."

"See you as soon as you get back."

"I promise."

One I managed to keep. If only barely.

CHAPTER FIFTEEN

The beach was pristine, the sand a color more similar to the slate gray of my locale in New England. It felt solid underfoot, though we knew further up footing would be less steady as it got drier.

I pulled my sneakers off and tossed them back in the dinghy, running up the beach like a madwoman with my arms behind me like an anime character. I was that happy to be on land, despite my avian nature.

"I can fly!"

"Me too!"

Cosmo followed right behind me, running up the beach barefoot and flapping his arms. He caught up with me quickly, of course. Despite all the laps in morning gym, dance practice in Drama Club, and stage combat rehearsals on board, Cos was more physically fit. He probably always would be.

"Hey Mavis, I like this."

Cosmo turned once he passed me, jogging backward. Because of course, he did. I would've too if I could have.

"Yeah. Stir crazy boat stuff. You know?"

"I know. Just had to blow off some steam."

I chuckled and kept on running until I couldn't anymore. Not from being tired or out of breath. But because of the captain and her commanding voice.

"Halt!"

One look back told me all I needed to know. Ed was halfway up the beach, hunched over with one hand on his knee and the other on his inhaler, held up to his mouth. He hadn't taken his shoes off and suffered for it. I should've thought of that, warned him. I would've jogged back toward him and helped him out. Hope's order had frozen Cosmo and me.

"At ease."

Like that, we could move again. Cosmo and I strode toward Ed, but Saya got there first.

"I told you not to. You didn't listen."

"I wanted to have fun, Say." He puffed his inhaler a second time. "Stupid body, always getting in my way."

The hair raised on the back of my neck as the pit of my stomach dropped. An unbidden thought invaded my mind. Ed's asthma wouldn't bother him anymore once he was a ghost.

"You should be more careful." Saya patted his shoulder. If she was like this with him all the time, no wonder he'd fallen for her once upon a time.

That day, Ed shrugged the gesture off. He stood, tucked his inhaler into a pocket, and grinned at Cosmo and me. He shook his head, pointed at his mouth, and shrugged.

"Saving your breath." I nodded. "I grok it."

"I got you, buddy." Cosmo got a shoulder under Ed's arm, then hoisted him on his back. "We're all birds now!"

Cosmo took off running up the beach again, this time with Ed on his back, which slowed him down enough for me to keep up. We hit the line where the woods met the sand and continued under the trees.

"Watch the terrain!" Saya called after us. If only Cos had listened to her.

"Excuse me, miss."

I looked around, then down what looked like a deer trail through the underbrush. I didn't see anything. At least not until my eyes adjusted better to the shadows.

"Hello there." I waved at the still murky shape.

"Oh, you *can* see me. Perhaps you are the medium I've been waiting for."

I peered into the shadows again. My eyes were fine, but the ghost stood partway inside a tree trunk, which made them difficult to make out. I'd never seen a ghost do something like that before. Pass through a solid object, yes. But stand in one, no. Was this one afraid of me?

"You mean you don't know who and what I am?" I blinked.

"I'm not entirely sure, no. We've been waiting ever so long for the promised one's arrival. Eons, it seems. Or longer."

The ghost took a step backward. I moved forward, around it so I wouldn't lose the mysterious being. And finally, I got a good look at him.

Tattered fabric draped his gaunt frame, held together at the shoulder by a tarnished brooch. Wild hair corkscrewed up from his head at all angles, and his bushy beard looked matted. He was green, like much of the forest, but in a sickly way. Again, different from other ghosts.

"I'm not a medium. I'm the Sirin. An Unseelie bird in the service of the king, but with a medium's talent. Like a blend of faerie and psychic."

"Blended. Yes, I see that now." The ghost nodded. "You've got companions, boys on the beach. Perhaps he's one of them. Bring them immediately."

I thought of fetching Ed, him running here, asthma and all. My first concern was for my friend, not this ghostly stranger. Following a ghost's instructions to the letter hadn't done Hamlet any good. So I went with my gut instead.

"If you've been here for ages, ten minutes isn't going to hurt."

"This is for the good of all the realms."

"All." I raised an eyebrow. "Last time I checked, there were only two."

"Ah, but you haven't checked. And after all this time, such knowledge may be lost."

"Let me fetch my friends. It might take a few minutes, though."

"Shortcomings of flesh. I'd almost forgotten."

I headed back toward the beach and the beginnings of a cone of driftwood in a sandpit—a brilliant idea. The sun had neared the horizon, and I didn't relish the idea of sleeping on the island without a source of light and heat. The ocean breeze had a chill. Cosmo collected firewood while Ed sat, piling the wood into a conic structure.

"Hey Ed, there's a ghost in the woods. Said something about needing a medium," I made air quotes, "as foretold. I'm totally confused. He's a weird color for a ghost and undefined. Seemed not all there because he mentioned something about the good of all the realms when there's only two."

"Let me have a look. Sounds like he's close to becoming a wraith, which makes this a dangerous situation."

Wraiths were lost souls. Tattered and frayed by the ravages of time, forgotten about and forgotten themselves. They could do incredible damage and were almost impossible to stop without a fully possessed medium. And Rob was back in the mundane.

"I read about them but never imagined one would look like that. We haven't gone over wraiths at Messing, though."

"I know enough about them. Encountered one before." Ed sighed.

"He said something about being here for eons. If that's literal, no wonder he's going wraith. He didn't even know I was the Sirin."

"In the Under, we're our true selves. Ghosts here usually take one look and see stuff like that."

"Was it the amulet, do you think? Should I take it off?"

"No. He might be completely demented, but there's a slim chance he predates your feather and just doesn't know what Sirin means. We don't want to give him a shock like that if he's almost lost himself."

We took our time making our way to the tree at the head of the deer trail. The ghost wasn't there.

"Let's follow that trail." Ed pointed. "You see the pale splashes on the trunks?"

"Yeah. Is it ectoplasm?" I winced.

Ectoplasm was ghost blood, bits of their energy broken off.

"No. It looks deliberate. So either your ghost has something to show us, or this is an ambush."

"Hey." Cosmo was behind us. "Saw you wander off and thought you could use a little lion guard."

"Thanks, Cos." Ed nodded. "Yeah, we might."

"Should I go back and get the others?" I asked.

"No. I don't want them in this." Ed shook his head. "Cosmo is exactly who we need."

"Thanks, buddy." Cosmo punched Ed's shoulder.

We headed into the woods, walking as quietly as possible. Cos was great at it, Ed passable. I sounded like a bull rampaging in a china shop. I'd never been the outdoor type, except for flying.

Eventually, we reached a clearing where the ghost sat beside what looked like a ruined well. A tumble of bricks, blocks, and even upturned flagstones from a bygone courtyard littered the ground. The well stared up at the starlit sky like an eyeless socket.

"It's not here anymore. I waited all this time for nothing." The ghost's hands twined in his hair, pulling and tearing it out in clumps. If he'd been alive, he might have wailed in pain.

"That's nothing nice," Kasa said near my shoulder.

"Hey, take it easy." Ed stepped beside the ghost, holding out his hand.

The ghost stilled, then let go of his hair. What remained in his hands dissipated on the breeze.

"You. It *is* you. But I failed. It's no longer here."

"That's okay. You've met me, as foretold, right? If it's true fate, I'll find it. Whatever you were supposed to show me, telling is good enough for now."

"Oh, but it isn't. You'll need it, and the sooner you have it, the better. I can't imagine how they managed to move it."

"Who?" I asked.

"The Calamity." The ghost shuddered. "It ruined this place."

"Take it easy now, friend. I'm Ed Redford. I didn't come here for any calamity. I'm here to help."

Ed put his hand on the ghost's arm. It didn't pass through the way it did for me when I tried touching them. Maybe he was more advanced. Or perhaps the Sirin's powers didn't include that ability. What happened next would have been a miracle if such things existed.

All the ghost's frayed edges knitted back together. His garment fell in angular pleats to his feet, his brooch untarnished, and his gaunt frame filled back into a healthy wiriness. His hair twisted itself back into neat coils. And his beard, while still bushy, unmatted itself and resolved into a neater shape.

I glanced at Kasa a few times during the transformation. She'd always looked as defined as the island ghost did by the end.

"Oh. Oh, thank you. I was at my wits' end but barely felt it." The ghost appeared to take a deep breath, of what I wasn't sure.

Ed sagged against the largest flagstone, fumbling for his inhaler.

It was then I realized what he'd done. Gave his energy to the ghost to restore and save him from a wraith's fate. Now there he was again, puffing on his inhaler for his trouble. The ghost noticed it too. He turned to me.

"Ed must find the Cronus Sphere and restore the cosmic balance."

"The what?" I blinked. Cronus was one of the Greek gods of time, I thought. But I hadn't heard of any sphere or had any idea what it might have to do with balance.

"That's my quest. Balance." He stopped to take a few more breaths before continuing. "I don't know about a sphere, but I want to help. Tell me what happened here."

"Yes. I can't remember exactly, besides the Calamity, which couldn't touch it. After that, in the fog of my memory, somebody moved it. Perhaps it was the one who tried and failed two generations ago. Perhaps he had the strength to bring it somewhere safer."

"What is the Cronus sphere anyway?" Cosmo asked.

"Tell him it's something to research later," Kasa whispered.

I passed the info along, keeping my voice low.

"Cos?" Ed asked.

"Yeah?"

"Have a look around. Use those shifter eyes. Check and see if there's anything. Clues about who that was."

"Sure thing. Gotta shift, be back soon." He handed me his amulet. "Hold this for me, Mavis."

The moment I took the amulet, Cosmo shifted into his lion form. Unfortunately, that tore up his clothes. Fortunately, he'd been wearing a fleet uniform. There were trunks of them on board the ship, so replacing it wouldn't be a problem.

"Now that you've given your message, how else can I help you?" Ed asked the ghost. "Someone I can give a message to, a place you'd like me to move your anchor? Or maybe there's a task to help you move on?"

"We can't move on, not out here. The way's closed in the uncharted sea. But I thank you for asking. I have no anchor. Unless the entire island acts as one for me."

"Well then. We haven't done introductions. You already know my name is Ed Redford. This is my friend Mavis Merlini. The lion is Cosmo Gitano. And the other ghost here is Kasa. She was a coyote shifter."

"I am Cyrus. Well met, Ed Redford and friends. I know not my fate once all this is through. But it is a relief to know that you seek the sphere."

"I wouldn't say we seek the sphere exactly." Ed sighed. "Our mission is restoring balance here in the Under. The monarchs are united, but the realm's still not stable. They've sent us to rectify it."

"Then you do seek the Sphere, whether you know it or not."

He seemed about to say more, but Cosmo growled from a patch of wood near the far end of the clearing. I hurried to his side, where he stood with one foreleg lifted.

"Here." I slipped the amulet over his neck. He shifted back to human form, turned his back to me, and rubbed his left wrist.

"Hurts like a bastard." He pointed at his forearm.

"What does?" I squinted. Ravens aren't nocturnal, and the flashlight was with Cosmo's discarded clothes. "There's nothing there."

"Think I stepped on something. Now there's pain all up my forearm."

"Are you sure it's not carpal tunnel from all the homework, Cosmo?" I snorted.

"I hope you're kidding. You're kidding right? Crap, I asked a question."

"Look, I don't see anything on your arm. Or in it for that matter, no wound or anything."

"Yeah, I smelled blood before but that's gone now. That's good news. And if you don't see anything, it's not ghost stuff. I'll buck up and be okay."

"Did you find any clues?"

"Yeah, let me show you." He stood, and I averted my eyes.

"Just a sec."

I jogged back to where he'd shifted before, grabbed his indestructible trench coat, and gave it to him.

"I don't get what the big deal is." Cosmo shrugged it on. "I was only naked."

"You're shameless. You know that?"

"Nothing to be ashamed of. Everyone's got a body."

"You're so innocent, Cos. Never change." I couldn't help but grin.

It was true. Leave it to Cosmo Gitano to always assume the best. He wrapped the trench coat around himself and tied the belt, then beckoned.

"I found carvings in the rock over here. They don't look all that old." He chuckled while pointing at another. "This one has a date. Pretty cool, even if it's retro."

"Retro how?"

I looked closer. The first carving was a set of initials, a little heart drawn around them. I pulled a notebook out of my satchel, jotted them down, then moved on to the next carving. This one had five sets of initials, arranged around a five-pointed star. I copied it entirely this time because the symbol might be as significant as the date under it from back in my grandparents' day. My grandma would have been college-age, though she hadn't gone. Her initials weren't there. Not even her maiden name, I checked.

But one of them was familiar. And another had the last initial A.

"TM." I scratched my head. "Do you think that could mean Thomas Mendez?"

"I don't know. Do you even know a guy named Thomas Mendez? Oh no, not again."

"I do." I headed back to the flagstone near the well, where Ed still rested with our new ghost friend.

"Hey Ed, do you think our friend here is ready to answer a question?"

"I'm feeling much better, Miss Mavis. Ask away."

"Okay. The medium who was here before that you said visited after the calamity. Was his name Thomas Mendez by any chance? He might've gone by Tommy."

"Yes. That was his name."

"Good." I nodded. "We happen to know a friend of his, one who might have been here too."

"One still living?" He raised his eyebrow at Ed. "Do tell."

"I met him recently, but we only know his surname," Ed answered. "He's still in contact with Tommy's ghost. Via an anchor. A ring."

"Describe the ring, please."

Ed did.

"I see. Yes, it sounds to me as though this Thomas and the friend you mentioned were among the five visitors."

"Do you think we should ask the monarchs? They must've known if they got this far."

"They probably can't talk about it, or they would've told us already," Ed answered.

"Good point." I sighed. "Looks like it's library time again."

"And Dead Man's Party." Ed nodded. "We can walk right up to Tommy and ask. If he was under a ban while living, it might not extend after death."

"Brilliant." I grinned.

"I'll caution you on one thing," Cyrus said. "The storm surrounding the Calamity was atrocious. I wasn't the only one who suffered injury. The visitors got here after it passed, but they traveled through it on their way home. Though Thomas himself lived, not all made it out of the Under after that encounter."

"This Calamity thing is no joke." Cosmo winced. "Capital-Q quests suck."

"They warned us of the danger." Ed nodded.

"Yeah, not really sure why they wanted you bringing a garden-variety lion shifter along."

"Hey, you're not garden-variety." Ed patted his shoulder. "You're the only lion shifter I want watching my back."

"Thanks, Ed."

"May the two of you maintain your bond. You'll need it on the path you're walking."

"That sounds ominous." I grinned.

"And she's smiling." Cosmo blinked.

"I eat ominous for breakfast."

"Keep that tenacious attitude." Cyrus nodded. "It will serve you well."

"Listen, no matter what happens, Cyrus, I'll check on you next time we pass this island," Ed said. "If I can't make it, I'll send someone. I want to make sure you don't fall to pieces out here by yourself."

"Many thanks, friend Ed. But time grows short, and your journey is long."

"Well, I guess that means we ought to go."

"Yeah, Hope's already hollering for us." Cosmo shrugged. "She's gonna wonder where my clothes went. I'll tell her I was off being a goofball."

"You were a goofball." I elbowed him.

"True story, Mavis." He chuckled.

The camp on the beach wasn't for us. Hal and the crew used it as a base to resupply the ship with food and water. The boatswains from both the Fleet and the Navy took to the air and flew overhead with enchanted charting devices.

"I've got things covered for now," Hal told us. "We'll make a cartographic record and get underway once we're finished with that and supplying. The monarchs will call you when you're needed here."

"I'm still not sure how we get back."

"This." Hope held her left arm up. She wore a watch on a thick, shimmering band.

"That's silk from the Tsuchigomo." I blinked.

"It's a sympathetic connection to a unique creature. It'll help Sid's portal open onboard instead of the beach. Until we find a place to drop that old spider off, anyway."

"I've got your return portal." Hal concentrated and waved one hand in a clockwise circle.

The gesture reminded me of cleaning glass but without a cloth. After that, the portal opened right at the tide line. We waved goodbye and walked through.

On the other side, Matron Klein, Sid, Rob, and Horace waited for us.

"You're paler than me," Rob scolded. "Get upstairs and eat something."

"I missed you too Rob." Ed grinned.

"Sorry Horace, I met a ghost but not Bianca. He was from Ancient Greece, I think."

"Tell me all about him, but later. Rob's right about Ed, but you all need to eat."

We did as asked. Neither of the ghosts had heard of Cyrus, but they thought we had a good plan to investigate further.

CHAPTER SIXTEEN

Finally, we all got a chance to show off. Despite the Harvest Moon dance, most of us wanted to do something besides wear once-in-a-lifetime clothes and hobnob at a different school.

Hawthorn Academy had its charms. I liked it there well enough. However, Gallows Hill and the boardinghouse were literally my home by that point. What happened there felt like it mattered more, somehow.

Entertainment wrestling was first on the schedule, slated for Monday during the recreation period. There was art too, but that was on display in the halls all week instead of done in a presentation. Since the art kids were pretty introverted, that was a good thing.

On Tuesday, we'd have a science fair during Rec, then Bishop's Row with cheer squad performing between matches after school. First and second-year had two teams, while third had one.

Ed was concerned it'd run over, preventing us from visiting Tommy and Old Grandpa at Dead Man's Party. I reassured him. Matches were short. We'd make it there.

The variety show was on Wednesday. Stepping out in front of danger was all fine and well, practically second nature with my upbringing. I still felt like we didn't get enough practice, but kept those worries to myself. My nerves were all over the place as a result.

Ramon had the opposite attitude. All through Lecture and Forum, he was his usual relaxed and genial self.

"I can't wait." He elbowed Wyatt. "We're gonna wreck it out there, and everyone's going to go nuts."

"Finally think we've got it down." He nodded.

"Entertainment wrestling doesn't go first," Fiona said. "Last year that was band, according to Dr. Aranha."

"Oh," Hope said. "When do we see them?"

"They play in the gym right before wrestling goes on." Saya sighed. "I forgot they existed until I saw the schedule. Blaine was in band at Trout. I should care more."

"It's all good." I shrugged. "We've been busy. Besides, apples fall on all sides of the tree, Saya."

"True story." Wyatt nodded.

"I should have known, too," Kiara said. "We've got some band folks in the variety show, a string quartet. They're very talented. It must be a challenge, doing more than one activity."

"It's hard but not impossible." Hope grinned. "Science fair's the same day as Bishop's Row, and I happen to know there are athletes presenting projects."

"You're one of them, I bet." Julian smirked.

"Maybe," Hope said.

"That's our friend Hope." I chuckled. "Captain of the overachievement ship. How you found time to do a project is beyond me."

"My secret identity is Captain Caffeine, that's how." She winked.

Everybody laughed at that.

Fortunately, we'd gotten back from the Under on Sunday. Hal probably wouldn't be done with all his mapping until after Rec Week. Or even longer. All our quest outings had been on weekends so far, which wouldn't be such a great thing later.

In spring, Bishop's Row consumed weekends for our team, competing with the other schools. Only the third-year division did that, but the cheer squad was singular. Saya would have obligations, at least on some Saturday mornings. Maybe our journeying schedule would be different by then.

We went out into the hall on the way to Lecture from morning gym. Up on the wall between classroom doors, I saw that Rec Week activities had already started.

"Look, it's the art show." I pointed out the paintings and collages gracing the walls.

Cosmo's eyes traveled everywhere except the walls or the rest of us. His gaze darted floor and ceiling because there wasn't anywhere else to look. Finally, he set them on the door to Lecture, hustling toward it without speaking to us.

"Was it something I said?" I blinked.

"Nah, just nerves," Ramon said. "Cos has three pieces on display. He wasn't gonna tell anyone. Says it was last-minute and his stuff's not good. Maybe he's worried about that."

"Or maybe it's because none of us even mentioned art. I'd better go apologize, then."

"It's not that simple." Hope sighed.

"Why?" I blinked.

"Sad to say Cosmo is a truly terrible artist." Saya shook her head. " So, maybe it's better that nobody talked about it."

"Guy's like a brother to you. How could you say that?" Ramon blinked.

"That's dirty pool." Wyatt snorted. "Cos can't be that bad."

"Sadly, I wouldn't have said if it wasn't true. For one thing, he's colorblind. For another, poor Cosmo just hasn't got the fine motor skill for drawing. Even with years of practice, he can't draw a cube."

"Plenty of artists are avant-garde." I sniffed, throwing Saya's mannerism back in her face.

"True, but those master realism before trying anything off the wall. They put emotion into their work, even. So he lacks life perspective as well as skill."

"I don't want to hear any of that art is pain crap." Wyatt shook his head. "If you gotta create, you gotta create, am I right?" He elbowed Ramon.

Ramon looked at me and shrugged.

"Yeah, Wyatt. I agree. Creative arts should be fun. Stuff you like doing. It can draw off any experience, not just trauma. It's obvious he likes it, or he wouldn't bother. Especially not when you doubt him so much, Say."

"I'll concede your point for now." Saya clicked her tongue. "But if you see his work and find yourself agreeing with me, try not to be shocked."

"Hey, where's Kiara?" Hope changed the subject.

"She went into the Lecture classroom." Jaxon jerked a thumb at it. "Right after Saya started defending her opinion."

"Gotta go." Brandon hurried toward the door, opening it and heading inside.

"I guess we all should." Jillian shrugged. "Get in there, I mean. Ambersmith doesn't like it when we're late."

"Don't have to tell me twice." Wyatt snorted. "Still think princess dragon owes the lion king an apology, though."

We filed in, Saya at the back of the crowd. As I took my seat, I watched her beckon Cosmo toward the corner. The two of them had a conversation, but not a particularly positive one judging by the looks on their faces.

I made a mental note to seek out Cosmo's artwork on the walls later that day. Maybe Saya was wrong. Even if she wasn't, he was a friend who'd supported me. I wanted to return that favor. If my variety show performance were awful, I'd still want my friends showing up for it.

In Mediumship, I told Ed what Saya said about Cosmo's artwork.

"You can love something and not be talented at it. That's why it's a hobby." Ed sighed. "Mostly, Hertha encouraged him to draw and paint when he first came to live at her estate because otherwise, he destroyed things."

"Are you agreeing with her?"

"No, it's my opinion. Cos won't ever master art, but he loves it, and that's what matters. Thanks for sticking up for him, Mavis. You've got an amazing heart."

I froze, unable to reply. Ed was honest to a fault but wrong about that. He had to be about a bad omen bird like myself. I didn't dare contradict and risk driving him away, either.

We sat staring at each other, silence unsteady instead of comfortable. He looked as awkward as I felt, hanging in that moment.

Somehow I knew, if either of us broke that silence, it might break our bond. Or alter it irrevocably in some unknown way.

His ghost averted that disaster by butting in like a nincompoop.

"You've got a bad something else, Ed." Rob pulled a funny face. "Rhymes with art and heart, but it's not either!"

Class started so Ed couldn't laugh out loud. Instead, he slumped breathless in his seat, holding his sides.

That afternoon, our rec groups met in their usual places, then reconvened in the gym. The entire band stood in the middle of the court, all in uniform and holding their instruments. The rest of us, minus the folks in wrestling, took seats in the bleachers, watching and waiting.

They played mostly music I'd never heard. Pop stuff, which the crowd seemed to love. Their uniforms looked heavy, and their instruments even more so. How anybody managed to do marching band without extrahuman strength was beyond me.

Apparently, mundanes had been doing it for centuries. And out in the heat or the snow and other inhospitable weather conditions to boot. You had to admire them for that, even low-rated bands.

The Gallows Hill marching band wasn't one of those. They already rocked and would be amazing by spring Rec Week and the extramural events. They finished and marched off the court to the sound of a cheering crowd.

I'd never seen any wrestling at Gallows Hill. Still, I knew something of what to expect. Before the Reveal, the extrahuman version used to be underground. Now, there were all types of leagues with divisions and belts at a professional level because entertainment wrestling was a televised sport.

Each of our school's wrestlers had personas, gimmicks, and entrance music, but they had divided into groups based on their weight or style. It was just like televised wrestling—plenty of drama and even more choreographed but not fake combat.

I expected to admire Ramon as Angry DelSangre. He'd chosen an underdog persona with a bat and blood costume. The concept worked well for a dhampyr and set him apart from the shifters and changelings in his weight bracket. In practice, he stood out because he wasn't afraid to take risks.

Ramon's moves mainly involved launching himself off the top turnbuckle, even managing a few flips in the air before landing on his opponents with an elbow or knee. Despite the fact that his opponents were often shifters with enhanced strength, he held his own. He was a face, sympathetic to the audience.

Jillian was a heel, the kind of wrestler people love to hate. As the She-Wolf, Jill displayed undeniable skill but with a boastful attitude. Her natural directness, along with her stature and muscular build, brought the persona to life. Timid, gentle Fiona was her tag team partner. She went by the name Tiny in the ring.

The She-Wolf was all gnashing teeth and challenges declaring the best. Tiny stomped gleefully around the ring, catching her opponents in bear hugs and chokeholds with apparent affection. They ended up flat on the mat and gasping for air. She did it all with an enormous, innocent smile on her face. The crowd loved her.

The big surprise was Wyatt as Big Red. He never made the cut for Bishop's Row. The way he told it, Wyatt settled for entertainment wrestling. You'd never think that watching him. As the only freshman in the heavyweight title class, he held his own against older students. They didn't let him win his match, which Ramon said wasn't easy for anyone, let alone someone with a big ego. At first, it wasn't clear whether he was a face or a heel.

"Big Red? More like Big Red Stain," his final opponent said.

That elicited a resounding chorus of boos from the audience. Nobody liked it when the guy stomping on the underdog piles on an insult for good measure. I appreciated the effort, time, and sheer physical effort the entertainment wrestling students went through.

How the Drama Club could hold a candle to them, I had no idea. At least we had Bishop's Row and the science fair before worrying about that.

CHAPTER SEVENTEEN

On Tuesday, we had the science fair at rec time and Bishop's Row after school. After lunch, I headed toward the gym, where they'd set up the tables and projects during the earlier break.

Across from the entrance, a painting on the wall caught my eye. I stopped and stared, scratching my head and wrinkling my nose.

"That's Cosmo's," Horace said. "If you don't like it, don't say anything, okay?"

"I'm baffled. He's sixteen. But it reminds me of finger paintings by a kindergartener."

"Hush. The walls don't have ears, but other students are walking behind you right now."

"But why?"

"It's not my place to answer."

Horace leaned against the wall, a challenging feat for a ghost.

"You mean I'll never know?"

"You can live with wondering. He's better off keeping that secret."

"Good point. Curiosity gets the cat, but I'm a raven. I should know better."

"Having as much information as possible without directly asking is a sensible survival tactic. You don't need it for this. Try to let it go."

"Thanks for the reminder. And I'm sorry."

Horace blinked.

"Bet you never had this problem with Bianca."

"As perfect as she was for me, Bianca came with her own set of flaws. There's no need to apologize because hypervigilance wasn't one of them."

"I'm lucky. Could have wound up with a prankster like Rob."

"Rob's exactly who Ed needs. But—"

The bell rang.

"We ought to move along, see what all the brainiacs made."

"Brainiacs?"

I turned my head to see the woman who'd paused beside me in the hall.

"Yeah, I said brainiacs. You have a problem with that?"

"I resemble that remark." The young woman grinned. "I'm Doctor Lynn Frampton, one of the brainiacs judging the science fair." She held her hand out.

"I'm Mavis Merlini." I shook with her. "Just a student, but no science, I'm afraid. I bet you won all your science fairs."

We stepped into the gym, where tables bordered the court.

"I never did projects like these."

The tables were full of contraptions, thingamabobs, whatchamacallits, and gizmos. I had no clue what they were for. Most were advanced, the work of seniors and juniors. Lynn's comment baffled me.

"What do you mean? You're a doctor."

"I did Undergrad and Med School at Providence Paranormal. But my high school was a totally different animal."

"Psychic, then?"

"No, I'm mundane."

"Get out!" I smiled. "Don't tell me you're *that* student, the first mundane at a magical college?"

"Yeah, it was a piece of cake academically. The hardest part was all the hullabaloo over being non-magical."

Lynn Frampton wasn't humble. Some people might have found her off-putting, but her confidence inspired me.

I saw Kiara and Brandon waving from behind their table.

"That's my roommate over there. I didn't get to see her gadget yet."

"Well, it was nice to meet you, Mavis. I'm sure we'll see each other again sometime."

"Nice meeting you too, Dr. Frampton."

I crossed the room, where my roommate greeted me.

"Welcome to the future!"

"What did you make, Kiara?" I gestured at the kabuki brush on the table.

"It's illusion cosmetics." She smiled. "Well, not totally illusion. There's water in it. It takes a picture of makeup you like from anywhere so you can wear that look. Like a filter on Picstagram, but for your actual face. Do you want to give it a try?"

"Sure."

"Great!" Kiara bounced on her toes. "Come on over here."

Brandon had an array of images from fashion magazines. I picked one out with some complicated contouring. Kiara held the brush over the page while holding a button on the side. She handed it to me.

Dr. Aranha approached the table. She stood watching as I used the brush on my face. Kiara held up a mirror, and sure enough, my face was expertly contoured.

"That's an interesting piece of work, Miss Knight." Dr. Aranha nodded approvingly. "Excellent application of first-year skills and good teamwork. It could use its own mirror, perhaps a preview function. But I don't expect you to learn those methods until midway through second-year. Keep up the good work!"

"I like it, too." I chuckled. "If I had this the night of the dance, I wouldn't have got mascara in my eye."

"I know, right." Kiara clicked her tongue. "I wish it was done by then, too."

"Hey, can I check that out?" Jillian leaned over, peering at the device. "Will it work with a pic from my phone?"

"Yeah, it can do that," Kiara said.

"Wicked cool." Jillian smiled.

"Have fun. I'm going to go look at Hope's project."

"Tell her I said her gadget was cool," Jillian said. "I saw it a few minutes ago."

"Okay, later."

The item on her table looked like a regular spyglass. Brass, but mostly normal.

"Jill said your project was cool, Hope."

"Wow." Hope blinked. "Have a look for yourself."

"Okay."

I picked it up, turned it over a few times, and peered at its surface. Maybe it really was just a garden-variety spyglass. To any outside observer, that's what it looked like.

Then, I put it to my eye. It was far more than that.

"This is amazing. I can see so many things. You must've had help from a magus."

"Hal added some energy to it on board, but the idea and design were all mine."

"I can't imagine there's anything else out there like this."

"There is. I've seen it."

"Yours is better."

"I'm not sure it's better. But you're right. I saw magic monocles at Providence Paranormal College in the Magic Theory lab. They only have one lens each. This has three. But I made it a spyglass to keep one eye free. It's easier to compare mundane with magical that way."

"Hey Horace, can you stand in front of me for a minute?"

He had a golden aura, totally different from everybody else's. Even the other random ghosts.

"Something's interesting," Hope said.

I told her what I saw.

"Then it's not gone." Horace gasped.

"I'd love to know what he just said," Hope said.

I repeated it for her, then handed the spyglass back.

"Maybe it's about him and Bianca," I added. "Because they're destined."

"Maybe. You should ask Ed about gold auras next time you see him."

"I hope I don't forget." I sighed. "So many things are going on. It's hard to keep track."

"I'll remember." Horace nodded.

"The judges are here," Hope said. "I'll be busy for a bit."

"See you later then."

"Yeah."

I wandered around the room, not in the mood for any more science projects. They weren't mandatory, so nobody else I knew had one. Eventually, I moved into the hall to look at art. I found another bafflingly juvenile painting in watercolor this time. Once again, it was Cosmo's.

His paintings were strangely distinct. They certainly provoked an emotional reaction, which explained why the teachers chose them for display. The truth was, despite the crude and unskilled execution, the subject matter hit home. The finger painting was of someone caught on a street, in a truck's headlights.

This watercolor of a pond should've been common, even bucolic. Except the waters were a still, sickly shade of green. Dangerous, not relaxing. Had Cosmo been in situations like this? Or did he draw from his friends? If so, how did that work for a regular lion shifter?

I meant to ask, but Cosmo worked with Hope in Lab. They both left early to get ready for Bishop's Row along with all the other players. They'd have sandwiches in the cafeteria, warm up, then get changed into uniforms for a start time of five.

The rest of the students left school for a quick meal at home. For most of my classmates and me, that meant the boarding house.

The dining room had three varieties of chili, along with toppings including cheese, salsa, guacamole, sour cream, and nachos. The line was long but moved quickly since everything was self-serve.

I got there first and ended up sitting at the table thinking, barely touching my food.

"Your chili is getting cold." Ed wagged a finger at my bowl, then sat down with his. "You need that. We're dashing to Koto after the games."

"You're right. Hey Ed, I saw something weird today. I was wondering if you knew what it was."

I told him about Hope's spyglass and Horace's aura.

"That's strange for sure." Ed nodded. "I've never seen an aura like that myself. But it sounds familiar. Might be luck energy."

"Luck energy?" I blinked.

"Yeah. Dragons and tanukis can see it, but only the latter can manipulate it. It consumes a charm, though, so it's not something they do every day."

"Didn't Cos say Blaine's wife is a tanuki?"

"She is. But she can't see ghosts. So this gold aura might have been on Horace for a long time without us knowing."

"He thinks it has something to do with Bianca."

"It might." Ed stirred his chili. "I can't imagine anything but luck reuniting the two of them at this point."

"Maybe we should borrow it. Look at everyone we can. And ask Old Grandpa or Tommy about Horace's aura."

"Those are sound ideas. But it's Hope's call. She made the thing for our quest. We'll need it in the Under."

"That's a good point."

"Less talking, more fooding." Wyatt plunked his bowl down. He'd already finished half the chili in it.

"Did you skip lunch or something?" I asked.

"Nah, stress eating." He wolfed more down. "Still annoyed about not making the team."

"I grok the stress." I pointed my spoon at his now-empty bowl. "But not the eating."

"Redcap stress eating is pretty common." Ed gave him a grin and his nachos.

"You know it." Wyatt crunched chips. "Do you ever wish you'd been born a redcap?"

"Doesn't matter." Ed chuckled. "Medium's my game. Small medium, though."

Wyatt hadn't heard that one before apparently. He guffawed, slapping the table so hard Brandon had to hug his bowl before it tipped over.

"My smallest brother here practically invented medium-bad jokes." Saya raised an eyebrow at Ed, sniffing.

"Thanks, Blaine two-point-oh." Ed smiled broadly.

"That's an enormous compliment, considering what a genius he is." Saya raised an eyebrow.

Like that, all the tension between Saya and Ed crumbled like a decayed rubber band.

After chili, we went through the magic door to campus. It led into the gym, set up with a regulation-size Bishop's Row court. The bleachers were out on both sides of it, already quite full with students, parents, faculty, and staff.

"Guess we'll be in the nosebleed seats." I shrugged.

"Nope, Ramon and the twins saved you some seats," Saya said.

Sure enough, our friends sat there, waving. We headed toward it, but Saya made a beeline for the locker room.

"Oh, right. She's on the cheer squad." I winced. "I almost forgot."

"Good thing she didn't," Ed said.

We joined our friends and got seated. Ed went next to Jillian while Kiara and Brandon went on the other side of Jaxon. Fiona climbed down from a few rows up and sat on the other side of Wyatt from me.

"Thanks." I hugged Ramon. "You're the best boyfriend ever."

"Gotta be, to keep up with you." He put his arm around me.

"Aww!" Fiona smiled.

"Eww, you mean." Wyatt made a gagging noise. "Who wants to bother with dating."

"Last time I checked, you did." I rolled my eyes. "Until Kiara got together with Brandon."

Wyatt turned away and faced Fiona.

"What were you doing up there, anyway?" Wyatt asked. "Starting a fan club for your favorite ship?"

"Talking to my fans, actually." She shrugged. "Well, Tiny's fans."

"Oh." He stared at the court. "Well, here comes our year."

Both of the first-year division teams strode out from the locker room, one in white uniforms with red numbers and the other in red with white numbers. Hope and Cosmo were on the white team.

"Red team looks intimidating." Ramon winced. "Hope our friends can handle them."

"Cosmo's aces with those orbs," I said. "Don't worry. We practiced in the Under, but I couldn't really keep up."

"Hope probably could, though," Fiona said.

"She did." I grinned. "He blocked almost everything she threw at him, but he never tagged her."

Cosmo was brutal with the orbs. He conjured quickly and never seemed to run out of steam. Also, he threw with deadly accuracy, resisting all efforts to fake him out. If he been on a battlefield, he would have turned the tide.

Hope was in back, playing reverse point, the MVP position. I wasn't surprised to see her in it, either. Now that her true nature was no secret, she used her wings to dodge and counter orbs at impossible angles.

They called the game for the white team. They'd play again, facing whichever team won second-year.

Cheer squad was school-wide and included students from all three years. Saya was the only first-year on it. They'd need to recruit more from us next year, however. A good portion of the group were third-years, including Wanda.

"I love this song!" Kiara clapped her hands. "If I knew they did routines like this, I might've tried out."

We watched them dance through their routine, cheering after the performance. They'd be back with more between games.

Brett the dragon shifter was the only person I knew by name in second-year, playing on their blue team. The second-year students were such excellent players that the tryout standards must've been extremely high. Like Hope, he used his wings. However, they hadn't made him reverse point, which was a good thing despite his extra mobility. Brett took too many risks, but because his team captain played cautiously, they won.

The cheer squad came out again, this time with different costumes and music.

"Does anybody know why they're doing so many routines?" Fiona asked.

"This is how they decide which one to do at extramurals," Brandon said. "I tried out for squad and didn't make it. That's what they told us. It's three routines per semester. The other schools only do two per year."

"Wow." I blinked. "That's a lot. Some musicals have fewer dance numbers."

The winning first and second-year teams played off before facing the seniors. Of course, the white team lost to the second-year blue team. It was a near enough thing that Hope's division might squeak out a win next semester. The second-year team didn't have as good a dynamic, despite their experience level.

The cheer squad came out again with yet another popular song. I recognized this one because they played it at the Dodge Street Café the night Ramon asked me out. *Rain on Me* with Lady Gaga and Ariana Grande.

I didn't pay much attention to the squad doing their thing out there. Instead, I held hands with my boyfriend, enjoying his company and forgetting my nerves for a while.

Third-year Gallows Hill Bishop's Row was serious business. Magi tended toward sportsmanship and camaraderie. Messing Academy psychics valued professionalism on the court. Our third-year players were another animal entirely. I'm not only saying that because most of them were shifters.

These were star players. The kind fans would follow because each had personal flair and individual style. The egos were big enough to make the court seem crowded. It wasn't a bad thing, exactly. But the teamwork aspect faded into the background here.

The third-years won in just over a minute. Like that, we were out the door and down the street. I walked Ramon home with Ed following. On the way, I told him our plan to visit the ghost.

"Sounds solid." He nodded. "Get some rest after that."

We kissed before he went in. As Ed and I headed out of The Point and toward downtown, I looked over my shoulder.

I had too much to do, it seemed. Wishing I could include Ramon in more of it had become an all too common occurrence.

"We should be rehearsing," I said to Ed as we walked up Washington Street. "Instead of chasing ghosts."

"Or out on dates. I know. We got plenty of time on the boat, at least."

"Why do they always pick teenagers to go save the world, Ed?"

"It's not always teens." He sighed. "Sometimes it's grown folks. Or kids. Retirees have more time. Less energy, though."

"Maybe that's why." I shrugged.

"If I grow up to be some mysterious being who gatekeeps a cosmic power, I'm gonna be more sensible with my employment terms."

"So you'll ask for applicants on Glassdoor or Indeed?"

"I don't know about that. But no child labor. And better pay for sure."

"Hire Old Grandpa Ambersmith." I chuckled. "You can ask for his resume tonight."

We laughed the rest of the way down the block but managed to compose ourselves by the time we reached our destination.

At Koto, the bar was empty upfront. However, I heard the music from out back, exactly as Ed had described it.

"Oh, Ed," The bartender called, beckoning him over. "Your friend isn't here this evening. Such a shame."

"What happened?" Ed blinked.

"I'm afraid he's ill. He called his son, who brought him to the hospital."

"Is he in the ICU?"

"I'm not sure. I only heard someone mention chest pains."

"That sounds awful."

"He walked out of here without much help. So hopefully, he'll be back next week. In the meanwhile, our incorporeal guests are still here if you care to join them."

"You might get more information from the ghosts back there," Rob said.

"Maybe Tommy stayed," Horace added.

"Come on, Ed." I beckoned to him and walked past the bar. "I'll show you how to get to the hospital after we finish here."

"Thanks, Mavis. I'll try to make it quick. I know you wanted to practice after this."

"This is more important." I shrugged. "Besides, I always wanted to see this place."

We walked through a beaded curtain and into a room full of ghosts dancing. Ed was right. It was just about the coolest thing I'd ever seen in my entire life. Or likely to see once that was over too. It was even more festive and joyous than the party for ghosts at the king's lodge. If I had to choose between them as places to spend my afterlife, I'd pick the back room of the Koto over the king's any day of the week.

Tommy wasn't there. Ed looked all over for him. Christian the DJ hadn't seen him.

"Of course not." I wave my hand. "He went to the hospital. Let's go."

"Your friend's smart, Ed." Christian grinned at me. "Bring her back sometime."

"Already got a double date in the works for that." Ed grinned. "See you then."

We headed out of the room, back through the bar and restaurant, and out on the street.

"I'm totally lost. No idea where the hospital is." Ed shook his head.

"Salem General is on the other side of Gallows Hill campus, past Salem State College. If we keep walking, we'll get there eventually. I'd call a Swyft, but that's not exactly the best idea."

"I'm not sure why, but okay. You're the local."

"It's my fault, Ed." I patted my chest. "Crow thinks our mother can track me by this amulet. Getting into one of those cars is asking for trouble."

"Somehow, walking the streets isn't?" He raised an eyebrow. "I'm not sure why you think one is worse than the other."

"Mom's got Branwen running a Swyft racket."

"Oh. It's like that." Ed's lips flattened into a thin pink line. "Fewmets. If I ever get that cosmic power, I'll hire a lawyer to sue her to next Tuesday."

"Look, if I thought it was safe for you, I'd call you a car and fly myself. It might not be. You got in Mom's face at the museum, so she knows we're friends."

"I can't believe it's this bad, and you didn't mention it."

"We have more important stuff on our plate than her, you know."

"I get it. She seems lower priority. Still, this is the kind of stuff you tell your friends. Besides, my family's the opposite of yours. Maybe they can counter each other."

"I don't know. They're in Rhode Island."

"I bet Cosmo's brother has dirt on her. Also, Hertha Harcourt's talons are long and not anything your mother wants to mess with."

I didn't ask Ed about his brother or mom. I knew she was still at Butler Hospital and Fred still on tour.

"This really is a long walk." He glanced at the school as we passed it. "You weren't kidding."

"At least it feels quicker when you've got company."

"True story."

We kept walking, passing the Salem State University gym before reaching the hospital. Once there, we went straight to the front desk.

"Hello, we're here to see Old Grandpa Ambersmith." I smiled at the receptionist.

"You're a Merlini. That's interesting." The receptionist typed something on her computer without looking at me. "Nobody in that family is listed, of course."

Ed puffed his inhaler, then spoke.

"How about Ed Redford?"

"Yes, the Ambersmiths have you on their list. Let me get you a visitor's badge, Mr. Redford."

"Mavis here is my plus one, so please get two."

"I hope you're powerful, Mr. Redford. If she starts any trouble, you're responsible."

He clenched his fists, and his cheeks blazed with color.

"How da—"

I cut Ed off.

"I'll behave as though I'm visiting the Sidhe queen, I promise."

"Well then, here's a badge." She handed it over. "The ICU is on the third floor, just go down the hall and take the second right until you see the elevator. He's in 345. Remember, visiting hours are only for another thirty minutes, so be brief."

"Thanks," Ed said. "For nothing," he added under his breath.

"Gotta love hospital security," I said. "I'd want them keeping people like my mom out, too."

"Gotta hate people judging you all the time for crap you didn't do."

"I'm used to it." I sighed. "Thanks for sticking up for me. Again."

"That woman was awful. But overall, I'm glad hospitals have lists."

"It sounds like you're speaking from experience here."

"Secondhand. Bianca and Olivia had some trouble when Tony was in Rhode Island Hospital."

"You mean the night he died."

"Yes. Of course, you looked that up."

"Right. Your article wasn't the only thing I found. Like I said, rabbit hole."

"More like a massive sinkhole." Ed shook his head. "Honestly, I'm not sure how you put up with all our drama. With the number of unbelievable things we've been through, I'm surprised you didn't run away screaming."

"Listen, my family doesn't get into the papers. If they did, it would've been you running away screaming."

"Touché, Mavis."

"Looks like we're here."

The elevator opened on the third floor. We found the room. Old Grandpa himself was sleeping, rather soundly. To the point where somebody came to stop us from entering.

"Hey, Mr. Ambersmith is asleep. Maybe you should come back another—"

"Hello, Doctor." Ed grinned.

There was a familiar face.

"Don't give me any doctor crap. It's just Lynn. You're here to see this guy's ghost pal, aren't you?"

"Tommy Mendez, that's right."

"Have at it then. Keep your voices down. My patient needs his rest."

"Thanks, Dr. Frampton." Ed waved.

She left us, and we finally went in. Thomas Mendez was an elderly-seeming yet well-defined ghost who floated slightly above the floor. In that, he reminded me of Rob and Horace. But his expression wasn't anywhere near as friendly.

"Redford." The ghost gave me a side-eye. "You never said the Sirin was a Merlini."

"I didn't think that was important." Ed shrugged. "She's my friend from before the Sirin thing happened. So if you've got a problem with that, I'm out of here."

"I don't. It's just interesting. Maybe a little dangerous."

"Dangerous was part of my repertoire before this happened to me," I said. "Anyway, I thought the Mendez family was Switzerland in the state of Salem's family affairs."

"That's the party line, but I'm dead now and don't have to stick to it. Your mother's a nasty piece of work. So are most of your siblings. Poor Cornelius busted his ass. It's all her fault he didn't make it. Be careful."

"I will. I'm taking him with me if I get out."

"You mean when." He shook his head and chuckled. "That feather's a ticket out of anywhere. You lucked out."

"I want to leave on my merit, not by accident."

"She really is different, isn't she?" he asked Ed.

"My friend, like I said. Now that's out of the way. We went on a little voyage in the Under. Across the sea. Should ring a bell."

"No." Tommy's eyes went wide. "They didn't."

"Who didn't what?"

The monarchs. They didn't send you on a quest?"

"They did, actually."

"Thank goodness because we went against their wishes. It was a disaster."

"So the artifact you mentioned that made Old Grandpa able to see ghosts if he has their anchor. That's the Cronus Sphere, right?"

"Don't say it here. Not in this realm."

"Sorry. Am I right?"

"Too smart for your own good is what you are."

"It's dangerous, then."

"No, it's mostly harmless. There's a prophecy, a long list of qualifications to use it, which I thought fit me but didn't. The real danger out there is the Calamity."

"Somebody out there mentioned that. Who or what is it?"

"Nobody knows. Some kind of storm or its bringer. It makes a massive cyclone originating from out past the map's end."

"Who else can we ask?" I held up my tablet with my notes on it. "There were four more with you."

"You're looking at one of them." Tommy jerked a thumb at Old Grandpa. "He's lost that memory. He was our magus."

"All right, who else?"

"Well, you know they're all dead and mostly moved on. You might ask Paolo Micello. I think his father might've told him a few things."

"Paolo's dad was with you?" I blinked.

"Yeah, he was our changeling. Untithed."

"So you had one of each type then. Extrahumans, I mean," Ed asked.

"We did. It was the only way to get around the monarchs."

"So, there's a vampire?"

"Didn't make it."

"Oh. I'm sorry."

"His ghost might still be in the Under, though. Have you met one?"

"Yeah. His name was Cyrus."

"Not our guy. Check the next island over. That's where the Calamity shipwrecked us. We lost our sense of direction and went the wrong way. The entire place is dangerous. Full of territorial talking animals."

"We've got a lion shifter with us. He can handle that," Ed said.

"What else you got?"

"Alkonost, Sirin, water dragon, djinn with space magic, and me."

"You're gonna need something undead, eventually."

"How about an undeath magus?" I asked. "Our djinn's married to one."

"That might work. I'll look into it. I know a guy, but he doesn't talk to solids, not even mediums."

"Solids?" I scratched my head. "I don't get it."

"You're new to that feather. It's what we call the living."

"It makes sense. It's almost complimentary."

"Funny you say that. I thought the opposite before I died." Tommy Mendez nodded his head. "Drop by Dead Man's Party next week. If this old coot is stuck at home or here, I'll go anyway. Make it easier on you folks. I can tell Ed didn't like walking here."

"How?"

"I'll answer that." Ed grinned. "Ghosts can sense weariness in mediums."

"She looks perfectly fine. But you, Redford. Get a good night's sleep."

"Thanks. You remind me of an old friend."

"Okay, your time's up," Dr. Frampton said at the door.

"Thanks, Lynn. We'll see you again soon, Tommy. Tell Old Grandpa we hope he feels better soon."

"Will do."

Ed and I managed to squeeze in one more practice that night after visiting the hospital. We even had an audience in the lounge since Hope and Saya were studying with Kiara. Wyatt was there too, supposedly for snacks. However, I'd seen him taking notes as I walked in.

"Well, let's see it then." Wyatt snorted. "I missed it the day of auditions."

"Yeah, Wyatt's a litmus test since we all saw it." Kiara nodded.

"It'll be way easier with a stable floor than aboard a ship." Hope chuckled. "Have at it. Don't make me order you."

"Here goes nothing." I set my satchel in the corner and cracked my knuckles. "Sorry for not having costumes."

"That's okay. They've all got big imaginations." Ed grinned.

"Thanks." Wyatt blinked.

We ignored the self-deprecating redcap and went on with our performance. At the end, with the big finish, Wyatt jumped out of his seat.

"No fracking way!" He stepped back. "That was freaky, you guys are scary, but like in a good way, you know."

"I guess we're good then." Ed elbowed me. "If we get that kind of response in the cramped lounge without props or costumes, we'll do great."

"Guess I shouldn't have worried too much." I shrugged. "It's out of character for me at any rate. The one I'm playing too."

"I'd never have imagined you as Peter Pan, Mavis," Saya raised an eyebrow. "I must admit you nail it. There's something to be said for hard work and getting to know a character."

I wasn't sure what to say to that. I'd practically lived Peter Pan, though she didn't know that. I would trust her with that information. She had some of it. Still. it didn't feel right, dumping my trauma on someone who had enough of her own.

"Well, lights out is coming soon," Kiara held her tablet out toward me. "Do you want me to send you these notes?"

"That'd be great, thanks. I'm missing too much studying, I think. Hope my grades don't suffer for it."

"You're super smart, Mavis. I wouldn't worry," Wyatt said. "Even if your brain's full of feathers."

"Smart is as smart does." I shrugged. "Dropping the ball is bad news. No matter how quick-witted, without enough hard work, failure happens."

"Well, if you need help, just let us know. You've got no shortage of study buddies," Hope said. "I can always make a general study order if asking is hard."

"No, don't do that. Punishing everybody else for my mistakes isn't cool. Order that individually if I mess up too much."

"Yeah, not it on that." Wyatt grabbed a handful of trail mix packs, opening one and pouring it into his mouth before he left the room, waving one hand in the air behind him.

"Just keep bringing your homework everywhere, and you'll be fine. For now, we need rest," Ed said. "We've run all over town this evening, after all."

"You can always depend on the wisdom of mediums." I nodded. "Good night, everybody."

I headed upstairs, too nervous to rest. So I went into the bathroom and had a reasonably long bath. It helped relax me enough. I settled into bed without any trouble falling asleep.

I doodled on my tablet half the time in Lecture. It wasn't that I couldn't take notes, only that I wrote so fast I had extra time. My idle hands needed something to do, or I'd end up pacing the room. That would get me detention I didn't need. Maybe.

Mrs. Ambersmith's hardcase act might be her personality or actual concern we'd get into her debt. Still, I didn't imagine she'd let students walk around in the middle of her lecture. So I kept my hands busy instead.

I drew circles interlocked and patterns. Made some symbols nagging at the back of my mind. Astrology, I think. They framed my notes, zigzagging over, around, and under different bullet points I copied from the board. I didn't stop, even when my hand got cramped.

Once out of Lecture and into Mediumship, it was easier. We had a substitute who showed us a magipsychic 3D display. There were replicas of ghosts to interact with. So I played pretend with the fake ghosts while the real ones chuckled in the corner over how absurd that was.

"I imagine their programming isn't particularly accurate." Donna sniffed. "Our regular instructor is a magus, after all."

"My grandpa, Thomas Mendez, made everything for this class before he passed away," Diego countered. "So shut your trap, Donna."

"What did you say to me?"

"He said shut your trap. It's going to get you in trouble." Allen slapped a card down on the desk between them. I glimpsed the devil.

"Your cards don't scare me."

"Maybe they should." Gia shuddered. "He means what he says, Donna. Being careful is never a bad idea."

Donna turned her back on us, stalking away. Gia followed.

"She should get over herself," Diego muttered under his breath.

"Ditto." I rolled my eyes. "It's distracting, and I'm trying to study."

"If she doesn't care about that, let her fail." Ed shrugged. "Nobody can blame us for not caring about her academic fate when she acts like this."

"It's not academics, though." Allen joined us. "Her problem's something else. Out of school, and nothing nice."

"How bad is it?" I raised my eyebrow. "Did you get the Tower again on her draw?"

"No, but it's pretty bad. Danger for her and her family."

"Oh?" I blinked. "From where?"

Allen flipped a card. Two of Cups reversed.

"Old friend turned enemy." He swallowed, glancing at me as he tucked the card away. His face turned a clammy shade of green.

Before Allen could say more, he put a hand over his mouth and the other in the air. The substitute nodded, and the clairvoyant rushed toward the restroom.

"Is he gonna be okay?" I asked.

"The Arnolds have a side effect sometimes," Diego said. "Nothing like it in our family, but they toss their cookies when foreseeing something particularly bad."

"She did it to herself," Gia said as she walked along the row behind us. "And I don't care. Don't tell her I said that."

"Wow." Diego blinked. I made a zipping gesture over my lips and nodded at Gia.

I moved on, finding another pretend ghost on the other side of the room to interact with. Ed followed.

"Maybe we should care though," he said. "Strong emotions connect people. Even negative ones. Whatever's going on with Donna could spill over on us, considering she kind of hates you, Mavis."

"There's no kind of about it, Ed." I sighed. "She hates me, says it every chance she gets. I don't know why. I'll keep my eyes and ears open. But there's not much I can do."

Deep down, I did know. I didn't realize it until too late.

I couldn't eat lunch. I thought Allen's nausea was contagious. Stomach flu instead of precognition. But no, it was nerves of course. The variety show was right after lunch. Despite the positive feedback and the fact that we had the entire song down, I was terrified.

Brandon and Jaxon opened the show with their tap number to *King of New York* from *Newsies*. They'd used glamour bracelets for their costumes and hammed it up out there.

The string quartet went after them, playing a medley of songs from video games. From the wings, I saw Cosmo going nuts about them in the front row. I didn't recognize any of the music until he mentioned it later.

Kiara went out and sang *Popular* from *Wicked* all by herself. After hearing her practice, I wasn't surprised by the quality of her performance. The audience loved her, too.

The roster had our act right between Wanda and Hayden. His act was completely novel. She was at the professional level, a performance art equivalent to the third-year Bishop's Row team.

Wanda sang *Wishing You Were Somehow Here Again* from *Phantom of the Opera*. She could have been an opera singer. As a triple threat with that much talent, I had no doubt she'd end up on Broadway. Half of her family were professionals already.

In contrast, choosing Drama Club was my thing, different from my entire family. No other Merlini had been here before, waiting in the wings with their stomachs churning. A step on stage was another step away from them. Maybe that, instead of stage fright, was the true source of my anxiety.

Between Ramon in the audience and Ed on stage with me, I could take it. I only wished Crow was there, too. Especially after the fact. Even though extrahumans are used to a little magic, an unexpected kind happened for me out there on the stage.

A Wonderful World Without Peter flowed through us and out to the audience like a river into the sea. The big finish delighted everyone in the crowd. I heard some screams, so we'd startled a significant portion of the audience—no mean feat for a medium and a bird shifter at a school full of shifters and fae.

I couldn't bring myself to watch Hayden and Howie, but everybody else was in the wings doing exactly that. They were hilarious, and the act was unique. Despite being from another school, Hayden might win.

We rested in the green room, Ed leaning against the wall as I slumped in a chair. Diego was there too but left to perform his monologue. We wished him good luck as he went.

"I still wonder if we should have reversed roles," he said. "Because of how you're a hair taller than me."

I had an entire inch on Ed. We adjusted his glamour bracelet and used the hat to give him the illusion of height.

"Maybe we can if you want to use this to audition for the spring musical." I shrugged. "But I don't know. Peter is—"

"A lot like you. I get it. I don't feel much like Hook. But you know, the old codfish grew on me. It was fun, pretending to fight. Nobody else lets me do that. They're all afraid I'll get hurt."

"I'm glad we're friends, Ed. Thanks for recommending Snapple to a wayward bird. And everything after that."

"Me too. Even if I think standing up to Donna is a bigger deal than beverages."

"Hey, come on out here." Kiara beckoned from the door. "They're ready to announce prizes."

We headed out of the green room and into the wings, joining the line of other acts. Diego and Kiara both got honorable mentions. Hayden came in third. We clapped, watching him step up to accept the ribbon, his face crimson. His humility made sense. All the pride belonged to the duck strutting before him like a monarch instead of a surly waterfowl.

My ears felt filled with cotton as they announced second place. Mr. Hickson's words were like gibberish except for our names. Ed's eyes widened, and he froze. Kiara came to our rescue.

"Go, go." She patted our backs, and we had no choice but to step forward.

I stopped after one. What right did a Merlini have, winning anything here?

Ed grabbed my hand and dragged me to the front of the stage. We took a bow, and Ed took the ribbon from Mr. Hickson, then handed it to me.

After stepping back, we watched Wanda take first place.

Back at the boarding house that afternoon, a flier on the dining room door announced a celebratory dinner with place cards and everything.

I wasn't sure what that entailed, so I went upstairs and had a quick shower. The nervous sweat was still sticky, despite my performance finishing two hours earlier.

I'd neglected my laundry and only had the school sweats. In the basement, I started washing a load, but it was time for dinner as I put them in the dryer. Gym sweats would have to do.

"That's not the choice I would've made," Saya said. "For an honorary dinner, I mean."

"They're clean, comfortable, and I just want food."

"I suppose they show school spirit. But you're a guest of honor and—"

"And any type of Gallows Hill uniform is appropriate at a Gallows Hill function." Matron Klein grinned then opened the door. "Right this way."

She sat me at a table with Ed, John Clayton, who captained the third-year Bishop's Row team, and Hope. Also joining us was Cosmo, whose painting of the person in the headlights won an award.

"You first-years are tearing it up," John Clayton said. "A division win, placing in variety, an art ribbon, honorable mentions all over the science fair and entertainment wrestling. You'll be role models for the next few years."

"Thanks, but technically I'm a Messing student." Ed shrugged.

"You do Drama Club at Gallows Hill. Gallows Hill drama kids look up to you. It's the nature of the beast here. Goes double for the high profile students, like Hope. You too, Mavis."

"I appreciate the sentiment, John." I shrugged. "Doesn't really apply to me, though."

"That's ridiculous." Cosmo snorted. "I look up to you already, and I'm in your year."

"Right back at you, Cos." I grinned.

"I misjudged you that first day, Mavis." John shook his head. "Maybe you meant me to. Considering that aptitude for performance art. I mean, jeepers."

"She's something else." Hope nodded.

"I'm sitting right here, you know." I smirked.

"We know. You'd better tell your brother about all this. He'll be proud."

"I'll do that. Anything you want me to pass along?"

"Yeah, thanks to Wyatt and his deep-dive into court documents. Tell Crow I'm rooting for him. To get better and get out of there."

"I will."

We spent the rest of the dinner conversation on lighter topics. After everything between the Under and the mundane realm, a break from serious business was exactly what I needed.

ABOUT A GIRL

PART THREE

I told myself I'd prioritize studying after the Rec Week hullabaloo. I failed.

My new friends and teachers were amazing. Still, being at school was like moving to another planet. I was an alien, managing the social aspects but behind on how to manage time without do-or-die stakes.

Short-term goals were easy, done on the fly by instinct. The light at the ends of those tunnels was painfully obvious. I couldn't grok anything farther ahead than next week. It was a weakness, like Cosmo's color blindness or Ed's asthma. Except in my head instead of my body.

Planning for the future when you can't see one is next door to impossible.

Mr. Hickson chose Kiara's one-act play for the performance show-case. We auditioned for that at the end of Rec Week. I didn't make it in. None of the roles fit me, and I didn't try too hard.

It seemed like a good idea, giving myself more time to study. Instead, it meant trying to do schoolwork alone. Until then, I didn't realize how much the others being around helped me focus—especially Kiara, who was busy directing her play.

"Shot myself in the foot," I murmured to Horace in the library.

"How do you mean?"

"Everybody thinks I'm doing fine. That's because they don't see me daydream or fall into rabbit holes when they're not around to make me focus. I need help but don't want to bother anyone."

"You won't be bothering them," Horace said.

"I disagree." I shook my head.

"It can't hurt to ask."

"It can. They've got their own problems. What if they think I'm too much trouble?"

"It's only your grades. No reason to bother the people who want you around." Horace rolled his eyes. "Don't sabotage yourself, Mavis."

"Crow says cycles can break. It's not quick and easy, Horace. I know you're trying to give good advice. I refuse to take advantage of my friends."

"Okay then. Consider your boyfriend. He's not going anywhere. And Ramon's no slouch at school."

"Good idea, Horace. Thanks, I'll take it."

I didn't. It's not that I meant to lie to my ghostly pal or that I didn't intend to continue hitting the books. I deliberately spent more time with Ramon, but that wasn't academic. At least Kiara wasn't annoyed at us monopolizing the room more frequently.

We had a double date with Ed and Jillian at Dead Man's Party, but Ed and I went over early to talk to Tommy.

"So, how about that hermit ghost?" Ed asked. "What did he say about vampires?"

"It's not easy on them. The uncharted sea's got a real day and night. Mostly, we brought a vampire for tracking. Corporeal is better than anything else. Maybe a critter will do."

"Critter?" Ed blinked.

"A magical creature, the kind Hawthorn kids have for familiars," I said. "They have affinities. We can ask Hayden or Rita about that."

"Those magi don't part with their familiars." Tommy shook his head. "Better off asking the Morgensterns. They might have rescues or strays. Sorry I couldn't be more help."

"At least we've got a lead." I grinned.

"Thanks, Tommy," Ed said.

Ramon and Jillian entered the building. We went on our date, and he went back to the hospital. Fortunately, we didn't need Old Grandpa's ring. All that practice in Lab had paid off. My powers let Ramon and Jillian see and hear the ghosts in the back room, and we all had a blast.

Despite the fun, all my time seemed borrowed. Life felt like a game of hurry up and wait with the monarchs. Or Mom's other shoe to drop.

Eventually, I marched to Principal Klein's office and knocked on her door.

"When's that test, ma'am?"

"I know you don't mean exams," she said. "Have a seat, Mavis."

I did.

"Director-General Rockport tried to confirm appointments with your mother twice. Both times she said the date was inconvenient. It's still up in the air."

"She's doing it on purpose." I sighed. "Holding it over my head, trying to stress me out before exams."

"Perhaps."

"Why doesn't Rockport do something?"

"The Registry has procedures and protocol. The Sirin's abilities are obscure but documented, so it's not considered high-priority. He can back-burner the matter for months. Maybe it's a good thing."

"It's driving me insane." I stood. "Not knowing."

"I underst—"

"You don't!" I slapped the table, tipping over a picture there. "Nobody can! Not even Crow or any of my other siblings. Because none of them took off and found something she wants. They're not stuck in this sick holding pattern. Wondering when she'll strike, what she'll take, and from who. What if she hurts one of my friends? What if she hurts Ramon?"

"Miss Merlini, we have chill-out chambers for a reason."

"I don't need one. I'm totally rational here. I knew it'd happen someday. That you'd stop believing me."

"If that's true, sit back down, put your wings away, and lower your voice."

I hadn't even heard the back of my shirt tear. Some actress I was. I followed her suggestions. I noticed something in the process.

The photo I'd knocked over laid on the desk, face up. An elementary school-aged girl with her chestnut hair in braids stood beside an older version of a familiar logo. Moonstruck Music, on the side of a conversion van. Her unsmiling face looked familiar. A glance up confirmed my suspicions. Almost.

"Is that you?" I blinked. "The girl by Paolo's van?"

"It is." She nodded.

"Is he your father?"

"More like a brother. His parents fostered me."

"Were your parents killed in the Boston Internment?"

"They're undead and well, actually. Though I only found out about that a couple of years ago."

"So what happened?"

"I was in an illegal blood ring. The bust was all over the local news. The Micellos called CPS and took all five of us in."

"Wow." I blinked. "Until they found your parents, right?"

"The rest found their parents. Ginny and Neil kept fostering me. That picture's on my desk as a reminder."

"That's heavy."

"That's the point. Fate deals some of us a heavy hand. The only way to stand up under its weight is with help."

"You don't look happy in that picture. Or even grateful."

"Ginny always said I didn't have to be either of those things. Neither do you. If you're fed, clothed, sheltered, and cared for, the rest will follow when you're ready. "

The bell rang.

"I should go."

"I'll give you a hall pass if you need to change."

"It's lunch. I don't." I stood, more sedately this time. "Sorry. Guess the old Merlini temper didn't skip me."

"You're under enormous pressure, Mavis. Don't apologize. Just remember that everyone needs help sometimes. And keep your appointments with Counselor Goldfarb."

"Yes, ma'am."

That afternoon, only a few of us went to the park. Hope stayed after school at Lab to try applying unliving energy to her spyglass with Dr. Aranha. Saya had cheer squad practice. Brandon said it was too cold and Kiara stayed with him. Ramon walked as far as Tropica Mart, leaving to help his parents with all the extra Halloween-related business.

Fiona and Wyatt walked over with us, but Fiona stopped as we neared the common.

"I'm meeting Hayden at the Witch's Brew over on Essex," Fiona said. "It's, well, sort of a date."

"The guy with the duck?" Wyatt blinked.

"Yeah. We've been chatting since the dance."

"That's awesome," I said. "Hayden's hilarious. You won't be bored."

After she left, Wyatt spotted the food trucks at the common for Haunted Happenings.

"There's no way I'm throwing frisbees on an empty stomach," he said. "Catch you all later."

"Is it always going to be like this now?" Ed asked Jillian.

"November first, it'll be a ghost town." She chuckled. "Literally, for you."

"For real?" Cosmo asked.

"She's not lying." I sighed. "Living in a tourist town is a blessing and a curse."

When we got to the park, Jaxon joined a group of shifters playing dodge ball. Ed and Jillian went around the other side of the tank to get a little privacy. I nudged Cosmo.

"Let's walk."

"Okay. Guess you're missing Ramon for a bit."

"We see each other a lot, actually.

"Uh, yeah. I know." He blushed. "I can hear you two."

"Oh no." My mouth dropped open along with the pit of my stomach. "Magic cat ears, for the lose. If it bothered you, why didn't you bring it up before?"

"Because it doesn't. Bother me, I mean. Ed's been going at it with Jill. That's different."

"How so?"

"I know they're careful, Ed told me. Uh, are you?"

The question's magic and its gravity hung in the air between us. This conversation was totally uncomfortable for my friend. Still, he cared enough to have it anyway. Even though he needn't have worried.

"Oh. Uh, we're not getting X-rated, Cos. I'll go to the nurse if we decide to do that." I studied his face. "Is that all?"

"No." He swallowed. "Saya keeps trying to set me up with someone because I've never been on a date. I don't like it."

"With who?"

"This girl on our team." He wrinkled his nose.

"Should she introduce you to a guy instead?"

"I know what gay is. I'm not into guys, either."

"Cosmo, I don't want you to take this the wrong way. But you compliment all of us on how we look. Pretty much every day."

"Tony says don't miss the moment, that if your words can help, speak up. I see you all worrying about that stuff."

"So you say it because it's nice?"

"Because it's true. I notice beautiful stuff. Art, trees, sunsets, people. But in a hands-off way. Except food. The only thing I'd passionately embrace is a cheeseburger. Nobody else agrees with that. Mavis, is something wrong with me?"

"No." I shook my head. "Not at all. Cosmo, you're one of the purest people I know. You be you."

"I wish you'd tell that to Saya."

What Principal Klein said earlier came back to me, how the only way to stand up under pressure is with help. So I offered some to Cosmo.

"I can if you want."

"Please. She still sees me as a little kid, sometimes."

"Okay."

I sat with Saya at dinner and told her everything. Except the things Cosmo overheard.

"Tiamat's scales. He's asexual!" She shook her head. "I should have known."

"Well, now you do."

"I'll apologize next time I see him. And lay off on the dating tips."

"He'll be happy."

"Good." She nodded. "Thanks for the talk."

The following week, it was too cold for the park even if crowds hadn't filled it.

"There has to be someplace else to go when it's frigid outside," Ed said as we painted sets in Drama Club. "I'm going to miss hanging out if there isn't."

"Yeah, I know what you mean. Don't want to freeze my tailfeathers off all winter." I nodded.

"What about the Dodge Street Café?" Kiara suggested.

"Right, the café's open all day. So we could hang there in the afternoons before the bar opens." I nodded. "I'll pitch that to the rest of the section later."

"I'll get word to Allen." Ed nodded. "Donna's poor dogs will miss out, though."

"Sucks to be her." Diego snorted. "But yeah, I feel for the puppers. They don't like working for her."

"How do you know?" Kiara asked.

"Empath, remember?" He glanced at me. "It sometimes sucks, picking up everyone's angst."

My emotions weren't Diego's fault, but what he said angered me. It hit too close to home, making me uncomfortable in the auditorium for almost the first time.

We didn't go out that week, which should have been a perfect time to study. I confined myself to the lounge with my tablet after school instead. The information didn't stick.

"Actually looking at your notes is a good start," Horace said.

"Starting's the problem. What subject? The pure faeries or shifter types?"

"Whichever you studied least."

"That's all of the above." I sighed. "At least I know everything by sight in Lab for the practical. That won't do me any good on Hickson's paper exam."

"Maybe it could if you add drawings to your notes."

I jumped out of my seat and rushed to Horace's side before I remembered he was incorporeal.

"I could kiss you!"

"Uh." He glanced at the door.

"Dunno what I walked in on here, but I won't look." Wyatt had his eyes on the snack table, hands against his temples like blinders.

"No, it's okay. I was talking to Horace."

"Huh, okay." Wyatt dropped his hands, the tension going out of his arms. He grabbed an armful of snacks from the table. "Ghost man must have done something good."

"Study advice."

"You don't need it. Been alone with your notes practically all the time."

"Whatever."

"Whoa." He blinked. "You haven't been studying."

"Everybody thinks you're a meathead, just like everyone thinks I'm a brain."

"I get it. Wrong on both counts." He unwrapped a granola bar and crunched it. "Let's hear the invisible man's idea."

I told him.

"It could work. But only if you do it."

"That's the hard part."

"John says to reward yourself." He waggled another granola bar at me. "Like this. I just finished studying, so I get snacks."

"That's helpful. Thanks, Wyatt."

"Like it's a surprise. Thank me by studying. I'll get on your case if you don't. Later."

After he left, I sat back down with my tablet and some paper at the coffee table. Horace had gone off somewhere, so I had no more excuses. Or distractions besides the ones in my head. I stated my intention, hoping to silence them.

"Let me get these doodle notes done, and you get a bubble bath."

It worked. At least for a while. I managed to make a new set of pure faerie notes on paper, giving me a way to check them without the distractions on my tablet. The dinner bell rang before I got halfway through my visual guide to pure faeries. After the meal, I kept that promise to myself and had a bath.

It took the rest of the week, but I managed to make all the offline notes I needed.

The next week we hung out at the Dodge Street Café because it was sleeting. Early November was like that, unpredictable in the weather sense. Haunted Happenings was over, along with its crowds. Town was a less distracting place as a result. Also more dangerous for me to be out and about since I couldn't hide in throngs of tourists from my family anymore. Moving indoors was a good solution to both problems.

It felt different, less comfortable. Not due to the surroundings, but because of money. We'd file in, and everyone ordered a beverage or snack except me. I'm sure they noticed. The staff did, at any rate. However, nobody offered anything.

My friends didn't notice how poor I was. They knew my mom was horrible. I hadn't told most of them and asked Ed and Ramon to keep it secret. So it was my fault. Knowing that didn't make me feel any better.

The beginning of the month had me worried about its end. Thanksgiving break. All my friends would go home to their families or have gatherings right there in town. I wasn't invited. Or at least nobody had asked.

"I don't expect an invitation. I know Matron Klein will make something for me at the boardinghouse. But it feels lonely. More than that, I don't know. Like, hollow in my heart," I said at a counseling session.

"You're not the first student at Gallows Hill in this situation. You're not alone, Mavis. Though for various reasons, I can't get into specifics."

"That helps in a general sense, but it doesn't change how I feel. None of my friends are going to grok this."

"Don't be so sure. Last time, you told me most of them don't know what's going on. Before that, you said you stopped talking to Ramon and Ed about family problems because you didn't want to be a downer."

"I talk to Horace, sometimes. You know, the guy haunting me?"

"That's good, Mavis. Bonds of friendship come in all shapes, sizes, and forms. Ghosts are great friends who listen, give advice, and have fun with you. However, you can't share a meal. Pick things up again with Ed or Ramon. They've helped you before."

"Counselor Goldfarb, I don't want to be a downer." I sighed. "They've all got their problems. I don't want to dump mine on them too."

"Think of it as helping your friends understand. They notice you're upset and don't know why. The only way they will is if you tell them."

"That might take time."

"This holiday is coming whether you're ready or not." Counselor Goldfarb nodded. "So, consider a chat with your brother. You haven't mentioned visiting him recently."

"Not since before Rec Week." I blinked. "Oh no. I'm a crappy sister."

"You made a mistake. I bet he'll be glad to see you."

"I'll go see him this afternoon."

The bell rang.

I went back to class, finishing out the day. Ramon walked me to the bus and took it over to Danvers with me. He waited in the lobby, admiring the paintings as usual while I went inside.

"I'm sorry for spacing," I started.

"Thank Odin." Crow hugged me so tightly he lifted me off my feet. "I don't care if you're in the Under or distracted with school. It's been too long."

"I'm sorry."

"Don't be. Just don't forget about me."

"Never."

I gave him an update on things.

"Keep on hitting the books even though the midterm exams aren't as big a deal as finals. You can get a D on midterms and still pass for the year."

"I'd rather not do that. How about you in here?"

"Check it out. I'm almost at level yellow." He gestured at his flannel, which was still orange but with a lot less red in it.

"So they're going to let you out soon?"

"Yellow's a long stage, with service to do. Also, a slew of written apologies to the people I hurt. The staff is still trying to figure out exactly what that entails. Because I put in a request, you see."

"About the Under?" I held my breath.

"Yes. Everyone on that boat of yours has to voice their thoughts before the monarchs even consider it. They need an answer back from Hal Hawkins, considering we've clashed before."

"You really have come a long way. Proud of you."

"Kind of hard to believe. Feels surreal, remembering the night I threatened him. And shitty. He could barely walk without help, and I pulled a knife on the guy."

"It's almost like you were another person then, right?"

"Absolutely." He nodded. "I already got word back that Hal, Cadence, Logan, Aliyah, and Xan got my letters to them, which is the most important part as far as healing goes for any of us. I can always pick litter and clean graffiti like the other yellows if the boat doesn't work out."

I filled Ramon in on the bus on the way home.

"I don't like what he said about exams, Mavis. It's too easy to use that as an excuse to slack in class."

"I don't plan on it."

"Whatever your plans are, you're not getting any studying done with me. I think I'm too distracting."

"What can I say? You're amazing."

We sat silently, hand in hand at the back of the bus, heads turned to stare into each other's eyes. At first, I thought he wanted a kiss, but he leaned farther than that, tilting his head to the side. A whisper in the ear, then.

"Mavis. I love you."

"I love you too, Ramon."

"That's why I'm not coming over to visit until after you've had study time with another one of our classmates. It doesn't matter who. They're all doing pretty well, even Wyatt."

"I hear you. I do. I'm working on that by myself already."

"So share your method. Let's call it insurance, and give me a chance to study with someone else, too. Because I've got the same problem, getting distracted by you."

The bus stopped, and we stepped off together. We parted ways on Washington Street because it was close to lights out by then. I could barely feel the ground under my feet.

***

"You're coming with me after school today," Saya said in a singsong voice.

"Part of Ramon's studying strategy, I presume?"

"No, to State of Grace. We need dresses for the Yule Ball."

"Oh. Right. I was going to wear the one from Harvest Moon."

"You'll do no such thing. You're coming with me. Fiona too."

"I guess I can't say no."

Really, I didn't want to.

We spent part of the afternoon at the dress shop. This time Fiona and I got more involved with our designs, recommending things to each other.

It wasn't study time, but Ramon couldn't have foreseen Saya's act of fashion kidnapping, which ended up extending beyond that appointment. She took us down to the wharf and asked my advice on a bunch of regular clothes. Then, she didn't buy anything. It mystified me.

That mystery solved itself the next day. Because when I returned to the boardinghouse after Ramon and I walked Ed back from school, a stack of parcels sat at the foot of my bed.

"They came by pixie carrier. I've got no idea what they are or where they're from," Kiara said

"I guess there's only one thing to do." I opened them and discovered every outfit I'd admired at the wharf shops the day before.

"Somebody's got an admirer." Kiara smiled. "I wonder how Ramon paid for this."

"It wasn't Ramon. It was Saya." I explained.

"I don't know where she got the idea I needed a wardrobe." I shook my head.

"Hmm, mysterious."

Kiara busied herself at her bookshelf, apparently organizing paperbacks. However, she'd done that over the weekend. Like that, I figured it out.

"Thanks, Kiara."

"You don't have as many secrets as you think, Mavis. I can't take all the credit. It was a group effort."

"Then I need a whole stack of thank you notes. Who do I address them to?"

"All the ladies in our section. Ed and Cosmo, too."

"You're all awesome. I don't deserve you all."

"Everyone deserves friends."

I still said nothing about the peril of Thanksgiving. I couldn't risk deflating that moment.

CHAPTER TWO

I was a good little student and hit the books for the next few days. Still, I couldn't focus on any of it. I blamed angst over Thanksgiving, threatening to eat me alive. The last thing I wanted was another outburst like the one in the principal's office.

Counselor Goldfarb was booked solid, and I didn't want to use the chill-out chamber for a session with a random counselor. So I went to see Crow again, even though it'd only been a few days since last time.

I went alone. I didn't need Mom noticing I'd brought Ramon to Danvers twice in one week. Going alone made me uneasy, but I didn't want to risk any of my friends. So I flew in a straight line instead of relying on the bus or its route.

When I saw my brother, we walked along the pond for a bit, discussing the small improvements he'd made to his cabin. After that, we sat and skipped stones again. That didn't last long. He set his rock down and didn't say a word until I paid attention.

"Something's eating you."

"You're right."

"Thought you started counseling, Mavis."

"I did." I shook my head. "Counseling won't help me solve this problem."

"Then tell your brother." He shrugged. "If it's not a counseling thing, maybe I can help."

"It's Thanksgiving," I blurted. "Everyone's going home for it. I don't have one of those."

"Matron Klein lives in that boarding house. She must be making dinner."

"Yes. But it's just her and me."

"What's wrong with that?"

"You wasted a question."

"There's no such thing as a wasted question if it's for you."

"Thanks." I hung my head. "I don't want to feel alone. Matron Klein kind of saved my life. But she's my principal, not my family."

"There's no turkey here, only stew. Come visit anyway."

"Is that an invitation?"

"Yeah, of course. You're always welcome wherever I am. The sanitarium's open for visitors on the holidays."

"I hadn't even thought of that."

"Most people don't. I'm one of the only people in here who even get visits. Because folks find the idea of a place like this disturbing."

"If this place is helping you, I'm comfortable here. So make lots of stew. I'm coming over for Thanksgiving."

"You're a rare bird." He sighed. "Rarer still is the one who thinks it's hilarious."

"You mean Mom?"

"Yeah. Mom."

Something happened. A change I felt coming before I saw it. Crow's flannel shirt gradually changed color, the yellow deepening until it turned blue.

"Oh, no way." He blinked. "Never had that happen outside of a session."

"Proud of you. So, what happens now?"

"The monarchs will hear my request." He smiled. "I might have something other than wilderness survival to do in a month or so. Can't believe it."

"I can."

"I don't know how. We've got almost nothing in common, despite the home life."

"No, we do. We never give up."

"Almost did. Would have, if it hadn't been for you."

"That's an overstatement." I couldn't look him in the eye.

"It's not. You're not the only person who visited to encourage me. But everything you do has more weight."

"Who, if you don't mind my asking?"

"Bar's uncle Paolo if you can believe it." He chuckled. "I've got no idea why he even cares, but I'm glad for it."

"Maybe he just has a good heart." Or he owed someone else. I didn't want to burst Crow's bubble by saying that.

"Did you know he and Mom used to date in school?" Crow shook his head. "There I go again wasting a question."

"There is no such thing as wasting question on me, remember?" I elbowed him. "Yeah, I heard that through more than one grapevine."

"Maybe he feels something for her still. That's the only thing I can think of."

"Doesn't make much sense to me. Or he would have helped the rest of our siblings." I shrugged. "He's a troll. Maybe he owed a favor."

"Probably." Crow shook his head. "But probably not. They're feuding. A faerie favor to Mom would have defused that. It's highly possible he owes someone else, though. Guess it'll be a while before you solve the mystery of the helpful Micello."

"That's okay. I've got bigger fish to fry." I wrinkled my nose. "Homework-shaped fish."

"It's getting close to your lights out. You should go."

"I'll be back soon. See you on Thanksgiving."

"Can't wait."

I told Matron Klein the next day about my Thanksgiving plans.

"I'm glad to hear that. I'll still have dinner here, however. Perhaps you'll bring a dessert with you. I'm a bit of a stress baker."

"The bus doesn't run on Thanksgiving. I'd have to go as a bird."

"I'll drive if you want to bring pie."

"You're not upset, are you?" I swallowed. "I mean if dinner in an almost empty boarding house was your thing to do."

"No, it's not the only thing, just a new one."

"Thanks for not making this weird."

"Nobody makes things weird, Mavis. Our feelings change with time and growth. Remember that."

"I'll try."

I hoped she was right. And that my growth was toward success instead of failure.

With the angst over Thanksgiving resolved, studying should have been easy. It wasn't, even without being in the one-act play. I was only helping Sid with props, not much of a commitment until after exams.

Mostly, I found myself taking too many study breaks. Ramon kept his distance, so it wasn't his fault. Without anything else to blame, I couldn't escape the truth.

It was my birdbrain and its wiring. I'd be in the library going over class material and exam preparation worksheets. Then something shiny, some tidbit of unrelated knowledge as yet unearthed, would catch my eye.

Off I'd go down the rabbit hole like the day I researched Cosmo and his family. Except this time, it wasn't snooping. I ended up reading an awful lot about local current events, especially from last year. My mind drew me toward that mystery Crow mentioned on my last visit.

Who did Paolo owe, and how was helping me paying off that debt? Why did he continue helping Crow? What did he care about Morgan Merlini and her wayward family, especially after she'd burned him over their pack? The Micellos were so stable. It didn't make sense for Paolo to embroil himself in Mom's drama.

Unless that was the heart of the matter. Maybe Paolo's family wasn't always well-off. Could he have made a deal with someone to change that? When did it start? Back when he was a student here, maybe. Mr. Hickson never mentioned who else was in that pack besides him, Paolo, and Mom.

The next day, I found myself in a section of the library with shelves—the one devoted to old yearbooks.

I found one from the year my mother should've graduated but didn't. Flipping through, I found all the usual suspects. Paolo, Mr. Hickson, Dr. Aranha, and Mom herself. Reading the name Morgan Canto on paper jarred me, even though I'd known her maiden name for months.

Seeing them all looking so young was surreal. Especially because I wasn't even the age they were in the pictures.

I flipped through the clubs and rec activities, hoping to find more about Paolo and my mother. Like an activity in common. Maybe I just wanted concrete evidence that they dated.

I found Mr. Hickson on the Drama Club page as expected. For the photo, he stood wedged between two other students, twin boys with pale skin, black hair, and blue eyes. Justin Cormack and Kyle Cormack. They looked so much like me that I wondered who they were. Cousins of Dad's, maybe.

My mother was on the entertainment wrestling page with Paolo Micello. They'd been tag team partners, which supported the dating rumor. The heavyweight champion that year was Gary Clayton, who bore a striking resemblance to Wyatt. I flipped further and found Charlotte Aranha, whose surname hadn't changed. She was in band.

"Still no freaking clue." I sighed.

"Those aren't textbooks or notes, birdbrain." Wyatt leaned against a nearby bookshelf. "Thought you needed more studying."

"This is your business how, exactly?" I sighed. "I don't have time for dudebro angst today, Wyatt."

"It's your angst if you flunk, not mine. Don't get why it's more important than grades."

"You saw how it is at my house. I'm digging for old dirt. In case of emergency."

"Oh. Well, that's my dad's actual old yearbook. He donated it. Check the back page."

I did. Sure enough, on the last page, there were exactly two signatures. None were the folks I'd looked up.

"I can see why he got rid of it. Looks like he was about as popular as you are."

"Hey, I'm not here to get insulted."

"I don't know what you want, Wyatt."

"Same."

"It's none of your business, anyway."

"Dunno what got into you, but if it's back in the day stuff you want to know, maybe don't piss me off."

I mulled that over. Things at the nest were not normal. Maybe Wyatt's life was. Perhaps his dad discussed the good old days, unlike my family. He might know something.

"Whatever. Probably, your dad's old stories don't include what I'm looking for anyway."

"You won't know unless you ask."

"Point taken." I shrugged, carried the yearbook to a nearby table, and set it down. Then I leaned over it, pointing at the Cormack twins.

"Who are these guys?"

"Couple of chuckleheads. One's a raven who went here. The other's a magus, over for Drama from Essex Regional. Part of your mom's pack, so Dad always kept his eye on them."

"Any particular reason why?"

"Company they kept. There weren't horrible on their own, though."

"Let me guess, Morgan Canto and Paolo Micello."

"Yeah."

"I imagine Paolo wasn't that bad."

"Back then he was. Rebelled against everything under the sun or moon as Dad tells it. The only reason they never messed with him is because, well, look at him."

Wyatt turned the page to where Gary Clayton stood on the top rope, looking positively feral and gigantic.

"Okay, I grok that. So he didn't run with them."

"No way. Redcaps are overt. We've got no business in a trickster pack."

"There had to be at least one more. I wonder who it is."

"So Dad said that pack had Morgan as alpha, Micello the beta, Jedi Hickson was omega. The Cormack twins were in it too. Then a girl you wouldn't expect."

"Can you show her to me?"

He said nothing, only flipped pages until he found who he was looking for.

"Carmella, she's a shifter. Dog, to be exact."

"Why does she look familiar?"

"That's Donna's mom."

"Donna the summoner?" I snorted. "You're kidding me."

"Nope. Dad went on exactly one date with her. She creeped him out big time, so he cut her off. After that, he had some trouble. Random bad luck, among other things."

"So Donna's part dog shifter."

"She summons dogs, remember? God, I did it again. Asked you a question."

"This is your first time today, don't worry."

"Do you think that's why Donna's got it in for you? Mother—"

I cut him off quickly and made a shushing gesture. The last thing we needed was the troll librarian kicking us out.

"Maybe. If Mom had friends in high school, she only has enemies now. So this is a total stumper."

"I don't agree." Wyatt shook his head. "Donna hates you. Your mom throws threats around like they're water. Your bully's in your face to protect her mom. No offense, Merlini. But I don't think you've got a grip on what most families are like."

"I can't argue with you on that. But try not to remind me in the future. I'm painfully aware, on a nearly constant basis."

"Then let it work for you instead of against you."

"Get my brain gremlins under control? Easier said than done."

"You either work with what you got, or it works against you.

That's what Dad always says. Anyway, that's all I got, so drop the year-book and get your notes."

I turned away, flipping through the yearbook again to look at random pages. But Wyatt didn't leave.

"Hey, uh. I don't want to ask a question. But I kinda need a favor."

"So that's why you're helping. I figured."

"Right. fine. I'll skedaddle."

"No, wait. What is it?"

"It's Fiona. I wanted to ask her to Yule Ball, but she's gonna say no."

"Unsurprising, considering how you acted the first week. Besides, Hayden's showing her a lot of attention. They'll likely be exclusive soon."

"I was kind of hoping you'd put a good word in for me. Maybe she'll change her mind."

"I can't do that, Wyatt."

"Come on, help a guy out. I've seen you with Ramon. You believe in love."

I raised my eyebrow and snorted out a laugh.

"You're not in love with Fiona. You barely know the girl."

"I want to."

"Look, a good word's not enough, even if it came from the Sidhe queen. Dating's like studying. You've got to do the work to make it work."

"Who died and made you the love doctor?"

I felt something, a sensation on my skin. The best possible description is it felt like how glitter looks. That was my first faerie favor, and I didn't want to botch it.

"Can't keep my big mouth shut." He hung his head. "I'm an entire wreck."

"Just in need of a few small repairs. Since you owe me a favor now, I know exactly what I want out of you."

"Oh no. Get it over with."

"I want you to work on yourself, Wyatt. Grow some empathy."

"That's awfully open-ended."

"I'm not done. You'll finish your task when you have a date for a dance. Someone who genuinely wants to go with you because they like you. That gives you eight chances."

"That's, uh, generous." Wyatt blinked. "Guess I better scram now. Before I get in any more trouble."

"You're not in trouble, Wyatt. Consider it enlightening. For both of us."

He said nothing to that, only made a hasty retreat. I got my tablet and noted everything down. I considered doing a few library database searches, but the bell rang.

I should have been doing my homework, anyway.

Matron Klein hadn't been kidding about stress baking.

I saw muffins, cakes, apple pies, pumpkin pies, trays of cookies, biscotti, and even a few loaves each of banana bread and zucchini bread. She put about half of these into two boxes. The aromas wafting up from them were heavenly.

"If you carry one, we'll only make the one trip, Mavis."

"Okay." I hefted a box. "Why are we bringing so much?"

"Only the pie on top is for you and Crow. The rest, I drive around town to places like the senior center and community outreach."

"All of it?" I blinked.

"The zucchini bread is spoken for. But yes. It all gets given away."

"Wow. Is it an old family tradition?"

"It's a tradition, but new. From right before my divorce, in fact."

"You can't just make traditions, I thought."

"Yet here you are, helping out with a home-grown one. You can make your own if you want."

I chewed on that the whole way to Danvers. Getting kicked out was a loss I'd been numb to for months. Still, it was a total one. Not only a roof over my head or the contents of my room but everything else I'd grown up with, like traditions and people to share them with.

That loss wasn't like them all dying. Instead, I was the ghost. The nest was only blocks away from the boarding house. If I wanted to be there, the best I could do was look through the windows and pine for them.

I had nothing, but not no one. Stephanie Klein had lost everything when she was younger than me. Yet, here she was, running a school and giving back to the community that gave her a second chance.

If she built her life back from nothing, maybe I could do it too.

She dropped me off in the circular driveway at the front of the sanitarium.

"I can pick you up. Just send a message on your tablet."

"I'll probably fly back." I held the pie up. "You gave me a paper dish and everything."

"I'll see you later, then."

She drove off, and I went inside. The faeries let me in, sending me to Crow's cabin for the first time in months. The logs had mortar between them now, a testament to his hard work. A garland of yellow and orange leaves framed the door. I pulled the handle, went inside, and blinked at my surroundings.

The table held two place settings, at its head and foot. Yellow plaid bandannas served as placemats with orange ones as napkins, tied into tubes around metal utensils with bits of twine. A wax pillar candle embedded with cloves sat in the middle, wreathed with more autumn leaves.

"I can't believe you decorated."

"I can't believe I'm hosting Thanksgiving dinner at age nineteen, but there you go."

"Brought pie." I set it behind the candle.

"Thank Frigg." He smiled. "I ended up finding everything but dessert."

"It's like she knew," Horace said. "Your principal, I mean."

"Hmm." I nodded.

"You brought Horace."

"Yeah." I nodded.

"There's no other chair, sorry."

"Horace says ghosts don't need those to sit. Hold on."

I concentrated, focusing on my powers. A moment later, Crow clapped his hands slowly.

"I see you now, Horace. Welcome to this old house."

"Thank you," Horace said.

"He said—"

"I heard him. This is amazing. Never heard of them teaching that at Gallows Hill."

"Learned how to control it in Lab with Dr. Aranha. As far as anyone knows, it's unique. Even Ed can't do it."

"I'm not the only one working hard, then." His stomach growled.

Mine did too.

"Heh." He snickered. "Guess it's time to eat."

We had vegetable stew, but it wasn't as plain as last time. Crow also had bread, baked on sticks over the fire to go with it.

"They gave me some basic dry goods when I hit yellow. Salt, yeast, sugar, flour."

"I'm impressed with Danvers Sanitarium," Horace said. "It's a good place."

"It's saved my tailfeathers, that's for sure." Crow nodded. "You talk like you've seen worse."

"I have. That's not my story to tell."

"Good." Crow nodded.

"How?" I blinked.

"That means Horace didn't get stuck in one."

After we finished the stew, he brought out a second course. It was quail instead of turkey, with sides of button mushrooms and sauced berries. Also, something that looked familiar but next to impossible to forage in there.

"Where'd you get mashed potatoes?"

"They're typha. You know, cattails. The roots aren't potatoes, but close enough."

"You're learning almost as much in here as I do at school."

"They focus on practical stuff. Survival skills. Some bird shifters can identify edible forage with the right training. They taught that fact in school, but not the process."

"It suits you."

"I feel the same way. Maybe I can find a job in the wilderness someday."

"I hope the monarchs grant your request first. Get you even more experience out in the middle of nowhere."

Crow put the dinner plates into a bucket of water, then got two more off a shelf and served up the pie.

"This is so good. There's no way you made it."

This fact didn't bother me. I burned pasta on the regular at the nest.

"Matron Klein says she's a stress baker."

"Tell her I want her recipe."

"I will. I'm not sure where you'll find pumpkins here though."

"I'm thinking of when I'm out."

"Maybe we'll find a pumpkin island on our voyage. I'd bring some back. If you're on board, you can find out for yourself."

"The Under's got all kinds of different flora and fauna. I've been reading up on that in the books here. But yeah, I think some of my skills could come in handy. That went in my letter."

"A not-so-little bird told me it's already delivered," Horace said.

"Is that why Hope left early?"

"Yes."

"Wait." He faced Horace. "Mavis's captain, the fracking Alkonost, sent that?"

"She didn't just send it," Horace answered. "She read it, too. Insisted on delivering it herself."

"I'm no clairvoyant, but I think you'll make it." I beamed.

By the time I left the sanitarium, my belly was full of delicious food. And my heart, full of hope.

CHAPTER THREE

The two weeks in December went by too fast. I tried to study every day, but apparently it hadn't only been the Thanksgiving dilemma distracting me.

My brain was the real traitor. I'd blamed stress, trauma brain gremlins, but with them gone, that wasn't right. Some other monster lurked among all my other problems. It took the spotlight as soon as I'd managed to fight back against the rest.

I'd stare at my tablet, unable to swipe to the next screen. Read the same page of written notes three times because somehow, turning over to the next one was a herculean task.

I wasn't lazy. I was desperate. I needed to do the work, had given both family and friends advice along those lines for months. Here I was, unable to follow that very path.

The day before exams, I stood in the hall outside Lecture as usual. I felt my chest contract as though a giant invisible hand gripped it. The light was too bright, the sounds too loud. I couldn't breathe.

"Hey." Fiona stepped behind me in line.

I sprang back, wings out and teeth bared. Had I really just threatened my friend? Why couldn't I back down?

Eyes suddenly wellsprings, I ran full tilt toward the nearest chill-out chamber, flung the door open, and collapsed inside. Fortunately, on something soft. A cushion on the floor.

"Panic attack detected," a voice droned. "Lavender aromatherapy deployed. Deep breathing exercise engaged."

A blue dot appeared on the wall in front of me. It expanded with the words "breathe in" on it and contracted with the words "breathe out."

"Adjust respiration to match the graphic."

I gave it my best try. It wasn't easy, but that never stopped me before. So I persisted and won the battle with my breathing eventually.

The entire room smelled of lavender by the time the blue dot faded. The wall it had been on opened, revealing a small office. I stood, stepped inside, then closed the door behind me.

And found myself face-to-face with a member of Mom's old pack. One of the twins who'd been in Drama Club with Mr. Hickson. I read the placard on his desk.

"Counselor Kyle Cormack, Ph.D. Magus," I said.

"Student Mavis Merlini, Sirin." He gestured at a chair. "Have a seat."

"I'm okay now, though."

"Then this will be quick." He tapped the tablet in front of him. "I've already got your file, thanks to the chamber."

"Can I get another counselor, though?"

"I understand you typically see Buttons, but they're with another student. I can assure you that we're all equally qualified."

"You're in my mother's pack," I blurted.

"So is your Forum guide."

He was right. Paolo, too. I trusted both him and Mr. Hickson. The only difference between them and Dr. Cormack was that I hadn't known their pack status before I met them.

"Oh." I blinked.

"Please be seated."

"Fine." I sat.

"You had a panic attack. It's common here on exam weeks. Our goal here is to help you avoid another."

"Sounds sensible. But how?"

"If your stressors are over academic topics, we can offer you tutoring after school. If they're home-based, we have community resources. If you're trying to manage an SLD, we'll look at your accommodations."

"What's SLD?"

"Specific learning disability."

"Gods." I blinked. Droplets, the precursor to tears, scattered from my eyelashes.

Dr. Cormack handed me a tissue. I took it and dabbed my eyes.

"Some students have all of the above. I see from your file that you've never undergone evaluations."

"Definitely the other two, though." I swallowed.

"Tell me about the academic problems."

I described my difficulties with getting started, along with the lack of focus once I did. I ended with the random rabbit holes.

"It sounds to me like you've got an SLD, Mavis. Another indication is a relative with one, as they run in families."

"My brother got diagnosed with dyslexia recently."

"If I had my way, I'd evaluate you today. I'm sure you're aware your mother would refuse. You could request one as part of mental health services, but without her consent, you'd need to fund it."

"Yeah, I know." I sighed. "I don't even have ten dollars."

"The main reason for official diagnoses is to put accommodations in place. We can't do that for you without a diagnosis. However, there is one way for the school to release funds."

"How do I get that to happen?"

"This is the hard part. You'd have to do poorly on your exam. Without failing it outright."

"Oh no." I shook my head. "No. I'm not failing, don't worry about that. A friend did the math. I'm doing well enough in Lab to pass with a D, as long as I get thirty percent on the written exam."

"That's the spirit."

"What if I get twenty points? Do I flunk completely out, or what?"

"No. They combine scores from the spring finals with the fall and take the average. You'll need an A, but if we can get accommodations in place, that's probable."

"That's a relief."

"I see a note in here. Principal Klein spoke with you about becoming an emancipated minor."

"I haven't even looked into that."

"I'll get the process started and send you the requisite paperwork. You'll need to appear in court in about six months, and they may not grant your request. The fact that you even made it will help next year when you turn seventeen. More of your education will be in your control, and an attempt like this opens more doors."

"I probably don't need any more help than that diagnosis and whatever comes with it. But thanks."

"Ultimately, filling out that paperwork is up to you. I'm sending it anyway. You can complete and submit it any time before you turn eighteen."

"Will she know I've got it?"

"Not until it's in. However, the school can send her notices. The principal has noted here not to send any materials to your parents without your consent, so that's up to you.

I thought for a moment. Mom had the abilities test with Director-General Rockport hanging over my head. If Dr. Cormack sent a notice about emancipation, she'd have to deal with the same thing. Being on even footing with her could give me leverage.

"Send it."

"That's an interesting choice considering the reservations you voiced earlier."

"After some thought, I realized it's part of the herring pile."

"Explain."

"Everybody knows red herrings. The big distracting thing that ends up being fake. Not everyone falls for those. So sometimes, the best idea is a bucket of actual herring instead. What can she do if there's suddenly fish everywhere? Not much."

"That's a creative way of putting it. Usually, I hear the straw on the camel's back."

"See, it doesn't fit. The camel is trying to be a camel and carry straw with a quantity problem. The herring pile is offense, tactical, something you use to confuse and overwhelm an enemy."

"I think I understand the difference now." He nodded.

"I'm weird."

"Not so much. In fact, you remind me of someone else who fought a wily foe."

"Did they win?"

"I'm still waiting to find that out."

The bell rang.

"I missed Lecture?"

"The chamber sent a message to your teacher. She'll have a recording uploaded to your tablet before Forum. For now, I understand you've got a class at Messing Academy."

"Yeah, I do." I stood and glanced at the wall to my left. But the door I'd come through was gone. "Thanks, Mr. Cormack. How do I get out of here?"

"Behind you. It's the usual door to my office. Don't be a stranger, Mavis."

"I won't."

That turned out to be a promise I kept.

That night, I put my tablet and my notes on my desk and didn't look at them again until the next morning. I went down the hall and checked the lounge, looking for something to do or someone to talk to.

Everyone else was cramming, of course. I'd visited Crow on Sunday. He'd told me not to drop by until after the exam. I decided to do laundry instead since the weekend would be busy, and I didn't want to run out of clothes.

Down in the basement, I found Ed. He'd had the same idea, but for an entirely different reason.

"I forgot they don't have exams at Messing."

"Laundry basket, and not a book in sight." He narrowed his eyes.

"Don't, Ed," Horace said. "It's the last thing she needs right now."

"Self-care night."

"Mavis, what hap—"

"I'm not talking about it until after the exam."

"Okay." Ed nodded. "Self-care night, it is. After we finish the laundry."

I wanted to stay in, thought it'd be safer for Ed that way. I'd been reducing my time around town alone with Ramon to protect him from the inevitable repercussions of being my boyfriend. The downside to that was making all of my male friends potential targets.

I told him as much, expecting a response in line with Ed's usual circumspection. Instead, he laughed.

"I don't have any family in town for her to harass. If she bugs me, I've got Rob."

"I've got Horace. He can't do much but cheer me on."

"Yeah, but you can't do this." Ed grinned at his ghost. "Hit it, Rob!"

They merged again, like at the variety show but more completely. Ed was still himself, but also Rob at the same time. I wished I had Hope's spyglass to see what they looked like through it.

"It's cool. But—"

Then, Ed-slash-Rob lifted an empty dryer with one hand.

"Fewmets!" I stepped back. "Put that down, guys. Before we get in hot water with the Matron."

He did, then brushed lint off his hands.

"We can go out, no problem. So, let's get loaded potato skins at Dodge Street Café."

"I still don't have any money."

"You do."

"Huh?"

"Check your satchel."

"Fine."

I'd need my coat upstairs if we were going outside anyway, so it wasn't a big deal to fetch that. There was no way money appeared in my satchel for no reason. I'd been at school long enough to know there was no such thing as a money faerie.

Ed-slash-Rob followed, whistling a tune.

Sure enough, there was a brand new wallet in my satchel with money in the billfold section. Not an indecent amount, but enough for a snack and beverage out once a week over break. I almost asked Ed how it got there, but I recognized it from a shop on the wharf.

"I've already got a list of possible suspects in this reverse heist. It's short, one name."

"Saya's got a sense of humor after all." Rob-slash-Ed chuckled.

"Dry for a water dragon." I grinned. "So it *was* her."

"We told her you'd figure it out. Put your coat on, and let's go."

I did. We stepped out in the hallway. Ed-slash-Rob kept walking past their room. I stopped in front of the door.

"You too."

"Don't need it when we're like this."

"Just so people won't freak out, maybe. Please."

"Since you asked nicely." They went in and got it.

The merged duo set a pace brisk enough to give Cosmo a hard time. I barely kept up. They weren't winded.

The Dodge Street Café had a swing band playing. While we waited for our potato skins and soda, Ed-slash-Rob got up and danced. They didn't need the inhaler.

We chatted about mundane topics such as books, movies, music, and theater. As we walked out the door, I asked them something I'd been wondering.

"What were you whistling earlier?"

"*Peddler of Connecticut.* A favorite song from back in the day. For Rob, not Ed."

"Haven't heard of it."

"You know *Modern Major General* from *Pirates of Penzance*, of course."

"Yeah."

"It's like that."

"Sounds cool. Haven't heard it."

They hurried past me, then turned and walked backward, like Cosmo. And he sang it.

The song was pretty much a list of all the items a long-gone peddler had for sale, arranged as a tongue twister. They sang it once, then repeated it faster. By then, we made it back to the boarding house. I'd almost forgotten about the hoped-for near failure I'd need to pull off the next day.

"Thanks, guys," I said. "I needed that."

"So did we." Ed-slash-Rob nodded.

We went upstairs.

"I should start winding down, or I'll never get to sleep."

"Goodnight, then. See you tomorrow."

I went into my room, collected my hairbrush, toothbrush, pajamas, and a copy of *Milk and Honey* by Rupi Kaur courtesy of Kiara's bookshelf. Then I went into the bathroom to have a lavender bath and didn't get out of the tub until I'd finished the book. In my room, plaiting my hair, I had an epiphany.

For some reason, even when we know we need rest, we resist it. Giving in and taking the time to do nothing important for a while made a difference. As much of one as Ed merging with Rob had on his asthma.

Possession had its benefits. I wasn't remotely ready to try it myself. Not until I had some idea what the drawbacks were.

There were more than I could have guessed, but I didn't find that out until the next day.

The next day, I woke feeling refreshed, but Ed leaned on the table, eyes bloodshot.

"What did you do?" Saya chided him. "I know you weren't up all night studying. I've got half a mind to send you to Nurse Wilson."

"More. Coffee." He held his mug. I poured.

"He was sleeping like a log when I got in from our cram session," Cosmo said. "Sawing them, too. Small medium, huge snores."

"We went for snacks last night." I didn't rat him out about the possession. "Bunch of things, I forget what."

"You look fresh as a daisy." Saya shook her head. "Oh. Something must have had peanuts in it. That's not so good for him."

"I'm right here," Ed mumbled.

"Yeah, he's got a mild allergy, asthma stuff." Cosmo nodded. "Explains the snoring and the red eyes."

"I'll get him some antihistamines."

Saya left her half-eaten breakfast on the table and strode from the room. A few moments later, she returned with a pill in a small plastic cup. Ed washed it down with more coffee.

"Have some French toast."

Cosmo put two slices on Ed's plate, then four on his. He poured syrup over his, then held it out to Ed, eyebrows raised.

Ed shook his head, picked up a piece of his dry eggy toast, and took a bite. I did the same with mine so he wouldn't feel weird. Horace nodded and gave me a thumbs-up. Rob was nowhere in sight.

After breakfast, the morning routine was the same as usual with the trip through the portal, gym, and washing up in the locker room.

After that, we stood outside the Lecture classroom. I went up to Fiona while we waited.

"Sorry."

"You haven't even said hello yet," Fiona said.

"About yesterday."

"Everybody gets nervous around exams. It's okay."

"I don't want to scare my friends off."

"Not happening." She shook her head. "I'm sticking around."

"Thanks, Fiona."

The bell rang, and we went in. Mrs. Ambersmith and Mr. Hickson both stood at the front of the room. Once we were seated, they walked through, handing out our tests, pencils, and the answer booklets then went back to the front.

"This test consists of one hundred and one questions," Mr.

Hickson announced. "Twenty-five are true and false. Twenty-five are short answers. The rest are multiple-choice. You'll answer each of them to the best of your ability. If you finish early, the library is open."

"This is a half-day. Your Lab practical is after Research. You have the entire Lecture period to complete this exam." Mrs. Ambersmith tapped her tablet. Behind her on the wall, a timer started a countdown. "Begin."

The sound of rustling paper filled the room. After that, mostly silence. I did my best, just like Mr. Hickson said. It was worse than I imagined.

I'd gone in expecting to guess at half the questions. But it was more like two-thirds of them. On one of the short answers, I wrote nunya business. True and false were relatively easy, but multiple-choice was more like multiple guesses.

I was painfully aware of time passing. Kiara left for the library first, with Brandon on her heels. Hope followed a few minutes later. Ramon was right behind her. Wyatt and Jaxon got up at the same time.

Nearby, I saw Fiona close her answer booklet, then open it again to double-check her answers. Jillian finished before Fiona got two pages in. I kept slogging through, too often stumped.

Fiona shot me an apologetic glance over her shoulder. Cosmo was still there in the same row with me, plugging away.

His brow furrowed. He spent a lot of time reading each question. Cosmo held his shoulders low and leaned back between pauses to mark the paper. We both worked hard, but my effort was desperate. His was circumspect and finished ten minutes before time up.

Same storm, different boat. Story of my life.

By the time I'd put an answer down for every question, I had three minutes. Not enough to check back over. So I went and turned it in, unable to look either of my teachers in the eye. At least I wouldn't be late to Mediumship at Messing.

Old Grandpa Ambersmith had us in pairs, practicing terminology with flashcards. I made a beeline for Ed.

"So, about that exam." Ed elbowed me. His eyes were clear but puffy.

"I didn't cry if that's what you wanted to know."

"Thanks for not telling Saya about last night."

"I figured she'd go all dragon force if she knew." I peered at the definition on the card. "Anchor."

"The mom act was all I could handle before coffee." He read the term on the next one. "Wraith. A ghost who's forgotten themselves."

"You drank a gallon."

"No, but close." He gave me a half-grin.

"Where's Rob?"

"Having his self-care day." He held another card up.

"Solid. Ghostly term for a corporeal person." I chuckled. "Didn't even need a class to learn that one."

The quiz at the end of Mediumship felt a lot more comfortable than the exam. When I returned to Gallows Hill campus, I got in line outside Lab.

"I'm not sure I'm ready," Cosmo said. "Especially for the glove."

"I hear you."

"You saw Ed at Messing."

"He looked a lot better."

"Good."

Dr. Aranha let us in. The stations were at even intervals on benches around the room. I had no trouble identifying the faerie artifacts, pure or otherwise. Practical was a breeze.

This time, I was the first student to finish. Wyatt handed his booklet in as I headed out the door, a testament to his familiarity with everything fae. In the hall, he whistled.

"Nice job for someone who'd never seen a gnome toenail until September."

"Uh, thanks."

Hope walked into the hall.

"Odd reversal from Lecture." She grinned.

"Not so odd." I shrugged. "I'm a birdbrain, and I know it."

Kiara came out next.

"Missed you at the cram session, Mavis."

"I needed a night off."

"Glad you got one, then."

Ramon emerged, shaking his head. Brandon came with him.

"That bad?" I asked.

"Think I might have mixed up gnome dentures and pixie jewelry."

"Don't beat yourself up over that," Brandon said. "I'm a faerie shifter and still get them mixed up sometimes."

Jillian, Jaxon, and Fiona came out of the lab in a line.

"Saya's done," Jillian said. "She's still in there for Cos. Moral support."

"It's the gloves, isn't it?" Hope asked.

"No. He only wrecked one pair." Jaxon shook his head. "It's something else. A pain in his arm."

"Yeah," Fiona nodded. "Dr. Aranha offered to let him go to the nurse and finish it later, but he said he'd rather get it done."

"That's cats for you." Jillian shrugged. "Once they get their claws in something, it's hard to let go."

In the end, Hope ended up escorting Cosmo to the nurse's office. Despite my near-certain failure on the written exam, I felt lucky. Because, despite his obvious expression of pain, nothing was apparently wrong with him.

Everybody else went out to celebrate with pizza. I headed back to the dorm and slept until my stomach woke me up for dinner. I grabbed a sandwich and went back to bed, utterly exhausted.

CHAPTER FOUR

On Friday, Mrs. Ambersmith announced that we wouldn't get our exam scores until Monday. I'd have to tether my impatience through classes, Yule Ball that night, the performance showcase on Saturday, and a visit to the Under on Sunday. At least I'd be well and truly distracted.

Azrael Ambersmith delivered our wardrobe to the boarding house that afternoon. Since I'd missed my fitting, I decided to try mine on. Kiara joined me, showing off her stunning mermaid-cut gown with cap sleeves in gold velvet.

This time, I'd gone with kale green instead of monochrome and chose a higher neckline with an A-line fit instead of bias-cut like last time. The back plunged, leaving room in case my wings put in a surprise appearance.

Grace had added a shimmering, translucent taffeta overlay.

"I love that outer layer," Kiara said. "It really enhances the green."

"Thanks. Yours is going to steal the show, though."

"We'll see." I peered into the shoebox that came with the gown. "At least these look more comfortable."

They were ankle boots, green with speed laces and a squared toe. No pinched toes or blistered heels for me this time.

"I love mine." She opened hers, revealing gold patent pumps with kitten heels. "And I can't wait to get our makeup done in record time with the glamour brush."

"Same here." I nodded. "We can spend more time on our hair."

"We'd better set these aside until after dinner."

Downstairs, Cosmo sat sulking at the table beside Wyatt, who was inhaling stacks of hamburgers.

"What's up, Cos?" I asked.

"That girl from our team asked me to the dance." He wrinkled his nose and pushed food around on his plate. "When I said no, she cried. Felt like the world's biggest jerk. Ugh."

"That sucks."

"Maybe," Wyatt said between bites. "At least it wasn't Donna."

"Wait. Is that why you're stress eating? She asked you to the dance?"

"No." He ate faster, taking bigger bites. Probably to avoid answering.

"Mavis, we need to talk." Hope tapped me on the shoulder.

"Okay." I pulled the chair beside me away from the table.

"No, not here."

"Uh, okay." I got up and followed her to the lounge.

"Ed told me Donna got out in front of everyone at entertainment wrestling and asked Ramon to Yule Ball."

When I opened my mouth, a stream of words Mom usually said came out. After I stopped, Hope spoke again.

"He said no."

"I know. I can't believe she asked."

"I needed to see your reaction."

"That makes no sense."

"Listen, Mavis. Donna's trying to get you in trouble. She tried it at the last dance with Fiona. We didn't see it coming then. We do this time. You don't want to get suspended. So no winging out, no matter what she does."

"We could stop her from coming."

"It's too late to plan something like that. Besides, it'll only make her more determined to hurt someone worse if she doesn't get a little dig in now."

"Easy for you to say when it's nobody you care about."

"We're a crew, and I'm the captain. Whether I care or not, I'm bound to protect all of you."

"If only they taught us about crews and packs in first-year."

"It's not on me to give you those details. I know you're capable of extra research. And controlling your temper."

"I'll do my best." I narrowed my eyes. "But it's Ramon. I love him."

"I get it."

I doubted that but didn't say so. I'd never even caught Hope checking anyone out. Mostly, she seemed cold, even a little heartless. Maybe there was a different reason for that. Maybe she did love someone, just in secret. She was almost too good at keeping those.

"I'll do my best to avoid Donna. That's better than waiting for her to act and bottling my feelings."

"Whatever works for the two of you."

"Last time, you had Fiona's back. Sent Wyatt out there to cut in."

"I did no such thing. He acted on his own."

"So no help from my captain is the way it goes, I guess."

"I'll do what I can. Saya's who I'd normally put on something like this, but she has her issue to deal with tonight."

"Brett again. She mentioned having another date arranged."

"Right." Hope nodded. "So, here's my suggestion. I'll call Ramon, give him a heads-up that we're on guard. You ask Horace to tail Ramon. I'll have Ed put Rob on Donna and stay alert. Jillian will follow his lead if there's trouble."

"Decent enough strategy. But Donna summons scary faerie hounds."

"That problem's got a faculty solution. Any faerie teacher will notice her summons and kick her out." Hope put a hand on my shoulder. "Mostly, we want to avoid her inciting a brawl."

"Okay." My stomach rumbled. "I'm going back to dinner."

"Good talk."

I didn't dare tell her it was no such thing.

The boarding house kids got to the gym before everyone else. Saya wore pink and silver tulle like the sugar plum fairy. Hope had another pantsuit in flowing red chiffon. Brandon's suit was mahogany wool with gold velvet accents to match Kiara. Cosmo's very basic tux was white with an ice blue vest and tie. Wyatt wore a crimson woolen coat with a white shirt and black vest underneath. He'd turned his cap into a top hat.

Ed wore a black tuxedo, classic with tails, and a pine green cravat. He glanced at me.

"You, uh, look really nice, Mavis."

"Ditto. But you said you'd dress formal goth for this one."

"Jill said tuxes are classy."

"Oh."

"Hope told me about the Donna plan."

"Good."

"I would have had your back anyway."

"Knowing what to expect isn't a bad thing, though."

"Except I was there when Wyatt gave her the heads-up. You two aren't getting any friendlier. I can't figure out why."

"As long as we can work together, it doesn't matter much, right?"

"That's reasonable. I hoped you'd be friends."

The off-campus students arrived before I could ask why. Jillian squealed and made a beeline for Ed. She wore a clingy forest green sheath dress with spaghetti straps, covered in flashy sequins.

Jaxon sauntered after them, hands in the pockets of the off-white slacks under his mint satin Nehru jacket. Ramon was at my side a moment later.

"Donna—"

"I know all about that, don't worry. She's likely planning something horrible, and Captain Dunstable's got our backs."

"You've got a plan for everything else, so I should have known." He grinned and looped his arm through mine. "I'm the luckiest guy here. Brains and all this beauty, too."

"Grace gave you shantung again." I stroked the deep green fabric covering his forearm.

"I like the texture. And your reaction to it."

"My lady." Brett bowed deeply in front of Saya and offered her his arm.

"Say what you want about him, but dude's got manners," Cosmo said.

"Meh," Fiona said. "I get a bad vibe from him."

"I love how your dress came out." Cosmo gave her a thumbs-up.

"Me too," I said.

"Thanks, it has pockets. And twirls!" She spun, the cranberry damask circle skirt flaring out gracefully from the corseted waistline. The back of her dress laced up with a golden cord, and Grace had given her a square neckline, just as flattering as the v-neck from the Harvest Moon dance.

"Hayden will love it," Cosmo said.

"You think so?"

"Yeah. Bet you two will spend the entire break together after he sees you in this."

Coach Tremain blew his whistle as Mrs. Ambersmith strode into the room. She stopped in the middle of the gym and clapped her hands. A handful of students, all changelings, met her there. Kiara went with them, forming a circle and joining hands.

"What's going on?"

"That's the Ball Committee," Fiona said. "They're putting the decorations up."

A moment later, we all stood in a forest clearing, surrounded by evergreens and holly bushes, and bathed in clear, bright moonlight. The chairs were all logs or toadstools, while the refreshment and DJ tables took on the appearance of granite henge structures. The floor beneath our feet turned to crystal but retained the gym's traction.

"Magical decorations for a magical school," Kiara said when she returned.

"They're gorgeous," Brandon replied. "Like you."

The music started as our guests from the other schools arrived.

Hayden quickly joined Fiona, and they hit the dance floor. Wyatt sat on a toadstool. Diego came in with Rita on his arm, waved, then got right to dancing.

"Help." Cosmo ducked behind me. "It's that girl from the team."

"I've got you, bro." Hope escorted him to the dance floor, where they did the chicken dance even though that wasn't playing.

"Waiting for Donna sucks," I said.

"It does." Ramon nodded. "At least we're waiting together."

He had a point. Donna took her time to show up. When she did, Rob floated behind her. The strap on her handbag broke as she walked in the door. With a strangled growl, she stomped off toward the bathroom. Rob winked at me before sailing after her.

Ramon and I finally felt comfortable enough to start enjoying the dance. For the first hour, we only stopped when we needed drinks, relying on Horace to warn us of impending trouble.

But my hypervigilance wouldn't let me ignore the bully. So I noticed something.

Random minor misfortunes followed Donna the summoner. Toilet paper sticking to her shoe. Clips coming out of her hair. Spilling her punch on Mr. Hickson's shoe. Gia and Peg tried to help her fix these issues, but that only frustrated Donna more.

"I'm going home," she announced halfway through the dance.

"Good riddance to bad rubbish!" Rob blew a raspberry as she left the building.

Ramon headed to the bathroom so I sat to wait for him.

"No, Brett." I heard Saya speak from farther down the row. "I already told you I'm helping load in for the performance showcase tomorrow morning, early."

Her date sat between her and me with four empty stumps between us. No, three were empty. The one directly beside him held two cups of punch.

"I didn't say you should leave with me at the end. I'm talking about now." His grin had too much leer in it.

"They'll know we're not on campus if we do that. It's magical, remember?"

"We don't have to go to my house. This school is huge. I know all sorts of rooms nobody's using."

"Let's just have our drinks instead."

"Fine." He held a cup of punch toward her. "If you want to stay boring, whatever."

On the seat near his beverage, I saw a little glass vial. I stood, put my posture off-balance, and clomped noisily toward my friend with the goofiest imitation Cosmo face I could plaster on.

"Heya, Saya!" I faked a hiccup. "Gimme a sip?"

"It's not for you, failfeathers!" Brett snatched it back from her. "I mean, uh—"

"How uncouth." Saya sniffed. "There's no excuse for such behavior from a dragon of your breeding."

I giggled, this time for real, as Brett backpedaled over various apologies. I added in a little uncoordinated swaying for good measure, then slapped a hand over my mouth as a grand finale. I even stuck my pinkie out for fun.

Saya stood and hooked her arm through mine.

"It seems my classmate needs an escort to the ladies' room. Do excuse me."

I only pretended to lean on her, which she noticed of course. Saya was more observant than most of our friends gave her credit for. In the bathroom, I maintained the charade until a magus finished washing her hands and left.

"What do you really need help with, Mavis?" she asked.

"He put something in your drink, Saya."

"Fewmets." She sighed. I noticed for the first time that evening how weary she seemed. "Mavis, that was me. *I* put something in our drinks."

"What?"

"Insisted on it, in fact."

"But why?" I blinked. "It's obvious he's down for just about anything. And I've seen where you're looking whenever he walks in front of you."

"That's the problem. Which is why I asked Nurse Wilson for that chastening powder."

"So it's not a roofie?"

"The exact opposite."

"Wow." I shook my head. "Thought you needed help but it turns out you're a self-rescuing princess."

"Strategic princess, if you please." She chuckled. "Brett is certainly strapping. And Mother has no qualms about me laying an egg while still in school."

"Wouldn't you have to drop out?"

"Laying an egg isn't like being pregnant. It's a week of craving fish at most, then three days in the hospital. After that, the egg's at home in Newport while I'm here, immersed in Lecture, Forum, and Lab. It wouldn't hatch for nearly a decade. In this case, Mother recommended the chastening powder. She hasn't gotten the entire background check back, only lineage and hatching records."

"Good call on her part." I nodded. "He might have proof of being a hatchling, but that's not permanent. Who knows what he got up to before meeting you?"

"I'm a bit baffled here, Mavis." She tapped her foot slowly. "You're discussing this with me like it's, well, normal. Instead of trying to save me from my own culture."

"Because that's how it is for you. Living with all these rules *is* your normal. I grok that, Saya."

"Hmm." She tilted her head, bowed it. "In any event, I've run out of powder, and there's no way of knowing whether Brett drank his punch. So, I ought to formally end the date for now, just in case."

"Since you can't trust him, walking on eggshells is a good strategy."

"Please ask Hope to deliver the message to Brett. But don't tell her why, for Tiamat's sake. She doesn't like hearing about our sex lives. Or in this case for now, lack thereof."

"Absolutely." I nodded.

Outside the bathroom, Saya marched directly to Dr. Aranha by the gym door. After speaking briefly, they went into the hallway.

"Hey, you're back from something." Ramon was at my elbow.

"Helping a friend. Come with me, just finishing that up."

I found Hope chatting with Ed near the stone DJ table.

"Hope, Saya wants you to tell Brett that their date's over."

"Hmm. Must be a reason."

"Yeah, she'll tell you later."

"Then I've got this."

"Ditto." Ed nodded. "Now that nobody's on Donna duty."

"You have a date." Hope jerked her thumb at Jill, who pouted over by the punch bowl. "Go get her and hit the floor already."

"Oh, right." He went over.

We stayed until the end, chatting and dancing with our friends. Matron Klein insisted on ushering all the dorm kids back through Sid's portal instead of walking home.

I clutched Ramon's arm, shaking. Had the emancipation papers gone through? Had I made a horrible mistake? Did Mom have the school under siege?

When Ramon and the other off-campus kids pushed the street door open, I understood.

Sometime during that last hour, it had begun snowing.

C H A P T E R   F I V E

The performance showcase was on Saturday at Hawthorn. Technically it started just after dinner. But for us in the Drama Club, it was an all-day affair.

We spent all morning and some of the afternoon moving our sets in, arranging curtains, testing the lights, and making sure the wings had enough clearance for one of the props. It would have taken forever with only the Drama Club. Everyone in first-year section two helped out. We had a late lunch at the boarding house and rested up.

After dinner, when we headed over again, I was more nervous than excited, but it was a near thing. Performing might've been less stressful than remembering cues for props and which was which.

Messing's interpretive dance production was literally over the top. The dancers weren't technically on the stage. They performed their entire routine hanging from long silk ropes. Diego said that was all the rage at outdoor festivals. How they managed to keep themselves aloft baffled me, but I enjoyed their performance.

I couldn't see the poetry slam because we had to set up. I was backstage, checking on all the props. Kiara handed out the glamour bracelets for costumes, which was a good thing. We had extensive costuming for this show.

"There's no way we could have done this play without glamour bracelets," she said.

"We haven't done it yet." I gave her a grin I hoped wasn't too weary. "Get ready, though. It's about time."

"Right."

Kiara's play was called *The Time Traveler's Club*. It involved a group of people trying to meet at a sign for the eponymous club. They came from different eras, with monologues about the challenges they faced on the way to the meeting. Each had different means of navigating to that place at that exact moment. Kiara said she got the idea from a meme, something she saw on the Internet a few years ago. She hadn't been able to set that inspiration aside, so she'd written her play about it.

Diego played the lead, a quirky scientist from the future who'd made the sign for what seemed like a dire purpose. In reality, he only wanted to make friends with similar interests. He killed it, of course.

Ed as a Victorian author based on H.G. Wells gave him a run for his money. I realized he'd borrowed heavily from Horace, basing many character mannerisms on our ghostly friend.

Wanda's Renaissance duchess put everyone else to shame, though. Despite the fact that she ended up poisoning two of the other characters before Ed's and Diego's characters sent her back to her time. Jaxon's 1950s lab assistant and Rita's Mayan priestess got an antidote in time, though. The future scientist saved the day.

As a work of fiction, Kiara's play was intriguing and innovative. So many of our shows, movies, and musicals were fantasy-based. Most of the time, they didn't showcase science in a setting devoid of the magic we all lived with daily. Not since before the Reveal, anyway. No wonder she loved Heinlein so much.

Finally, it was intermission. We headed to the gym for the entertainment wrestling elimination match.

Ramon and Wyatt teamed up to knock Chainsaw, a third-year heel wrestler, out of the ring. In an apparent face turn, Wyatt saved Ramon from getting knocked out by Donna but ended up out of the ring himself.

Jillian and Ramon had a mini-match, where he almost tricked her into falling over the turnbuckle. She managed to pin him for the three-count, making it a clean win with a high-five afterward.

Fiona stomped into the ring. She chased Jillian around, trying to "hug" her tag-team partner with an air of oblivious amiability. Jill kept apologizing, trying to grapple her, but Fiona had too much leverage as an ogre.

Chainsaw came back and walloped Fiona over the head in an illegal move. Jillian went into a wolfy rage and tossed him back out, winning the title. It was pure fun, utterly entertaining, and the kids from the other schools loved it.

"If I'd known it was that cool, I totally would've gone over for this instead of writing songs," Arick Magnuson said.

"If it weren't for work-study, I would have been right there with you," Xan said. "Maybe they have entertainment wrestling at PPC."

"Scholarships for Bishop's Row." Lena raised an eyebrow.

"Maybe you can do both," I chimed in.

"Not a bad idea." Xan nodded.

"I know you were watching me. In the park." I slapped my hand over my mouth.

"Mind the magus," Rob said to Ed.

Ed nodded, then studied Xan's response.

"Guilty as charged." He snorted. "Not for the reasons you think though."

"You'd better not be stalking her," Ed said.

"Not like that."

"Then how?"

"It's my job. Security."

"Yeah, for here." I nodded. "Not out in town."

"Somebody asked you to do it." Ed narrowed his eyes. "Who?"

"Your principal." He sighed. "I wasn't supposed to tell you, but you weren't supposed to notice."

"You thought we wouldn't notice a mysterious person in Hawthorn hoodies? Or wonder who it was?" Ed shook his head. "Your stealth skills need work."

"I'll stop if you want."

"Don't," I said. "I kind of appreciate having extra backup around. We're at Dodge Street Café now that it's cold."

"Good to know." Xan nodded.

"Hey." Rob wagged a finger at me. "We're extra backup. Me and Ed, in case you forgot."

"Rob," Horace said. "You two can't walk around merged all the time."

As Coach Tremain and the Hawthorn coach packed up the ring, Ed and I stepped away from the quarreling ghosts. We stopped outside the locker room, waiting for our significant others and friends.

"I agree with Horace, just so you know," Ed said. "Rob's been incorporeal for such a long time that he misses being in a body."

"Ghosts that age are rare."

"Yeah. We're both stumped on what he needs to move on. I understand how he feels. Wanting a type of life that's always out of reach."

"I grok it, too. Maybe when you find the whatchamacallit in the Under, you'll know."

"I've still got no idea what that even is, let alone does. Besides, it's not any kind of anchor. So I won't hold my breath."

"I'm going to keep hoping."

"For once, you make no sense to me, Mavis."

"The feather changed my entire life, including my perspective, recently. Why can't something like that happen for you?"

"My luck doesn't work that way. Probably, we just have to get it out of the Under so the Calamity's away, and we can find that anchor. Even Tommy Mendez doesn't think I fit the bill to bear the thing. Sorry if I sound like a downer."

"Be one if that's what you need right now." I patted his shoulder. "If you need picking up, just ask."

He only nodded. The rest of section two joined us, chattering about all the kayfabe. Our wrestlers emerged and walked as a group back to the auditorium.

The band didn't march, but all the same students participated, sitting on stage arranged and dressed in formal orchestral fashion. They played a different medley this time, mostly scores from movies and TV. Once again, nearby Hawthorn students waxed impressed. I didn't know this batch, however.

"I hope the headmaster can do something about boosting attendance," a girl with a dog said. "I'd love to have activities the other schools want to do here."

"Yeah, tall order. I wish we had a band," a boy with a nightingale remarked.

I wondered how that would be possible. Hawthorn didn't do much recruiting. Maybe an ad campaign with familiars, because those sure were cute. Apparently, I was on to something.

The Hawthorn Academy familiar's parade was adorable. Each student participating led their familiar on stage to do a trick or show off a power. Xan Onassis had his dragonet flying figure-eights above his head. Arick Magnussen juggled his bookwyrm from one hand to the other like a slinky. Hayden was there with Howard, who quacked out a tune.

A plethora of cameras clicked and flashed from the aisles. I spied Headmaster Hawkins and some of the teachers taking pictures. Hopefully, they'd put those to good use.

Their Creatives group had a singer-songwriter, an earth magus doing clay sculpture entirely with magic, and a cheer squad member with a solo dance routine. They all had talent, but three performers didn't make for much of a showcase.

At the end, Hawthorn had a mixer, but first-year section two skipped it, along with Ed and Diego.

After the long, full day, all we wanted was sleep.

CHAPTER SIX

On Sunday morning, someone knocked on my door. I looked at the clock, then shuffled into my slippers and to the door.

"It's zero dark thirty," I said without opening it. "Go away."

"Monarchs, Mavis," Hope said. "Rise and shine."

I groaned because there wasn't anything else I could do. After that, I grabbed some of my nicer clothes and stuff I'd need in the bathroom, then stepped into the hall. Hope stood there, hands on her hips.

"No shoes is no good."

"Freshening up first. Deal with it."

"Thought you were an early bird."

"Not after yesterday."

"Fine. We're meeting in the dining room in twenty minutes. Don't be late."

"Or else." I snorted.

"It's monarchal rules, not mine."

"Said I'd be there, gods. Let me pee."

She said nothing more. In the bathroom I found Saya using a curling iron while Cosmo brushed his teeth. Both were fully dressed, with Cos wearing his amulet. I heard the shower in the gentlemen-only side.

After getting toothpaste, soap, and shampoo from the cabinet, I went to the ladies' side, took care of the basics, then had a quick shower. Yes, I brushed my teeth in there. Washed my face, too. I didn't exactly have time to do it any other way.

Once dressed, I went out to the sinks, still rubbing my damp hair with a towel. Saya and Cosmo were already gone, but Ed was there.

"You want to get that totally dry so it doesn't tangle."

"Why?"

"The queen's super formal, and we'll be seeing both her and his majesty today."

"I suppose she'll be upset if I don't put on makeup."

"No, Hope gets away without that all the time. Decent clothes and tidy hair is enough."

I put it in a plait.

"Good idea," Ed said. "That'll do. Look, I wanted to ask—"

The alarm on Ed's phone went off. "Guess there's no time for that."

"For what?"

"Never mind." He pushed the door open and held it for me.

"Okay. I still need my shoes from my room. How much time do we have?"

"Three minutes."

"It's enough."

I swapped my slippers for a pair of ballet flats with ghosts on them. Out in the hall, Ed saw them and smiled but said nothing. Unlike last night after the wrestling match, our silence was comfortable again. Whatever he had to say couldn't be bad.

The gremlins had left bagged breakfast and coffee to go for us. Sid emerged from the kitchen, leaving his chef's apron on a hook inside the door before leading us downstairs.

We ate our food while Sid made the portal. It took him longer than usual. Horace told me he was moving the location and being careful to get it exactly right. At least that gave us time to get the egg sandwiches and coffee down.

Hope put her trash in a wastebasket, then stepped through without any comment. The rest of us thanked Sid before doing the same. I realized she wasn't hard on him or us. Our captain was nervous. Whatever the monarchs summoned us for was a big deal.

Instead of the beach, we emerged in a hallway outside a set of double doors. Hope frowned upon seeing them. Ed did, too.

"Let's do this." Cosmo elbowed each of them in turn. "Come on, old guard."

Hope pushed the door open, revealing a throne room. Sidhe guards inside announced each of us, including name and title.

"Under-born Captain Hope Tolland Dunstable, Alkonost, daughter of Sir Albert Dunstable Esquire and Captain Gemma Tolland-Dunstable. Under-hatched esteemed dragon, Miss Saya Thetis Harcourt, daughter of Hertha and Wilfred. Master medium, Edward Aion Redford, son of Duke Neil and brother to Sir Frederick. Under-born esteemed guest, Cosmo Leon Gitano, brother to the Gamayun's betrothed."

As we walked, I recognized that comment had to do with the initial mystery surrounding their origins, still unsolved. Unspoken, actually. Because they were all at least my comrades, at best true friends, all I had to do was ask. But later.

"Under-born Mavis Rhiannon Merlini, Sirin," was all I got for an introduction. I didn't really mind not hearing my mother's name, though.

The monarchs stood on a dais, watching us approach. A round table, its seats carved with names, stood to the right. I recognized two: Ed's brother Fred and Hal Hawkins.

Hal himself was only somewhat present, incorporeally by some magic I didn't recognize right away. The djinn knelt before the monarchs, a gleaming object at his knee.

A lamp, of course. Hal's lamp, which one of the monarchs must control.

"Kneel when you get there," Cosmo said. "In case they forgot to tell you."

"Thanks, Cos." I wondered how he managed to be the only one with his wits about him. Whatever bothered the others apparently didn't affect him.

We all knelt until we heard His Majesty's voice.

"You may rise."

We did, even Hal.

"With the exception of the Sirin, who made the request, you may also each make a statement," her majesty said. "No more than three sentences, expressing either your support or refusal of the addition to Under-born Cornelius Owen Merlini, brother to the Sirin, to *The Odyssey's* crew."

"We'll hear from each of you in the order of your announcement. As Sir Harold holds the highest esteem, he may decide whether to open or close arguments."

"Close, Your Majesty," Hal said.

"So be it. Captain Dunstable, you may speak."

"I've never met Cornelius, but I hear he's strong and brave. Mavis has proven both loyal and resourceful, and the idea for this request is hers. She knows her brother best, so I say yea."

"Miss Harcourt." The queen nodded.

"Despite my tender years, I learned it's unwise to judge a man by his blood kin. I trust Mavis implicitly, but the records I've read of her brother's misdeeds are troubling. Apologies to my trusty friend the Sirin, but I say nay."

"Master Edward," the king said.

"I only need one sentence to say that Crow should join our crew, on account of his past misdeeds being under duress, but I'm saying more. The effort he's made toward rehabilitation is downright inspiring, and the advice he's given Mavis, crucial to her well-being. Horace Lancaster has made his acquaintance and attests that he's not only her brother by blood, but in his heart and soul, so I say yea."

"Guest Cosmo," the queen said.

"Yeah, I'm gonna say no. Crow— I mean Cornelius is working hard, and I admire that, but he's not all the way there. I'll be the one who ends up fighting him if he backslides or goes rogue, and I don't want to hurt Mavis by harming him, so I say nay."

"Sir Harold, close arguments, please," the king said.

"I forgive Cornelius and have just yesterday sent a letter to him by way of my wife saying as much. Mavis would benefit from her brother's presence, and he has skills the rest of us sorely lack when it comes to island exploration. My argument decides this, so I say yea."

It took every ounce of willpower to refrain from bursting into tears. My brother would get his chance.

"Captain Dunstable and Sir Hawkins will remain to discuss the logistics of bringing Cornelius aboard," the queen said. "The rest of you may return to your realm. We appreciate the time you've taken to make your statements and expect no quarreling over the arguments given, for better or worse."

"Discussing what transpired here is the proper course," the king directed. "If hard feelings interfere with completing your quest, we may enact a monarchal ban to prevent quarreling over this in the future."

"Yes, Your Majesty." I gave my deepest curtsy, which I'd been practicing. "You have my deepest admiration and respect."

On the way back through the doors, we stayed silent. Back at the boarding house, everyone else was in the dining room having breakfast. I could have joined them. The egg sandwich hadn't been very filling.

However, the king's instructions made sense, and I wanted to follow them as soon as possible. Cos was in the lounge, playing a game on his phone, so I started with him.

"I meant what I said, Mavis," Cosmo said. "It feels all wrong, saying stuff like that about a guy I never met, let alone your brother. But I'm the toughest guy on that boat. It's my responsibility to think like Tony about danger. I'm sorry for being a jerk."

"I grok that, Cos. You're not a jerk and I'm not angry. Mostly surprised."

"I don't grok that."

"I had no idea what we were walking into when we went. I bet you weren't allowed to say anything."

"Bingo." He grinned and opened his arms. "Bring it in here."

We hugged, then I headed up the stairs and knocked on Saya's door. She opened it and immediately got teary-eyed.

"Whoa, hey. Saya, don't cry."

She didn't stop, but she let me in before running to get a tissue.

"I didn't want to say no. But I'm literally partly named after a goddess of wisdom. And I'm on board to help Hope with matters of prudence. It was the wisest thing I could think of."

"You apologized right in that argument, Saya. You're sensible, and I might have said the same thing if the shoe was on the other foot. It's hard to trust someone just because they're related to one decent person. The rest of my family is a case in point."

"I know. Thanks for believing me."

"Back at you, savior of my wardrobe. Believing each other is kind of the foundation of friendship, right?"

"It is." She nodded. "I suppose you'll see Ed next."

"He said yea. Should I?"

"It's customary to thank the yeas in situations like this."

"I'll do that, then."

When I went looking for him, Ed wasn't in his room. Or the boarding house, either. Even Rob was nowhere in sight. Horace was in my room, empty with Kiara at breakfast.

"He went to Jillian's. Said he's not ready to talk about what happened in the Under yet."

"That's not good." I sighed. "They go home for winter break tomorrow."

"Plenty of time for them to talk in Newport."

"I won't be there."

"He didn't ask you, then."

"Uh, what?"

"Just look for him at lunch."

Hope and Ed came back at around the same time but from different directions. I wanted to go directly to Ed, but Hope stopped me in the hall.

"You've got to talk to—"

"Everybody, I know. Cos, Saya, and I did that already."

"You didn't mention Ed."

"He went out. I just saw him go into the dining room." I grinned.

"You're here now. So I want to say thanks for speaking in favor and giving my brother the benefit of the doubt. Most of the time, he doesn't get a chance like that. It's nice to know you think I'm resourceful, even if we butt heads on the regular."

"I stand by my words. Also, something Hal said. We need his skillset. Cosmo and Saya both made good points, and as captain, I'll have them in mind while getting to know him. I expect the same from you."

"I'm not a captain, though. His Majesty didn't have me tithe to any rank. Everyone mentioned roles on board. It's been unclear this entire time what mine is, exactly. I feel redundant."

"You can never have too many mediums. You're my counterweight, Mavis. The monarchs created our feathers to make balance in the realms."

"I guess I don't understand. All that seems to happen is us arguing."

"That's exactly the point. Light and darkness aren't inherently good or bad, but you need them pushing and pulling on each other. If not, we end up with either tyranny or chaos."

"It sounds like you've been there and done that."

"It sounds like you're onto something. Do the research."

"It'd be easier if you told me."

"I'm not under a ban. It's just for counselor's ears only."

"Okay." I nodded. "I still need to thank Ed."

"Have at it, then. I should find Cos and Saya. See you later."

"Later, captain."

In the dining room, Ed sat picking at his food. I got a ham sandwich and corn chips, then took the seat beside him.

"Hey, thanks," I started.

"I'm sorry," he said.

"Wait, for what?" I blinked.

"I didn't do my job on board."

"I don't understand."

"I'm supposed to make sure we stay focused. You've been struggling with that all semester. I couldn't think logically and went with my heart. Voted to put your distracting brother on board because I couldn't bear to see you separated from him like I am from mine."

"Stay focused? Me? Crow's not the cause of that problem. I'm going to need more than your help to solve that." I told him about my visit with Dr. Cormack.

"I had no idea." He shook his head.

"Nobody did. Not even me."

"So I ended up making the right call after all. Even if it was for the wrong reasons."

"Maybe there's no wrong reason to give a damn." I patted his hand. "Thank you for caring. I wish I could make it so Fred's with you, too. I might be wrong. But I'd rather err on the side of my friends."

"Time for that ask." He drew a deep breath. "Will you come to visit over break? In Newport, I mean."

"I want to but promised to spend Yule with Crow."

"Not the whole break, only a day trip. You can take the train to Wakefield, and I'll ask one of the adults to send a car."

"Absolutely!" I smiled. "Thanks, Ed. I could never have asked that myself. I'll call you on the office phone. Matron Klein already permitted me to use it."

"Awesome." He grinned. "Now I'd better go bury the hatchet with Saya and Cos."

"Are you okay about that? You sort of ran off earlier."

"Yeah, went over to Jill's, but it wasn't because of our crew. Being in that throne room was intense. I'll live."

"Good. Because as much as I like having ghost friends, I like you better alive."

"Ditto."

He got up, and I finished lunch by myself. But not entirely alone. I was part of a crew, after all.

CHAPTER SEVEN

Monday was a half day. I got my exam scores in Lecture. D-minus, just above a failure. Messing was already done for the semester, so there was no Mediumship. I headed to the library after Lecture, passing the courtyard where other first-year students occupied themselves with last hurrahs before the break.

I took a seat in the far corner, ready to do some reading about trickster packs, when somebody sat down across from me.

"Mrs. Ambersmith, you're the last person I expected to see here."

"Your grades must improve, Miss Merlini."

"I know."

"Dr. Aranha says your lab work was almost perfect. You know the material. I frequently see you here, reading on advanced topics. I want you to spend some self-discovery time over break."

"Dr. Cormack's helping me with that, now that my score came back the way it did. He's evaluating me for SLD."

"That's good news. Here's more. Principal Klein wants to see you in her office to discuss a different evaluation."

I disagreed with Mrs. Ambersmith but wasn't about to argue.

"She could have called me over the PA system."

"That's too disruptive and frightening, so she sent me."

I almost laughed at the irony of a dhampyr principal considering a loudspeaker announcement more disturbing than my dour redcap teacher.

"Thanks, Mrs. Ambersmith." I rose. "For the message and your concern."

I walked away without waiting for her to say more. If there even was more. On the way to the office, I passed Cosmo and Jaxon tossing paper airplanes at each other, utterly oblivious to anything else.

"Have a seat," Principal Klein said.

"As usual." I took one.

"You're scheduled for your SLD evaluation with Dr. Cormack in two days, December nineteenth." She pushed two pieces of paper toward me across the desk. "And your other test with Director-General Rockport is January third, the week before we come back to school."

"She scheduled it, then."

"Yes. Only after getting the court's notice of intention to emancipate." Principal Klein grinned. "Well played, Mavis."

"No bird likes fire under the tailfeathers, ma'am. My brother taught me that. What I can't figure out is why he didn't file one of those in his first year."

"You'll have to ask him because I'm not privy to his reasoning on that. I did suggest it, but he dismissed the idea out of hand."

It hit home at that moment. Crow promised he'd get me out of the nest. If he'd received emancipation, he couldn't have. I couldn't bring myself to say that out loud. Instead, I entered the dates, times, and locations in my tablet's calendar with periodic reminder alerts.

"You could use a phone."

"I still have one. It just doesn't work for anything but 911."

"Perhaps you'd like it to."

"You've given me more than enough necessities. A data plan for my smartphone's optional."

"I've been considering adding landlines to the hallways at the boarding house over the break."

"Nobody will use them if they're out in the hall with no privacy."

"If only there were still such things as phone booths." Horace sighed. I chuckled.

"That was your ghostly friend. Horace, I believe."

"Yeah." I repeated his lament.

"Horace, you may have something there. Although there's no room for booths in the hallways, there's plenty in the basement. I'll put in a budget request. Thanks for the idea, both of you."

"Thank you. For everything."

I left the office. This time, I caught Jaxon's paper airplane on the way down the hall. Out in the courtyard, Wyatt pointed at the paper vehicle and waved his hands over his head. I tossed it at him, then headed toward my friends.

Fiona, Jillian, and Kiara sat together gushing about a new rom-com. Hope, Brandon, and Saya played Go Fish with an old deck of cards.

Ramon looked up and smiled. Going to his side felt like coming home.

After school, we said our goodbyes to out-of-town friends. Wyatt and his brother John got on a train to Boston, along with Brandon. The Claytons would get another train to Worcester while Brandon took a bus to Hartford.

Fiona had to get home to pack for Yule with her grandparents in Fall River. The Thornes were off to a wolf-moot in upstate New York for the break, so they piled into a well-packed van with their parents and left Salem.

It was too cold to linger, and Ramon had to work at the Mart, so I plodded back toward the boarding house. I paused at the sound of light footsteps.

"Wait up, Mavis," Kiara called.

I did. We walked, not speaking until we reached the boarding house.

"Are your parents late?"

"A little. But I'm not leaving."

"I saw you packing up yesterday."

"The museum's closed until New Year's Eve, so that's when we take a vacation. We're having it here. I'll be at the Hawthorne Hotel with them, but around to hang out when they're antiquing."

"Wow, Kiara." I smiled. "I thought I'd be all alone here, rattling around like the last bean in the can."

We laughed at that, then had snacks downstairs. When her parents texted that they were ten minutes out, I helped her wheel her suitcase halfway across town to the hotel.

Maybe winter break wouldn't be as boring as I'd feared.

On Tuesday, I brought Ramon and Kiara to Dead Man's Party. Old Grandpa sat on his usual barstool, Tommy hovering nearby.

"You kids have fun," he said.

"We will." I smiled and waved.

I didn't notice someone had followed us. Kiara did.

"Oh, hi Diego! Have you been here before? Did your grandpa tell you about it? Where's Rita? Is she in town or home for break?"

"Uh, yeah, yeah, and back out west." Diego counted each of his answers on his fingers. "I'm, uh, meeting someone who didn't go home for break from Hawthorn."

Xan Onassis sauntered through the door a moment later.

"Do *not* tell me you put Diego on your security detail, Onassis." I tapped my foot.

"Sorry, I can't tell you otherwise." He shrugged. "Empaths are good at stuff like this."

"Uh, like what? I'm Kiara. What's your name besides Onassis? Are you a third-year? How do you know Diego? Is that a dragonet? Are you wearing eyeliner?"

Xan blinked. Diego answered, counting each phrase again.

"Keeping track of who's got bad intentions, he goes by Xan, yes he is, he knows my big sister, yes, and yes."

"You're good at that, Diego." She smiled.

"Uh, thanks, I guess." He shrugged.

"And Xan, your dragonet's adorable."

"She totally is." He gave the critter chin scratches. "And such a good familiar."

"I don't need babysitters in here with all these ghosts." I jerked a thumb at Diego. "Especially not one my age."

"Well, I guess the more, the merrier," Ramon said. "Koto's a public place. There's no reason not to have fun while we're all here."

"He's got a point." I sighed. "Party's started, but I'll make it so you all can see it."

I revealed the ghosts and watched the reaction with Ramon, who'd been here and done this already. Christian played nothing but floor-crowding tunes, so we danced the hours away until closing time.

"I guess you two can come back." I gestured at Xan and Diego. "You're acting more like buddies than babysitters."

"We'll be here every Tuesday over break," Ramon said.

He also let them in on our plans at the Dodge Street Café. I didn't mind. Two more guys in the mix would help confuse Mom more about my dating status.

Outside, a van stood waiting. I almost turned and ran before noticing the logo on the side. Moonstruck Music.

"Thought you'd want a ride," Paolo called through the open window.

"Yeah, sure." I nodded. "Thanks."

Ramon, Kiara, and I all got in.

"We're walking," Xan said to Diego before he got in.

"Okay."

Paolo dropped Kiara at the hotel and Ramon outside the Mart. He pulled up short of the boarding house, parked, then turned in his seat.

"I know you've been visiting that brother of yours."

"Yeah."

"Good. I don't hear much about how he's doing."

I wasn't sure why I told him everything I could about Crow's progress. Something about it felt right. Like it followed the strings

Paolo pulled to get him in therapy instead of prison. I sensed more to it than that but couldn't suss it out.

"You two need each other. He's progressing faster because of that. I'm glad you kept visiting. Yule's coming up."

I'd gotten familiar enough with reading between the lines of faerie conversation to grok what he wanted to know.

"We're having dinner together in the sanitarium. The last one before he starts his service in the Under."

"I have something for him if you're willing to carry it."

"Okay."

Paolo rummaged in his glove box. He came up with a ring similar to Tommy's with the gem-studded horseshoe signet design. The stones were jet black, some kind of semi-precious gem I couldn't identify. The rest was carved from something, not wood, maybe antler or bone.

When Paolo handed it to me, his glamour slipped. One look at his face and I knew.

He'd carved the ring from his tusk. The tip of the left one was broken off and had always been the entire time I'd known him.

He'd been wounded, maybe even in that duel with my mother all those years ago. Yet he'd taken a defeat, that loss, and made something beautiful out of it—a gift for another young man, damaged in an entirely different way.

"I'll tell him Merry Yule from you."

"Thank you, Mavis." His voice sounded hoarse. "That means more than you know."

<hr>

The next day after lunch, I went to the eerily empty Gallows Hill campus for my SLD evaluation. It was boring, and I zoned out or went on tangents more often than not. At the end, Dr. Cormack told me that was a good thing.

"You have ADHD, Mavis. That's why you can't focus no matter how you try. I'm sending your results to Counselor Goldfarb to add support for that to your sessions. It'll depend on the outcome of your registry testing, but the next step is seeing a metaphysician. Luckily, Nurse Wilson is certified. If you end up needing mood-altering magitech, she can help. We need an IEP in place to get you academic accommodations first, though."

"The school already lets any shifter who needs it get up and move, though."

"There's more we can do to help you. ADHD isn't only about fidgeting or trouble sitting still. It's a question of focus. What it's on and whether it stays."

"Does that mean I have a chance of passing next semester?"

"Absolutely." He nodded. "Now that we know the nature of the beast, we can help you tame it."

"Thanks, Dr. Cormack."

"Thank me by working with us. I'll see you again the day before school to go over the strategies we develop."

"Okay." I nodded. "See you then."

The next day was Yule. I didn't have any gift for my brother besides my presence. Plus a tin of snickerdoodles from Matron Klein's stress baking collection.

She didn't drive baked goods around on Yule. Like the Micellos who raised her, she was Roman Catholic. In the spirit she'd inspired in me of new traditions, I asked if she'd stop by the PCC before heading to Danvers and let me donate some other cookies that would go stale before the twenty-fourth.

"What a lovely idea," she said.

Though Crow and I had spent a good deal of time at the Pagan Community Center, I hadn't been there since the end of elementary school. There were no familiar faces, but plenty of children were waiting on their working parents to appreciate the treats.

The pure faeries vanished me to the inside of Crow's cabin, thankfully. The snow outside was thick and deep, making the log home even cozier by comparison.

My brother sat by the fire, roasting fish on spits and stirring the stew.

"If you told me I'd love ice fishing last year, I'd still be waiting for the punchline."

"Love it or not, thanks for going to all that trouble for my dinner."

"Our dinner," he corrected. "The last one here for a while. Maybe ever. Think I might miss this place."

"Why?"

"It saved me. Not my life, but my sanity."

"Didn't it also save your heart?"

"You helped me save that. Along with my future."

I fiddled with the cookie tin, unable to find any words at all, let alone the right ones.

We had dinner, chatting about Yule Ball, exams, and the evaluations.

"You got one up on me with that diagnosis alone. I bet Mom's still wigging out about those papers."

"Did you refuse emancipation because of me?"

"Not wanting to abandon you figured in, for sure. Mainly, I wanted to prove I was tougher than Mom."

"I grok that."

"You're kicking her ass now, figuratively anyway. Keep it up. Might be the only way to win."

"It didn't work for Paolo." I reached into my satchel. "Who asked me to give you this, by the way."

I handed over the ring.

"Whoa." He held it up, admiring the glittering stones in the blend of fire and candlelight. "This is powerful."

"Is it? I couldn't tell. I thought it was pretty impressive, made from that broken tusk of his. What's powerful about it?"

"For one thing, the gems. They're shadowstone, from the Under. Full of unliving energy. Troll tusk rings have wild magic, bestowing a dragon's strength once a day. Unheard of outside of troll families.

They break down pretty quickly unless they pass—" His eyes went wide. "Gods, Mavis. I'm—" He swallowed.

I understood immediately.

"Paolo's your dad."

"What if he's yours, too?" Crow shook his head. "Explains why we're not like the rest of our siblings. Why he helped us."

"He helped me to clear a debt. I don't think he's my dad." I shook my head. "Explains why he went out of his way to help you all the time."

"Not as much as he could have, though." Crow closed his hand over the signet. "Or maybe only at the limit of what she allowed him to do."

"Because their pack's still active."

"Right."

"Dr. Cormack's still in it too. And Mr. Hickson."

"I wonder what she's got them doing."

"Sabotage," I said. "Probably hoping she'll dissolve the pack. Hey, did you know you're Under-born too?"

"Had no idea until now, but it pales in comparison to my heritage. That's an odd thing to find out."

"It came up in the discussion about you joining the quest. Everybody else on it was also born there. Except for Ed."

"This is a lot to process."

"Yeah." I pushed the tin toward him. "Let's talk more about it on the boat, with more minds to bounce things off. For now, cookies."

"Cookies it is, then." He opened the tin, unleashing a divine aroma. "Principal stress baking strikes again."

"Yeah. Don't go to dinner without them."

"Seriously, ask her for lessons," he said with his mouth full. "Or marry someone who takes them."

"You marry someone who does instead." I stuck out my tongue. "Or her, she's divorced. I kid."

"I know. You kid, I adult."

We laughed together. By the time I was ready to go, he'd put the ring on. It fit his index finger as though made for him.

Early in the morning on New Year's Eve, I was all set to catch a train down to Wakefield, Rhode Island. Alone, because Ramon had the flu and Jill had traveled down the day before. We'd have a small party, observe the change to a new year, and have a sleepover at the Harcourt mansion.

I hummed to myself down Washington Street until I got to the Army barracks and saw an all-too-familiar crow perched there.

"Should have known," I mumbled, picking up speed.

At the roundabout at the end of Washington, I saw them again and got a better look.

"Scram, Branwen." I made a shooing gesture at my sister.

"Caw!" She took off but flew toward the train station instead of away.

I used the crosswalks even with the scant traffic. A long set of concrete stairs led down to the Salem Commuter Rail Station, a spacious unwalled shelter beside an elevated platform. I wasn't even four steps down it when I saw what my mother had done.

"Fewmets."

Crows covered the shelter's roof. Not mundane in this weather, either. Besides shifters, magical corvids existed. The sort that bonded with magi of a mind to befriend them. Their sheer numbers meant they had no such obligation.

The last person I wanted to see stood beneath all those empowered crows. My mother, Morgan Merlini. An alpha shifter of their type. The only creature those unbound birds would obey for miles around.

I couldn't go. Not down to the station. Not on the train, to Wakefield and a car and Newport and a mansion. Not with my friends. And no way of knowing how she discovered my plans, either.

I'd be stuck in town, surrounded by enemies.

I walked backward up the few steps I'd taken, not daring to turn my back on them.

I fell, of course. Like Ed on his first day of school, into an ice-rimmed, salty puddle. I picked myself but didn't take the time to brush myself off. I'd lost this one, so a hasty retreat was the best course.

"Mavis," Horace said. "Don't run. Face them."

"Can't."

"You're the Sirin. Those birds won't attack you. It's only your mom and siblings in your way."

"That's more than enough to stop me."

"There's plenty you can do."

"There's not." I shook my head. "Unless I want the police getting involved on her side."

He floated along beside me, mulling that over.

"Call them first."

"With what phone?"

"It dials 911, you said."

"Mom always has an explanation for times like this. Just a family, seeing our youngest off for a holiday, is what she'd say. The burden of proof on me, no matter who calls first."

"That's messed up."

"Yeah, but at least I know going in. Thanks for trying to help, Horace. But it looks like this outing's shot."

After a shower and a change of clothes, I called Saya on the new basement phone to explain.

"I'd ask Blaine to fly you down, but he's in Crete, looking over clay tablets for clues about our quest. Mother's, uh, indisposed."

"Fewmets."

"Yes." She sighed. I heard a series of *beeps* as she put me on speaker. "We'll miss you."

"Yeah." I heard Cosmo's voice. "This sucks. I was gonna kick your butt at Guitar Hero."

"I wanted to introduce you to some of the local ghosts," Ed commented. "Next time."

"We'll see you on the fourth when we're back in the boarding house," Hope said. "But call us five minutes to midnight. We'll still be together for the New Year."

"I was going to call Ramon from your place."

"Give him this number. We can do a conference call," Saya encouraged.

I said goodbye, then called Ramon to give him a heads up about the change of plans. He sounded sad but still congested from his flu.

"Gonna get rest, set the alarm. Talk to you later, *mi amore*."

"Get well. Love you."

After that, I spent all my time upstairs reading the book and music for *Kiss Me, Kate*. We'd have auditions shortly after school started again, and I wanted to be ready.

Playing the soundtrack Mr. Hickson uploaded to our tablets helped take my mind off all the disappointment. So did the video links to the dance numbers. It looked like a fun show, though I didn't see a role that fit me.

My stomach insisted on dinner so I went downstairs and found chili in a crockpot, then went up and had a bath. By the time eleven o'clock rolled around, I felt soothed enough not to snap at my friends.

The call wasn't even close to a substitute for actually being there. But it outdid last year when I'd watched the ball drop on Picstagram alone in my room.

So the evening wasn't an entire failure, despite Mom's best efforts.

CHAPTER EIGHT

Scars
Crow

Picture this.

You're sitting on a log outside a survivalist cabin where you labor each day crafting yourself luxuries like utensils, fresh meat, and toilet paper. At least it has a perpetual cauldron of stew so you don't starve. Randomly, a voice booms out news that has jack-all to do with the wood you're chopping or the fish on your line.

Brownies must love startling people.

At first, it bugged me, but I changed my mind after it started announcing my sister's visits.

It wasn't boring, at least. That day, I expected it.

"Your escort is here, Cornelius Merlini." The voice sounded overhead.

"I'm gonna miss hearing you talk, pal." I smirked. "Never change."

"Please pack any desired belongings you've acquired during your stay into the provided bag."

My old rucksack appeared on the log beside me. I lifted the flap and found the clothes I'd worn to my sentencing inside. I didn't care much about those, so I carried them into the cabin and left them on the table.

My stay at Danvers Sanitarium felt longer than the true passage of time. The glamour they used to make the cabin and its surroundings was total. I lived in a microcosm, seven months to Mavis, almost two years to me.

The first thing I did was put on my amulet. The one that let me shift my clothing along with my body. Aside from saving me buttloads of embarrassment, it hid my reminders.

Scars wreathed my shoulders and the tops of my arms, chaotically placed. In another sense, they neatly marked out nearly two decades of hanging between defense and despair. They weren't self-inflicted, but for the longest time, I considered them my fault. After years of therapy, I knew better.

Early on, the man I called Dad made them. After Mavis was born, Mom took over. Still, the worst things she did to me hadn't left marks you could see. I took the guilty by insanity plea because I'd had enough of tearing down.

Maybe that's why I took to making my mark on the cabin by building instead of breaking. I'd been more productive than I thought possible, making several things, some too big to bring. They gave me a mattress and rudimentary bed frame, but I'd carved and sanded the headboard. That wouldn't fit in my bag.

The bowls and a small knife came with the place, but my ladle, spoons, and forks were my whittling. Would I need them on board a ship built and outfitted by both faerie monarchs? Not likely.

I brought the utensils anyway.

Along with them went a collection of more practical items. Flannels to wash my face. A pair of slippers that used to be a brace of rabbits. My dyslexi-specs, which made words stop jumbling on the page.

I couldn't leave behind the blanket I'd finally finished the week before, a patchwork of my worn-down flannel shirts.

As I folded it, I ran my hands along it, marking my progress by the colors. Red to orange, orange to yellow, and yellow to blue. My sewing improved along with my mental health, stitching jagged, too long, and uneven with snarled thread in the red, no snarls in orange, even stitches in yellow, and finally neat, even, and small for the blue.

"I've come a long way," I said to nobody in particular. Or maybe the cabin. "Think I'm gonna miss you, wannabe tiny home."

I banked the fire out of habit more than anything else. Probably, the fae would end up erasing this place once I left. Still, it felt right. Besides, what kind of shifter would I be if I didn't go with instinct?

On the way out, I closed the door behind me, another habit. A glance down at the carved tusk ring on my hand reminded me that everything had changed.

Paolo's gift persisted instead of crumbling to nothing. So, it wasn't a fluke. I was half-Micello, an odd bird with troll heritage. I'd try to remember that whenever I had trouble fitting in with the fae navy. Or faevy. I chuckled.

"Okay, I'm ready for vanishment to wherever."

I closed my eyes. That helped with the nausea most of the time.

"No vanishment, only portal."

"Hawkins."

I opened my eyes, expecting to see the man himself sitting in his magic wheelchair at the bottom of the steps.

Instead, he waved at me from the other side of a portal, standing with his legs on the deck of a ship. He looked healthy, filled out instead of bony, and pretty snazzy in the queen's colors. The deck moved, rocking on the ocean.

"Watch your step."

"Yeah, noticed that. Thanks."

I stepped through and managed not to fall. I knew the portal had closed when I couldn't smell the sharp mid-spring air anymore. A few shades and sprites in uniforms for their respective monarchs bustled about, doing work around the deck.

"As first mate, I formally welcome you aboard." Hal Hawkins held his hand out. It wasn't only his physique that looked better. His skin did too, bronze and glowing instead of ashy and dull.

"Thanks. Ocean's done you some good."

"As the wilderness has for you. Which is why you're here."

"Yeah." I nodded. "Your critter's not with you. The ferret or whatever."

"Nin's back in the mundane with my dad. She's mated, having a litter. We can't bring a Pharaoh's Rat into close quarters with Saya anyway. She's a dragon. They're natural enemies."

"Right, right." I'd almost forgotten that lesson at school. It felt so far away. "Gonna want a five-cent tour."

"Five centaurs would be a handful on board." Hal chuckled.

"You know what I mean."

"Yeah, couldn't resist. We can do that while we wait for Faith." He started walking up the deck toward the mainmast.

"The wife must be happy about that."

"We both are. She's here on business, too."

"I won't be the only one getting fitted for a uniform, then."

"You will. She's not staying."

"Bummer for you."

"I'll deal." He shrugged. "Still going to be a long visit. She's bringing an unbound sha to join our crew."

"Those yappy undeath dogs, I remember. Didn't know we'd need that magic here."

"We didn't either. Mavis and Ed found a clue that it's important. A vampire's going to be in constant danger here. So we're going with a magic dog."

"Thank the gods I'm not allergic, then." I sighed. "Is it housebroken?"

"You'll find out and help it learn if not. Part of your job is taking care of the pup. Who knows, maybe you'll make a friend." He tilted his head and pointed up. "That's the crow's nest, where you'll be a lookout. Nice to have a literal crow instead of only Kasa. She's a ghost but friendly."

"Cool." It looked peaceful. I could handle spending time up there.

We kept walking until we reached the front. It didn't take long. The ship was a masterwork but small. Hal stopped near a set of steps.

"Up there's the helm. That's my job so don't worry about learning to handle it for now." He pointed at the door. "That's how you get below decks, where the cabins are. Come on and see."

He led me down some stairs. It was brighter than I expected. Wisps hovered around pegs at intervals on the wall. A clever job to give what otherwise would have been fae pests. I stopped in my tracks. An enormous cat basket sat under one of the wisp lights.

"Don't tell me we have a panther infestation."

"It's Cosmo's." Hal chuckled. "He likes sleeping in lion form."

"Oddball." I snorted.

"Say that to his face." Hal made a couple of sounds that tried to be coughing but weren't.

"Right to his whiskers."

We burst out laughing. He shook his head, beckoning again.

"It's a good thing he wanted the basket, actually." Hal opened a door at the back of the boat. "There's a hammock in there for you. But mind the—"

"Spider man!" I stepped back.

"Not like the comics, more like that old song by The Cure." Hal nodded. "But completely different. He's a yokai."

"If this is supposed to be a joke, it's not funny." I shook my head. "Gonna take that hammock and sling it up someplace else."

"I'm perfectly humorous once you get to know me." A voice came from inside the room.

"Uh, sure. Bet people laugh out of fear, but your jokes actually suck."

"The young medium staying here has said exactly that on numerous occasions."

"Well, that makes it all better, then." I rolled my eyes.

"This might not be the room you want, but it's the room we've got, Crow," Hal said. "Or we can build you a nest next to Cosmo's kitty city."

"I miss my old cabin," I muttered. But I went in. "Okay, spider man. Tell me a joke."

"Why do bees have sticky hair?" He stroked his mustache.

"Dunno."

"They use a honeycomb."

"Ugh, that's terrible!" I wrinkled my nose and hung my bag from the hook by the top hammock. "Name's Crow. I'm helping as lookout and exploring the islands."

"They call me the Tsuchigomo." He inclined his head at me. "I'm being moved to a more secure location." That didn't fool me. I knew location was doublespeak for prison. Takes one to know one. "Well met. I'll see you later."

"Later?" I blinked.

"We've got to get you a uniform," Hal said. "Follow me."

I did. We ended up at another set of stairs that led into the ship's bowels, where they stored supplies. Hal opened two chests, one golden and the other purple.

"Which court?"

I glanced down at the ring on my index finger. "Unseelie." Like my actual father, I didn't add.

"Here you go." He pulled a paper-wrapped parcel out of the purple chest and handed it over. "His majesty's not too particular about how you style it, as long as the insignia shows."

"No way he gave me a rank."

"It'll only be an identifier on yours. Like when Cos or Mavis put one on."

"Cool, cool." I nodded, then glanced around, looking for a place to change. Nobody had seen my scars since Cadence DelMar. "Uh, there must be like, a head to hit in here."

"You don't need one."

"That letter accepting my apology was extra nice but not enough for me to start stripping."

He gestured at the parcel I still held, the paper undisturbed. Somehow, the uniform was on me, and my sanitarium clothes were folded and packed away. Hal handed them to a shade, who brought them to our cabin for me.

We went up above deck after that and to the back of the ship. Hal pulled a pocket watch from inside his uniform coat, then began setting up the tools to make another portal.

"The Under's fracking cool."

"Yeah, it is." He nodded. "Is there anything else you'd like to see?"

"Just the top of that crow's nest."

"Have at it, then." He nodded. "Faith will be here soon."

I shifted. It felt different than in the mundane realm. That made sense because the Under revealed our true selves. I fluttered my wings and tried hopping. Immediately, I knew the difference.

My crow form was bigger. Heavier, too. And there was more brown at my wingtips than usual.

"Ocean's done you some good, too," Hal said.

I opened my beak, intending to caw. That's what happened when you tried having a conversation with a magus in your animal form. Not in the Under. Or maybe not when your father's a faerie.

"No ocean, only troll."

"I wondered about that when I saw your ring," Hal said. "The Under doesn't let us keep many secrets."

This time I only nodded, not wanting to reveal any more. He nodded in reply and returned to his work.

Finally, I soared up, rising above the busy djinn. The crow's nest was *my* style. Not the bird I'd been, stuck under Mom's talons and obsessed with escaping at any cost.

What felt like ages ago, I'd lost hope. Back on a different boat, I gave in, followed Mom's orders for the New Order cause, which I'd never believed in.

Somehow, I thought I could preserve the people I cared for, the ones who mattered to me. Protect them from the threat of displacement, enslavement, or murder. If I helped the magisupremacists get their juggernaut rolling, I expected *quid pro quo.*

Just like my mother.

After the magi defeated me, I realized my worst crime wasn't cutting Onassis, clobbering Magnussen, or pushing Cadence overboard. It was believing Mom's line, no matter how briefly, that only the contents of my heart mattered.

Since then, I thanked Hodr in my prayers each night that I was stopped and given a second chance. Because what I got wrong that night was that everyone mattered. Not only the people close to me.

Finally, I was heading in the right direction. If not at full speed, then at least with visible progress. That was enough for this new me.

Eventually, I noticed the woman up there with me, braids blowing back over her shoulders in the wind. Her eyes studied the horizon, and she didn't move a muscle. She ignored me, which I didn't mind.

I had no idea I shouldn't be able to see her until a month later.

CHAPTER NINE

Mavis

January third was a Friday, and the abilities test was at Gallows Hill.

I walked with Principal Klein, Horace, and Dr. Aranha into the lab. Director-General Rockport was there, standing in front of Dr. Aranha's desk. He peered at a console beside the whiteboard, displaying the expandability function that let us shift and use powers without wrecking the place.

"Yes, this location will suit our needs perfectly," he said.

He turned, and the light reflected off his bald head. The attire he wore was what my family typically referred to as a "cop suit," the sort of thing a detective or federal agent had in their closet.

He'd looked way more intimidating in the video I'd seen of an extramagus evaluation than here in a familiar classroom, especially with my mother in the room and Branwen at her side.

I've said before that Mom was tiny. Fierce also described her. I'd hoped time and distance would have softened her effect on me. After hearing about her high school days and my discovery about Paolo's broken tusk and Crow's parentage, it didn't.

I trembled. Horace put his hand out, unable to physically comfort me with it. The fact that he cared enough to try helped.

"Let's begin," Rockport said.

His voice and that statement let me focus on him instead of Mom. My chest swelled with strange gratitude.

"Okay." I nodded. "What am I going to do?"

He rattled off a list of feats, most of which I'd heard of before if not seen. He did it all without any reference—no list on paper, electronic, or magipsychic device. As though he did this so often, he had it memorized.

At least I was in experienced hands.

"Start with your animal form."

I changed into a raven. Easily, I might add. That was a piece of cake after getting the feather at any rate.

"Noted," Rockport said, though he made no physical notation. Did he have covert magitech on him, perhaps? "Shift back."

I did. With my clothes on, because of my necklace.

"Ability and presence of amulet verified." Now his voice reminded me of the one in the chill-out chamber. "Set it aside for the remainder of this appointment."

I removed my amulet and handed it to Dr. Aranha. I didn't miss Mom's eyes narrowing. If she knew I'd had it all this time and used it to track my whereabouts the night she kicked me out, why had she made that face?

It didn't matter now. I had abilities to verify.

"Wings."

I set my cardigan on a nearby bench and unleashed them, grinning a little. I'd worn an outfit Saya bought, a halter dress that fastened around my neck with an open back. I could almost hear her voice in my head, saying it was her go-to for wing situations.

My friends were with me, even if they weren't physically present.

"Noted."

Rockport called out several other features from my bird form. I attempted to shift each one partially and surprised myself.

Feathers appeared in my hair, down my arms, across my back and chest. Stiffer and heavier than the ones on my wings, but sturdier. I imagined Cosmo's reaction, probably something about nice armor. My grin grew, along with my confidence.

"Noted." Rockport was awfully repetitive. That predictability comforted me. He wasn't interested in taunting or harassing me about how these abilities made me different. This was just accounting. "Physical evaluation complete. Begin elemental demonstration."

Hope had air magic. I knew because she used it at sea in the Under. Cosmo said they all thought it came from her mother, not the Alkonost's feather. That she would have been an air magus if she'd never picked that up. So maybe I had an element, though it seemed unlikely.

He called out all the elements magi used. I tried to imagine my hands bursting into flames, wreathed with air, flowing with water, obscured by shadow, glowing with light, heavy with earth.

He declared all of those negative. The last two weren't so easy.

"Invade my mind," he said.

"What?" I blinked.

"Say how you perceive me at this moment," he expounded.

I focused, looking him in the eye, feeling nothing but confusion I knew came from my mind.

"Like a teacher," was the only answer I came up with.

"Mind negative."

"That's a relief," Bran mumbled. Mom shushed her.

I realized now another reason my mother agreed to this, finally. Tactics. She'd read everything about the birds and their feathers but had never seen them in action.

That changed today. It looked like their biggest fear, mind magic, the one power that might give them trouble, wasn't part of my repertoire.

Dr. Aranha held a section of braided red hair on a tray in front of me. I didn't recognize it from the practical because it wasn't faerie. I wrinkled my nose at it, inexplicably repulsed. Rockport raised an eyebrow at that.

"Use unliving energy to move the vampire locks."

I looked down at my hands, unsure how to even attempt conjuring an element without having seen it. I'd never spent much time around vampires.

Except at Tropica Mart. And with dhampyr. I stared at the hair, holding my hands palms out in front of the tray. They tingled the same way the rest of my body had when I revealed ghosts. Were those powers connected, somehow?

Right when I thought I was on to something, the feeling faded.

"Unliving negative."

"Wait, Director-General," I said. "Something happened."

"Explain."

I did, with my back to my mom and sister.

"Unliving inconclusive." He nodded. "Single evaluation in six to nine months."

"All this again?"

"No, only inconclusive results. Elemental evaluation complete. Begin psychic talent demonstration."

Again, he called out a list of psychic talents this time, with instructions to try each one. I wondered how he'd manage mediumship. His method shocked me.

"Find the hidden ghost."

I glanced at the principal first, looking for some reassurance. I knew with absolute certainty I was as much a medium as Ed. If there'd been a ghost in here, I would have seen them the moment I entered the room.

Once again, I managed with a friend's help. Ed would tell me to look closer, not at the room. At the people in it. An instant later, I had it.

"She's with you, sir. You're a medium."

"Mediumship confirmed." One corner of his mouth twitched.

"Only one other ever found me so quickly," the ghost hiding in his shadow said. "Good job." She smiled.

"Thanks." I smiled back.

"You're confirmed already, Miss Merlini," he said. "No need to demonstrate further."

I wondered about that. Because I'd revealed Horace in this very room. The faculty at two schools knew I could show ghosts to anyone. For some reason, Rockport didn't ask me to demonstrate that and confirm.

Maybe he'd seen a recording. Or maybe that wasn't so important, only a potential feature of mediumship that not everybody could do, like possession. That made sense. He hadn't asked me to try that, even though I had a ghostly partner with me. He moved on.

"Summon a pure faerie."

I'd seen both Sid and Donna do that so I knew how it worked. Nothing happened, of course.

"Summoning negative." Along with all the other psychic talents.

In the end, I had more abilities than expected. The inconclusive unliving element had me excited, though I wasn't sure how I'd learn to use it if it fully developed. Whatever Hope did for her air, I imagined. In any case, it'd be useful on our quest. However, nobody in the room needed to know that.

"Evaluation complete." Rockport said. "The school, the parent, and the subject will each receive an official record in three days."

Without further comment, he sauntered across the room and out the door. His ghost looked back at me on the way out, smiling and clapping. Horace tipped his hat at her.

"You know her?" I murmured.

"Tessie was there at my evaluation years ago."

"In 1910?" I snorted.

"I'm almost eighty years younger than that." He gestured at his appearance and winked. "Aesthetic preference."

"I'm closing my classroom now," Dr. Aranha announced.

Principal Klein tapped her foot on the floor with her arms crossed over her chest. Mom didn't like that but knew how to take a hint. She and Branwen left without a word.

"Chilly," Principal Klein said.

"Um, Doc?" I asked. "My amulet? Can I have it back?"

"After I make a few small repairs to it." She grinned. "It's about time I did that."

"How?"

"She helped make it, of course," Principal Klein said. "And your brother's. Though I didn't know they had spyware built into them until an incident a few days ago."

That explained how Mom knew about my New Year's Eve plans. Along with why Klein had meals prepared for me that day. I hadn't even thought of that.

"I've already been to the sanitarium, by the way," Dr. Aranha said. "Crow's was fixed just in time for the service portion of his rehabilitation."

"You're not in her pack, too, are you?"

"No. She hired me, along with an associate. An odd job, all the way back when we were undergrads. I won't need his help to fix your problem. You'll have this back at gym on Monday morning."

"So it's been the amulets all along then, how she's kept track of me. That got harder for her."

"Likely." Dr. Aranha nodded. "Morgan Canto always had backups to her backup plans. After she got married, that tendency only grew."

"She's right," Principal Klein said. "I don't think you're out of the woods in that regard yet. But it's a start."

The entire day felt like that—a start, the beginning of a different path. I took a walk to Tropica Mart and hung around with Ramon while he did his last Friday shift before the end of break. He was working the next day too, but I promised to bring our returning classmates by to say hello.

"I'd better go do laundry before folks start returning with a mind to wash the gym clothes they didn't bring home." I chuckled.

"See you tomorrow." He gave me a peck on the lips.

Just before dinner, Wyatt and John arrived at the boarding house.

"Yo, Merlini!" John held up a hand.

"Yo yourself." I slapped it.

"Had a decent break, I hope," Wyatt said.

"Ups and downs, but not bad," I said. "No ghost pepper chili moments, at any rate."

"Good."

They headed upstairs with their bags. I sat at a table by myself but wasn't alone for long.

"Mavis!" Kiara plunked her suitcase by a chair, then sat in it. "I missed you. And everybody else."

"Missed you too."

We enjoyed our meal with Wyatt and John, talking about holiday celebrations. I didn't mention mine at all. At first, I thought I'd evaded contributing to the topic entirely. Or that my friends were so wrapped up in their holiday fun that they'd forgotten me. I was wrong.

"We tried calling you on the basement phone number, then Klein's office," Wyatt said. "She said you were out."

"Yeah." Kiara nodded. "The same thing happened at our house."

"Went to see my brother."

"Told you." John nudged Wyatt. "Cough it up." Wyatt sighed and handed him a ten-dollar bill.

The Rhode Island crew returned after dinner. We had just enough time to say goodnight before lights out. Saturday and Sunday were a blissful blur of oddly comforting excitement.

We made the strangest sandwich combinations we could think of at Saturday lunch and asked each other for advice on which outfit to wear the first day back. Later, we sipped froth-topped beverages at the Dodge Street Café while Diego slayed Sunday's poetry slam.

Like normal high schoolers. Something I never thought I'd get a chance to be.

After Dr. Aranha returned my amulet, I marched through the gym to meet with Dr. Cormack. Nurse Wilson was in his office when I arrived. On the desk between them sat my file and a blue plastic bin with the cover off. Before I could peer inside it, Dr. Cormack spoke.

"Have a seat."

I did.

"I'm taking a few vital measurements while you discuss things," Nurse Wilson said. "Pay me no mind."

That ended up being easier than it sounded. Instead of shining lights in my eyes or squeezing my arm with an inflatable cuff, Nurse Wilson used purely magical methods to examine me.

"We've worked out two strategies to try for accommodating your ADHD. The first is intended for use while testing."

He reached into the plastic box and took out a small purple case. Inside was a set of what appeared to be wireless earbuds. When he shook them onto the palm of his hand, they got harder to see.

"These are umbral earbuds. They'll damp down ambient noise so sounds like flipping pages and scratching pencils won't distract you. They will, however, allow sounds like fire alarms and the teacher's voice through."

"That's brilliant." I chuckled. "But I have no money. How much are they?"

"You've got an IEP. They're on loan like a library book. So, no using them over the summer or taking them on vacations, for example."

"Good to know, thanks." I put the earbuds in their case, then zipped it into the interior pocket of my satchel.

"You'll need them for a remedial quiz each Friday your first month back. It cuts into Rec a little, but it's a requirement for any student on academic probation."

"If I'm in there by myself, what do I need earbuds for?"

"One other student in your section is on probation, too."

"Who?"

"Cosmo Gitano."

"Then I'm in good company." I felt relieved if a little bad for my friend. At least we could be study buddies.

"I believe I've got a dosage range pinpointed, Kyle." Nurse Wilson said.

"Good."

"Thought we were waiting on meds."

"Mundane ones are a last resort for shifters and changelings." He pulled a small black chest from the box, decorated with several gemstones. "Inside this is an enchanted bracelet, made by combining psychokinesis with water and earth magic. It balances dopamine and norepinephrine. Amanda can explain how it works in practice."

"You wear it here at school and off-campus while studying. Activities where, without focus, you'd otherwise struggle." She tapped each of the gemstones in a pattern I couldn't follow. "It's not meant for constant use."

"So it's okay to not wear it at gym or out with my friends. Got it."

"Don't wear it to bed, either," she added. "Or for an hour before that. Some people take it off for meals because they say it reduces their appetite."

"If that sort of thing happens, or you feel too focused, come and see us," Dr. Cormack advised. "We'll also need to adjust the levels for the next month, so you'll need to visit my office thrice weekly until we find the right settings for you."

"It's a loaner too, like the earbuds, I bet."

"No, it's yours. You'll need it recharged every six months, but school breaks will give you time for that. While you're here, recharges are covered with your IEP. Once you graduate, you'll have to find a metaphysician clinic for that."

"You can open this and try it on now." Nurse Wilson handed me the gemmed box.

The bracelet was bangle style, carved from gray stone with tiny pink metallic flecks. After I slipped it over my hand, it reduced in size until it was small enough not to fall off.

"Whoa."

"It's formolite," Dr. Cormack explained. "If you happen to shift while wearing it, the stone adjusts. It only gets big enough to come off when you want it to."

"How does it know?"

"The psychic enchantment includes that feature."

"How do you know so much about it?"

"Decades of school." He chuckled. "And look."

He pulled the cuff of his jacket back and showed me his formolite bracelet.

"Wow." I smiled. "Thanks, both of you. I hope it works."

"Remember, if it doesn't, or only works for a little while, come see us for an adjustment."

"I'll try to be patient."

The bell rang.

"Off to Lecture with you, then," Nurse Wilson said.

I waved at them and headed to class.

Lecture felt different. I didn't feel the need to doodle quite as much as before break, though I made a few spirals between lines anyway. My patience was longer, even for the boring part about bird shifters that I knew already.

Mediumship was always pretty engaging, but that day I felt extra sharp. Nothing escaped my notice, and I didn't once pay more attention to a Messing ghost than Old Grandpa Ambersmith.

In Forum, I remembered to ask my question about how bear shifters kept from hibernating all winter. I only went off on five tangents over the lunch table instead of ten.

Drama club was pretty much the same as normal except I didn't mind laying down for those breathing exercises as much. Lab was a similar experience, too.

It wasn't perfect, but definitely better already, and I'd only had accommodations for one day. If it got even better than this, nothing could stop me.

Not even Mom.

CHAPTER TEN

Hope strode into the lounge on the last Thursday in January with a basket of dirty clothes under one arm.

"We've been summoned."

"No way." Cosmo looked up from his notes, blinking. "I'm still not done studying. Us slackers have that check-in quiz."

"Bad enough we have to miss Rec," I added. "I have my last adjustment appointment tomorrow, too."

"It's for tomorrow, actually," she said. "After school. Don't worry. See you at dinner."

Hope headed off to do her laundry.

"That's better." Cosmo nodded. "Stupid quiz. At least they give us the grades back right away."

"I know, right?" I jerked a thumb at my tablet. "We still have time to hit the ebooks."

"Can't believe you're stuck in remedial with me, Mavis."

"Same." I sighed. "That's academic probation for you."

"But you're, like, smart."

"So are you, Cos. And like I told everyone, it was unmanaged ADHD."

"Right, the brain gremlins."

"Hey!" An angry voice called from the snack cart. "Jerkface! Check your language, or this cart goes bye-bye."

The gremlins stood in stacks, replenishing the granola, trail mix, Power Bars, and beverages. Their leader hung from the cart's handle, shaking their fist at my friend.

"Ugh, sorry." Cosmo stood and bowed. "Forgive my mistake, oh bringers of snacks. I was wrong."

"More like it." The leader whistled. "Carry on with wayward munch!"

We watched them finish, then leave. After that, I got up for another cup of tea. We managed to finish reviewing everything before dinner. I was stumped. Because Cosmo didn't seem to need much work. He'd ended up with a higher grade than me on the written exam but lower in Lab.

"Was it test anxiety, Cos?" I raised an eyebrow. "Or those dragon molt gloves?"

"Dunno." He shrugged. "I don't understand things the same way the rest of you all do, I guess. It takes me more time like I'm always going to be remedial."

"Maybe we should keep meeting like this. Even after we don't have to."

"Would rather be at the Dodge Street Café or extra Bishop's Row practice."

"I know." I nodded. "Have you seen Dr. Cormack? Maybe you could get evaluated. Hertha and Tony wouldn't object to an SLD eval, right?"

"No. It's not that." He sighed. "It's about time you knew. Sit back down, Mavis."

"Okay."

"You know the Tsuchigomo. We go way back."

"Oh?"

"My dad had connections to some bad dudes back before I was born. He used them to get my mom to do what he wanted." He swallowed, wrinkling his nose. "It's hard to talk about. I don't understand that part much."

"I think I do." Magipsychic brainwashing was horrifying and very illegal. Its rarity was the only reason Mom hadn't done do it to us.

"Right. Your mom's like my dad." He sighed. "Anyway, when she got pregnant, he sent her to the Under. He wasn't Under-born himself, so he wanted a kid he could control who was. Unlike Tony."

"Makes sense. Your brother sounds like a rebel."

"Right." He nodded. "This is the weird part. I was born six months before Tony died."

"That's impossible." I blinked. "I know time runs differently in the Under, but still."

"Time's out of whack there. But here I am, and that's not why. There's more to the story."

"Okay."

"After she had me, somehow it unwashed her brain. She was psychic, a precog. By then, Dad was in federal custody. She had a vision about his ally coming after us. So she made a deal with the Tsuchigomo."

"I'm still not sure what he does."

"He weaves years."

"Oh." I blinked. "She bought strength for you with time."

"See, you're super smart." He sniffled. "Told Hope you'd get it right away."

"Hey, you need a hug?"

He nodded. I gave him one. A few moments later, we leaned back, and he continued.

"Did your Dad's ally get her?"

"Yeah, but she was practically on her deathbed by then." Tears he utterly ignored flowed down his face. "The Tsuchigomo help cost more than my early childhood. He took almost the whole rest of her life, too."

"Gods, Cos." I scooted closer to him and put my arm around his shoulders. "I'm so sorry."

"Thanks." He leaned his head on my shoulder. "You're a good friend, Mavis. And you get the other part too, probably."

"You're learning differently because you're younger than the rest of us."

"Yeah, so no point in one of those eval things. Even if I want one after seeing how it helped you."

"There is."

"They might figure my real age out, though. And send me to elementary school or whatever."

"Does Principal Klein know?"

"Well, yeah." He sniffled again, lifting his head. "Yeah, she does. Like she knew Hope was the Alkonost."

"Wouldn't she have the final say in keeping you here? If she thought you didn't belong in high school, she would have said no way before now. If you want the help, get it. I'll come with you."

"I'll think about it over the weekend." He wiped his eyes with his sleeve but dragged a hanky from his pocket for his nose.

"Good."

Matron Klein's handbell rang for dinner in the hall. I waited as Cosmo went to the first-floor restroom to wash his face, an odd feeling filling my heart. I knew how protectiveness and love felt because of Ramon. Mutual and balanced, a partnership.

This emotion for Cosmo was different, positive and caring but heavier on me than him. Like helping him learn and grow was a sacred duty. Horace hovered at my side.

"Is this how Crow feels about me?"

"A good question to ask him this weekend. He's onboard already."

"Can't wait to get there, then."

<hr>

I ended up with an A-minus on the quiz and Cosmo a solid B. Apparently with better focus, I knew more than I thought I did. And studying with someone helped him.

At Rec, Mr. Hickson announced auditions for principal and supporting roles in the spring musical.

"They'll happen on Monday. Anyone in the school can try out, but don't expect Bishop's Row players or cheer squad. They don't have time for anything but the big dance numbers."

"What about band?" Jaxon asked.

"They're our orchestra," Mr. Hickson informed us.

"Cool."

"Remember, you can audition singly, in pairs, or in groups. You'll need sixteen bars of music and a monologue or scene."

"What about dance?" Brandon asked.

"We'll break you into groups and have you follow the pixie." He gestured at a tiny blue person perched on the piano. "This is Trixie. They'll teach you a short series of steps for the dance portion of the audition. If you have questions about how it works, ask me so you can avoid owing them."

After that, we milled around, chatting amongst ourselves about the show and the audition.

"The show looks like it's got something for everyone," Kiara said.

"I read, watched, and listened to it over break," I said. "Gonna go out for chorus. Don't think there's a role for me."

"Do the principal auditions anyway," she advised. "These older shows don't look like they've got a lot of roles for us gals, but Mr. Hickson isn't averse to bending some of the genders. And you've already played a guy this year."

"True. Even though the playwright wrote Peter Pan with a woman in mind. Are you going for a particular role?"

"Lois Lane. It's a part with lots of dancing, which I love. I'll probably be opposite Brandon, which will be so much fun."

"I'm rooting for you." I flipped through the libretto again. "If genders bend, maybe you'll be opposite me." I winked at her. "Anyway, we can try out and let Hickson put us where he thinks we fit."

"That's what I'm doing," Diego said. "I'm not much of a dancer, so the wait and see mentality is less nerve-racking."

"Two roles like that, Batista and Howell," I said. "You'll get something."

Before Rec let out, Ed tugged my sleeve. "Hey. Go out for the gangsters with me. We already know we're good as a stage duo. They get a whole number with a soft shoe routine."

"The comic relief?" I blinked. "Figured that's Hayden's bag."

"Yeah." He nodded. "We can be funny too, though."

"I'll put it down, then. But don't be disappointed if it doesn't happen."

"Never." He grinned. "We can talk more about it onboard if you want. Anyway, see you at dinner."

"See you."

Lab let out early, letting me get to the adjustment appointment ahead of time. Nurse Wilson wasn't busy, so she saw me right away.

"I know we adjusted down last week because you got hyper focused."

"Yes." I nodded. "This week, that didn't happen. I think it's good for now."

"That's what we hope to accomplish in the first month. Remember, brain and body chemistry fluctuate with stress and hormones. So, even though our appointments are monthly now, come back any time you feel off in either direction."

"Too much focus or too little. I get it. It feels like I'm a microscope in the lab sometimes."

We chuckled together.

"That's clever. I haven't heard that analogy before." She smiled. "Have fun this weekend, Mavis."

"Thanks, Nurse Wilson."

I walked out to find Ramon waiting for me in the hallway.

"Since you're in the Under tonight, thought you might want a walk together."

"Always." I took his hand.

Off-campus students were allowed in the boarding house on weekends, including Friday afternoons. We headed inside and upstairs, making up for the time we'd lose to my quest later on.

CHAPTER ELEVEN

"Ahoy!" A sprite called. "Captain aboard!"

The whistle sounded as I stepped through the portal, bringing up the rear as usual. After it closed, I felt a familiar tap on my shoulder.

"Crow?"

"In the plumage." He smirked. "Until a second ago. I just landed on deck and shifted back. Cover your ears, by the way."

I did. He drew a deep breath, then shouted at the top of his lungs. "Land, ho!"

A small dog with short black fur and a frenetically wagging tail danced at his feet, barking up a storm.

"All right, already." Crow scooped the canine under one arm. The dog quieted immediately. "You've got no patience, Nut."

"Aww!" Cosmo smiled, clapping his hands. "Puppy!"

"Sha, actually," Saya said. "They're magical dogs, familiars to undeath magi, originating in Egypt. Some obscure records imply they're also friendly with vampires and mediums."

"You seriously called her Nut?" Hope blinked. "Hope it's short for peanut, not a crappy word for mentally ill folks."

"I resemble that remark, captain," Crow said. "And it's Nut, like the Egyptian goddess of the night. Sir."

"Who named her that?" Hope asked.

"My friend Logan Pierce said she chose it herself," Hal said. "He talks to familiars."

"She's got no magus, though." I pointed at her collarless neck.

"Someday, she might decide to bond with one." Hal nodded. "For now, she's here to help us sniff out unliving energy."

"Looks like she's already made a friend." I jerked my thumb at Crow's hand, now coated with Nut's doggy drool.

"Can I pet her?" Cosmo asked.

"You let her sniff your hand first." He nodded. "You're Cosmo, right? It feels like I already know you all."

"Yeah, back at you." Cosmo held his hand out for Nut to smell. "Mavis talks about you all the time."

"All good, I swear." I grinned. "This is Saya." I gestured at her. "You already know our captain. And—" I looked around for Ed.

He was halfway across the deck, speaking in heated whispers with Kasa.

"Just a sec, ghost problem," I said. "I'll be back."

"This is serious." Ed shook his head. "It's not your fault, Kasa. None of us had any reason to think he could do that."

"What's going on?" I asked.

"Your brother. Look."

She raised her hand high in the air and waved in his direction. I turned and found him waving back at her.

"Odin's beard!"

"I said Zeus's before, but yeah. Pretty much my thoughts too." Ed sighed. "Got a boatload of oddballs and misfits over here."

"Wasn't it you who said misfits get things done?"

"Let's hope I'm right. If only we had any idea how he's doing it all."

"All? What else happened?"

"The sha loves him," Kasa said. "Barely leaves his side. They don't like heights, but she even let him bring her up to the crow's nest a few times. It's like magus bonding, but he's a shifter. Albeit enormous for a crow."

"Oh!" I blinked. "I think I know what this is. We figured out at Yule that he's half-troll."

"Halves aren't a thing in the extrahuman world," Ed said. "That's like saying I'm half-redcap because my dad's one."

I told them about Paolo, the tusk ring, and the shadowstones studding it.

"Maybe it's that ring." Ed nodded. "If an undeath magus helped Paolo enchant everything."

"That's possible." I reminded Ed about Mom's old pack and Dr. Kyle Cormack. "I tested inconclusive for unliving energy at my abilities test. So maybe the stones are enhancing something for him from Mom's side of the family."

"Wow." He shook his head. "There's a lot of unknown here because we don't know what they did to it or why. I'd say that explains a lot. And that we'd better tell the captain."

"Agreed."

We called Hope over and shared our information and theories.

"Your reasoning is sound. I think it's not too important to look this gift crow in the beak. Someone needed to take charge of the sha on this mission. I'm glad it's someone on board full time."

"I wonder if that makes a difference," Ed said. "Cos would have loved that job."

"You're right. But then we'd have to bring Nut back through with us to the rooming house and school. Unbonded familiars can make a lot of trouble."

"Fair point," Ed conceded.

"All the same, I want both of you to get comfortable with the sha. Cyrus said the other group's vampire was a full member of their team. We all need to play with the dog."

"This is the best mission ever." I smiled.

"True story," Ed agreed.

We headed across the deck to join the group playing fetch with Nut. A while later, the ship dropped anchor off the coast of the next island.

I detached from the group and headed to the landward side of *The*

Odyssey, peering at the shore. Hope sauntered over and handed me her magic spyglass.

"Thanks." I held it to my eye.

That glass made all the difference. I spied a rocky stretch of beach, bordered above the tide line by palms and other subtropical trees. A few adjustments to the eye lens showed me more ocean past the flora.

"It's pretty small," I told Hope.

"That's fine. We stopped to resupply, mostly. Turn the butt end and think of a drinking fountain."

I tried that. The spyglass zoomed in on a stand of low palmettos to my right. Blue peeped through the branches.

"Freshwater, I guess."

"Yes."

"They should have given you first prize at that science fair."

"I was robbed." Hope chuckled. "I didn't want it winning. Mostly, I needed confirmation it'd suffice for this voyage. The judge's remarks managed that."

"Well, enter something else next year."

"No time with all my duties. I chose Bishop's Row as my one indulgence." She sighed. "I won't need college. There's always work for the Alkonost."

Maybe this was a word of caution that she meant the Sirin, too. Didn't the Gamayun have a fiancé and a career at a law firm? Perhaps Hope needed someone to disagree. She'd declared us opposites, after all.

"The captain who marries the sea lives a lonely life."

"Lonelier still the one who eschews the company of her crew."

"I can't argue with that. But don't forget to live life a little. I learned that the hard way."

"Noted."

I handed the spyglass back and prepared to disembark to help locate and gather supplies.

Crow identified all the useful plants on the island, including a small grove of citrus trees. This time it was Saya who discovered another clue in our quest. Another stone with carvings on it, much less crude than the last. Not in English, either. It had an alphabet, but not from a romance language.

"It's a grave," she said. "Look at the skull with angel wings at the top."

"Not angel." I shook my head and pointed at the single feather at the bottom. "Mystic bird."

"Ooh, you're right." She knelt in the dirt. "The dates are much earlier than that other group Cyrus told us about, though."

"The birds used to go on missions in the uncharted islands back before the monarchs reunited," Hope said. "Sometimes, they even had to fight each other. I bet one of them buried the other after something like that."

"Or it had a run-in with that Calamity. A storm would be a hazard for any flying being," Saya pointed out.

"Those dates, if they're mundane Gregorian, are colonial," I said. "Better get Ed. We'll need to talk to Rob."

"I can do better than that." Saya pulled a length of paper and a block of charcoal from her bag. I recognized them immediately.

"Grave rubbing, brilliant." I grinned. "We can use our school tablets to translate it."

"No." Hope shook her head. "That's going straight to LORA."

"I've never heard of her."

"Not her, what," Saya said. "LORA's a data analysis program for extrahuman legends, lore, and events. Kimmie made it."

"Your sister-in-law?"

"Yes. Maybe you'll meet her this summer."

I hadn't thought of visiting Rhode Island since the New Year's Eve debacle. I didn't have the heart to tell them the problem I had that night might be recurring.

"I. Uh, yes. Maybe."

Saya packed up her rubbing and the charcoal. When we got back to the dinghies, we found most of them loaded up with victuals, the sprites and shades ready to ferry them to the ship and back again.

"Your brother's truly skilled." Saya grinned.

"He's off hunting boar with Cos now so there's meat on board," Ed called from his seat on a rock. "I said no thanks."

"We found a grave." I jerked my thumb back the way we came. "Wanna take a ghost walk?"

"Sure."

We took it easy, no reason to rush. Ed and I took turns beating back underbrush with borrowed sabers. After a visit to the spring for a drink, I brought him to the grave.

"No sign of ghosts. Which isn't unusual in a place this deserted."

"Why?"

"Without any company, the ghost of this poor soul would have gone wraith centuries ago."

"Then why isn't the wraith here?"

"Wow. That's a good question, Mavis. I don't know."

"I'd say we should ask in Mediumship, but Old Grandpa probably doesn't know, either."

"I'm still going to. But at Dead Man's Party instead. It's quest stuff, not anything I want Donna overhearing."

"Good call."

The sun edged toward the horizon. On the way back, we kept a brisk pace. Ed only had to use his inhaler once but was pretty wiped out by the time we got back on board. He went to his cabin and got a nap. I managed to wake him up in time for bacon.

After dinner, Hope gave orders to set sail for the next island and send notice when they saw land. We would have asked Hal to send us back through the portal, but it would have been the middle of the night in the mundane realm. We slept on board and emerged in the boarding house basement on Saturday afternoon.

Apparently, Under lag was a thing, but at least relatively easy to manage.

When we got back, the first thing Saya wanted to do was show the gravestone rubbing to Rob. He hid from everyone. Even Ed couldn't coax him out of hiding. Nobody knew why, either.

"He must know something about the grave, or he wouldn't avoid me like this." Ed sighed.

"If it's something with an official record, our database will find it without him," Saya said. She uploaded the rubbing to LORA as intended but had to wait for the results.

"He'll come out for Dead Man's Party, Ed." I patted his shoulder. "We were planning on that anyway, right?"

"Yeah." He nodded, then looked at the ceiling and spoke in a louder voice. "I hope he doesn't let me down by skipping out on auditions."

The muffled sound of a raspberry being blown somewhere on the floor above gave both of us a little hope.

On Monday, I went with Cosmo to see Principal Klein. She understood why almost immediately and assured him they had the resources and faculty to help him right here at Gallows Hill. With his agreement, she made him an appointment with Dr. Cormack.

"It's so weird. I thought I was a unique case." He shook his head. "Klein said extrahuman kids have gaps in their education for all kinds of reasons. Like the wolf shifter she told us about, who grew up in a mundane wolf pack."

"How do you feel about that, Cos?"

"Way better." He grinned. "I'm lucky, living with folks like Blaine and Kim who answered any question I could think of. I'll still have to wait until that appointment to see what Doc Cormack thinks I need."

We went on with our day. At lunch, Ramon took me aside.

"There's an all-ages karaoke at the Dodge Street Café on Valentine's Day. I want to bring you."

"I want you to take me." I blushed. "Oh. Um."

"We'll make it happen, then." He blushed, too. "*Dios.*"

Nearby, Jillian cleared her throat.

"Uh, yes?" I asked.

"I'm trying to get Fiona and Hayden to go to that. They've only been on casual dates since Yule Ball. I need help."

"Okay." I nodded. "With what?"

"Try and get Hayden to ask her when you see him at Drama. I tried, but Fiona says it's not ladylike to ask a guy out." Jill rolled her eyes. "Like, whatever."

"I know." I chuckled. "I'll put the bug in his ear, but no guarantees."

"Thanks."

"Is this about karaoke?" Kiara asked. "Let's make it a quadruple date!"

"Quintuple," Saya said. "Brett just messaged me to ask."

"Sounds like a party," Ramon said.

I heard a flat clatter. When I turned, I saw Wyatt striding away, his lunch tray only halfway on the return counter.

"Maybe not." Ramon winced. "I'll talk to him at wrestling."

"No, I've got this." I went after him.

"Magic duck man better make up his mind is all I'm saying." Wyatt didn't even turn his head as I caught up to him. "Or I'll move on his girl."

"That's a better thing to say than you could have."

"I'm trying to do the work, Mavis."

"I know. I noticed."

"She doesn't."

"Somebody will."

"I get it. But in the meantime, I get none."

"You're backsliding."

"You're caring too much."

"No. That's impossible."

"You shouldn't have wasted your time pitching me a soft task."

"If it's so soft, you can do it."

"That's not what I mean. I'm a blunt instrument. You can't smash a soft task. Takes finesse I don't have."

"What's harder, the ball or the bat?"

"I don't need riddles."

"Pretend it's a mantra."

"No. Yoga sucks."

"You have time. Keep going."

"I will. Away from you."

I stopped and let him stride the rest of the way down the hall and into the gym. I pressed my forehead against the wall and sighed.

"That didn't look very friendly," Mr Hickson said.

"You should have heard us in the cafeteria before he stormed off."

"I did."

"Oh." I looked up at him. "How did you do it? Help your friends when you were my age."

"I failed. Then kept trying."

"Did you know Paolo was Crow's dad?"

"I suspected for a long time but only found out over the summer."

"Is he *my* dad?"

"No."

"How did you find out?"

"By setting myself up to fail, yet again."

"That makes no sense."

"I'm a coyote, and this isn't a classroom."

"Let's go in one, and I'll ask a second time."

"It's also not academic."

"You said there's no such thing as a stupid question."

"I don't usually tell students this until second-year, Mavis. Not all questions have answers. And some of those have very clear ones that simply aren't mine to give."

"I think I understand."

"Do you?"

Magic thrilled along my skin like goosebumps. My teacher was no fool. He knew we were playing a dangerous game. Favors weren't allowed to stand between students and faculty.

"Maybe. But I could be wrong and fail worse than with Wyatt before."

"If you do fail at anything, no matter why, because of what, or on behalf of who, never stop trying."

"Whatever." I rolled my eyes. Now I knew how I must have sounded to Wyatt with the platitudes. No wonder he walked off.

"I want you to promise."

"Why?"

"Promise me thrice."

The conversation felt weird since its beginning, but it had grown utterly bizarre with this exchange.

"I'm not ready for that kind of commitment."

"Prepare yourself, then. Get back to me when you do. But don't wait too much longer."

He turned his back on me, squeaking the auditorium door open and stepping inside.

I had almost ten minutes before the bell, but I couldn't go back to my friends, not after that. Instead, I headed toward the office to wait for Sid to make the portal for the exchange students.

"You made the right choice, Mavis," Horace said.

I wasn't sure. But I'd have no way of knowing without more information. Who I could trust to ask about it mystified me. Maybe it was one of those things I'd have to decide for myself.

The portal opened, and students walked through. Ed and Diego came in before Hayden and Rita. I glanced between the groups, unable to decide who to speak with first.

Horace came to my rescue, hovering along the hall beside Hayden.

"Hi." I said.

"Oh, uh hello."

"We're all going to this karaoke night, sort of a quintuple date thing. And we're wondering if—"

"Fiona's old-fashioned, I get it." He nodded. I wasn't crazy about the tightness around his eyes when he spoke again. "I'll ask."

"Something up with you two? Haven't seen you around Dodge Street Café since the first week of January."

"Don't," Rita said.

"Look, it's Hawthorn stuff," Hayden said. "Tense there right now. But magi business only, sorry."

"Gotcha." I nodded. "Break a leg at the audition."

"Right. You too."

We got into the auditorium, which Sid and Mr. Hickson set up like the variety show auditions. We all got seats well behind the rows blocked off for Mr. Hickson, Sid, and an unmistakably familiar figure. I approached Wanda and asked a question.

"Is that Cadence DelMar?"

"It is." She nodded. "She created our choreography months ago and taught it all to Trixie, who's coaching us. But she's making calls on the dance roles."

"Wow."

"Yeah, it's pretty awesome."

I nodded and went back to sit with Ed.

"Rob showed, but he won't leave the light booth," he said. "Better than nothing."

"He's such a drama queen."

"Can't exactly fault him for that, considering where we are."

We chuckled.

"Shh," Jaxon hissed behind us. "They're starting."

They called Wanda up first. She got up with that eagle shifter buddy of Brett's and sang *A Heart Full of Love* from *Les Misérables*. After that, they read a scene from *Merchant of Venice*.

Unlike variety show auditions, there wasn't much applause. Everybody was too nervous. They sat, and the next name got called.

Another second-year and a third-year tried out together. I hadn't met them, mostly because they avoided me. I couldn't blame them for that. I did appreciate their rendition of *Tonight* from *West Side Story* and the scene from the same show to go with it.

I realized there were way more first-years in Drama Club than any other grade. I wondered whether we'd lose people to more difficult academics or other time demands. I hoped not. I'd rather see us grow. Mr. Hickson called another name.

Diego. He opted to do his monologue first, Polonius's from *Hamlet*, to thine own self be true. Then he passably sang the title song from *Camelot*. Diego wasn't the greatest singer, but I saw his strategy. He wanted to play Henry-slash-Batista, Kate's and Bianca's father in the play within a play. He had plenty of Shakespeare lines and only sang with the entire chorus. I crossed my fingers for him.

Next, they called three names. Brandon, Kiara, and Jaxon. They did *Don't Tell Mama* from *Cabaret*, taking turns with the verses. Their scene was from *Love (Awkwardly)*, a comedy I hadn't seen or read. I already knew she wanted to play Lois-slash-Bianca, so Brandon must have been going for Bill-slash-Lucentio and Jaxon either Gremio or Hortensio. Plenty of dancing for all of them.

Rita sang *Morning Person* from *Shrek*, then did an Emily Webb monologue from *Our Town*. If it weren't for Wanda's strong audition, she would have been a good Lilli-slash-Kate.

It was my turn, so I got up and sang my selection, inspired in part by my monarch and journeys in the Under. *Pirate King* from *Pirates of Penzance*. And I bent gender some more by reading from Hamlet's famous soliloquy.

"Solid," Diego said when I got back, which was extremely high praise.

Hayden went next, singing an old standard instead of a show tune, *Young at Heart*. Then he surprised us all by giving us a Romeo that could have rivaled Diego's.

Ed finished up. He sang *Guys and Dolls* from the musical of the same name, then did Puck's opening speech from *A Midsummer Night's Dream*.

Nobody else auditioned, despite how we hoped to get noticed more after the performance showcase.

"Looks like we're still bottom rung rec," the third-year guy said to the girl he auditioned with.

"Not so much." She nodded at us. "Nice pirate king, especially after that Pan."

"Thanks!" I waved. "Nice Maria!"

Maybe she really was busy and didn't have a problem with me after all. Perhaps I could say the same thing about Cadence DelMar.

Cadence went around the room and put us in groups for the dance audition. She split Kiara, Brandon, and Jaxon up. When she got to me, she smiled.

"I'm glad to see you in here, Mavis."

"It's way more fun than sports."

"Cheer squad's fun, too." Cadence raised an eyebrow.

"Wanda told me."

"Hope you don't have two left feet."

"She doesn't," Ed said.

"Hmm." She pointed at the group with Hayden and Jaxon in it. "You go there, Mavis. Ed, you're with Rita and those upperclassmen."

We split up. The dance Trixie the pixie showed us wasn't too complicated. When they put the music on, it got harder. We had to do it three times at different speeds. I felt subpar next to Jaxon, but Hayden made me look like Bob Fosse.

"Why didn't you do comedy?" I asked as we headed off stage.

"Dancing's my weakness. Going for Harrison Howell."

"Wow." I grinned. "That explains everything. I think you've got a shot with how you read Romeo."

"Coming from you, that means a lot."

I didn't understand why until the next day.

Apparently, I'd nailed it. I'd gotten the part I wanted, Second Man with Ed as First. Wanda was Lilli-slash-Kate, and Kiara Lois-slash-Bianca, of course. Rita was understudying both roles. Diego got Henry-slash-Baptista and the suitors Gremio and Hortensio were Brandon and the third-year guy who did West Side. His partner who'd complimented me would sing the opening number as Hattie, the stage manager.

Jaxon was Bill-slash-Lucentio, which meant he'd have to kiss Kiara. Brandon didn't pull a Wyatt and stomp off. However, he got even quieter than usual.

The eagle shifter's name was George, and he got the male lead, Graham-slash-Petruchio. Hopefully, we wouldn't have ego problems. According to Saya, we should be on the lookout for those with him.

With that settled, there were no more distractions. Ed and I agreed to head over to Dead Man's Party with our questions for Old Grandpa and the gravestone rubbing.

Ramon and Jillian asked if they could go with us.

"We could leave a little early, get fancy coffees and celebrate," Ramon added.

"Sounds like a plan," Ed said. "As long as you both don't mind us having that chat with the old guys for a few before going in to dance."

"We get it," Jill said. "Faerie business."

After dinner, we met them at the Dodge Street Café and drank our coffee on the way over. Old Grandpa was there, glued to his usual stool. I went in the back with our dates for a minute to reveal the ghosts so they could have fun. Then I went back, where Ed had already begun explaining everything to our medium-adjacent teacher.

"So basically, we want to know if you think it was a Sirin versus Alkonost battle or some other group after the, uh, thingamabob."

"The monarchs haven't sent their birds after that, not while they were separate," he said. "I know my faerie history, and that's not part of it. But they might have been chasing someone, or something, that was after it."

"Could it be the Calamity?" I asked.

"Mayhap." He nodded. "Tommy, what do you think?"

"I think your gravestone's in Hebrew. Not even an ancient version, either." Tommy nodded. "And yeah, those probably are Gregorian dates. Colonial-era."

"Are you Jewish? Can you read it?"

"No to both." Tommy shook his head. "It looks an awful lot like what old Doctor Ambersmith had to study from her synagogue back when we were in middle school, though."

"Right." Old Grandpa nodded. "Bat Mitzvahs read from the Torah, so she crammed it like crazy when we were in seventh grade. Yeah, now that I think a bit, it does look like what she had in her Hebrew notebooks."

"At least it's a language LORA can translate," Ed said. "And she can use the dates, maybe find a record of who the Sirin, Gamayun, and Alkonost were back then. Thanks, fellows."

"No trouble at all," Tommy said.

"If you don't mind, I have a, well, town history question."

"Go on," Old Grandpa said.

"Tell me about Jedi Hickson."

"Your teacher's a reasonable man. I advise you to ask him yourself."

"See, that's the thing. I'm not so sure his circumstances are reasonable." I told the three of them about the strange conversation in the hall.

"Always figured Cornelius wasn't Owen's chick." Old Grandpa said. "The threefold promise is strange, though. Tommy, do you know if Jedi Hickson frequents psychics?"

"No idea. He's never been to my family's house."

"You think he's had a reading or heard a prediction?" Ed asked.

"It's possible. Or maybe he's got a mundane source, warning of trouble for Mavis. The reason is mysterious, but I can't think of too many ways it'd be a malignant request."

"That's helpful. Sorry for all the family drama."

"We're two bored old men, too often ignored. Don't apologize for considering us wise and asking us questions."

"Right." Tommy nodded. "We kind of like these chats."

"Thanks," Ed said again.

Jillian beckoned to him from the back room. I could see Ramon in there, dancing already. We bade the older gentlemen a good evening, then had one of our own.

Rob came back while we were out but evaded the question with random and senseless acts every time we tried bringing up the subject or the grave rubbing. Ed decided to give him three more days, but he had a plan.

CHAPTER THIRTEEN

"Zero dark thirty kinda sucks, Ed." I yawned, still in the sweats I'd worn overnight. "It's too early for the coffee cart, even."

"It's the only time nobody uses the laundry room." He gulped down the last of the stale coffee he'd prepared the night before. I was jealous of his foresight.

"Let's do this." I lit the pillar candle at Ed's feet, then stepped back.

"Okay, Rob." Ed called from the middle of the almost completed salt circle I'd made on the floor. "Time to have that chat."

He held his hands over his head, closed his eyes, and concentrated. Moments later, two steady streams of silvery-white energy unfurled from his hands. They reminded me of smoke from a candle after being blown out. Instead of drifting away, they continued upward.

With time, they got more solid than smoke until they resembled the silver thread of a projection psychic. Ed was still firmly grounded in his body. In his earlier explanation, he said they were like snares.

Trapping Rob seemed unkind. Ed said we didn't have a choice. If Rob stayed away for too long, their connection might break. At the ghost's age, he could go wraith in a matter of days.

I got the impression that our colonial ghost associate wasn't all there to begin with, but I hadn't said anything about that to Ed. Or Horace either.

"You can't make me." Rob's voice came from the ceiling.

"I can, and you know it." Ed snorted.

"Never managed before." I saw Rob's boots appear above Ed's head, followed a few seconds later by his calves.

"Seen Mom do it a million times." Ed panted.

"Where's she now?" Rob pulled back before his knees came through the ceiling. "Oh, right. Weaving baskets."

"Low blow." Ed balled his hands into fists and pulled his arms down. "Gotcha."

Rob roared out what sounded like a last-stand battle-cry. Maybe it was, to him. But Ed prevailed, drawing down the ghost. Once inside the circle, I poured the last of the salt, closing it. With intent, because otherwise, tactics like that didn't work.

"You're telling us what you know about the gravestone in the Under now, Rob. It's for a quest, one about to get more dangerous. We can't wait any more."

"You can." Rob wailed. "You tyrant!"

His face sprouted several small wounds, leaking ectoplasm. Another spot of it bloomed at his midsection. I put my hand to my heart. Ed seemed nonplussed, like a preschool teacher witnessing a toddler tantrum.

"There's possession in it for you if you tell us what you know. Here and now."

"I'm driving."

"No."

"You can't compel my words. I'm driving, or you live without what's in my brainpan."

"You don't even technically have a brainpan anymore, Rob."

"I want to drive. That's final."

"Fifteen minutes, you get control of the meat suit. That's it."

"Thirty. At the time of my choosing."

"For taking my body for a joyride, yes. You still spill the beans here and now. Quizzes and dates with Jill are off-limits."

"You're no fun."

"This isn't about fun, and you know it. Are you taking the offer?"

"Fine."

"Great. Now pay up."

"Show me the stupid paper."

I unrolled the rubbing, holding it up outside the salt circle to let Rob get a good look at it. He hovered in front of Ed, peering at it.

"It's the final resting place of Ruth Toro. Former Sirin and once my partner."

"Partner?" I asked. "As in medium?"

"No." He shook his head. "Partner. She was the daughter of the first rabbi on this continent. I was a gentile among other things, so we couldn't marry. I offered to convert, but that wasn't good enough for her father. I love her still."

"Oh." I blinked. "I'm so sorry. How did she die?"

"The gravestone only says she fell in battle. LORA will tell you that much."

"You know more, though. And we have a deal." Ed insisted.

"The king called on her. A dragon flew over the king's lodge, one in the Under, without his consent. I wanted her to bring the rest of our pack. She said the queen already sent the Alkonost." He sighed. "That they'd be safe, working together."

"She wasn't."

"Thank you, Second Mate Obvious." Rob shook his head. "I tried following her. That's how I died."

"Walking through portals doesn't kill you," Ed said.

"It wasn't that. It was the musket to the back."

His face shimmered with more ectoplasm from his eyes.

"Who betrayed you?" I asked.

"The summoner who opened the portal, of course. I saw everything because he hadn't closed it."

"What happened to Ruth?" Ed asked.

"Doesn't care about me, just his information." Rob snorted to cover a sniffle. "The dragon killed her, of course. He was the biggest one I'd ever seen."

"Describe him," Ed said. "What color? Any breath weapon?"

"That's the thing. He wasn't any one color, which was entirely confusing. Polychromatic, I'd call his scales. He didn't need to use his breath to kill Ruth. She was the bravest person I've ever known. She flew right at his underbelly with her spear. He folded his wings and dropped on her."

"Oh, Rob, that's awful," I said. "Did this happen on an island? Thin strip of land, like a sliver from whittling?"

"No. But after that crash, the island might have looked like that." Rob sighed. "He was massive enough to sink half of it."

"Okay now. Who killed you?" Ed asked.

"Our summoner. The one from our pack. I forget his name."

"For crying out loud." Ed shook his head.

I rattled off names from town at random, hoping to jog a memory. Then, I went through Hawthorn magi from the newspapers last year. Nothing helped. I tried the ones in the old yearbook from Mom's days in High School.

"Canto. Hickson. Cormack."

"Wait. Hickson rings a bell. But that wasn't the summoner. Someone else from our pack, a wolf shifter." Rob's eyes widened. "Keep going."

"Hmm." I wracked my brain for the maiden name of Donna's mother. But it didn't come up. "I have to go look in the library for the last one to try, Rob. But I think it might help. I know this agreement's for here and now, but will you hear just that one last thing later today?"

"For you, yes."

Ed blinked.

"I can tell you at rehearsal or here at the boarding house."

"Here," Rob answered. "In this very room. It's safer."

"Okay."

Rob spun and faced Ed.

"Can I go now, master?"

"Don't be like that."

"Change starts with you, pal."

"This was hard for both of us," Ed said. "But I had—"

"No. I don't want excuses. We made a deal. Enjoy feeling competent for now. Because it only gets harder from here."

Ed dropped his hands and smudged the salt. Rob flew in loops toward the door, singing *A Peddler of Connecticut*.

I snuffed the candle and swept up the salt while Ed tapped his phone, entering the information we'd gathered into LORA.

"What do we do now?" I hoped he had a strategy to mend things with Rob.

"We wait." With his back turned, he lifted his arm and wiped his face on his sleeve. Then he turned and waved the phone, smiling only with his mouth.

I didn't have the heart to coax him into talking about it. My confidence was shot after the failure with Wyatt. If Ed spurned me the same way, I didn't think I could bear it.

"Come on, let's get coffee and breakfast," I said instead.

He nodded and followed.

I met Rob alone that afternoon with the name. Ed begged off and had a nap instead, but he gave me his phone for LORA reporting purposes.

"Catellus."

"Yes." Rob hung his head. "Antonio Catellus, a summoner with a dog shifter father. We grew up together. His mother was a converso from Spain, also a summoner."

"Converso?"

"Forced to convert to Catholicism by the Inquisition. We had a lot of people in Rhode Island like that. Refugees, mostly. She was Jewish, married a gentile to avoid getting murdered. Antonio's home life wasn't happy. He's the one who killed me."

"I'm sorry."

"Thanks."

"But why? Why would Antonio kill you?"

"Ruth, of course. You remind me of her so much."

"Thank you."

"You're an odd bird."

"Better than boring."

"I know. Ed tells me that's your mindset."

"Are you two going to be okay?"

"The circumstances of my death have always been a touchy subject."

"Because that's how ghosts move on."

"Sharp as a tack." He tapped his temple. "He's not ready, but it'll happen to me someday. I can't wait much longer, either."

"Does he know?"

"Haven't told him in so many words. But you're equals in intellect. He's at least somewhat aware."

"Why all the antics? The raspberries and pranking?"

"Tears of a clown, Mavis."

"I grok that." I sighed. "Wish I could help."

"There's nothing you can do for me. But hold on to that wish. Let it be your center. Everyone needs help because none of us make it alone."

"I will."

Like that, I knew exactly why Mr. Hickson wanted me to make that threefold promise. Yes, he knew something, a problem he probably couldn't divulge, any more than Paolo had been able to tell Crow he was his father.

He wanted to help me.

The next day, between gym and lecture, I found him leaving the teacher's lounge.

"Mr. Hickson."

"Mavis?"

The magic at the beginning of a favor prickled my skin. I kept going.

"I promise, if I fail at anything, no matter why, because of what, or on behalf of who, I'll never stop trying."

"What are you doing?"

The magic tickled this time, somehow stronger than when Wyatt ended up on the hook. I drew a deep breath and said the words again.

"I promise, if I fail at anything, no matter why, because of what, or on behalf of who, I'll never stop trying."

"You don't have to do this."

"I want to. I understand now."

"I changed my mind. What if you—"

"Don't ask. Not a single time more or I'll run to the principal, and you'll get punished. Let me do this."

"Never give up has killed people, Mavis."

"It's saved people, too. I've got priorities. So, I promise, if I fail at anything, no matter why, because of what, or on behalf of who, I'll never stop trying."

With the third utterance, a blast of wind laced with the secret woodsy scent of the Goblin King's forest rushed between us.

"Pray to Loki for guile and Odin for wisdom." He shook his head. "You'll need it."

The bell rang. I wasn't as religious as Crow, but that night before bed, I did exactly that.

Two weeks later, LORA still hadn't returned any answers. I asked Saya, who said adding new information made the search and compile start all over again. That was fine for the time being. We had plans.

The Dodge Street Café ended up packed for all-ages karaoke. We each only got up to sing once but had fun anyway. Everyone else showed up too, not just the folks on dates.

Cosmo dragged Jaxon and Wyatt through the door. Diego showed up with Allen and a couple of Messing girls who had nothing to do with Donna. Hope had invited the rest of her Bishop's Row team to come with her. I saw Chainsaw the entertainment wrestler hanging out in the corner with Wanda and her cheer squad friends.

Although Hayden showed up, he kept glancing at the door. I also noticed the absence of any other Hawthorn students. Not even Onassis, who Principal Klein hired to keep an eye on me. I asked him again if he was okay.

"Me personally, I'll live." He leaned closer. "Since Rita's not here, I can tell you a little something. Trustees are meeting. Makes everyone nervous. Can't say what it's about."

"Is it a campus issue? Because you keep looking at the door."

"Ah, no." He shook his head. "No. It's the thing I'll live from."

"I know paranoia trouble when I see it."

"Right, I know. I mean, I bet you've seen some shit. But I can't talk about it."

I knew how to put two and two together. Hayden's problem was Hawthorn's problem. He was from Peabody, the town next door. That meant parents.

"Hmm. Look, if you do get into trouble, call the boarding house phone. I'll help." I wrote the number on a napkin.

"Hopefully, I won't need it. But thanks."

He relaxed a bit but not entirely. I went to Cosmo, asked him to walk Hayden back to Hawthorn. He agreed and brought Wyatt and Jaxon with them when they left.

Ramon walked me home. We took our usual detour at the left side of the building. On the way in, I met Ed, who'd done the same thing with Jill on the other side. I winked at him, but he only nodded. I figured he was tired.

That night, I had trouble getting to sleep. Once I did, I was out cold.

"It's a short rehearsal period, but you're all doing an amazing job," Mr. Hickson said at the beginning of March. "You'll be ready when the show goes up at the end of the month."

"Can't believe it's almost Rec Week again." Kiara smiled.

"Can't believe we get to participate in it," Diego said. "Especially after all the rivalry and bad blood a couple of years back. Who knew?"

"Principal Klein." I chuckled. "She seems to know everything. No wonder people believed she was psychic."

The show moved along with the rest of the semester. Mediumship was a cakewalk with my new accommodations and Lab only slightly harder. I realized the way those classes ran dovetailed with how my brain worked in the first place.

Lecture and Forum were dense. That was by design. We had so much to learn, an enormous foundation to build on over the next two years of high school.

Finally, I felt confident about it. Until I remembered my birthday was coming up. I brought it up with Counselor Goldfarb.

"I don't want to celebrate it," I said. "I would rather treat it like any other day. But I'm not sure whether people know."

"The faculty do. I can make a note not to acknowledge it in your file. As far as your friends go, you have to think around the matter."

"What do you mean?"

"Go over what could happen if you keep quiet. Then compare it to what happens if you tell them and ask them not to celebrate."

"If I keep quiet, one or more of them might go out of their way to find out, like by asking my brother or something. Kiara would throw me a surprise party. Saya, too."

"Go on."

"If I tell them, the reaction might be mixed. I have no idea what a few of them might do. But if I go to Hope first, I could ask if she'd order the crew to leave me alone on my birthday."

I blinked.

"Not so hard when you think it through." Counselor Goldfarb grinned.

I talked to Hope that afternoon.

"No festivities on March fourteenth." She nodded. "No problem. I wanted an outing at the park if it's nice on the Ides the next day, though."

"I can handle observing the Ides."

"Great. I'll give the order at lunch tomorrow. And tell Ed tonight."

I'd forgotten someone.

On my birthday, I went down to breakfast ultra-early so I could eat before it got crowded. A cupcake sat on a plate in front of my usual seat. I stepped back without sitting.

"Matron Klein? Did you do this?"

"It's me." Ed burst through the kitchen door, wearing a befloured apron.

"Uh." I swallowed. "Didn't Hope tell you?"

"Yes, she ordered Ed." He grinned. "But I'm driving."

"Oh." I blinked. "Rob. You know I didn't want—"

"A big fuss." He nodded. "It's only a little cake. I don't expect you to have a happy birthday. Just something to sweeten a sour day."

"You used your thirty minutes on this?"

"And on the other twelve cupcakes." He muffled a belch behind his hand. "They're all gone. Yours is the last one."

"You're the nicest glutton I ever met." I sniffled. "I could kiss you. Uh, like a brother."

A timer went off on Ed's phone.

"Time's up." Rob unwound himself from Ed, waving as he floated toward then through the ceiling.

"Oh, God." Ed stared down at the apron. "What did he do? I promised Hope I wouldn't—"

"You didn't. It's okay."

"You're crying."

"They're good tears." I picked up the cupcake, pulled the paper liner off one side, and took a bite. "See?"

"Are you sure?"

"Don't get in debt. I already discussed it with Rob. I'm fine."

He untied the apron and pulled it over his head, then headed into the kitchen to put it away. I finished my treat, disposing of the paper wrapper in the trash by the coffee cart. After Ed came back, we had a proper breakfast even though he'd technically eaten a dozen cupcakes.

The rest of the day passed without anyone else mentioning my birthday. The lows I usually experienced every March fourteenth still manifested, but they never once consumed me. My friends didn't make a fuss because I asked them not to. My brain fell in line for an entirely different reason.

Just a little cake.

<h1 style="text-align:center">CHAPTER FOURTEEN</h1>

Spring Rec Week had the same structure as the one in fall, except the Spring Fling dance at Messing was three weeks later, the night before Extramural Day instead. As a result, we moved it up in the week.

Artwork went up on the walls that Tuesday morning. I looked for Cosmo's right away and found he'd improved. He still used finger-paints for one, but he also had a work in oil pastel—a mouse pulling a thorn from a lion's paw.

"I really like that new medium, Cos," I said.

"It's a mouse. They can't see ghosts."

"The stuff you colored it with, not like Ed."

"Oh, yeah." He chuckled. "Just trying to be funny. John's helping me with jokes. Says I sound like I'm ten sometimes. Which, I mean, he's not wrong even if he doesn't know the whole story."

"So it's working out?"

"He's there whether I have questions about library modules or social stuff. So yeah, it is working. Thanks for believing in me and saying nice things about my art, Mavis."

"It's only the truth."

Everyone loved entertainment wrestling. They did their usual divisions, with Ramon cementing his status as a face and Jillian dragging Fiona into a major heel turn by using the ropes to pin an opponent.

The big finale was a grudge match in a cage between Chainsaw and Wyatt. The storyline had it come about because of how Big Red stopped Chainsaw from cheating at the end of the elimination match.

Chainsaw beat Wyatt, who went to a lot of trouble selling serious injuries. After the referee called the match, Ramon ran in to escort his stretcher out of the ring. Outside the locker room later, Wyatt walked out only slightly bruised.

"Worst part was him using the cage like a cheese grater on my face." He chuckled. "Thank goodness for redcap shark skin."

"The best part is, this sets us up to be a tag team next year," Ramon said. "I can't wait!"

"You guys are going to be stars," Jillian said. "Show us up for sure."

"We won't make it easy for them, though." Fiona laughed.

"Good." Wyatt glanced at me. "Harder is more fun."

On Wednesday, Kiara had a new and improved version of her glamour brush at the science fair. Now it lasted longer and helped cover scars, extending its uses beyond cosmetic and into therapeutic. She ended up placing third, surpassing her earlier honorable mention. I congratulated her with a hug.

"I can go to State in June if I want." She grinned. "Mom and Dad are going to be proud."

"I'm already proud of my genius roommate." I smiled. "Great job, Kiara."

That afternoon, the early dinner was pizza instead of chili, and the Bishop's Row teams had their meal at the gym. Saya stayed on campus since the last time she'd been later than Wanda liked for cheer squad.

"I'm already nervous for tomorrow," I told Ed.

"Me too." He nodded. "But we've got our song down cold."

"Right. It's a little weird, playing folks who are only so funny because they scare everyone at first."

"I don't think so." He shrugged. "Isn't that a little like how it was for us, back in September? Bad omen bird and creepy ghost dude."

"Touché, Ed."

We finished our pizza and headed back to campus with Wyatt, Kiara, and Brandon. I got a little concerned. Kiara took Brandon's hand, but he shook her off halfway there.

"Are you okay?" I asked in the din of the crowd before the matches started.

"It's the show. I wanted that role so bad, but I didn't think. We didn't do it at all in rehearsal, but tomorrow I have to kiss Jaxon. I'm so not into him, and Brandon feels awful. Some genius I am."

"Have you talked to Wanda about it? She has to kiss George, and I know they don't like each other that way. Maybe there's a stage trick or glamour technique to avoid any actual kissing."

"Oh my God, Mavis! You're a lifesaver. I'll do that and bring Brandon with me."

Cheer squad did their first routine to *Go!* by My Chemical Romance. I thought it was a stronger performance than any they did in the fall. It didn't hurt that I loved that song.

The whistle blew, and the first game started. Instead of pitting the year divisions against each other like last time, they did it by putting the teams with the least wins first. That meant red team played gold team. Then the winner played orange. Hope's white team would play off against whoever won that. Brett's blue team played the third-year black team. Then the last ones standing faced off.

It was important because the winning team went to extramurals a few weeks later. Gold team defeated red, but orange won the next match. I could have made twenty bucks if I'd taken Wyatt's offer of a bet on that. But he would have won it back if I let it stand.

Cheer squad's rendition of *The Man* by The Killers was an utterly ironic lead-in to the game that came after it, considering the only team captained by a woman won.

Hope's first-year team was even better than in the fall. They trounced orange in just under a minute, setting a record for first-year wins at our school. They'd made it to the playoffs for extramurals.

Cheer squad finished their three-performance set with *Nine in the Afternoon* by Panic! At the Disco. As much as I loved the alternative set this time around, they'd probably end up picking a pop routine from fall for extramurals.

Black team beat blue team again, which was no big surprise. After the coin toss between white and black, Hope popped wings, immediately rose in the air, and tossed her first orb directly at the third-year playing reverse point.

The ogre playing mid on black team dropped his glamour and expanded his size to intercept it. We almost won in that first moment because of Hope's tactic.

We almost lost in the next.

Their other mid threw at Hope. Or where she'd been anyway. I knew flying well enough to understand what had happened. She'd folded her wings and dropped to avoid getting hit, and snapped her ankle and two toes in the process. Even a magical shifter couldn't heal multiple fractured bones in the minute she had for a time out. Hope was out of play for the rest of the match.

Cosmo took her place, and another player came off reserves to take his previous position. The team did their best, but it was a game of attrition after that. Downhill for the white team, unfortunately.

"We're the ones to watch next year," Hope said later. "That's all I wanted. Good job leading them after I fell, Cos."

"You make it sound like war."

"It's how magi did it back in the day," I said. "For matters that extended beyond duels."

"Glad I'm not a magus, then." Cosmo grinned. "Or a history buff, either."

<hr>

The musical didn't run during Rec like the variety show. Instead, we had a full dress rehearsal during the school day and returned later on Thursday to put on our production. We were exhausted and nervous at the same time.

"I can't eat," Ed said at the early dinner.

"Same." I nodded. "I don't want to eat either."

"Doesn't help to have pizza again." He pushed his plate aside.

"You need food, Ed. Honestly, Mavis. Don't enable him or he'll waste away."

"Yes, princess mom friend." I bowed my head.

"You're lucky I like you so much." She sat, placing two coffee mugs full of hot water and two packets of instant oatmeal in front of us. "Now. This isn't pizza, and it won't coat your vocal cords. Eat."

"Guess we'd better do what she says." Ed tore open one pack of oatmeal and poured it into the mug. "Don't anger dragons."

"I'm no good with ketchup, but you're right." I copied him.

Once we'd each had a spoonful, Saya got a slice of pizza and ate it in a series of dainty bites. With a fork and knife.

Maybe taking her advice at mealtime wasn't the best choice.

"Oh, good call on the oatmeal." Kiara sat on my other side. "I just came back from the Mart with microwave chicken soup, but I'll probably be hungry by intermission."

"That's okay." Brandon's voice surprised me. "Wanda says post-show donuts are a tradition."

I caught Kiara's eye and raised my eyebrows.

She grinned and nodded.

So they'd solved the kissing problem, then. I'd have to ask her how to do it eventually, in case I ever got stuck in a romantic role.

We went through the portal to school an hour before curtain up. It was six, but they didn't open the front of the house until quarter to seven. I paced the green room, weaving my way through the rest of the cast. We had two of Wanda's friends from cheer squad in the five big dance numbers. I wondered how they managed stage fright.

Kiara's glamour brush was a miracle for stage makeup. We used pictures from the Broadway revival to set each character, then applied it in a handful of strokes. It saved us so much time and effort. Everybody thanked her.

Sid and his crew of gremlins were at the ready to move the sets around. Mr. Hickson acted as both stage manager and props. We had faculty members running lights and sound. Blended voices filled the space on the other side of the curtain.

Everything was ready.

Rita went out with the chorus behind her to open the show. Ed and I waited backstage because our first cue wasn't until after three musical numbers.

"Downside of character roles." I sighed.

"Hurry up and wait." He shrugged. "Once we're on, it'll go fast, like variety."

Ed was absolutely right. While rehearsal, even the full dress, seemed to abide time's usual passage, the performance whizzed by. What was different, though? We had the same cast, music, sets, and costumes as every other time. In the middle of intermission, I had it.

It was the audience.

Their energy, emotional investment, and reactions to us made all the difference. The crowd lent a fourth dimension to the triad of book, music, and actors.

"How to time travel," I mumbled.

"Kiss," Horace said. "Read. Write. Music. All of these are in this play."

"You forgot breathe," Ed said.

"Easy for ghosts to forget." Rob snorted. "Cut him some slack. Get ready. They're halfway through act two."

"I swear, you two share a brain sometimes," Diego said. "You sure you're mediums and not telepaths?"

"You just didn't hear the ghosts, is all," Ed said.

"Seen weirder things connecting folks. Later, my cue." Diego left to join the rest of the company for Jaxon's solo to Bianca.

Horace tilted his head, eyes closed, swaying to the music.

"I used to sing this to her sometimes," he said at the end. "Brings back memories. The good ones."

"One more number until our big act." Ed grabbed my hand.

"We've got this." I squeezed.

We let go and headed out of the green room, already hamming our movements up in the wings before setting foot on the stage. We sang *Brush Up Your Shakespeare* and did the soft shoe steps at the dance break.

Everybody laughed. Down in the front row, I even caught Matron Klein dabbing the corners of her eyes breathlessly. From the looks of things, she'd needed a good laugh for a long time. I felt honored to help with that. A little vindicated, too.

I was good for something besides following Mom's orders or getting into trouble. It felt utterly amazing.

We took a bow, then sauntered off the stage. Instead of going back to the green room, we stayed in the wings, watching the show's remainder from there. There was plenty of room with the rest of the cast on stage for the closing numbers.

We came back out for a curtain call at the end of the closing number, *Kiss Me, Kate*. We got an enormous number of cheers during our bow, and the entire left section stood. I spotted Hope there, with half of first-year between our section and the Bishop's Row players. Ramon sat with all the wrestlers, even Chainsaw.

The green room was a flurry of glamour bracelets off wrists and onto hooks, deactivating makeup, laughter, and plenty of hugging. And donuts.

I managed to snag a powdered jelly. Ed got a Boston cream. Kiara's had rainbow sprinkles, and Brandon a maple glazed. They held hands while they ate.

"Nah." Diego waved a hand at the pink box. "Watching the weight."

"Me too," Rita said.

"More for me." Hayden took two chocolate frosted. "And maybe, uh, a friend."

"For my sister." Jaxon got one of the other jelly donuts and a cruller, then headed toward the door. "Our section's waiting in the hall."

"How'd you know?" Kiara asked.

"Twintuition." Jax grinned. "Come on."

We followed him out, and sure enough, everyone was there. Hayden gave his extra donut to Fiona, bowing with a flourish. Howie quacked and waddled around the pair of them.

"Awesome!" Jill hugged Ed.

"Thanks, Jill." Ed smiled but winced a little. "That's my rib."

She moved, circling him with her arm, and the wince vanished.

"You were amazing." Ramon twined his fingers with mine.

"Thanks."

"Here." He pulled his hand out from behind his back, holding a single red rose out. "It's only from the Mart, but—"

"It's perfect." I took it. "Like you."

Also, like the rest of the night. We left campus in an entire group. We all walked Fiona home near Irzyk Park, then back toward the Mendez house for Diego and Hawthorn for Hayden and Rita.

By then, the adrenaline had worn off. We made it back to the boarding house, hanging around on the front steps while Jillian and Jaxon waited for their dad to pick them up. After that, Ramon headed home while the rest of us went inside.

"It's over," I said to Kiara in the mirror as we put our hair up. "Can't believe it."

"Yeah. And the rest of it almost is." Her soft grin held a hint of sadness. "Got a lot of ideas for next year, though."

"Of course you do." I smiled. "You're always thinking about the future. It's one of my favorite things about you, Kiara."

"Wow, thanks!" The sadness left her smile. "It's an amazing thing to have in common."

I lay in bed awake, staring into the darkness, listening to her sleeping breaths. How was that forward-thinking something we had in common? My question still had no answer when sleep took me.

By Friday, I was sleepwalking through the day. I hadn't slept well after the show, despite being utterly exhausted. Immediately after school, I went upstairs and had a good soak in the tub. At dinner, I almost fell asleep on my plate of lasagna.

"Go sleep, Mavis," Wyatt said. "You look like hell."

"Thanks, bloody cap man," I mumbled.

"You can't," Hope said. "At least, not for more than an hour. Under time, eight-thirty sharp."

I wanted nothing more than to sleep halfway through Saturday after that grueling Rec Week. But a summons was a summons.

After an utterly inadequate nap, I stepped through the portal in the basement with Hope, Saya, Cosmo, and Ed. On the other side, Hal handed Cosmo a small envelope with a golden wax seal.

"From her majesty," he said.

"To our trusty friend Under-born Cosmo Leo Gitano, we give both greeting and instruction regarding the inhabitants of Aesop's Island."

"Wait, how'd she know its name?" I scratched my head, yawning again.

"I did a recon mission with this." Crow held up Hope's spyglass. "We set it up to record, and Hal gave her majesty a full account. Keep reading, Cos. She must have unearthed some old information."

"Aesop's Island," he repeated. "It is our intention that Cosmo, whose forebears are Etruscan lions, take the lead in contacting and dealing with this island's inhabitants. May your searches be fruitful and as conflict-free as possible. Her Royal Majesty, the Queen of Stone and Light."

"Wow, Cos," Hope said. "Your first time on point. How do you feel about it?"

"Uh." He shrugged. "I've read the fables. Probably it's full of animals. Maybe ruled by a lion. Aesop's Island's the right place for me to get my feet wet with leadership, I guess."

"The sun's just coming up, so it's a good time to go ashore," Hal said.

"It's eight o'clock to us, though." I yawned.

"You don't have to go if you don't want, Mavis," Cosmo said. "I'm not tired. I'll bring folks who aren't as tired. Maybe it's better if we don't show them our mystic birds right off the bat. But we probably want to bring shifters if the queen put me in charge."

"I'm good to go," Crow said. "Kasa was a shifter before she died but says she's staying here. She didn't see any ghosts on recon."

"You're hearing her now?" I asked.

"Nah, it's sign language."

"She didn't tell me she taught you that." Hope blinked.

I heard Kasa's spoken answer as she signed but let Crow deliver it.

"She says it was needed."

"True." She nodded. "Anybody else?"

"I'll go along as well," Saya said. "In the spirit of shifter solidarity. And because Cosmo can't steer a dinghy to save his life."

Nut barked, running rings around Cosmo's feet.

"Yeah, okay. Nut's here to track magic, so bringing the pupper is a no-brainer."

"Good." Hope nodded, then blew her whistle. "Ready the dinghy. And wish Cosmo good fortune."

I did exactly that, extending my well-wishes to Crow, Saya, and even Nut. After that, I shuffled down the stairs below decks and tumbled into my bunk, asleep in seconds.

CHAPTER FIFTEEN

The Lion Leads Tonight
Cosmo

Saya was right. I couldn't steer the dinghy. Rowing it was another story. I whistled while I worked, delighting Nut who barked along.

When we landed, I got my feet wet for real. Soggy shoes always annoyed me, so I got ready to shift into lion form. Saya stopped me.

"You forgot your amulet." She held it out.

"Thanks." I took it and looped the cord over my head. "Maybe I don't have to shift just yet."

"Honestly, Cos. You've got to start remembering your clothes so you don't ruin them."

"Yeah. You're right."

"Give the kid a break," Crow said. "Not all of us like the water as much as you do."

"You do have a point." She sighed.

Nut dashed up the beach, growling at a weathered tree stump at its edge.

"What's up, pup?" I went after her and smelled what was wrong a moment later. "Oh."

"Don't tell me you ate cheese again, Nut," Crow said.

"She didn't," I said. "It's a warning sign. The kind dogs leave at fire hydrants and the like."

"Well, it smells utterly horrid." Saya wrinkled her nose. "What's it say?"

"Two legs, keep out, basically."

"It figures," Crow said.

"Also says wings are legs."

"Thank the gods."

"Let's shift and get on with it already," Saya said. "I'm not nearly as exhausted as Mavis, but even dragons get tired eventually."

Nut danced on her hind legs as we all took on our animal forms. Saya's seafoam green scales gleamed in the sun. Crow stretched his impressive wings. Nut hopped up between Saya's wings, curling into a ball there like the hollow between the dragon's shoulder blades was a set of encircled arms.

All I did was wince. My left forepaw felt cut down to the bone, even though I had no hint of an injury there, not even a whiff of blood.

It felt like the unseen injury I'd first noticed back on the ruined island, but more intense. This puzzled me. Nurse Wilson hadn't found anything wrong.

I'd played countless Bishop's Row games and made half as many works of art since then without any pain at all. If I couldn't see or even smell a wound, there was no possible solution to the problem except keeping calm and carrying on.

I paced ahead, leading like Hope and the queen asked me to. It didn't seem too dangerous so far. My brain thought maybe this would be easy. But my heart said maybe not.

At first, I smelled only sea and forest. The farther we went, the more scents joined, followed by rustling in the underbrush along our path. All animals, as the warning marker had hinted.

By the time I saw the clearing in the distance, my nose picked up too many animals to count. None of those island-dwelling followers entered with me, sticking to the safety of the trees. With good reason.

At its center, basking on a great, gray rock, lay the biggest lion I'd ever seen. And I'd gone to Africa on a big cat's retreat last summer. He lifted his head, opened his mouth, and spoke.

"You, cub. Enter and bow before your king."

Saya stopped, still on the path behind me. Crow fluttered down to one of the branches over her head. Only Nut followed as I approached the massive beast. He ignored her so I did, too, letting her sniff practically every inch of the clearing besides the rock itself.

On closer inspection, I realized he was old. Definitely as old as Saya's mom Hertha, who'd hatched before Vikings first landed on Iceland. Maybe older than that. But he wasn't elderly in a frail way, like how Mom looked before Richard Hopewell struck her down.

Classmates called me lion king sometimes as a joke. But they wouldn't dare if they could see me now. This guy was the real thing.

I wasn't sure how to address him in more ways than one. He'd declared himself a king, but I wasn't sure whether that was slang for lion here or a real title. Also, my vocal cords didn't work in a human way while shifted. Not in the mundane or faerie realm.

I was good at trying things that weren't supposed to work anyway. So I opened my mouth, as the lion on the rock had. The island itself must have had magic because words came out.

"Sir—"

"Majesty," he corrected me. No big deal, I was used to that.

"I'm here on another monarch's behalf, Majesty. The Queen of Stone and Light."

"I'm familiar with her. Does she still wage war on the King of Forest and Shadow?"

"No, Majesty. They've reunited and sent the ship that carried my friends and me here."

"You brought a dragon." He sniffed the air. "A hatchling, and young. Step forward, dragonling, and introduce yourself."

"Good greeting, Your Majesty," Saya said. "You see before you Under-hatched esteemed dragon, Miss Saya Thetis Harcourt, daughter of Hertha and Wilfred. I am most honored to make your acquaintance."

"Pretty manners for a scion of the foulest tyrant to ever darken the sky with his wings. And his daughter, Hertha the Horrible."

I held my breath, waiting to pounce in case the old lion meant it as a threat. On his branch, Crow let out a series of croaks. At least I had backup.

"As you say." Saya lowered her snaky neck, bowing to the creature who'd just insulted her.

She was a total badass in the manners department.

"I suppose you're here for your grandfather's hoard, such as it is."

"Your Majesty, I know nothing of my grandparents on either side. Only that they were hatchlings themselves, or I wouldn't be as you see me now. Who was my grandfather?"

"I won't sully my mouth with his name, nor your mind with its knowledge. But if the dragon's hoard is not what you seek, then what is your mission?"

"We're exploring, trying to find and fix something," I answered. "Your Majesty."

"Ah. The Calamity."

"They didn't give it a name, Majesty. But I'm not sure that's it."

"Explain."

"The Calamity's a storm, I thought. One that destroyed another island."

"Where did you hear this?"

"A ghost named Cyrus."

"Then a medium travels with you. Interesting. Yes, very interesting indeed."

"Why?"

"Should you have the misfortune of facing the Calamity, your medium will understand. If she doesn't go mad in the process."

"He," I corrected. Then remembered who I was talking to. "The medium's name is Ed, and he's a guy, Your Majesty."

The real lion king stood, then stretched with his forelegs pressing against the stone. He flicked his tail three times, then sat on his haunches and stared at me.

"A boy?" He sniffed. "Yes. I smell him on you. A most curious contradiction of aromas. Camphor and the bones of dead leviathans. Gunpowder and honeyed blood. Decrepitude and youth. Curious indeed."

"If you say so, Your Majesty."

"Tell me, what is this medium's full title? As the Queen of Stone and Light gives it."

"Master medium, Edward Aion Redford, son of Duke Neil and brother to Sir Frederick," I managed to rattle off.

"Aion, curious. No mention of companions?"

I sat blinking and twitching my tail. What could he mean? Ed's girlfriend? Probably not. Companions was plural. But mediums hung out with ghosts. And the ghosts of mediums bonded with them, Ed included. He only had one friend like that.

Still, Hope said to be careful. Not say too much. I'd given Ed's entire name already, so that cat was out of the bag. However, I could still answer the question without mentioning Rob directly.

"Not in the Under, Majesty. He's only got one ghost in the mundane."

"Still, more promising than I hoped. His voyage is still new."

It wasn't a question. The king of Aesop's Island knew something. He wasn't sharing, either. I felt far out of my depth.

"Yeah."

"Perhaps my time has come at last." The elder lion chuckled. "Or maybe yours, Cosmo son of Gino. Step back upon the path, elegant hatchling, and keep to your perch, bold crow. This matter is between lions alone."

"What matter?" I blinked.

"Why, the matter of this rock and who rules it, of course," he said. "You must fight me for it."

Somehow I knew that whoever claimed the rock in the clearing would reign over the entire island, with rights to everything on it.

"Uh, that's not my reason for coming here."

"It's my reason for granting you passage." His tail flicked from side to side. "Prepare yourself, youngster. You have until the sun touches the far side of this stone of mine."

I tried, but the pain in my paw had grown worse during the whole mind-boggling conversation, throbbing like the time I'd crushed my hand getting out of a car.

"Psst."

I looked over my shoulder in the direction of the sound. A blade of grass twitched and quivered. I approached, favoring my left front paw. It hurt so badly by that point, that I could barely think straight.

"Down here." The voice spoke again.

Nestled in a patch of tawny seeded grass, I spied a small gray mouse. I lowered my nose, hoping he was maybe a shifter or unknown type of pure faerie instead of another talking animal. An additional powerful ally would help with all the pain I was in.

My breath made the grass flutter, and lifted his fur. I smelled nothing fae or human about him. I almost turned away, prepared to die. Or at the very least, get myself disfigured.

"The thorn, sire," the mouse said. "Allow me to remove it."

"Sire? Thorn?" I blinked. "There's not even any blood. It's probably brain gremlins."

"I know nothing of gremlins, but sire, your injury is not in your brain, and is in fact most grievous. If the Thorn of Androcles remains embedded there, you've no hope for survival even if you win today's battle."

"What are you, a doctor?"

"That I am," said the mouse. "Galenus is my name. Please, allow me to help."

"Well, Galenus, thanks for the offer. However, I've got nothing to give you in return." I glanced at the shadow on the rock. Only a sliver remained. "I'm Under-born, so I know payment's important here. Even if it's the Uncharted Isles."

"Your friendship is reward enough."

"Wow." I chuckled. "You sound exactly like another friend of mine. Go ahead, Galenus. Take it out if you want to."

I set my paw on the ground between us, turning the pads up and velveting my claws. If I hurt the nice mouse doctor, even by accident, I'd never forgive myself.

The dull throbbing pain changed as the mouse went about his work. It brightened, then sharpened, like sunlight glinting off a blade. I growled. He spoke.

"*Mutua Benevolentia primaria lex naturae est.*"

It meant reciprocal kindness, the primary law of nature.

The coppery scent of blood filled my nose but only briefly. The pain faded as my shifter healing kicked in. The mouse held a gleaming wooden thorn in both paws, barely able to hold it up.

"Thanks, Galenus. You're a lifesaver."

"Sire, the thorn." He gestured at it, then me. "You bore the pain of it. It belongs to you now."

"No time!" Crow called from overhead.

I glanced at the shadow again. It had moved entirely off the rock. And old king lion was ready to pounce.

"Nut, run away!" I called to the little sha dog.

She dashed right past me. Before I leaped forward to lock claws with royalty, I saw her tail drop toward Galenus. He clung to it, letting her carry him, thorn and all, away from me.

Smart dog. Smarter mouse.

The king pounced and knocked me flying. I would have crushed my new doctor friend if Nut hadn't rescued him. I scrambled to my feet, loping along the tree line to try and get behind him.

It almost worked.

He spun on a dime, kicking up dust. The next time he leaped at me, it wasn't blunt force. He struck my shoulder with his claws out.

I'd never yowled before. Then again, I never got gouged by anyone that much bigger than me, either. My brother Tony had, though. And he'd come back from that with one of his nine lives. He always said it's okay to lose your voice, as long as you don't lose your focus. I kept my distance until the wound began healing.

"First blood." The king's tail swished. "And a shifter's healing. Do better."

Why was he encouraging me? At first, it seemed to make no sense. Not much did, with my short years and limited experience. I continued to fight, letting my instincts move my body.

My brain struggled to connect dots left by other people, like breadcrumbs scattered in the woods by lost children.

I tried pouncing on him. My solid but still growing body didn't have the mass to topple him, so I tried a grapple, imitating Fiona in the wrestling ring without the giggles.

That didn't work for long. I clung to his back for as long as I could, but he shook me off pretty quickly. I landed on my feet, thank goodness. It gave me time for more thinking.

He began a series of paw swipes that I managed to avoid.

The king was rude, especially to Saya. He guarded that rock like Hertha guarded her vault. And he'd only left off on both the rudeness and the rock after I mentioned Ed.

"What's. Ed. To. You?" I panted.

"Defeat me and find out." He purred. "Or think as hard as you fight."

He thought I fought hard? How? The king of Aesop's Island was an absolute juggernaut. I couldn't beat him any more than Galenus could.

But Galenus fought death on the regular. Another enemy nobody could beat. Those words he'd said to me in Latin made sense now. Kindness was the primary law of nature. Especially here, or the mouse doctor wouldn't have said it.

I dodged one of his massive paws more easily than I expected to.

The way to beat the king was with kindness. Hadn't I already done that?

No. I'd only been polite, speaking pretty. Kindness was care, giving to someone in need. But what was kindness to someone like him?

We batted at each other, a dance of claws, dust, and a thousand shallow cuts. He let me pause to breathe. I realized something.

The king was old. Was he tired, too? Not physically worn out but weary of his life and duty here. He hadn't come to greet us or sent his subjects to do the same.

"You're waiting for something." I chuckled.

"Ah." He swatted my face almost tenderly.

"Not death." I swatted back, less gently.

The king pressed me in the other direction, away from the rock.

My body gave me the last piece of the puzzle. I knew what he wanted and what to do, all in the same instant.

I ran away from him, almost back to the path where Saya waited under the trees. I pressed my chest to the ground, haunches coiled. He pursued, of course. I expected him to.

He slowed, the moment I'd been waiting for. I let loose my pounce, not at the king but at his throne.

I came up a breath short and heard him behind me, about to close on my back and drag me away again.

This was all about Ed and by extension, Rob. So I took a page out of the ghost's book and stuck out my tongue. The moment it made contact with the rock, the battle ended. I sat up, and the king stepped aside.

"How did you know?" he asked.

"Ed says nothing lasts forever. You've been here practically that long. Figured you're tired."

"Thank you." He yawned. "Under the rock is an item of interest."

"I can't move that."

"You couldn't defeat me. Yet here we are."

"Good point."

I gave it a try and moved the rock with ease. A scroll case lay beneath it, carved from marble. I batted it out with my free paw.

"Wow." I set the rock back down. "That's amazing. But also kind of scary. What if I hurt my friends by hugging them?"

"This extra strength only persists on Aesop's Island. You leave it behind when you set sail."

"So you'll be stuck as king again when I go home?"

"No, young king." He shook his mane. "This island is yours to rule. But since you are so young, you may appoint a regent to watch over it until you're ready to return."

"I choose Galenus, the mouse."

"A mouse valiant enough to pull the thorn from your paw." He chuckled. "You would entrust him with the strength of a thousand lions?"

"Yeah, I would."

"Then so be it." He lifted his head to the sky and roared.

A collection of stars brightened against the darkening sky, shining down on the former king. Somehow, that starlight changed into something more solid.

"A ramp?" I blinked.

"For my ascension. I thank you again for your kindness, young king. Take your scroll back to your friends, and return when you are ready."

"Will I see you again?"

"In a manner of speaking. I'll always be out of reach, but never too far away."

He paced up the ramp. I watched him go so I know he didn't diminish in size or fade from view. Instead, his form increased, growing even more massive until it matched those bright stars.

He joined them, meshed in, became them.

Later, on the boat, Hope, Saya, Ed, Mavis, and Hal tried and failed to open that scroll case.

"Maybe we need an earth magus. One approved by the monarchs," Hope said.

"Unfortunately, I don't know any that well," Hal said.

"It can wait. As long as we bring it to them, it'll be safe until we figure something out," Ed said.

"I'll write to Mother," Saya said. "Maybe she's got something in her vault."

"Or the monarchs might already know how to open it, and we'll be all set faster than we think." Mavis chuckled. "But we're never that lucky."

Except she was wrong. I'd been lucky that day.

I stood on the deck, holding the Thorn of Androcles and staring up at the stars the old king had joined.

"What's eating you, kid?" Crow asked.

"Just admiring the stars. You're a tracker. You know all about constellations and stuff, right?"

"Yeah."

"So, what's that one?" I pointed.

"It's Leo. The lion, of course."

"Thanks."

"No problem. It's a good one for you to know, especially now."

"Why?"

"Wow." He chuckled, not unkindly. "You want to learn as much as you can before coming back here, King Cosmo."

"Good point." I sighed. "Left things pretty open-ended down there, didn't I."

"Yeah, and that's okay. I learned that some things take time. You can't rush or force growing up or this quest. Trust the guy holding your seat and do what you have to."

"That makes a lot of sense, Crow. Your advice is almost as good as Tony's. Thanks."

After Crow left to go on duty, I held my hand up to King Leo in the sky and waved.

CHAPTER SIXTEEN

Mavis

On Monday at the park after school, Saya insisted that three weeks was plenty of time to order formal wear at State of Grace as long as our measurements hadn't changed much.

"Uh, already ordered," Ed said. "Spring Fling's at Messing, and I'm on the committee. I've got to look my best."

"Went with him," Cosmo muttered. "Moral support."

"Who else has already been?"

"Guilty." Wyatt raised his hand.

"Same," Jaxon added. "Jill, too."

"We went together last week." Kiara held up her hand, Brandon's intertwined with it. "With Fiona."

"No Hayden?" Saya asked.

"They're going stag. Something about Hawthorn exams."

"Hmm." Hope hummed and put her hand up.

"Et tu, Alkonost!" Saya put the back of her hand on her forehead.

"I haven't been," Ramon said.

"Same here." I nodded.

"Thank goodness." Saya sighed. "We've got an appointment. In twenty minutes."

"Well, that's the end of field day for the three of us, then." I shrugged. "Somebody put the frisbees and stuff away when you leave."

"On it." Kiara nodded.

The appointment was more fun than I expected with Ramon there. I decided to let him make selections and leave mine up to Grace again.

"Make us look good together, that's all," I told her.

"Hard to improve on Mother Nature." She grinned. "I'll give it a go."

The next three weeks I filled with studying. The exam was a full week after Spring Fling, but I didn't want to take any chances. Not when I had to get an A-minus or better overall to make it to second-year.

Of course, I still went to field days and the Dodge Street Café when it rained. My tablet was an ever-present companion on each outing. Even the ones that were date-ish.

"I hope you don't mind, Ramon."

"I don't. It gives me a chance to peek at your notes. They're better than mine this semester."

Sid opened the portal once, the second week after our production. Hal sent a message through for Hope. She called us to a meeting in the lounge.

"It says he thinks they're just over a week away from the next island," she said. "He'll know more in five days."

"Oh no." Saya groaned. "We can't miss extramurals. Half of us are in it."

"I'll order him to drop anchor and wait a day or two. Thanks to Crow, they're still decently stocked." She nodded. "Don't worry."

"That's good news," I said. "It'll make things easier over the summer, too."

"About that," Ed said. "Saya?"

"We've certainly got room. Do you want to stay at the mansion? Or the carriage house, if that sounds too intimidating."

"I'll think about it," I said. "Talk to Matron Klein, too. She already offered to let me stay here, so it's a decision. But thanks, everybody."

Before I knew it, Azrael was dropping our orders off at the boarding house. I opened mine, gasping at the fabric. For a moment, I thought it glowed. But when I took it out, I realized that was the light hitting the shantung.

It was iridescent and ombre, deep royal purple with a rosy reflection at the wrapped v-neck bodice, lightening through violet, lavender, and finally ice purple. It had a full skirt with a crinoline underneath.

"Wow!" Kiara gasped. "I love it!"

For once, I felt as excited as Kiara sounded.

"Open yours!"

She did. It was a draped yellow chiffon, one-shouldered with mother of pearl beading.

"I love yours too!"

We jumped up and down, carrying on so loudly that Brandon burst into the room holding a broom, handle out.

"Oh." He breathed a sigh of relief, then called down the hall. "It's dress day, no murder."

"You owe me five bucks, Porter," Wyatt hollered.

"Murder?" I blinked.

"Yeah." He nodded at the window. "Like, of crows. The bad kind."

"Brandon!" Kiara put her hands on her hips and glared.

"Sorry."

"It's okay." I grinned. "Kind of funny, actually. We were loud, right?"

"Super loud." She nodded. "But with the best reason."

The dance was the next night. I had no trouble sleeping this time or focusing in class, either.

Since it was at Messing, I thought we'd take a portal. Instead, Saya led us out the front door.

She had a bus—the swanky kind, with drinks and plush seats.

"Don't worry, Mavis," she said. "Ed told me about the trouble with local transportation. This is Mother's, from Newport."

Brett, Ramon, the twins, and Fiona were already inside. Apparently, we were the last stop before Messing. I got to see everyone's outfits on the way, which was nice.

Grace had given us a spring color theme, matching existing couples. Ramon's suit was the same royal purple as the top of my dress, but his vest and tie were lavender. Brandon was in a blue suit with yellow accents.

Saya and Brett were in pink and red. Jillian and Ed wore blue, with his in grayer tones. It was a little odd seeing him in such a light color, but he was smiling at least.

She'd given Wyatt emerald green with mint pinstripes, which surprisingly suited him despite his red cap. Fiona's dress was pale orange in her favorite twirly skirt style, but with lace trim. Cosmo's suit was more whimsical, a deep iridescent beige that shimmered in rainbow hues when the light hit it.

When we arrived at Messing's gym, I realized I'd been right about the stark white walls. They were magipsychic tech. Each was a screen displaying slideshows on every side of springtime scenes. With the overhead lights dimmed, it was like being in a garden at night—a magical one with phosphorescent plants.

"It's gorgeous, Ed," I said.

"Uh, thanks." He kept his voice down.

"You *were* on the committee, right?"

"Yeah." He nodded. "It's on the down-low, though."

"Oh, didn't know. Sorry."

"Not your fault."

He headed off to say hello to Diego. Rob floated over and spoke.

"Jill doesn't like it. Same as his clothes. Hair too."

"That, well, frankly sucks."

"I agree. He doesn't." Rob shrugged. "What can you do?"

"Go dance, maybe." I pointed at the ceiling. Ghosts I saw on campus from time to time sailed overhead, wheeling through the air in a dance. "It looks like fun to me, anyway."

"Check out the nutcase, talking to herself."

"Go away Donna. The ghosts don't like you." I glanced over at my shoulder to find her alone. Pretty ironic after hearing her insult. "Nobody does."

"They like you but shouldn't. Just wait. That's changing sooner than you think."

"Why do you hate me, Donna?"

"You're dangerous."

"Look around." I gestured at Wyatt, Saya, Brett, Fiona. Then I pointed at her. "We all are. How am I different?"

"You already know. You're a Merlini. I've had enough of your family, threatening mine. My mother deserves to be free of yours."

So, her beef with me had something to do with that old pack business.

"I didn't pick my family. Let's call a truce. Neither of us needs this feud."

"I actually *love* my family, so no." She shook her head. "I'm on your case for them. Watch your back. I know what you're capable of. And I'm not afraid to do something about it."

"Are you sure you don't want to stop? We've had this conversation twice before."

She turned her back on me and walked away, humming.

"Whatever." I shrugged. "Can't win them all."

I went to join my friends. The music started, and we danced, sometimes in pairs and other times as a big chaotic group. They had a live band instead of a DJ, so there was a break.

The sound went back to recorded music, and we all grabbed refreshments. As I sipped some punch, I felt a tingle, like faerie magic. But nobody had asked me a single question that day, let alone three. Only one other thing did that.

A threefold promise. Donna's thrice-repeated threats.

"Oh no," I said as the music cut off.

Instead of the band returning, the deck of a boat on the ocean, sailing at night, replaced the flower images on the wall. A voice came over the speakers.

Crow's.

"It's me or the ocean, bitch."

My brother leaned forward, catching Cadence between him and the rail around the boat. He had one hand over her mouth. In his other hand, he held a dagger.

"The Boss knows about the DelMar exile. There's a new order coming to town. The only way you and your folks get to stay on land is you with me. Choose wisely."

He took his hand off her mouth and tapped his foot, waiting for an answer.

"Wow." Cadence blinked. "You can't even call her your mom anymore? How pathetic."

Crow slapped her.

The scene replayed, this time with a different voice over it. Donna's, of course. She stood on the stage, at the band's microphone.

"This is what we let into our school last year. We let his sister in this year. How long before she does something like this? The Merlinis have terrorized this town for too long. It's time to stand up and say no. Like Cadence did."

My stomach hadn't dropped so hard in months, but I'd had a lifetime of moments like these. If I couldn't rise to this occasion and prove Donna wrong, I hadn't really changed. Which meant she was right.

Also, I couldn't give up. Literally, because of my promise to Mr. Hickson. No matter what, who, or why. I had to act. But how? Stop the video, or confront Donna?

Ramon parted ways with me, snapping Ed out of his horror and pointing at the wall, then gesturing at the ceiling. I trusted them to take care of what was on the screens.

I strode toward the stage.

"Go, Mavis," Cosmo called after me. "You tell her!"

A chorus of our friends' voices mingled with his. They propelled me faster. Horace floated down from the ceiling, unable to do much but stay by my side. It was enough.

I took one of the other microphones off its stand and walked across the stage until I faced her, six inches away. We probably looked like we were about to drop the hottest album ever, making it all the more important to stay serious.

"Donna Ambersmith."

The utterance of her surname on the Messing campus elicited a series of gasps. At least I had everyone's attention. Especially hers. She paled, eyes wide.

"Here she is, right on cue to hit me."

"No. I'm challenging you to a formal duel to settle our differences."

"Lay one hand on me now—"

"Not now." I shook my head. "I said formal. I'm talking about the right and proper way. Square the circle in public, with seconds and supervision. Do you agree?"

"You'll never beat me in a fair fight."

"So be it. Do you agree or not?"

"You'll hit me if I don't, I bet." She gestured at the wall, where Crow's mistake still played out. "Like he did to her."

"No. But Donna, if we don't do this, we'll be at odds forever." I glanced over my shoulder. Hope and Saya stood below me, nodding. "I ask, a third time. Will you face me in a proper duel?"

"Fine, already. Tomorrow, between games out on the common. Natural abilities only, no weapons."

"Thank you." I inclined my head at her, then replaced the microphone in its stand. "I'll make arrangements immediately. Let's step aside for the band, now."

I stepped off the stage, not caring whether she followed me. Or about much else besides finding a Gallows Hill chaperone. Ed stood at my side as I scanned the room, searching for one.

"She's a summoner. It'll be daytime. That means Seelie hounds, the ultimate weapon against anything shadowy or unliving. I've watched one of them chew through a building to get to a vampire. Mavis. You're Unseelie."

"Your point?"

Cosmo appeared on my other side.

"You can't beat her with natural abilities. Or maybe not at all."

"I don't care if I win, Ed."

"Then explain it to me."

I spotted Mr. Hickson. Finally, I had a direction to move in.

"I have to prove her," I gestured at the walls, still playing Crow's shame silently, "prove this wrong. Or at least that it's different now."

"You'll get hurt."

"We all do, for worse reasons than this."

"Let me be your second, then."

"No, Ed," Cosmo said. "You're the strongest medium I know. But the right second should have different abilities. It's tactics."

"Who, then?" I asked.

"Hope will run into the same problem because Donna has both flavors of hound," Ed added.

"Should be a shifter. Mundane one, and strong," Cosmo said. "I—"

"I'm your second." Jillian stepped forward with Mr. Hickson. "Fae energy won't whammy me, and I've got tons of experience fighting on four legs."

"Hey!" Cosmo put his hands on his hips.

"Y'all love her like a sister." Jill gestured at both of them. "You're both too emotional about this. I know a thing or two about hounds to boot. Let me do this."

"Okay, Jill." I nodded. "Thank you." I sighed, looking up at my teacher. "You were right about the promise, sir."

"I imagined worse. It's still pretty dire." He grinned at my friends. "You've all been paying attention in class, at least. Because every one of you spoke correctly. Even Ed."

"Huzzah for extra credit." He shrugged.

More students and chaperones from my school joined us, making a cluster by one wall. Thankfully, the projections on it had reverted to the garden images. Ramon returned to my side, taking my hand.

"I'm still not clear on how to make it formal, exactly," I said. "Especially on short notice. The example from Lecture gave three days of preparation, with couriers and stuff."

"We'll have to draw up a written challenge, easy to do in a short time. Which is a good thing because she has to accept it by midnight."

"Let's get it done." I nodded.

"We'll need parchment and ink," Mr. Hickson said.

"I've got that." Mrs. Ambersmith opened her enormous red handbag, produced a roll of yellow paper with a fountain pen, and handed it to Mr. Hickson.

"Can I use the words I said up there?" I asked.

"Yes." He nodded, unrolling the parchment on a nearby table. "I'll write a formal address before it, a matching close, then we'll only need to deliver it."

"I've got the delivery thing," Ramon said. "Natural-born diplomat."

"Good." Mr. Hickson nodded, then wrote the date at the top of the parchment.

"Before you write more, Jedi, state that I'm supervising on Mavis's side."

"Donna's your niece, Dana."

"By marriage, yes. She's also a bully, which you know I don't tolerate. Not in my classroom, not in my family."

"True story," Wyatt said.

"Only if Mavis agrees."

"It's unexpected. Yeah, I do. Thanks, Mrs. Ambersmith."

"You're not the only one surprised, Miss Merlini."

Minutes later, we had the formal declaration in writing. Ramon delivered it with Jillian guarding him, part of her duties as my second. The response declaring date, time, and weapon came back at two minutes to midnight. Donna's second was her brother, an air magus at the regional public school. Mr. Markoff, the Messing summoning teacher, was her supervisor.

Earlier, I'd been excited about the extramural Bishop's Row tournament. I spent the night a bundle of nerves, emotionally unable to prepare for being part of the entertainment.

CHAPTER SEVENTEEN

Technically, I woke before dawn. What I'd done in bed didn't feel exactly like sleep, more like falling in and out of consciousness. It reminded me of being sick at age ten with viral pneumonia.

Downstairs, I drank what felt like a gallon of chamomile, trying to calm my stomach. It didn't do much. When breakfast rolled around, I forced some oatmeal down, trying to finish before anyone else arrived for the meal. I didn't manage.

"Mavis." John Clayton sat beside me with a plate of toast. "I heard the whole thing. Sorry about my cousin."

"You're not her keeper." I sighed and collected my bowl, spoon, and cup. "Sorry in advance for missing your last game. They'll have me with Nurse Wilson, getting checked for illegal enhancements while you play."

"This is a tough thing to go through in first-year."

"Could be worse." I stood with my dirty dishes. "I could be doing this without my friends backing me up. Like Donna."

"Takes a big person to empathize like that." He nodded. "I'm rooting for you."

I thanked him, then put my dishes away before heading upstairs to put on a pair of school sweats and a matching halter top. Yes, it was still chilly on May mornings.

But everything depended on my wings. And my honor.

We both got checked by nurses from all three schools before the Bishop's Row games even started. The teachers evaluated us, too—Dr. Aranha, Professor DeBeer from Hawthorn, and Mr. Casey, the Messing clairvoyance instructor. The entire time, we heard my school's cheer squad music, *Stupid Love* by Lady Gaga.

The nurses and faculty cleared both of us to duel. They put us in different tents with our seconds and supervisors to guarantee no tampering.

"We gotta talk about when I should step in," Jill said.

"That's my call," Mrs. Ambersmith said. "If I see anything unethical on either side, the second goes in."

"So if Donna cheats, I'm up against an air magus." I nodded.

"And if you do, she's fighting me." Jill cracked her knuckles.

"Remember, ghosts harrying Donna or her hounds is foul play. You're designated as a shifter, so no talents or elements used for direct offense."

"Totally unfair when we're talking about mediums in combat." Jill snorted.

"Possession is permitted," Mrs. Ambersmith said. "It's considered defensive."

"Oh, yeah." Jill nodded, grinning. "Do that, then. It's totally broken in a good way."

"I can't do it yet." I sighed. "Still new, remember?"

"Crap. Forgot, sorry." Jill sighed.

During the match between our team and Messing's, we tried to come up with strategies. Ways I could win against Donna fairly.

"The only thing I can do is evade and try to tire her Spites out. Popping wings is my biggest advantage because I've got more stamina that way than in raven form."

"If only you knew their anchors," Mrs. Ambersmith said.

"I'll look for them. With Spites, it's always something amber-colored. The shinier, the better. I remember from class."

"She's smart enough to have them wrapped up," Jill pointed out. "Look for bundles or bulging pockets. Same lesson, different fact."

"I'm pleased to watch you demonstrate what you've learned," Mrs. Ambersmith praised. "But I hear the second cheer squad starting. Be prepared."

Messing Academy's routine was to *Ex's and Oh's* by Elle King. The song was short, and I was painfully curious what they'd done with it at least until Principal Klein opened the tent's flap and beckoned us out.

We stepped on the fully warded field, watching an earth magus redraw the game court lines to make a circle inside a square at the center. Duelists had to stay inside the circle. The space left over in the square marked posts for our supporters.

I stood on one side as Jill took her place in the corner to my right and Mrs. Ambersmith the corner to my left. Donna's second and supervisor mirrored them on the other side.

The space we had looked impossibly small. If I relied on airborne evasion, I'd need to be extremely careful not to leave the circle. Fortunately, unlike mediumship, flying was a skill I'd mastered years ago.

We had an adjudicator, a neutral party chosen by agreement between our supervisors late last night. It was Coach Pickman from Hawthorn Academy. I'd never met her in person, which was ideal in this situation. As far as I knew, the same applied to Donna.

I saw my opponent walking to the other side of the squared circle, swathed from neck to ankles in a voluminous black cloak. A quintet of wrought iron pins held it together in the front. Her attire utterly eliminated any chance of my finding or interfering with her anchors.

"Approach, then bow," Coach Pickman called.

I walked forward, stopping with my toes just outside the line, put one hand over my waist and the other behind my back, then bowed to my opponent.

Donna barely bent her head.

The crowd collectively gasped, then went silent at that clear sign of disrespect. Before, they probably thought this was a garden-variety academic or romantic rivalry. Or that Donna had a valid point.

Duels were all about honor. She'd just made her disregard of it abundantly clear.

I kept my face still, imagining the surface of the pond in Danvers Sanitarium. Placid, to cover the roil of my anger at the summoner. I'd need to keep it contained, use it before it used me.

"Enter and begin!" Coach Pickman followed her words with a whistle blast.

We stepped across our lines at the same time. After that, Donna summoned her dogs of war. A set of Spites, as expected.

Neither of them was Lucius, who'd played with us at the park. That was a relief because the last thing I wanted was to see that hound harmed.

I unleashed my wings but didn't take off until the last possible second. The downdraft knocked the Spites back, not far enough for them to land out of bounds, unfortunately.

That had been my one chance of getting declared the winner. It hadn't happened, so I'd fall back on Plan B—a test of stamina.

I rose and dipped in the air, making passes above the hounds and alighting occasionally. Despite the cool breeze, sweat poured down my back between my wings and soaked my face.

The Spites looked fresh as daisies. Heads in the crowd shook, shoulders shrugged. The dogs couldn't win if I stayed in the air. If I landed, all three physical combatants would be injured while Donna remained unscathed.

The poor Spites were stuck following her orders. For all I knew, they didn't want to tangle with the Sirin. Blows in anger between opposite courts did threefold damage to pure faeries, and they were smaller than me. Beating up smaller opponents felt too much like something Mom would do.

I glanced down at Jill. She sighed and nodded. We both knew what I had to do. My opponent noticed our exchange of glances and smiled.

"Come down and fight, you coward!" Donna cried.

Replying to that would be a waste of breath. So I responded instead, not by fighting her hounds. But by the simple act of landing.

Just a hair out of bounds. I rubbed my eyes, sniffling.

"Nurses stand by!" Coach Pickman blasted her whistle and strode to my side. "Show me your eyes, Merlini."

"They're fine, Coach." I sighed. "It's wrong to do serious harm to harm compelled creatures. I forfeit."

"Strategic defeat, mitigating the casualties." She nodded. "Well done."

"Thanks." I folded my wings, willing my plain old humanoid shoulder blades to replace them.

"Merlini forfeits! Match, Ambersmith!" The coach let out three blasts on her whistle.

The crowd's response was a muddle of sounds, none of them cheers.

Donna called her hounds off. I bowed again, stepped over the line, and strode forward ready to shake on her win. She sneered and shook her head instead of my hand.

"Family full of bullies, and I end up with the one coward." She gloated.

"If you say so." I offered my hand again.

"I don't shake hands with New Order scum."

She put her hand on one of the iron cloak pins. I didn't ignore the threat but maintained a mask of confidence.

"I'm not one."

"But your mother—"

"Coerced my brother to fight a battle he never wanted. Like you just did with your Spites. Third and final offer." I stood, still waiting.

Donna took her hand off the iron and dropped her hand to her side. She couldn't argue, and she wouldn't accept my truce. Instead of helping bury our hatchet, she walked away from it, carrying her grudge for another day.

I held my head high as I walked off the field, Mrs. Ambersmith leading with Jillian a step behind. When I got back into the medical tent, they stayed outside.

"Freshen up. Then we'll meet our friends," Jill said. "Proud to call you one."

Horace followed me in briefly. "Ed's got a message."

"Let me have it."

"He says Donna might have won that duel, Mavis. But he thinks the real victory was yours."

After he floated away through the canvas, I finally had a few moments alone. I sat in the chair by the table with the washbasin and drew a deep breath, determined to power through a little more of the day for my friends.

Instead, I put my head in my hands and silently cried.

"Mavis?"

Ramon's voice would have had me all tingly in any case, but the magic from the question made the sensation nearly intolerable. The silent tears morphed into outright sobs.

I looked up at him through the blurry haze of too many tears. He pulled another chair over and sat beside me.

"Hey." He rubbed my back. "You take however long you need, *amore.*"

Maybe his presence was that soothing. Or perhaps I'd cried myself out. Either way, a few moments later, I reached for the basin and cloths. My hands shook so much I almost spilled the water.

Ramon took over, wetting the cloths and handing them over so I could wash my face. By the measure of kindness experienced in my life, my boyfriend was up there with Matron Klein, Paolo Micello, and Kiara.

He turned his back while I gave myself a little birdbath and changed my clothes. That year at Gallows Hill, I'd gained unique magic, watched my brother make incredible progress, and discovered true friendship. So many unexpected blessings.

Ramon DelSangre's heart put them all to shame.

"Thank you," I said afterward. "I love you so much."

"Good thing. Because I love you." He set the basin aside. "I hope you can make it through the barbecue at the park. If not, there's an entire crew of people waiting to walk you back to the boarding house."

"Already?" I blinked. "It's that late?"

"We trounced Messing. Their cheer squad won the award, though. And John Clayton's got a scholarship offer at Providence Paranormal. It's his parents throwing the shindig."

"Better get over to Irzyk, then." I stood. "I don't want to miss a thing."

CHAPTER EIGHTEEN

I wasn't worried about exams, despite the enormous stakes.

Ramon helped with that. He coordinated study groups in a variety of locations all over town, indoors and outside. Nobody got bored, with many declaring we should do this every year.

"Too bad we'd freeze in winter," was all Ramon said to all the praise.

Hope went to Sid, looking for a letter from the monarchs every morning. Everybody wanted to know if they'd cracked Cosmo's scroll case. She always came back empty-handed.

"Maybe we'll have to wait for summer." She shrugged. "That's okay. We all have enough to worry about with exams."

The night before the big day, I got to sleep at a reasonable hour. While I'd run myself a little ragged after the duel to distract myself from its loss, it wasn't a massive act of self-sabotage.

I sat with all my boarding house friends in the dining room, chatting to distract ourselves, which worked too well.

Because I almost put waffles on the letter.

"Seriously." I waved the waxy yellow envelope over my head. "Who puts something like this on a plate?"

It rattled a little. Something was inside.

"Thought it looked fancy," Sid said. "Came through a portal right before you all got here. Sorry."

"Oh." I blinked. "Well, uh, sorry for yelling. Thanks for delivering it."

"Yelling at the jack of all trades on final exam day is practically a Gallows Hill tradition." He shrugged. "I'm used to it, no hard feelings."

He headed back to the kitchen. I handed the letter to Hope.

"It's got your name on it, Mavis." She passed it back. "From her majesty."

"Open it," Kiara said.

"Read it for us, too," Cosmo added.

"Don't want to make like a lion and break any bans." I glanced at Hope.

"That's fine," Hope said. "If there's something sensitive in it, skip it in the narration."

I opened it and read aloud.

"We give you good greeting, Under-born Mavis Rhiannon Merlini. On this day, we extend our gratitude for your decision to spare our hounds most grievous injury." I blinked. "She's seriously overestimating my combat skills."

"Keep reading!" Cosmo chuckled. "The good part's always after the gratitude."

I cleared my throat and continued.

"After petitioning our most royal king and consort, he has decided to grant you the rank and title of ensign, in addition to the responsibilities therein."

"That's better than a page, like a squire but at sea," Wyatt said. "Nice."

"All I did was forfeit, though." I shook my head. "And tithing means being in the Under for a year and a day."

"Being in, yeah." Wyatt nodded. "With all the trips you're taking, it'll add up. Queen requires all that in a row. King's done it in blocks before. Like for my dad."

"That's good to know, Wyatt. Thanks. There's more."

I kept reading.

"Tell our esteemed guest Cosmo, son of Cassandra, that he handled his first mission most satisfactorily and that we appreciate his effort. In exchange, we return to him the Thorn, affixed to an amber chain taken from my vault. May it inspire and enhance him."

I handed the empty envelope to my friend. He pulled his gift from it and held it up, where it gleamed red-brown in the sunlight streaming through the window.

"Can't believe I walked around for months with this thing in my arm." He shook his head, then slipped the long chain over it.

The amber links adjusted in size until the necklace fit him perfectly. Saya peered at it, then nodded.

"It persists when you shift, Cos." She grinned. "Thank goodness. Finish that letter and get some food in your stomach before school starts, Mavis."

"Okay." I nodded. "We wish you and your allies all goodwill and success in your impending Trial by Academy. Her Royal Majesty, the Queen of Stone and Light."

"Trial by Academy." Ed chuckled. "Her majesty's always been whimsical with the flowery descriptions."

"It fits, though," I said. "The entire year's felt like one big series of tests."

"True story. Pretty much done for me, with no big exams. So I'm with the queen, wishing you all goodwill and success."

All the rules for taking the test were the same. Just about everything was, except for my accommodations. I put the earbuds in after our teachers recited their rules, so the sound of rustling paper didn't inspire last semester's sense of dread.

When I opened the final exam test booklet in Mrs. Ambersmith's classroom, I found the same format as on the mid-terms. Most of the questions were almost too easy. I knew it wasn't because of the queen's blessing. The reason was simpler than that.

I'd done the work.

Kiara, Brandon, and Hope weren't in the room when I handed my test back. Ramon was right behind me. On the way out, I saw Cosmo curl one hand around the Thorn of Androcles and spotted a formolite bracelet on his wrist.

Ramon and I headed for the library hand-in-hand. Once there, we joined the others from our crew at a table.

"You're out early." Kiara smiled.

"Yeah." I smiled back.

The rest of our section joined us in pairs, filing in just under ten minutes apart. Jill and Wyatt. Jaxon and Fiona. Fifteen minutes went by.

"I'm worried about Cos," Saya said.

"Me too." I nodded.

He walked in right after we voiced our concern, padding softly across the library carpet. He sat at the head of our table.

"How'd it go?" Hope asked.

"I know more than I think I know." Cosmo beamed like the sun. "Like Coach Tremain's old professor used to say."

"We all do." I smiled back.

"Bet you'll ace Lab, Mavis. Just like last time."

"Bet you will, too."

"We'll see."

An hour later, we walked out of Dr. Aranha's lab together. Cosmo hadn't torn a single dragon molt glove. And I found the practical just as easy as last semester's.

"Ten bucks, Thorne." Wyatt nudged Jaxon. "We don't need the grades back to know they rocked it."

"Never betting against the lion king again." The wolf shifter crossed the redcap's hand with a bill, then thumped Cosmo's back with one fist.

Outside in the balmy May sunshine, we settled on an extended field day. Ramon led us to Tropica Mart, where Saya sauntered through the store, putting together a picnic basket. We'd head over to Messing at the end of their day to include Ed, Diego, and Allen.

Only one more day of school remained for getting scores back and signing yearbooks. I had no doubt my back page would be full.

The PA system called me to Principal Klein's office at lunch on the last day of school. I left my yearbook with my friends and headed over. It had summoned me too early because the door to her office was closed.

A stroller stood outside it, empty. Before I could move closer to inspect it, the door opened. An auburn-haired girl maybe a little older than me carried her baby out and set him gently in the seat, smiling.

"I defended a dissertation with a six-month-old, Jolene. It might be challenging, but you can complete your diploma with Brody," Principal Klein said. "Remember to make an appointment with Counselor Amaral for childcare resources."

"Thanks, Principal Klein." She kissed the baby's head after fastening the stroller's harness. "I'm so happy to be back at school."

Jolene pushed the stroller toward the school social worker's office, humming softly to her child. Here was a girl who'd become a mother even younger than mine. Yet she seemed content, even confident about finishing school. And had my principal just implied she'd finished an advanced degree while parenting?

The entire situation seemed so backward to me. The idea that parenthood ruined opportunities was writ on my psyche like indelible ink. I wasn't sure what to make of this new contradiction. It wasn't the first time someone else's life challenged my worldview, so I knew what to do.

Watch. Discover. Learn.

"Mavis." Principal Klein held the door and gestured inside her office.

I nodded, went in, then took the seat closest to the door.

"I want to discuss summer with you, Mavis."

"Thought we did that already." I froze. "Oh no. You're not telling me I can't stay at the boarding house after all?"

"No, nothing like that." She shook her head. "It's two matters, actually. One is about you getting around."

"Salem's a walkable city. That's no problem."

"I'm referring to visiting out of town."

"Oh." I shivered, remembering New Year's Eve. "What should I do?"

"Come to me with plans like that. Sid summers in Bar Harbor, but if he's in town, you can travel by portal. If not, we'll schedule them so I can drive you to a different train station."

"Wow, thanks," I said. "What if she's watching the building and follows us?"

"She'll get frustrated if she tries that and bored enough to let her guard down. Because as part of your summer with me, you're having lessons in household management. We'll be back and forth several times a week to all sorts of places. The bank, the department store, the grocers. You get the idea."

"Will you teach me to bake?"

She threw her head back and laughed, a bright sound that ended the chill grip of mother-inspired fear. My spirits lifted enough to join in before she stopped.

"Yes." She nodded, dabbing the corners of her eyes. "Yes, I do believe I will. Now, on to that other matter."

"Oh no."

"Oh yes. They've set a date for your initial emancipation hearing. August third, at the district court downtown."

"Gods, I almost forgot about that." I shook my head. "Do your household management lessons include hiring a lawyer?"

"I'm surprised you asked that."

"I haven't got one."

"Hope didn't tell you, then."

"She's a woman of action, not words."

"Her father is representing you. He's got experience with extrahuman family cases."

"Thanks for arranging that."

"It was her idea."

"I'll thank her the second I see her. And thank you, Principal Klein. For this whole year and beyond."

The bell rang.

At Rec period, Mr. Hickson wasn't in the auditorium. Instead, a table stood on the stage with a sign tented atop it. Diego hopped up on stage to read it.

"Grading In Progress, Donut Club Today." He turned, smirking at us over his shoulder, and lifted the sign. Underneath sat a stack of pink boxes.

"Better get up there before he eats them all." Ed headed up the steps at the side of the stage.

"Wish I could have one," Horace said. "I miss chocolate frosted."

"Possession, my friend." Rob winked. "It's not only for romantic partners, you know."

"I know." Horace sighed.

"Hey, if you want to practice that over the summer, I'm game," I said.

"You're right. I'm doing you a disservice, refusing to try." He nodded. "It's a powerful skill once you get the hang of it."

"I don't want it for power, Horace."

"I know. All the more reason to trust you with its use. Let's table it for now, or you'll miss out on treats."

"Thanks, Horace."

Up on stage, I thought I'd missed out on a jelly donut. Rob floated down from the rigging above and presented one to me.

"Silly mediums and their floating food." Brandon chuckled, waving his maple frosted, and spoke again, drawing out his vowels in a shaky voice. "Oooo, it's a ghostnut. Spoooooky!"

"Silly selkie is more like it." Kiara giggled with her boyfriend before taking a rainbow sprinkle-filled bite of her pastry.

After stuffing our faces, we called Sid out to the piano, where he played songs from *Kiss Me, Kate.* We sang, danced, and reminisced until the bell rang.

In Lab, Dr. Aranha sent our scores to our tablets. I looked down at the screen, gasping as I saw my lecture grade, my lab grade, the semester total, and cumulative of spring's total with fall's disaster score. She went around the room, checking our reactions individually.

"A for spring. D for fall," she said.

"C-plus," I breathed. "I passed."

"And then some." Dr. Aranha smiled. "Good job, Mavis."

She let us out early. In the hall, Cosmo held his tablet up, grinning. I showed him mine.

"We match!" He laughed. "Two high C's, me and my friend from the high seas."

"Thanks for being a study buddy, Cos."

"Back at you."

I showed Ramon next. He caught me up in his arms, lifting me in the air as he spun us around in the hall. Sharing my success with him wasn't the same as flying, but just as exhilarating.

We had another field day like the day before, only shorter. As the golden afternoon sun poured the remains of its amber light over our group, I peeked at the back page in my yearbook.

Myriad messages of friendship wreathed the one at the center. *Love always, Ramon.* My eyes misted over, and I closed the book, tucking it back in my satchel as I joined him to watch clouds drift across the serene sky. Soon, Ed and Jillian joined us, passing the time in peace.

At the end of that day, I realized it was the closest I'd ever come to a perfect one because I'd done what Mom said was impossible—made it through a year at Gallows Hill.

Sometimes, the only way out was through. I'd never have managed with my head down and on my own. Finding the Sirin's feather gave me new powers. Discovering friends made as much of a difference.

The story continues with Gallows Hill Academy Year Two: Silver and Gold, available now at Amazon and Kindle Unlimited.

Grab your copy today!

AUTHOR'S NOTES

Thanks so much for giving Gallows Hill and the Revealed World setting a chance.

I'm a little misty-eyed after that ending, but also so excited to tell Mavis's story. It's delving deeper into the Revealed World than I went in Providence Paranormal College.

I'm greatly enjoying the crew's strange adventures on the far side of the Under. Cosmo's jaunt is only the beginning. Expect a bumpier ride as Mavis and her friends get closer to their personal truths in the mundane realm and universal ones in the Uncharted Isles.

I wanted to say a word before closing about the challenges some students face. The world we live in might not have formolite bracelets or umbral earbuds, but accommodations for people with learning challenges improve all the time.

You might know someone struggling like Mavis, Cosmo, or Crow with an undiagnosed learning disability. Or perhaps it's part of your experience. If so, these links are for you.

US: https://ldaamerica.org/

Canada: https://nildcanada.org/

UK: https://www.mencap.org.uk/

Australia: https://www.ldaustralia.org/

If you feel a bit lost, remember that there are two series in the Revealed World before this one. It starts with *Bearly Awake* at Providence Paranormal College and continues with *Fire of Justice* at Hawthorn Academy before landing with Mavis for this book at Gallows Hill. You can find everything on my Amazon author page here:

https://www.amazon.com/~/e/B00O6851HO

Thanks again,

D. R. Perry

Bobby Tremain's the first in his family to attend college, and also the first to see snow. A massive magical blizzard makes this not-so-average bear want to sleep all winter, but he needs to pass exams or risk flunking out of Providence Paranormal College.

Lynn Frampton's got a brain of epic proportions and an even smarter mouth. She went to college on the other side of the country to escape the town where everybody knows and fears her intellect. At college, Lynn's barely able to make friends, let alone influence people. At least she's at the top of her class.

Bobby needs Lynn's help to stay awake and pass his exams. She might just need his companionship, too. Can Lynn and Bobby find new hope together, or will their failures send them both packing?

Get it today at Amazon and through Kindle Unlimited

CONNECT WITH THE AUTHOR

Website: https://www.drperryauthor.com/

Join her newsletter!

Find more of D.R. Perry's books on Amazon.